THE EMPEROR OF SAN FRANCISCO

THE WICK CHRONICLES

BLUE BOX BOOKS

THE EMPEROR OF SAN FRANCISCO
THE WICK CHRONICLES

Published by Blue Box Books
www.blueboxbooks.com

ISBN 978-1-932461-47-3

Printed in the United States of America

THE EMPEROR OF SAN FRANCISCO

THE WICK CHRONICLES

BOOK ONE

MAX THOMPSON

THE
EMPEROR
OF SAN FRANCISCO

1

I watch the people. It's practically my job: I follow them around while they attend to the minutiae of their lives, observe and pass silent judgment, and interfere when the need or the whim strikes me. Their need for supervision cuts into some prime napping time, but it's part of the package. They feed me, provide treats both crunchy and meaty; they give me a warm place to live and dozens of beds to choose from, attention whether I want it or not, finger-scratches just behind my ears where I like it most and under my collar where I like it second most, and in turn I run along behind or beside them, paying attention to the minutiae of their lives.

(Okay, they usually carry me, but that's not the point.)

(Sometimes I ride on their shoulders. I haven't fallen yet.)

This has been my life for longer than anyone can remember. I was there when the King was a baby, I was there when the Emperor saved his princely six-year-old asterisk from the side of the bridge, I was there when he became King, there when he spawned—which was frankly kind of disturbing—and I'm still here. I know I was alive for a long time before any of them were born, but I've forgotten most of what came before.

The details sometimes come to me in wisps formed from faded pictures tucked into the back of my head, but I can never just sit back and think them forward in my brain.

No one really questions why I'm still here; the princess once asked how old I was, but the King told her—quietly, I don't know why, it's not as if my hearing was worse than any of theirs—that my age was something about which we do not ask, lest we jinx the ancient but still active kitty.

I was here before him, I know that much.

I may live forever.

2

I hate the water; I hate being out on the pier, where there are birds of every imaginable level of rudeness and where the water often behaves badly and laps up onto the wood, splattering on my fur. Oz—the Crown Princess of Pacifica, though I've never seen her wear a hat, much less a crown—on the other hand, loves to sit on one of the old, creaky benches at the end of the pier so that she can watch those rude feathery rats fly over the water, and wave at the ferries that come and go. When she gets tired of that, she turns around and watches the city, though I haven't figured out why.

It never changes; every day it's the same skyline, and has been for all of my memory. It used to be significantly dirtier and the city was quite a bit louder, but the views are all the same. The Ferry Building, the fountain on the Plaza, the jutting of buildings into the sky, often shrouded in thick, gray fog. The Embarcadero always runs along the water; Market Street always stretches out as far as I can see. It's the same thing, day in and day out, and has been that way for hundreds of years; the people worked hard to keep it that way.

Oz liked looking at it. I didn't get it, but understanding her wasn't my job.

She wanted to sit out there on a bench facing the bridge, so there I was, too, mostly minding my own business as I avoided droplets of ocean pinging off me. I wasn't too sure about the guy she was with, Prince Andrew of Midlam, but only because he was tall and loud and smelled like dog, and the last time I'd seen him he was tall and loud and smelled like cheese. I like cheese; dogs, not so much. I wedged myself between them—there was nothing in the rulebook that said I couldn't act as the royal supervisor right along with being the watcher—and stole the warmth that leeched off their legs.

"You know what I've noticed this summer?" she asked him. "No more uncomfortable looking dress slacks and starched shirts and perfect haircuts. You don't look regal at all these days. You look… normal."

He didn't; Andrew Van Hoff—Drew—looked anything but regal. He wore faded jeans that were worn to thin white threads in spots and beat up running shoes, his sweatshirt was frayed in spots at the hem, and his overly-blond hair was a jumbled mess of spikes and hair product; I'm pretty sure it was groomed every morning by that dog I could smell on him.

"You're not exactly princess-y yourself, sunshine," he countered.

She wasn't, either. The Crown Princess of Pacifica was tall, but not as tall as Drew; she favored jeans and t-shirts, she had short, black hair that was prone to odds and ends sticking out here and there—I may or may not help with that while she sleeps every night—and she'd spent her life playing against stereotypes that had held on for centuries and all the things people expected from her. While other little girls played house, she played racquetball against the Emperor and she trained in the martial arts; while they took ballet lessons, she hosted tournaments where the end goal was to hit other people until they either cried or a referee told her to stop.

I don't think she knew it, but that was almost by design. She had been a fiercely independent and stubborn toddler and her parents didn't want her to lose that innate toughness. The other kids her age were free to embrace or reject the old stereotypes, and to change their minds from day to day; they knew—peppered by reminders from the Emperor—what she was headed for, and knew she needed to be stronger than most to handle it.

I don't think she even owned a dress, and if she did, it had a thick layer of dust as it languished in the back of the closet and was probably ten sizes too small.

Oh yeah, I avoided the closet. Something in there made a horrible buzzing sound, and I didn't trust it to not be alive and hungry.

Oz and Drew had known each other since they were short, sticky people. Their kingdoms were strong allies; Midlam relied on Pacifica for military aid where their forces were thin, and Pacifica relied on Midlam for food staples that didn't grow well here but thrived there. They traded cattle for grain and wine for technology; they had a mutual goal of sustaining their people in comfort and safety, and the border between the two countries was left open.

The King of Pacifica and Queen of Midlam had been friends their entire lives, and the families met several times a year simply to spend time together. There were annual official meetings where business was conducted and deals were struck, but more often than that the Van Hoffs of Midlam spent a week or two visiting San Francisco, and the Blackshears of Pacifica took their spawn to Chicago.

The friendship they maintained rolled over to their kids. When the Van Hoffs were visiting, Drew and his older brother Carter played on the grass-lawn roof of the royal house with Oz and her younger brother Zed, and I stayed a comfortable distance away, keeping an eye on them. When they were older, maybe eleven or twelve—outgrowing the sticky stage but still loud and not-thinking a lot of the time—Oz and Zed spent part of the summer in Chicago with Drew, and then brought him back until school started.

Carter was older and not interested in spending much time with them. I rarely saw him, even when he was staying in the guest room next to Zed's, and knew nothing about him other than he was not as tall and did not have blond hair like Drew's, and he did not know how to walk quietly through the hallways.

I was familiar with Drew, but that didn't mean I fully trusted him as a person. He'd never done anything mean to me and had even tried to be friends, offering me bits and bites of food, but he was loud and not as gentle as I preferred. I kept my distance until he showed up at the start of summer without his family and moved into one of the guest rooms down the hall from Oz and Zed.

Even with the dog-smell, it was time to get to know him. He had been talking to Oz online and on the phone for years; they used video chat to see each other when they weren't visiting, and if she liked him enough to keep in touch with him that closely, I figured I might as well risk it. He wasn't as loud anymore—though he did have a deep voice that sounded like a shot going off if he raised it—and he patiently waited for me to come to him.

There was also the bigger picture that made me want to pay closer attention to him. When they were just starting to turn from little sticky things into medium-sized clumsy people, the King and the Prince Consort of Midlam joked that one day they would agree on a dowry and marry them off to each other, uniting the kingdoms into one. It was just a joke, something said to make the kids squirm and protest (and it did; Drew swore he would never get married, because, *girls*) but a year or two later Drew brought it up to Oz: "What if we really thought about that? I'm supposed to be King someday but I really don't want to, and you're supposed to be Queen and you're okay with that, and then we really could make Pacifica and Midlam one big country. We could bring back the United States."

She wasn't opposed to the idea. They made a pact to talk at least three times a week and to never keep secrets, and no matter what, to stay friends.

Drew was blunt, too. "Face it, your dad makes more decisions for Midlam than my mom does. If she didn't have him to advise her, we probably would have surrendered to Canada five years into her taking the throne. And Canada has never been a threat."

Oz thought that Drew's mother was a reasonable ruler, but he argued that she was kind, and kindness did not mean she was also any good at it. "I don't think I will be, either."

He wanted to study history—something she could show him personally, taking him on trips through the portals, going back in time—and he wanted to dabble in political science. That surprised her, because he was mostly interested in reading science fiction, and he was extremely excited about new stories where people traveled in space and shot each other with laser beams.

After Oz finished high school, he moved to San Francisco to finish his university studies. They'd told their parents that an education truly was the major reason he wanted to live in San Francisco, but no one was fooled. Midlam had some of the best universities in the world. The truth was that they both knew Oz didn't want to leave

San Francisco, and if they were going to get to know each other well enough to someday make a commitment, he needed to move.

So there he was, sitting next to Oz on a bench near the water, and I was in between them, doing my job. Watching. Listening. Keeping them six inches apart.

"That bridge," Drew said. "The Bay Bridge. I'm ninety per cent sure it's called something else in Midlam's history books."

"If you're old school it's still the Bay Bridge. Most of us call it the Emperor's Bridge. It's had a dozen names over the four or five times it's been rebuilt, but that's the favorite."

"Cripes, the Emperor. Crazy old dude, still makes me nervous. He always scared the crap out of me when I was little. It was like every time I was sneaking off to do something I wasn't supposed to, he was there, growling at me."

"Beloved crazy dude, not old. And he's not even that crazy. He's just particular and maybe a little strict with kids. For everyone else? He's an icon of the city, protector of us all."

"I stand corrected. Okay, it's the Emperor's Bridge. It'll take you to Treasure Island, where there is, to my understanding, no treasure."

"There's wine," she said. "And possible radioactive waste. But we put concrete over that part, so it should be fairly nontoxic."

"Well, I certainly feel safer now, thanks. How long does it take to walk to the probably-safe radioactive waste site, if one feels compelled to visit?"

"An hour or so on foot. Fifteen minutes on an air bike. I recommend the bike, since there's no place to stop and pee if you need to."

He shrugged. "I could just pee off the side of the bridge."

"You're just a classy prince, aren't you?"

"Oz, if you want class, you need to find another prince. Not having to be stuffy and pretentious is one reason I was so eager to come here. You have normal schools with normal people, your family is *super* normal and they've liked me since I was born. Everything I know about you says you're a lot like me, but better suited to the whole being in charge thing. I snap to judgment too quickly when I shouldn't and I'm slow to make up my mind when I need to be quick."

"So I won't need to poison you in your sleep in order to grab the crown if we merge Pacifica and Midlam."

"There might be other things you want to kill me for, but it won't be because I want the crown. I'm perfectly happy with the idea of being a kept man—as long as the one keeping me is my wife. I'm not, like, you know…my brother."

"Yeah, sure," Oz snickered. "I know all about the six girls you were stringing along your last year of high school and the ten others your first two years in college."

"My fantasy life doesn't count."

"And you're just fine with being the guy standing just to the right of the throne while I point at our loyal subjects and bark 'off with his head!' at random people. It won't bother you?"

Hey, I want to see that. I bet you would even wear the crown.

"As long as I get to keep *my* head. Besides, it makes sense for you to rule. Midlam's army is small and not especially well armed. Pacifica's military is much bigger and has all the cool war toys. I'm a science fiction geek who spends all his free time with his nose in books, and you're far more rounded. Plus, you can hurt people." He crossed his legs. "I've seen you kick."

"I didn't ask if it made sense. I asked if it would bother you."

Drew leaned back, snaking his arm behind her on the bench; I glared at him, a warning to keep his sticky boy-fingers to himself.

He must have felt the wrath of my glare, because his hand stayed right where it was supposed to, on the top rail of the bench, fingers resting on the back side, a good two inches from her back. "Midlam is traditionally a matriarchy, you know that. The only reason I'm next in line is because I don't have a sister and because my older brother would rather run naked through a blizzard than rule over anything more than a chess tournament. I was raised believing that women are better suited to head the state. So, no, it doesn't bother me. It means I can go about my business, indulge in my passions, and leave the country in more capable hands. Besides…you have that whole tripping through time thing going for you. You can access things I'll never be able to."

She doesn't trip, dude. She just walks right into the portal.

"That's actually an argument for me not being the head of state, if I want to keep doing that," she mused. "Once I take the throne, I'm basically stuck here."

"Doesn't your father still pop through time every now and then?"

"Rarely. It's not worth the risk. The last time he did, the Emperor—" she stopped and turned toward the sound that cut through my head like a tiny surgical blade. In unison we turned to look down the Embarcadero, almost like we'd practiced it; there was the shimmering of a portal, one that had never been there before.

If I could see it, Oz could see it; portal-blind Drew would just have to take her word.

She popped him on the arm several times in her excitement. "Look, look, look, look, look. Holy cow, I think a new portal is opening. And there's something in it, just beyond the opening."

Drew stood up, leaving my entire left side cold.

We need to discuss your manners, dog boy.

"Let's go, then. I've never seen someone come through one before."

*

I rode in Drew's sweatshirt with my head and front paws hanging out from its half-zipped front as they trotted down the pier and then up the street and along the Embarcadero. The new portal was a thin watery glimmer against the backdrop of the old Hyatt Hotel, and as we crossed the street we watched as first a leg poked through, then a hip, and the rest of the young man who was slowly standing up.

He moved like an old man getting out of a chair; the deliberation of unbending his back, the hand that went to it as he stretched a bit. He wasn't old, though; he looked almost as young as Drew, who was only nineteen.

In his excitement to meet someone fresh through a portal, Drew picked up speed, until Oz lunged and grabbed his arm. I knew what she was thinking: that portal wasn't supposed to be there. It was new and didn't look quite right; the colors were all wrong and the sound of it was just a little too different. Just beyond the shimmer of the opening was an oblong shaped—well, something—and things just didn't wait inside a portal. If you waited near one long enough and knew what to look for, you could see shadows of people passing in front of them in other Whens, but nothing ever hung in the pink mist of that null space.

"If you wait in the space," the King once told her, "you risk someone else running through and pulling you into a When you never intended."

Drew slowed down and walked beside her until they were near the Plaza, where the stiff young man was staring up Market Street, looking confused. He ran fingers through his short black hair, pulling at it a bit before letting go.

"This is wrong," he muttered when we were near.

"Wrong? How?" Drew asked.

"It's the middle of the day. Where is everyone? Where's the traffic? The vendors and the Farmer's Market? It was *just* here."

Drew followed his gaze up Market Street. "There are people. Just—"

Oz gently tapped his arm, and he stopped talking.

"When are you from?" she asked.

He blinked, and as if he had only then realized he wasn't alone, turned away from the length of Market Street. "From? San Francisco. Here."

Drew shifted from one foot to the other, and I could feel the want of speaking roll off him, but he held quiet.

"Seriously. What happened? I was *just* right here, and there were people practically shoulder to shoulder and the traffic noise was insane. Cars honking for no good reason, people shouting and jostling against each other."

"I'll ask again. When are you from?"

"San—"

"*When*," she stressed. "You're in San Francisco, but I think you missed your exit. You managed to create a new portal getting here, and I can see what has to be your ship hiding in it. I'm not asking where you're from, just *when*."

His mouth formed a silent "Oh," and then he frowned. "I'm from…I'm not sure."

"Tripping through those portals is tricky," she offered. "If you missed your exit or bounced through several in a row, it can mess with your head. It'll come to you."

He was breathing quickly, his eyes shining with panic. "You can see my ship? Am I breaking some law by being here?"

"Not everyone can see the portals," Oz said. "If you can see them and know the rules and how to use them, it's fine. No worries there."

"You don't even get in trouble if you can't see them, and just fall through," Drew added.

"Funnyman." She reached out, offering her hand. "I'm Oz, by the way. This is Drew, and the furball is Mister Wick."

"Mister Wick," he repeated as he shook her hand. "I'm—"

"Just call him Wick. He gets all self-important when we call him Mister."

He let go of her hand and began patting at his pockets. "I don't have any idea who I am. What—? How can I not know my name?"

Oz pointed toward the portal. "Maybe your ID is in your... whatever that is. Time-traveling egg? Seriously, it looks like an egg on steroids that was squeezed through a pipe."

I stretched to see past him; she was right. It was a long, squashed giant white egg that hovered a foot off the ground, and just beyond it, standing by the Plaza fountain with his hands shoved into his pockets and his head cocked to the right just so, was the Emperor. When he saw me looking at him, he sucked in a deep *oh-what-the-hell-now* breath, and began walking toward us.

You have company. He doesn't look happy. He doesn't look mad, either, but the unhappy is sitting right on top of his what's-going-on look.

"What are you babbling about, cat?" Drew asked. His hand went to my head, and if not for the Emperor approaching I might have let him scratch behind my ears for a good ten minutes.

The Emperor had been around almost as long as I had. He was a major presence of the city, spoke with a Scottish accent that came and went depending on his mood or how excited he was, and he was intentionally eccentric and often stern. Half the time he spoke with a formality that made him seem like a school teacher, but that was mostly a product of his accent; when he relaxed, so did his speech, unless he was deliberately poking at you. He also had the ear of the King—well, not the actual ear; that would be gross and the Queen would object—but the King paid valued attention to his opinions.

To most, he was the guy who wandered around the city and the guy you sent newcomers to for help. If you had no clue where to go to find a place to live, he'd get you into an apartment. Hungry? He'd find you food. Just passing through, but your shoes are wearing thin and you don't have money for new ones? In ten minutes he would have a new pair for you, plus a few pairs of bonus socks. He was a walking information center; if it existed in San Francisco, he could get you to it. If you were broke, he'd get you to it for free.

He was also weirdly moody, but everyone cut him slack on that. He'd saved the King's life when the King was just a little boy, and with that came respect. He went out of his way to be a guardian of the city, to get to know as many people as he could, and that made people like him. He could get away with moodiness; he'd earned the right.

He walked toward Oz and Drew and the new guy, his eyebrows knotted together and lips pressed thin, and I had no idea what to expect.

"You can't leave that there," he said to the new guy without acknowledging Oz or Drew. "Someone could walk into it and get hurt."

"It's in a portal," Oz said. "People pass through those all the time without even knowing they're there."

"People can pass through the portals they can't see, because there's nothing actually in their way. This—" he gestured toward the weird egg "—is huge and is physically here, even if it can't be seen." He turned to Drew and asked, "Can you see it? At all?"

"No."

He reached out to take me from Drew. "Walk. Slowly. Hands out in front of you, and head for the fountain."

Drew did as he was told, and five seconds later he bounced back from the edge of the portal.

"Pull it out of there," the Emperor said. "Or push it, I don't care."

"How? I can't see it."

He passed me off to Oz and stomped over to Drew. "Come on, then."

They went toward the back of the portal; Drew mimicked the

Emperor's placement of his hands, and together they pushed until the oblong white thing slid out from the portal, which closed behind it.

Ha. You just laid an egg, Emperor.

"Not so much a portal," the Emperor said. "A cloak."

Oz was already right next to it, running a hand over the smooth shell. I sniffed carefully, not trusting it to not bite me. Or worse.

"A time machine," she breathed.

It smells like burning.

The Emperor smelled it, too. "A time machine with a fried power supply. You must have had a hiccup along the way."

"That might explain your memory, too," Oz told the new guy. "Bounce here, bounce there, who knows? Look inside, maybe there's something that will tell you who you are and jar the rest of your memory."

The newby carefully set a hand on the top of the egg, his fingers splayed out like he was trying to pick up a basketball, and a door lifted from the side like a bird's wing. Oz and Drew moved to peek inside, while the Emperor took a few steps back.

He's not always a polite sort of person; neither Oz nor Drew would find that odd and the newby wasn't paying attention.

Ten minutes later, with three sets of hands digging through the clutter of papers and clothing and empty drink cups, the only thing close to an ID they found was a torn piece of paper with a partial signature scrawled across it. Oz talked while they searched, trying to explain to the Emperor about this newby's empty brain and wanting to figure out who he was.

"Finneg," Drew read out loud. "Does that sound familiar?"

He shook his head.

"It's all you've got," Oz said. "Until it comes to you, I suppose you're Finnegan."

"Finn?" Drew suggested.

"He's Other When," the Emperor said.

"We're looking for a name, not a label," Oz said.

Well, my name isn't really Mister Wick but I don't make a big deal out of it.

"Call him anything you want. But he is Other When. He's not

from now, and you have no idea why he's here or what he's here for. Or if he's telling the truth."

"But I—" Finn sputtered.

The Emperor held up his hand. "Whether you are or not doesn't change the most basic thing—you are from a different When. And this is where I'm going to seem unbelievably rude. You don't touch me, not ever. Not by accident, not by a brush of your shoulder as we pass, not by a stray hair. I will help you, but you will *not* touch me."

"Emperor," Oz started.

"No. Take him to your father, tell him what you know. I'll take care of his transportation and make sure it's secure."

"But no touching."

He nodded. "Of me. Don't detour, either, Oz. Take him straight to the King."

3

Oz did as she was told; she and Drew marched Finn up Market Street and turned on Powell, ignoring people who waved greetings or looked like they wanted to speak with her. People usually wanted to talk to her; she was the Princess, but she was friendly and accessible, and normally would have at least said hello. Over the summer people had gotten used to Drew drawing a lot of her attention and they kindly gave them privacy, so it might have seemed a bit less rude to them because they understood, but Oz was to sort of person who never wanted to intentionally ignore anyone and I don't think she was happy having to. Her cheeks were flushed and the tips of her ears as well, embarrassed that she might be making people feel unwanted.

She picked the closest door to the family residence and went in first, letting Drew bring up the rear, and it wasn't until they were in the elevator going up that anyone spoke.

Finn took a deep breath and spoke so softly he might as well have whispered. "This all looks familiar. All of it. Market Street. The cable car on Powell. I know you just took me into the Macy's building. Yet it doesn't feel right."

"Give it time," Oz said. "And it's not Macy's anymore. I live here."

"Your Emperor thinks I'm lying. So why would he just let you walk off with me? Why not call for police or security?"

"Because he really doesn't think you're lying. Neither do I."

"*I* don't even know. How could you?"

With a slight lift of her eyebrow and a twist of a grin, Oz said, "I have ways."

When the elevator doors opened and Oz stepped out, Finn hesitated. Drew nudged him forward and Oz, who realized he was not moving forward on his own, said, "I promise, my dad doesn't bite. He doesn't even growl."

"That's the Emperor's job," Drew muttered.

The elevator opened to the floor of the Royal Family apartment; to the right was the hallway that led to the bedrooms, with a staircase heading down near the end of the hall, and to the left there was a glass wall with a door that led out onto the balcony. The living room was straight ahead, and past that, the dining room and kitchen, with its little office nook for the Queen.

Finn looked past the foyer to the living room; there was laundry stacked on one end of the sofa and books scattered across the coffee table, a cat scratcher sat in the middle of the floor with flecks of shredded cardboard all around it, and a pile of backpacks took up an entire chair. He noted it all and then muttered, "Well, this is certainly normal."

"Expecting a palace?"

"Something like that. At least...opulent."

People live here, dude. Clutter happens.

The building the royal family lived in had once been a series of large department stores on the perimeter of Union Square and was known mostly as the Old Macy's Building. Oz described the family's main floor as having been everything from clothes and furniture sales to a restaurant, and it amused her to visit it any time she popped into the past via a portal.

"It's tons of fun to go back four hundred years and sit on the balcony with lunch just to watch pigeons sucker people into feeding them. Those little flying rats had cojones."

It became the home for the royal family a hundred years earlier; before then they'd taken space in an old Hyatt hotel near the Embarcadero, with spectacular views of the water and the Bay Bridge—and with all the drawbacks in security those views presented. It was a giant target on the edge of the financial district at a time when cars and trucks were still allowed on the bridge, and the King ignored the warnings that anyone could be on the bridge or on a ferry and have a direct line of site to the royal residence, or someone could blow the whole bridge up.

That seemed unlikely, and it was a fantastic vista for visiting dignitaries and personal guests. The King declared it safe and raised his family there, and hosted huge, lavish parties, all the while brushing off the idea that the old hotel was any more vulnerable than the rest of the city.

Three decades later, after a car loaded with explosives was stopped and sent flying over the bridge rails, both the Bay Bridge and the Golden Gate Bridge were closed to vehicle traffic. If you wanted into the city, you either had to drive south and come in from the 101, or you walked, biked, ferried, or took a Transbay train across.

When King Jackson—Jax—was a teenager, all of downtown was closed to traffic, other than licensed delivery vans. You could walk the streets, ride an old pedal bicycle, or hop on an air bike, but you could not drive a car anywhere downtown. The outcry was loud and the protests long; businesses would suffer, the tax base would crumble, and the city was doomed.

The city managed just fine. People in outlying neighborhoods used public transit for the most part, anyway; those who lived in the heart of the city walked everywhere as it was. Those most affected were the tourists, but with some help from locals, they figured it out. They learned the transit lines, rented air bikes and jetted around the city, exploring even further than they had in the past, they had purchases delivered to their hotels or shipped home, and still spent their money as they had before.

I liked it; the lack of loud, obnoxious cars meant I could go outside and breathe without choking on exhaust fumes, and I could run across the street without worrying about getting run over.

"My brother wants a castle," Oz told Finn as she led him through the living room toward the kitchen. "He's seriously disappointed that no one will tear down everything on Treasure Island and build him one. But his wish is probably the closest we'll ever get to living in a palace."

If the normal apartment in the normal building surprised Finn, seeing the King sitting at the dining room table baffled him. Wearing a plain black t-shirt, jeans, and sporting a heavy black five o'clock shadow, King Jackson, head of the House of Blackshear and ruler of Pacifica, sat at the table with his chin resting on his hands as he waited for his Queen to bring him a plate of the scrambled eggs she was making.

Finn, whether he wanted any or not, was getting a heaping plate of eggs. If Oz had come into the apartment with ten of her friends, they were getting eggs, like it or not. The Queen liked to feed people; her family did not leave the house without breakfast, she required they all be home for dinner when possible, and if you were in her house, you were family for as long as you were there. She cooked enough to feed a family of twelve, and the inevitable leftovers were foisted upon the Emperor or devoured late at night by Drew or Oz's brother, Zed.

The Queen turned around, frying pan in hand, and asked the King, "Jax, do you want bacon?" and in the same breath greeted Finn with, "Oh! So nice to meet you! Sit down, I'll bring dinner over in just a few minutes."

He started to protest, but the King pointed to the chair to his left. Finn sat down, quietly thanked her, and scooted closer to the table.

Sleepily, the King said, "Yes, we do breakfast for dinner. And if you don't eat, her feelings will be hurt and I'll hear about it until next Sunday."

"Not that my dad ever exaggerates," Oz said. She sat across the table and Drew—who still had me tucked into his sweatshirt— sat next to Finn. "But yeah, you don't get a choice. Eat, or forever offend her majesty. She might even cry."

"Oh, hush," the Queen said. She leaned over the breakfast bar. "Sweety, do you have any allergies I should know about? These guys love cream cheese in their eggs, but it's no trouble to make some without. Or if you can't eat eggs, I can make something else for you."

He took a moment to consider. "I don't think I do. I don't think it matters."

"Drew, put that cat down. And of course it matters. I won't risk killing you ten minutes after meeting you. Poison can wait for dessert if it's needed."

The King chuckled, but Finn missed it.

"No, it's just that…I'm pretty sure I'm dreaming. So nothing I eat will matter."

Drew pulled me out of his sweatshirt and set me on the floor; I jumped onto the empty chair at the foot of the table, even though the King was scowling at me.

I expected him to be amused, because the cat was sitting nicely at the table like a human, and I wasn't on the counter which drove him nuts, but after his three-second death glare that was surely designed to light my whiskers on fire, he turned back to Finn. "What makes you think you're dreaming?"

"I'm in San Francisco, which apparently now has a king, a queen, and an emperor who can tell a teenaged princess what to do…and she does it without arguing. I'm not sure how that fits in with the rest of the United States and where my brain cooked it up, but I have to be asleep."

Before Oz could jump in—and she surely would—the King asked, "And time travel? Does that make sense to you?"

"I think so. I don't know."

"Why didn't you take him straight to the doctor?" he asked Oz.

"The Emperor told me to bring him to you. I brought him to you."

He understood that; even he deferred to the Emperor on unofficial things much of the time. "The United States hasn't existed for nearly two hundred years, Finn. Pacifica and Midlam are monarchies that were born when it fell apart, and we're the two largest countries existing on former U.S. soil."

"You split the country down the middle? What, like cake?"

"I'm sure that would have been easier. It split into five main countries. New England, which is most of the upper northeast of the former U.S., Texas is its own gubernatorial state, and Florida, which comprises most of the eastern seaboard. New England is a neutrality, and Florida is a theocracy."

"Civil war?"

"Close. Between fighting over food, water, and religion, there very nearly was civil war. Texas seceded first, then Florida… sides were picked, people flocked to live where they were most comfortable politically, and the country was basically divided up. What became Pacifica voted to become a monarchy, and Midlam followed."

"How? How does that even work? A bunch of politicians fight to the death to become king?"

"No," the King said lightly. "The first monarchy was decided by an election. It was a five-year-long process with interim governors, and after that—" he gestured to his wife and daughter "—here we are. Midlam's path to monarchy was similar."

"Except we're a dedicated matriarchy," Drew added. "First born daughter rules."

"What if there isn't one?"

"Then you get me, the sister-less crown prince who doesn't really want the job."

"Yeah," Finn said as his food was placed on the table in front of him. "I'm definitely asleep."

*

Drew helped clean up and then took Finn to see the family doctor. After offering to help but being told to sit and rest, Finn watched the normal picture of family unfold; the kids cleaning in the kitchen while the mom cleared the table, dad on the phone asking his doctor to meet the new guy in his office, then lecturing the cat on the bad manners of jumping on the table.

"We own bleach, sweetheart," the Queen told him for the thousandth time. "Wick is fine."

I stayed right where I was, curled up on the warm spot where Drew's plate had been, and kept an eye on Finn, who was still baffled by the complete lack of regal bearing of the royalty he'd dined with. He accepted the destruction of the United States, listening to the short history lesson of how it collapsed under the weight of religious ideology fighting against personal freedoms, because he was positive that he was deeply asleep in a quiet bedroom somewhere and his brain was simply taking a vacation from reality.

He would play along, because sooner or later he would wake up.

When the elevator door closed behind Drew, the Queen dropped into her chair next to the King. "So," she started. "Neither of you think he's lying."

"He's not," Oz said.

"Not intentionally, anyway," the King added. "He has memory issues and is telling us the truth as far as he knows it, but that doesn't mean he's harmless."

"I watched his voice, and the color of the sounds he made never changed. I think that if he were even subconsciously lying that it would. I mean, even when he said he was dreaming…it wasn't hyperbole. He literally thinks he's deeply asleep and stuck in a dream."

"There's no point in lying when you're asleep," the King mused.

"But once he knows he's awake?" Oz went on. "Who knows?"

"I trust your gut feelings, Ozzie. We will treat him like a guest," the Queen said. "Set him up in the guest room next to Drew's and make sure he knows what time we have breakfast. And find out what size clothes he wears. He'll need something to sleep in and clothes for the next few days, at least. Jax, he's a little smaller than you are but I think you could lend him a t-shirt and sweatshirt for tonight. Sweatpants, too."

King Jackson knew better than to argue.

He might be the ruler, but they both knew who was in charge.

*

Oz left to find Drew and Finn; I waited behind, following the King from the dining room to the living room, because I knew that as soon as he could, the Emperor would be there. I could feel him moving through the hallways, waiting until the family was done eating, waiting until Oz had spoken with her father. He waited because he didn't want to interfere as the King met the newby, knowing that Jax might take his cues about Finn from his own behavior.

He didn't want to influence the King, yet he also did, and knew that he could.

He was human. I could hardly blame him for that.

Besides, he once went back 200 years to get me an entire bucket of chicken that was fried up by some army officer. He gets extra points from me just for that, and I shared it with him because he was so thoughtful. He also sometimes takes me with him—I don't care for that part—and buys me shrimp cut into Wick-sized pieces, so really, I shouldn't blame him for anything.

The Queen was the first to greet him, and before he could even get into the room she was fussing over him, insisting he was obviously hungry and needed food; he knew well enough that he would lose any argument, and agreed that yes, a sandwich would be nice. And yes, a cold beer would be fantastic. Yes, please, thank you…he smiled at her, and in that moment was genuinely happy and I had a fleeting notion that he missed someone and that I should know who, but it passed as he dropped into the comfy chair across from the King.

"The boy's vehicle is like nothing in existence," he said. There was no lead up to the topic at hand; he was jumping in, knowing the King would keep up. "If I stripped away its shell, I'd think I was looking at the bones of a new generation in personal air cars, but the engine—"

"Old? New?"

"It's not internal combustion. It's not thermal-driven. It's not magnetic. The power source is both complicated and simplistic. The back half of the inner compartment is lined with pods that look like small plasma-core batteries and half of them are dead, but I can't be sure without opening one."

"So open one."

"Jax."

"I know. 'Boom.' Give him a day or two to get some memories back and maybe he'll be able to tell you how they work."

He hesitated. "You believe him, then?"

"My daughter certainly does. At least she thinks he believes what he's saying. I'm caught between believing it and wondering where the hell he came from if he is being honest. The vehicle you describe is clearly from the future. What little details he recalls tells me he's from the past."

"Or lying."

"Lying well enough to fool Oz, which is a considerable feat. I could see some of the sound surrounding him, but I don't notice subtle changes the way she does. She'll latch onto him, too, you know she will. He's new and different and she won't be able to resist. I'm not sure that's a good idea."

"I'll make a nuisance of myself," the Emperor said as the Queen came back with his food. "I'll watch out for her."

"Good enough. But who will watch the watcher?"

I stretched, standing on my back legs to peer at the Emperor's plate—ham and cheese, I would be getting some of that—and then at his face.

He had a slight grin as he took a sip of his beer.

You know who will be watching you, right?

Anything else they had to discuss lost my interest. There was ham, and there was cheese, and in spite of the looks the Queen gave him, the Emperor tore off bite-sized pieces and fed them to me. When he was done, she took his plate, and with a heavy sigh said, "You spoil him."

"Old men *should* be spoiled."

"We don't discuss that," she said over her shoulder as she went to the kitchen.

"Really," the King said, "we don't. It feels like a jinx."

I didn't feel like it was a jinx; I was older than my own memories, and I was fine with that. I knew the Emperor was fine with that, and as he absently scratched under my chin he told the King that he could avoid it all he wanted, but I might be the equivalent of a thousand-year-old human and it should be celebrated, not avoided.

Give me some steak and shrimp, I'll celebrate anything you want.

"If anything happens to him—" the King sighed.

"We would all be heartbroken, I know. Wick is fine, Jax. You don't have to avoid the cat-sized elephant in the room. He shouldn't still be alive, yet here he is." And to me he said, "I don't think you plan on going anywhere soon, do you?"

Just to find the princess and the dude that smells like dog. Maybe the new guy, too.

"You're a good boy, Mister Wick."

Bloody hell. For sure I'm leaving now.

'Good boy.'

He said that on purpose, I think, trying to make me cough up the ham and cheese. I settled for one last head scratch, and then headed for the staircase at the end of the hall so that I could look for the princess, and quite possibly score another snack or two.

4

I found them down one floor in the staff kitchen, which was more of a break room for staff that the family didn't have—there were personal guards but no full time housekeepers or cooks, and there had never been nannies—and they were sitting on tall stools at the kitchen island. The lights were dim and the Princess's face was bathed in the glow from her phone. She pointedly set it down when I jumped up, and she said, "All right, Mister Wick. Dad said to not let you sucker me into anything. You already ate half the Emperor's sandwich."

That didn't matter. In ten minutes, maybe twenty, she would bend to my will. If not her, then Drew would. Drew, no matter how awful he smelled, was usually willing to sneak something to me. He believed that no food should be left uneaten, and he extended it to me.

I should get over my uncertainty about you. You smell like dog but I haven't actually seen one around here. Maybe you just need a shower.

I walked over to him and plopped down on the paper he had been looking at.

"That's my class schedule, Wick. I was looking at it."

And now you're not.

"Fine. I'm not ready for classes to start, anyway. That campus is huge and I don't know where anything is, and I'm pretty sure I'm going to throw up before I get to my first lecture."

That amused Oz. "You have over a month to walk around and learn the layout."

"Locked buildings," he countered. "There was no summer term."

"And with a phone call we can get in. I know you're all about the not-being-a-prince-while-you're-studying thing, but it has a few perks. If I call and say I want to show you around, they're going to let me in to show you around. They'll probably even give you a personal tour."

"And if your parents find out?"

"'What the hell, Oz?'" she said in exaggerated imitation of her father. "It wouldn't upset them. It's not like I'd be stomping my feet, telling some professor he has to freaking give you top level grades because I'm the freaking princess and I freaking say so."

"Are you sure? Because I wouldn't mind that at all."

"Ha. No. You pass or fail on your own merits but it would be nice if you pass, just in case we are together someday. I'd hate to have to introduce you like, 'Yes, this is Andrew, my husband, the Prince Consort, and third-year university failure. Oh, he majored in political science and history, but you know how it goes. No one told him he would have to, like, crack open a book and read while he was at it.'"

"I have to read?"

"I suppose we can hire someone to read your text books out loud to you, if you're that lazy."

"I might be." The door swung open and Finn came in. "Good, you found us. I'm not really good at giving directions and was worried you might wind up in the Emperor's apartment."

That wouldn't go over well. He hates company almost as much as he hates being touched.

"Is your room all right?" Oz asked.

"It's amazing. The view…damn."

"Seriously," Drew said. "We visited a lot when I was a kid, and I used to plaster myself to the window when I wasn't allowed on the balcony, just to keep looking outside. Something's always going on down on Union Square."

"Wait until the holidays," Oz said. "It's beautiful, with all the lights and the giant tree. There's even a skating rink and most nights there's live music."

"How long until then?" Finn asked.

"The decorations go up in three months. I hope if you're still here it's by choice and not because you can't remember anything and we have no idea in which When your home is."

He'd seen the doctor, who found nothing obviously wrong with him. He was poked, prodded, and scanned, and other than some scarring from having had his appendix removed as a child, and an old surgical staple over his sternum, there was nothing.

"The good news is I'm perfectly healthy. The bad news is I'm perfectly healthy."

"Not bad news," she said. "It just means that you probably did take a wrong bounce through a few different time periods, and you're a bit scrambled right now. In a day or two it'll all come back, and in the meantime you'll stay here with us so that my mother can feed you until you explode."

"She'll do it, too," Drew snickered.

"And the man who has gained about five pounds since he got here would know. Finn, I had an idea, I'm not sure if it will help at all…but you seem to know San Francisco, so maybe hitting up some familiar spots would help."

"Play like a tourist and go sight-seeing?"

She shrugged. "It's just an idea."

"No, I didn't mean it was a bad idea. It sure as hell can't hurt."

Clearly, he'd never seen Oz drive an air bike.

*

I did as the Emperor asked, when the King was distracted enough to not notice the drum-like tapping of his old friend's fingers across my back and a whisper was lost in the noise of the room; I waited until Oz and Drew had drifted apart for the night, and made my way through the cat flap next to the guest bedroom door.

Keep an eye on Finn. No problem.

Finn was already asleep, flat on his back, and he was bathed in the city lights that streamed through the nearly wall-sized window. I jumped up on the bed to watch him, listening to each sleepy breath that he took, every inhale and exhale, until he whispered, "Joe."

I crept closer to his head until my whiskers touched his cheek.

"Joe. Don't."

He reached up to brush the shadow of my whiskers from his face, and then rolled over.

I stayed there all night, napping when I was sure he would stay asleep, watching when I wasn't. He muttered that same name twice more, and he drooled onto the pillow, but there wasn't anything else to see or hear. I didn't want to risk climbing onto him to listen to his dreams; even curling up on his pillow and resting my head against his seemed like a bad idea, since I had no idea how he would react if he woke. An hour or two before dawn I sniffed at his face one more time, jumped off the bed, and left the room the same way I'd gone in.

The Emperor was waiting at the end of the hall, and when I stopped at his feet, he reached down to scratch behind my ears and then asked, "Why are you wandering about so early, Wick?"

Watching. Listening. The newby muttered a name. Just a name. Someone called "Joe."

He reached into a small plastic bag he'd fished from his pocket, and dropped half a dozen bites of steak on the floor in front of me. "Somehow I knew I'd find you wandering around this morning. Too many people to keep an eye on, eh? And here we are, saddling you with another charge."

Yeah, well, keep feeding me steak and I'll babysit him every night.

"He'll sort himself out sooner or later, you know, but I am glad you're keeping tabs on him. Maybe today we can find a way to jump start his brain."

I didn't think he knew about the plans Oz had made, but I was sleepy and content with the meaty bits, so I turned around and headed into her room, where I could curl up on the wide window seat and sleep until the first sun puddle of the day washed over me.

5

Drew lumbered out of the building a good ten minutes later than Oz and Finn; they waited for him across the street, sitting on the steps leading up to Union Square, barely talking through the haze that still had sleepy wisps wrapped around them. Finn held a cup of hot chocolate between his hands and he stared into it instead of looking around, and Oz's gaze was directed at the door across the street. If she had been more awake, she probably would have been irritated with Drew for taking so long, but she was still tired enough to not care.

He ran across the street holding bright red fabric scrunched up tightly in one hand, and as he neared he sputtered, "Your mom. Cripes."

Oz yawned. "She made you eat again?"

"Surprisingly, no." He flicked the fabric open and held it up for her to see. "She's been sewing. She took one of my sweatshirts and modified the hand pouch. Sewed the sides up and opened up the top. And she then cut off the sleeves so I wouldn't feel hot, because I'm apparently wearing it whether I want to or not."

Oz blinked. "Why?"

"Wick. She said, and I quote, 'I know you kids carry that poor cat everywhere. He's going to fall off your shoulder or you'll drop him. Wear this so he's safe and will be comfortable.' Seriously. She made a cat carrier out of a sweatshirt."

Finn snorted a laugh.

She loves me and wanted to give you to me as a minion.

Oz bit back a grin and told him to put it on, see how it looked. With a sigh, Drew pulled it over his head and then looked at me. "All right, fuzz bucket. Do you want to test sit this thing?"

It looks comfy enough.

I let him pick me up and ease me into the pouch. It was a bit tight around my tail, but with some wiggling I settled in, resting my paws on the top of the pouch. I had a decent view from there, and it was filled with just the right amount of warms.

It'll do.

The only thing about it that bothered me was that I couldn't see behind him; I could hear the Emperor approach, but I couldn't pinpoint exactly where he was and that made me nervous. People are tricky things; most of them can be trusted, but only so much. I wanted to know where he was, and tried to stretch to see around Drew's side.

"As if that cat wasn't spoiled enough," he said when Drew turned toward him.

"Not my idea."

The Queen thinks I'm too special to have to sit on your head.

The Emperor was a little too amused. "We could have just gotten him a stroller. Surely someone makes one for pushing around yappy little dogs."

Fine, and what part of you did you want me to make bleed?

"We're taking Finn sight-seeing today," Oz said. "I thought it might jog his memory."

"Not a bad idea."

"We could start—"

The Emperor held up his hand. "Let Finn decide. If you suggest places, you reduce the chance that he'll remember on his own."

"I know the city," Finn said, getting up. "The Embarcadero and the Ferry Building. Pier thirty-nine. Hiking along Ocean Beach and through Land's End and the Sutro Baths, then having dinner at the Cliff House. Getting burgers at a dive bar in North Beach. I remember it but it wasn't like *this*." He gestured around himself. "It wasn't this quiet. There should be thousands of people practically falling over each other on the sidewalks and dodging traffic on the streets. It should be fantastically loud, with cars honking and people trying to talk above it. There should be shadows from air traffic and light bouncing off metal and glass skyscrapers."

He took a deep breath. "I remember San Francisco, just not this one. This looks like the city when it was younger, early twenty-first century, but without...everyone."

Oz looked at the Emperor, one eyebrow raised as if she were asking him permission, or perhaps consenting him to tell Finn about the city.

"That's an intentional design choice," he said. "The city looks today almost eighty percent identical to how it looked right around twenty-fifteen. It's a tourist draw. People can come here and it's as if they're visiting a living piece of history."

"Minus the crowds and traffic," Finn mused.

"There's no need for heavy traffic downtown. People can walk, take sub-transit—" he gestured to the ground; the train ran under the streets "—or they can pedal a bicycle. If they're in a hurry or can't manage the hills, they can take an air bike. Personal cars are no longer allowed downtown."

"Why not?"

"Security."

"For my family," Oz added. "When my dad was a teenager, traffic was restricted from SOMA up to Crissy Field. You can still drive in South San Francisco, but pretty much from Sixteenth Street cutting cross the city, there's very limited traffic."

"All right, but why so few people?"

"If you're comparing to the early twenty-first century? Population across the continent as a whole is probably less than half of what it was then."

"You're remembering a city with nearly a million residents plus multiple thousands of tourists," the Emperor said.

"And now?"

"A little over one hundred thousand."

Finn mouthed the word 'wow' but then turned to the whirring

sound coming up behind the Emperor. "And that would be—?"

"My brother," Oz replied. "Oh, an air bike, if that's what you meant. My brother, Zed, on an air bike."

Air bikes were on the list of things I have never been fond of. They looked too much like those things that people rode on the water in the Bay—wave runners, I think—but with flat bottoms and noisy air jets that helped push them along the road. The magnets seated right next to the air jets bothered me—what if one flew over me and connected with the metal in my collar? I'd be taken for a ride I never asked for. They had longer seats so that three or four people could ride on one, but I'd only ever seen two on at a time, and it was usually Zed with a friend, going faster than he should, right over the middle of Union Square, where bikes were technically not allowed.

Zed sped up and then braked hard, making the front end of the bike lift a few inches, and then in one motion he slapped the ignition switch as he jumped off.

"Where have you been all night?" Oz asked him.

"Alcatraz. Talking to dead people." He turned toward Finn. "Hello. Who are you?"

Oz gestured to him. "Zed, this is Finn. Finn, Zed. Finn sort of popped up out of nowhere yesterday, and has a bit of a memory problem. We're trying to help him remember who he is and when he's from."

"Ah," Zed uttered, as if it made perfect sense. He held his hand out to Finn; he grasped hands to shake, but instead of letting go he moved in close, his face a bare inch from Finn's. "You smell... fresh."

I could feel Oz's horror roll off her. "Oh my God, Zed, you can't just go around sniffing people!"

He ignored her. "Fresh, like rain. Something new. A baby without the sour milk cloud."

"I showered."

"Ignore him, Finn," Oz said. "He does that. He knows it's rude, but he does it anyway."

"Why do you sniff people?" Finn asked him.

"I can sense things about them when I do. More than they want me to see, actually. I—"

"Alcatraz," Oz interrupted. "I didn't know you were working nights now."

"It's easier to tend to them at night. No distractions. Finn, have you seen the rock? It's beautiful, even looking at it from the shore."

"We're taking him around the city to try to jog his memory. He gets to choose where."

Finn shrugged. "Why not Alcatraz? Start there and work our way to the Golden Gate?"

Zed headed for his bike. "Hop on, I'll drive. They can catch up."

Finn looked to Oz for permission and she nodded. Half a minute later we were headed down the stairs to the garage under the Square to grab two more bikes. No one asked me how I felt about it, but I can tell you…I was not happy.

*

"Alcatraz used to be a prison, housing some of the worst criminals of the day, from the mid nineteen-thirties to the early nineteen-sixties. After it was closed, the infrastructure of the prison remained and became a weird little tourist attraction…then, roughly two hundred years ago, it was badly damaged in an earthquake and had to be torn down."

Finn was looking around, probably only half hearing what Zed was telling him. We were all cold and a little damp from the ferry ride that took us from the Embarcadero to the island, and no one was exactly happy.

My ear furs and whiskers were wet. I was three kinds of upset.

They should have dressed warmer. San Francisco is often cold during the summer and they should have known better. I didn't exactly have a choice selection of outfits to choose from, so my annoyance was justified.

"The prison couldn't be recreated, obviously, so it became our main mortuary. Since there are no cemeteries in San Francisco, most people are cremated here."

We were at the entrance to the biggest building on the island, which was only two stories tall and about the length of a football field. It was nondescript—just gray cement pocketed with a dozen square windows that made me feel even colder—but that was by design. When the building was first proposed, the committee in charge decided they wanted plain, ordinary, and a bit disinviting, simply to keep anyone in the near future from trying to reclaim it for money-grabbing touristy things.

What people saw from the shore was a mix of flowering vines, planted to block the building from view. The drab construction of the main building had worked—no one particularly wanted to visit the island unless they had a loved one there—but no one wanted it as a view, either.

"There are no cemeteries?" Finn stopped spinning on his heels to look at Zed. "You *have* to be cremated?"

"No, of course not. You just can't be buried in the city. Most families who want a traditional burial for their loved ones choose the Gardens of Sacramento, about two hours away. It's a beautiful place, but in the end it's still putting someone you love in a hole in the ground."

Oz slapped at his arm. "Zed…"

"I know. Not everyone shares my loathing of burial. I don't mean it's not respectful or tastefully done, but it does seem like a waste of resources and land."

He pulled the door open and ushered us into the lobby. Unlike the outside, inside had relaxing layers of warm and it was dry. In any other setting it would be a cheery place; the walls were pocked with colorful artwork, tall green plants were tucked into the corners and hung from the ceiling, and I felt like I was in the Emperor's living room. There were sofas and chairs, the walls were a nice bright yellow, and there was even a toy box with things to distract the sticky people.

He'd even had a toy box at one time, loaded with things to distract Oz and Zed when he watched them. The lobby didn't have his massive bookshelves crammed full with old, well-read books, but there were magazines and coloring books.

"The first thing a family experiences here shouldn't feel clinical," Zed said. "There's enough of that in the end for most people. They need to be able to sit down, catch their breath, and collect their thoughts. A lot of people need that, because the next thing is to sit with their loved one's body, and that can be difficult."

"And that's where Zed comes in," Oz said. "While families grieve, he comforts the dead, and in a way that comforts them, too."

He led us to the hallway that was just beyond a massive rubber tree plant; it had grown the height of the wall and was pushing its way across the ceiling, as if it threatened to swallow the entryway whole. The hall was brightly lit and lined with open doors and windows, except for one near the end. The door was closed and the lights bled around the edges of the curtain.

"Please try to pass by quietly."

Cat footsteps, dudes.

At the end of the hallway there were heavy double doors; on the other side was a huge room that was not decorated at all—it looked as cold as the outside, though I was not shivering and felt quite peaceful there.

It reminded me of the giant room where the basement pool lived, where the Emperor taught Oz and Zed to swim, though here there was no pool and no stench of chemicals. Instead, there were six tables lined up along one side, slabs on wheels that did not look the least bit restful, and on the one closest to the door was a woman with very long dark hair that cascaded down the side, and she had a soft blue sheet tucked neatly up to her shoulders.

Zed stepped over to her, and gently touched his fingers to her shoulder. "Good morning, Nikka. I brought a few friends to meet you and to say goodbye."

Oz leaned toward Finn and whispered, "Zed prepares people for their final goodbye. He usually does this in one of bereavement rooms with family who want to listen. He talks to them, reads them their favorite stories or sings to them. He learns as much as he can about who they were and speaks about their lives, what they dreamed about, what they hoped for and achieved in life."

"Why? They're dead, what's the point?"

Zed pulled a small basin and white washcloth from under the table. He tested the water with his finger and said that it was warm—he didn't want to send anyone off after a too-cold bath—and set it near her feet. "Everyone deserves that last bit of respect. Everyone, even the worst among us, deserves to have their lives acknowledged and then remembered, and everyone deserves to be mourned, even if it's the regrets of unfulfilled potential."

"I didn't mean—"

"I know. No disrespect intended. Nikka—" he slowly pulled the sheet away "—died alone and her family is gone. She's the reason I came home when I did this morning, to ask Oz and Drew to be here, to hear her story and to say goodbye, so that someone other than me will miss her."

The Emperor stepped toward the table. "Just tell us what to do, Zed."

We stood around the cold body of Nikka Johanson, and learned that she had been born in Seattle, where she met and married Brian Sorrel, and then moved with him to San Francisco to be a nurse and to care for those who were suffering and dying. She had a daughter, Tina, who died at the age of twelve, and her husband followed not long after, lost to the shadows of grief, drowned in spirits that did not haunt him but took him from her all the same.

Nikka loved animals, and in her mourning filled the hours that would have been otherwise empty by caring for the lost furry friends of the city and finding them homes; she gave them all her love and most of her money, and in the end died when she fell from a horse she had lovingly nursed from near-starvation to robust health.

We watched in silence as Zed finished bathing her and brushed her long hair; to reach the ends of it he had to go to his knees, and while he did he recited a poem that had been found in her pocket. It was scribbled on well-worn notepaper, the letters retraced several times, as if she had tried desperately to hold onto each fading syllable. It spoke of family and eternity, a wish for both and gratitude for having had it at all, even for time that passed in a blink. When Zed went quiet, his recitation of her life done and her body ready, the Emperor moved to the side of the table and placed a hand gently on top of one of hers.

"I knew Nikka, but not as well as I should have. I do know that she was unselfish and giving, and more importantly that she was unfailingly kind. I will miss seeing her chasing the cats around Union Square with her bag filled with treats, and I will miss her warm greetings as we passed each other on the street." He leaned over and whispered to her, "I will miss you, Nikka Johanson Sorrel. I will mourn you, and you will not be forgotten."

Oz and Drew moved closer to the table to whisper their goodbyes, and I wiggled to get free from Drew's grasp. He held tight, one finger looped through my collar, until the Emperor whispered for him to let me say goodbye, too.

Drew placed me at the foot of the table, and I made my way along Nikka's side, so that I could sniff her face. I knew her. She'd given me meaty bits and crunchy treats from time to time, and knew that I was not a stray but a loved family cat. She scratched my head right behind my ears where I loved it most, and told me I had the most beautiful green eyes she had ever seen. Most of the time she also asked me to go home where I would be safe, and watched to make sure that I went all the way across the street, and then in through my flap near the door.

You were more beautiful than most. Goodbye, Nikka of the Crunchy Treats. I will miss you.

With gentle hands placed on the edges of the table, Drew and Oz said their final soft goodbyes, but when I looked at Finn he was rooted in place at the foot of the table, his gaze fixed on Nikka's cascading hair, his hands clutched to his chest, and his eyes were filled with tears.

*

We waited for the ferry in the cold, locked into a breath of quiet thoughts. The nip of the air outside felt pleasant after the warmth of the mortuary, the bite of the fog comforting after having waited as Zed kissed Nikka's forehead, covered her again to her shoulders with the sheet, and then rolled the table to the next room.

When he came back, Finn asked what was going to happen to her.

"She'll be cremated today, and her ashes will be hard-pressed."

"What?"

"The dead are turned into diamonds, essentially," the Emperor said. "Rather than scattering the ashes or keeping them in an urn, it becomes something precious for their families to keep."

"But you said she had no family."

"Those with no immediate family become part of ours," Oz said. "Her remains will be kept safe in our home, either until someone comes forward or time just runs out."

There was an entire floor in the royal house that was meant for the storage of peoples' remains. I'd only been in it once, when I was looking for the swimming pool and got off a floor too early, but the Queen was there and let me in to see. It was a cheery place, even though there was no place to sit and the walls were lined with tiny, locked boxes.

It was the color that made it a happy place; the paint was the palest yellow and the walls were trimmed with a dark, reddish wood, and the lights that hung from the ceiling were cased in red. The room glowed, and I thought that when I was gone, this is where I would like to rest, although I was also sure if that happened while I was still part of the Blackshear family, I would be placed on the fireplace mantel in the living room.

I liked curling up by the fire when it was cold, so that was all right with me, too.

Zed added to Oz's thought, "I care for them the same, whether they have families here mourning them, or they're taking this step alone. When Nikka's stone is ready, I will treat it with the love and respect she deserves. I promise."

"That's a lot for a sixteen-year-old to take on."

"It's basic human kindness. No one is too young for that."

Now as we stood in the cold, Finn was staring at the Golden Gate Bridge, not speaking, barely blinking. He was focused on the San Francisco end, as if he was looking for someone waiting there. I tried to see what he wanted to see, but from where we waited, the people on the bridge were nothing but tiny moving dots.

When the ferry docked and we were boarding, he said quietly, "I'd like to go to the bridge next, if that's all right."

*

I'd never been to the Golden Gate Bridge. I'd seen it often enough, usually while perched on someone's shoulder and always from a good three or four miles away. Sometimes it was covered in thick fog, other times it practically glowed in the sunlight; this time there was fog rolling in giant balls over the bridge towers, but there were spots of warm on the street.

When Zed parked his air bike at the visitors' center and hopped off, he headed for the bridge without waiting for the rest of us; Finn was slow to dismount, instead taking in everything around him. He looked everywhere, from the visitors' center where one could buy anything from hot tea to sweatshirts, down the hill to Fort Point where soldiers once guarded the city, and once we were on the bridge he stared down its length, asking where it led.

"Sausalito, eventually," Oz answered. "You could walk there from here, though I would recommend taking the hill on the other side down to Fort Baker and then walking from there. Once you're on the Marin County side of the bridge, just past the Williams Tunnel, there's traffic."

"I think I've taken that walk," he said absently.

I burrowed into Drew's sweatshirt. I wasn't cold, but I could see how far it was to the water, and a bath was not on my schedule for the day.

Zed was a hundred feet ahead of us, bouncing on his toes as he peeked over the railing. When we reached him he began babbling excitedly. "Can you imagine flying under it? Oz, remember when that plane went under it during the air show and all hell broke loose? And then on his way back he squeezed between the towers and was chased by the air guard? They followed him out and he turned around and did it again. That was awesome."

She leaned against the railing and looked down, too. "I'm surprised you remember that. You were only five or six."

"We hardly ever get to see real airplanes. Hard to forget it when we do."

Finn turned and was staring toward the city, but he stayed where he was, in the middle of the road.

"You all right?" the Emperor asked him.

He didn't look all right. His face was pale, made worse by the grayness of the sky and the tendrils of fog that licked down around us, and he squinted as he gazed ahead.

"Someone wanted to jump," he said. "I can hear her. 'If I leap, I'll soar.' I think I stopped her."

Zed peered over the side again. "You can't jump from here."

The Emperor placed a hand on the rail. "You could, a long time ago." He lifted himself up, pushing with his hands, until he stood there facing us, feet on the railing with just the tips of his shoes hanging over and one hand on a tower, steadying himself. Finn rushed toward him, and stopped only because the Emperor held up a hand. "No touching."

Then with a flourish, he threw his arms out from his sides and flung himself backward, laughing when Finn screamed, "No!"

The air crackled around him and he hung there, stuck to the net that kept anyone from falling.

Someone should have told me about that. I would have relaxed a little.

"You can't jump off anymore, Finn. Once something goes past the sensors it activates the net and holds them in place for a moment and then"—he stepped forward, jumping down— "it pushes them back to the bridge."

"That was kind of mean," Oz said.

"Little bit, yeah."

Finn reached out, fingers extended to touch the net he could not see. When it sparked, he jumped back, shaking his hand against the stinging sensation.

"I didn't say it was comfortable," the Emperor said.

"It's bloody brilliant," Finn murmured.

"It catches a few unaware people every year."

"Why is it invisible?"

"Aside from the aesthetics? Across the board, the few people who have survived jumping from here said that as soon as their feet left the bridge, they changed their minds. They wanted to live. So the net is invisible to give those who *think* they want to jump that precious moment of clarity. Since it went up, I think there has only been one person who went on to find another way."

"How do you know? I mean, people who try to jump? How would you even know?"

Zed nodded toward the visitors' center, to the air bikes that were screaming toward them. "Technically, the Emperor just broke the law by activating the net."

"Technically," the Emperor echoed. When the bikes stopped, hovering a foot off the ground with engines still running and sirens muted, he turned toward them and with a wave of his hand, they left. "I can get away with things. The King likes me."

6

"My dad tried to climb one of the Bay Bridge towers," Oz said, waving over her shoulder in the general direction of the bridge. "He was six, and for whatever freaky six-year-old kid reason, he decided to climb it and got stuck partway up. The Emperor popped pretty much out of nowhere and climbed up after him, got him unstuck and carried him down. There were dozens of grown-ass adults down on the street, watching and screaming at my dad to quit playing around and get down, but only the Emperor bothered to help."

We were on the balcony; they had leaned forward in their chairs and looked down, watching as a band set up right in the middle of Union Square for First Friday Music, a monthly showcase for new and local bands. It was getting dark and I wanted no part of being so near to falling, so I curled up in one of the comfy chairs that kept me low and away from the edge, and just listened. Finn wanted to know why the King favored the Emperor so much, so Oz told him.

There was more to the story—there always is—but that was enough to satisfy him for the time being.

The Emperor went off on his own after we got back from the Golden Gate Bridge. He had "things to do and break, people to see and disappoint," which was just as well; Finn needed a mental break after and he had been brooding since.

The Queen peppered him with questions throughout dinner and he answered in short, almost clipped sentences while still managing to not be rude, but he didn't engage in anything unless asked, not until Oz and Drew dragged him out onto the balcony to hear the music.

When she was a little younger, Oz and the King often went back a few hundred years so he could teach her how to safely use the portals, and they almost always took the time to have lunch at the restaurant that took up the top floor of the building, and they always took a table on the balcony. After a major earthquake roughly two hundred years ago, the building had been reinforced and the balcony was moved five floors down, which made it ideal for watching things happening on Union Square.

When she told Drew a little bit about the history of the family home she said, "The views were amazing when the balcony was up higher, but if I want to see that now I can just go to the roof. Having it down here is a lot more fun."

I don't think he was impressed by it, but he liked the concerts every month.

Finn hadn't been all that interested in sitting out on a balcony at night, but Oz tried to convince him to join them. "There are concerts once a month, and the band playing tonight usually plays really old, like hundreds of years old, classic rock music. It's wonderful and amazing, and seriously beautiful."

He wanted to go to bed, to sleep until he could remember the woman on the bridge, but relented with a sigh. "Of course I'll go watch. Maybe I'll recognize a few notes from an old song and it will jar something loose."

It was while they watched the band set up, when Drew and Oz were focused on the activity below, that he asked about the Emperor and the King.

The quiet had suited them, but it only gave Finn more room to dwell on the things he could not pull from the depths of his brain.

I understood that feeling. There were hundreds of things I could feel worming around in the deep, dark parts of my brain, but the remembering of those things came and went as quickly as I realized I was thinking about them. Sometimes when the Emperor was sneaking little bites of his food to me, I had a notion that I would never not be hungry, even though there was plenty of food. Once, when one of the guards came into the building wearing his official uniform, with shiny rank bars and dangling medals, I recalled being in the army—or maybe it was the air force—but the idea came and went quickly, leaving only a vague thought that perhaps I had simply seen that on a video one of the people watched while I was curled up in their lap.

It was the hunger that constantly crawled around in the back of my head like a bug with a dozen wiggly little legs. I was a tiny guy, seven pounds at my heaviest, and I always wanted something more to eat, even when I had food right in front of me. The Emperor seemed to understand and would share his food with me as long as it was cat-friendly; the King's rule was that I only got tastes of their food if I was good and did not beg while they ate as a family.

I was always good. I knew I would be fed. But still, I hungered.

Finn's Swiss-cheese memory had to feel a lot like my hunger that would never go away.

"From what my grandmother hinted and the Emperor has outright said, my dad was a bit of a wild child. Even after that he got into a lot of trouble, and the Emperor pulled him out of a lot of it. I think he's the real reason there isn't traffic allowed downtown. It was better to close it off than risk killing the future king because he's too…teenagery…to stop and think that maybe racing a bicycle down California Street with a thousand cars around is not the best idea."

Finn perked up a bit. "Wait. California is super steep. It has, what, a twenty-five per cent grade? Start at the top and head down with no brakes and you're essentially flying."

"He reasoned that the cross streets slowed him down."

"And he *told* you about it?"

She laughed. "The Emperor did first. He doesn't seem to have a problem with ratting my dad out."

She was right; he didn't. But she was also only a few weeks away from turning eighteen and had never considered the timing of the Emperor's stories about her father. It was usually as he pulled *her* out of trouble, when she was torn between defiance and guilt;

he never absolved her from her behavior, but he wrapped a layer of *yeah-but-your-dad-did-this* cotton padding around it.

Tell him about the time you ran away to Sausalito.

She turned toward me. "What's wrong, Wick? Are you cold?" She got up and checked the cat flap by the door; sometimes it got stuck. "You can go inside if you want."

I'm fine. Cripes. I just wanted to hear that story again.

When the music began, Finn and Drew leaned forward so that they could see over the balcony, but Oz stared off into the sky, listening, and it looked like she was memorizing the stars.

After a while she sighed, "I freaking love this. So pretty."

"You're not even watching them," Drew said.

"I don't have to."

Finn looked up, then back down to the band, and back at Oz. He watched her until she felt it, and squirmed a bit uncomfortably.

"Tell me what you see," he said.

"Night sky, apparently," Drew muttered.

"No, it's more than that. What do you see, Oz?"

She looked over the balcony edge, pointing toward the band. "The drums and the bass, they're red. The guitar is blue. The vocals...shades of orange and yellow, sometimes gold and white."

Drew squinted, trying to see the musicians better. "The guitar is silverish."

Sure, let's see you explain it.

"I don't mean the instruments. The actual music. It starts as wispy ribbons and sparks, and as it rises it's like a rainbow of fog. It's amazing and wonderful."

Abruptly, Finn stood up.

"Show me a portal," he said. "Why you can see them and Drew can't makes more sense to me now."

*

Drew scooped me up as they headed inside for the elevator. On the ride down Finn was bouncing on his toes, the most animated he'd been since popping up out of nowhere with his giant malformed egg. Oz kept glancing at him sideways and Drew kept a tighter than necessary hold on me, until the doors opened and we were rushing toward the closest portal away from the cluster of people around Union Square.

I'm not sure what they were worried about. He was like a kid who'd just found out he was getting a new toy; he was excited, but not worrisome. The only thing that concerned me was that it was dark out and we might miss snack time if this took too long.

They ran down Powell and turned left on Market Street, stopping half a block down in front of a bookstore that sold very old and very rare print-bound editions. I'd spent a lot of time in there with the Emperor as he carefully flipped through pages of books he loved but would never own, because rare plus old equaled spendy, and he wasn't a spendy sort of person. Oz gestured to a spot that was close to the curb, one where a person could easily be mistaken for stepping off into the street as they stepped into the portal; it made sense back when there was traffic, that the portal would be right where someone could easily get to it and disappear without raising suspicion; maybe they just crossed the street.

It was easy when there were thousands of people and cars polluting the city.

"Tell me what it looks like to you," Finn said.

I knew what it looked like. It was like watching rose-tinged water slip over textured glass; it was a film of nothingness that had blurred edges to it, something easily looked through but easily seen, if one had the ability.

If Finn really wanted to know what it looked like, stepping in would have told him the most. When you step into a portal, it's like walking through a spray of pink that lasts only a fraction of a moment; blink and you miss it. It's not wet or cold, but it looks like early morning in October, when the fog is stubborn and feels like it has enough weight to hold a cat down and soak his furs.

The Emperor has a less poetic take on it. He once told me that it looks like what's left of a person after a bomb they've been holding goes off. Nothing of them remains—no bits and pieces of bone or skin or hair—except for that misting of blood, hanging in the air like smoke. I never asked how he knew that and I still don't want to know, but that's the sort of pink that it is.

I'd like to look at it more closely, but in all the times he's taken me through, the Emperor has never paused in a portal long enough for me to get more than a glimpse. I suppose I could ask him to specifically let me linger, but then we would probably wind up four hundred years back with all the noise and the people and those rude, food-pilfering seagulls, and I'd had enough of that.

Let the teenagers play with the portals.

Finn leaned in close to the edge Oz had outlined for him, and he listened.

When he could name it, he sounded almost reverent about it. "It sounds like a spark. Just the faintest crackle. It's like the sound of a single strand of hair being held over the flame of a candle."

"Can you see it?" she asked.

"No. But I can hear it. And if I can hear it..." He stepped back. "You're a synth. You see this *because* it has a sound."

"What did you call her?" Drew demanded.

"A synth. It's not an insult. She has synesthesia. She sees sound."

"Seriously? Oz, for real?"

She nodded.

I don't think I had ever seen her be so willingly quiet when others were speaking.

"And that's how you know I'm not lying," Finn went on. "You can tell by the colors that my voice makes. Can you also see the words people speak?"

"No, not the actual words. I see the sound surrounding you, and lies change color. You're mostly blue, and a little bit purple when you're upset. I'm not sure what your lie color would be."

"Isn't that distracting?"

"I'm used to it. I can usually ignore it." She reached over to scratch the top of my head. "I'm pretty sure he can see what I see. I know my dad can and I suspect the Emperor can though I'm not terribly sure. He can use the portals, but he's never mentioned being able to see one."

Drew exhaled sharply.

"What?" Oz asked. "I'm sorry, I've never thought to tell you. It's just normal for me and I have no idea what it's like to live any differently. I suppose I thought you just knew."

"It's fine. I just…hell, woman, I can *never* lie to you."

"I ignore the little white lies," she assured him.

"But not even to spare your feelings. You know, 'does this shirt make me look fat?' If it does, I have to actually say so."

"No you don't," she said, laughing. "I know your colors, Drew. You're a very soft blue, and when you outright lie? Raging red. And I haven't seen that since we were little and you tried to blame me for the water balloons you lobbed at my dad and the Canadian Prime Minister."

"Well, your t-shirt was wet and I thought they'd believe it."

"Tell me I'm not fat in my favorite white jeans and I'll believe it."

"You're not but would it matter if you were? I mean—"

"Holy hell," Finn muttered. "You two sound like an old married couple." He was staring at the portal again, one hand splayed out in front of him as he tried to feel what he could hear. When his fingers twitched, he grinned, knowing he had found the entry.

"How does it work? Clearly you step through, but how do you get where you're going?"

"I think it," Oz said.

"Just when you want to be? No specific time?"

"Just the When, unless you need a specific time. If I wanted to go back to last week, I'd just think of a day and step through, and it would take me to the same time on that day. If I needed to be there at midnight, I'd add that in. From here the portal looks whisper-thin, but it takes a step or two to actually move through it."

"Yesterday," Finn whispered, slowly pushing his hand forward. He repeated it until his hand vanished, his arm ending at his elbow. "This is fantastic. And it tingles."

Drew moved so he could look for the other side of the portal, where Finn's arm ended at the middle of his forearm. "Yeah. But now there's someone from yesterday freaking out over the hand hanging in the air."

"I'll give them a thumbs up," Finn said with a laugh. He slowly pulled his hand back, and he did indeed have his thumb sticking up.

"If you can hear the portal enough to use it, you can pop back home once you remember your When," Oz told him. "Well, you can as long as you're from the past."

"Why not the future?"

"Can't step into a When that hasn't happened."

"But if I'm from the future, that When has happened. Or will happen."

She frowned, contemplating. "I've been told to never even try. What if I tried to go forward a hundred years, but between now and then the world imploded and there's nothing left? I'd be stepping into my own certain death."

"Or you would just step forward and not go through the portal at all," Finn suggested. "But if I remember the date I left my When, it's there. I could get back to it."

Drew set his hand on Finn's arm, gently nudging him away from the portal. "Let's not try right now, okay? Oz might get in trouble if she helps you, and honestly, I think I'd physically hold her back to keep her from trying it with you."

I kind of wanted to see him try. Oz knew a bunch of different ways to hurt a guy, and there was no way Drew could stop her from doing anything unless she wanted him to.

Finn agreed, but a moment later asked if they could step back a few weeks, just to give it a try.

"Let me ask my dad," Oz said. "There are rules to using the portals and I've never taken someone through with me. I know it can be done, but—"

"Is this illegal? Or only allowed for certain people?"

"It's theoretically legal for anyone, but they have to know how and they have to know the rules. They also have to know these portals exist, and it's not exactly something we publicize. I can't stop you since you can obviously find it again, but I am asking you to wait until I can speak with my father."

"What about the Emperor?" Drew asked.

"It has to be my dad," Oz insisted. "If the Emperor was here right now and said it would be all right, I'd take you both through and let him take any blame, but my dad's word *literally* is law, so we'll ask him."

Finn agreed to wait; the portal wasn't going anywhere and it was late anyway.

He was right on that. It was well past food o'clock, and I still hadn't eaten.

*

The King was about to give his permission for Oz to take Finn back a day or two, even for a few minutes to see what memories it might stir, but the Emperor cleared his throat and uttered a stern, "No."

We were in the personal office of the King—the official office was at City Hall, and I had never been there—where the so-called throne was an overstuffed chair on a short pedestal, butted against the back wall, and the crown—which I had only seen on someone's head one time, and it didn't even fit—was on a shelf just above it. The King was sitting on the raised threshold of the fireplace opposite the throne, tying his running shoes, while Oz leaned against the edge of his desk, her toes barely touching the floor. Finn was leaning on the desk with her and the Emperor was in the big comfy chair near the window.

Someone new might wonder why the King wasn't in the nice chair, but it was pretty clear: to the rest of the world the Emperor deferred to the King, but behind closed doors he usually got the good spot. He didn't expect it; those things just happened. He could probably sit on the throne without the King thinking anything about it. If I sat there, he'd complain about my germs. Oz and Zed played on it when they were little, until they realized it was not just any chair. If anyone who was not family sat on it, his guards would rush in and start levels of unpleasantness from which I would run, yowling loudly.

"I'll bite," the King said. "Why not?"

"He still can't remember anything beyond a vague image of a woman standing on a bridge. If we expose him to another shift in time, who knows how much more his brain will be scrambled?" He looked to Finn. "It's not a great idea. Get some of your memories back before taking the risk of turning your brain into even thinner mush."

"That could take forever," Finn groaned.

"I was hoping you'd have begun to recall things already, but since you haven't—" He pushed himself up with a soft moan of middle age "—I have an idea. No guarantees, but it might spark something. Meet me on the Square in fifteen minutes."

*

Most of the area under Union Square was used for storage; it had once been a parking garage for cars and bikes, but when traffic was cut off the space was converted. On the first level was row after row of chain link storage units intended for downtown residents to use for their extraneous junk, but they were mostly empty and it wasn't unusual to find someone there teaching a child or two how to ride a bicycle. The second level was for official detritus and there was an unmanned kiosk where people could check out keys for the public-use air bikes parked against the back of the wall. Buried down deep was a level reserved for the Emperor and his playthings. I could get to it by squeezing through a gap near the floor by the locked stairwell door, but as far as I knew the only people with access were the Emperor and the King.

He came up on the elevator, carrying a short metal pipe in his hand, gripping it by an end that was covered in rubber. The other end was bare metal and it looked like brushed nickel, like the water faucets in Oz's bathroom.

Finn leaned toward Oz and whispered, "Is he planning on hitting me over the head with that thing?"

"Well, that might work."

The Emperor stopped about ten feet from Finn. "This is an electrical impulse memory rod," he said. "It works by sending small bursts of electrical impulses through your skin while you try to relax and focus on something other than thinking."

"Ok," Finn said to Oz. "So he's not going to hit me with it. He's going to electrocute me."

"Don't tempt me," the Emperor said. "It's very mild and feels more like a tingle than a shock. The key to this working is for you to relax. I'll hold one end, you hold the other, and for several minutes just close your eyes, breathe in through your nose and out through your mouth, and get used to how it feels. When I think you're ready, I'm going to ask you some questions. Don't think about them, just answer with the first thing that comes into your head, and don't worry if they make no sense or if you have no answer. I'm only trying to get you to the point where the answers flow, and asking simple, odd questions can help with that. The tingling you'll feel will help your brain fire off synapsis that aren't fully functioning right now."

Oz gestured to the pipe. "Do you want me to hold the other end? So you don't risk him touching you?"

"It's fine. He's been very respectful about that. I don't think he'll try."

Finn stood up. "No, I won't. I think you're a knob about it, but I won't try to touch you."

"You can think anything about me you choose." He pointed to a spot just a foot and a half from him. "Stand there, grab the end of the rod, and close your eyes. In a few seconds you'll feel your hand begin to tingle. Start breathing slowly and deeply, but not so deep that it's uncomfortable."

Finn planted himself where the Emperor indicated, his feet spread several inches apart as he found balance, and he reached out. "I swear, if this is a trick and I wind up with whipped cream in my hair or someone sprays water on me to make it look like I wet myself, I'm touching you."

"Fair enough."

Finn wrapped his fingers around the metal end of the pipe, took a deep breath, and closed his eyes. Everyone was quiet, so quiet that I could hear Drew's breath coming out of his nose, and quiet enough I could hear the faint hum when the Emperor turned the rod on. He kept his hand on the rubber, but I noticed that after a moment he deftly moved his little finger so that a sliver of it was touching the metal.

I don't think anyone else noticed.

"What is your name?"

"Finn."

"How old are you?"

"I don't know."

"Favorite color?"

"I don't know."

"Who was the woman on the bridge?"

"I don't know."

"What color is the sky?"

"Blue."

"What day is it?"

"Saturday."

"What day were you born on?"

"I don't know."

"If you could live anywhere, where would it be?"

"Here. San Francisco."

"When?"

"I don't know."

"What is the name of the woman on the bridge?"

"Jo."

"How many fingers do you have?"

"Eight. And two thumbs."

"What is six times two?"

"Twelve."

"How old are you?"

"I don't know."

"What's your favorite food?"

"Pizza. Pepperoni, absolutely no mushrooms."

"Left handed or right?"

"Right."

"What was Jo doing on the bridge?"

"She was going to jump."

"What did you have for dinner last night?"

"Meatloaf."

"Where is Land's End?"

"Near Ocean Beach."

"What's the cat's name?"

"Wick."

"What do you call Alcatraz?"

"Z Island."

"What's Oz's given name?"

"Oz?"

"How many days are in a week?"

"Seven."

"What's your favorite color?"

"Purple."

"What year were you born?"

"I don't know."

"How many states comprise the U.S.?"

"Forty."

"What is your given name?"

"Finn… Finnegan."

"Who is Jo?"

Finn's eyes snapped open and he let go of the pipe. "I wasn't supposed to stop her. I was supposed to let her jump. She wanted to soar, and I stopped her. I can hear her voice. She was telling me she could fly, and it would be wonderful."

Drew tensed and Oz stood up, but the Emperor hadn't told them they could speak yet. Finn's eyes were darting, watching something only he could see, and the Emperor hadn't moved at all, not even a twitch.

"She changed everything. I can hear someone telling me that, a woman's voice, whispering in my ear. She changed it all."

Very softly, the Emperor said, "Take the stick again."

He pushed it toward Finn again, but Finn wasn't hearing him.

"I wasn't supposed to save her. She does something, she wanted to stop…what? I can't remember. There was a speech… She's why the U.S. broke apart."

"That's not remotely logical, Finn."

"I can *feel* it."

"Take the stick," he urged.

"I have to go."

And with that, Finn turned and ran down the steps from the Square to the street, and was almost to Powell Street before either Oz or Drew thought to react.

*

As we turned on to Market Street, Finn was easing into the portal, slowly, and Oz sped up to catch him. She was less than ten feet away when it seemed to swallow him, and the Emperor barked at her to stop.

"Wait. Think before you follow."

Drew had his hands around me a little too tight, so I turned my head and nipped at his arm. He wasn't paying attention to me, though, and didn't react; he was staring at the space where Finn had been. "There's no time! Who knows what he's doing and when? Go after him, Oz."

"Drew."

"He could be tossing some poor woman off the Golden Gate Bridge right now!"

"It's a time portal," she reminded him. "And I'm the idiot who showed him how to use it. What the hell was I thinking? We don't know anything about him."

The Emperor was more forgiving. "He came here in a time machine. Somewhere deep down he knows how to move through time. Better that he did this now, when we can follow, than in the middle of the night when we would have no clue about which portal he used and when."

"What if he jumped forward?"

"Not likely. You warned him not to try and somewhere in that primordial soup brewing in his head, he understands the reasons."

"Unless he tried it anyway and walked into empty space," Drew offered.

"Yeah. Thanks for that." Oz reached for his hand. "Don't let go. Don't think about anything other than 'follow Finn.' Not anything. No stray thoughts about me, nothing about what you want for dinner, nothing about a book you just read. Just 'follow Finn.'"

"Wait, I'm not going." He tugged on the front of his shirt. "I have to hold the cat."

The Emperor reached out and plucked me from Drew's sweatshirt. "We may need your muscle. I'll take care of Wick."

He wanted to argue, but Oz had a death grip on his hand and was heading into the portal, dragging him along.

"He'll throw up on the other side," the Emperor said to me.

"How about it, old man? Fancy a trip to another When? Maybe the mice are bigger and you can catch one."

Like hell. My food comes out of a can. Or your sandwich.

"Don't worry about stray thoughts. It only matters what I think as we go through. But you already knew that, didn't you? We should tell Oz that sometime."

There's a lot you should tell Oz.

"We'll get to that later."

He stepped into the portal, and for a moment all I could see was the pink mist swirling all around us, but before I could blink and look around, we were through to the other side, and Oz was running at full tilt to catch up to Finn.

7

The Emperor didn't run. He watched—with a bit of amusement because Drew was trying to get a good look all around him while also trying to appease an orange-clad monk he had run right into when coming out of the portal, helping him up before taking off after Oz— as Oz and Drew got further away from us, chasing Finn down Market Street and then up the Embarcadero toward Pier 39.

"Not a real monk, Wick," he muttered. "No worries. He's only shouting obscenities because Drew had no wallet to lift."

He didn't follow them. Instead, he went into the Ferry Building and looked around until he found the thing he wanted, all the while holding me with one arm tucked under my belly. The noise of it all startled me at first; this was the San Francisco Finn had expected, with people crushing past each other, the din of voices exploding in the air.

Let's go back. I don't like this. I've never liked this.

"It'll be fine, Wick. And look" —he tapped the newspaper he had found— "it's twenty-sixteen. I have currency for this When. I'll get you a treat."

He bought himself a cup of coffee and some shrimp bites for me, and we sat outside on a bench, taking in the sunshine and watching the mass of people and cars that filtered past us.

The city was alive, and its heartbeat was a cacophony of horns blaring and voices shouting. It was the monster that wanted to swallow me in one bone-crunching bite; the people who wandered through it were the angry souls that chased me from corners and shadows, and made sure I was always nauseatingly hungry.

It was the place from which I wanted to be saved, not the place I wanted to stay.

"This," the Emperor said, tilting his coffee cup toward the city. "This is what the city designers were going for after the earthquake in twenty-two-forty. They wanted to make it look like this, the old city, so that visitors would find it charming and would want to stay for a while."

Good for them. They kept the shrimp, that's all I care about.

"However—right now there are over a million people in the city, and few of them can actually afford to live here with any reasonable level of comfort. Look around, Wick. In ten seconds you'll spot at least three people who survive here without a home. People treasured this city, but they never figured out how to truly help those living in it. Some who are just getting by can't do more than glance, because they know…one bad paycheck and it might be them, and that's terrifying. It's easier to pretend those other people don't exist. And the government? They would bomb the first country to blink too hard at them and not consider the expense, yet feeding and housing those in need—all of a sudden they became cost conscious.

"Then the earthquake hit. And you know who the only ones prepared for surviving the fallout were? The same people who were routinely ignored and shunned for not having enough money to afford a place to live in the city and who had no way to get anywhere else. Survivors found themselves with no skills to get by—the homeless were the ones who saved them. It certainly wasn't the government."

Okay. Today is teach-the-cat-some-history day. Get me more shrimp and I'll pay attention. Otherwise it's yadda-yadda-yadda.

"The answers were always so simple, Wick. And yet people look to convoluted solutions. Look at you, you fix your problems, right? Hungry? You go find food. If you find some friendly cat outside and she's hungry, you share. Don't deny it. I've seen you."

Yeah. I don't hunt. But I'd like to find more shrimp right now. Or steak. I'm not picky.

"I prefer the When of the current Blackshear monarchy, Wick. Feed them, house them, provide jobs and medical care. Keep them on their feet, don't wait until they have to be pulled up."

You're preaching to the choir. More shrimp?

Instead of going to the Ferry Building and getting more shrimp, he picked me up and then stood to wave for a taxi. While Oz and Drew ran after Finn, we rode in the back seat of a car that smelled like last weeks' litter box had been used by a drunk teenager who had eaten an entire bag of expired cheesy poofs.

I'm not sure I wouldn't have preferred to bounce around on the Emperor's shoulder as he tried to run. That at least would have been mock-worthy; he was thin and looked like he was in shape, but truthfully I don't think he'd run more than a city block in the last twenty years. He swam, he played with heavy things in the gym, but running as an activity was left to the King.

We got out of the taxi at the visitors' center near the Golden Gate Bridge, and I sucked in deep breaths of fresh air as the Emperor pushed through the mass of tourists to get to the fence. Finn was on the path that ran along the bottom of the hill, and he ran past Fort Point and up the stairs, with Oz not far behind him. When he reached the top step, before he could turn toward the bridge, the Emperor said firmly, "Stop."

I didn't think he would—I was surprised Finn even heard him—but he turned and came over to us.

"How?" he asked between breaths. "It was miles—"

"Roughly seven miles from the portal to here. And you made it in good time, too, less than an hour. Wick and I took the easy way, in a taxi. Even so, I'm surprised we beat you here. The traffic is insane."

Oz hit the top step and with an angry burst was on him, grabbing him by the arm and jerking him toward her. "What the hell, Finn?"

The Emperor brushed off her anger. "Where's Drew?"

She let go of Finn and looked down to the path leading up to Fort Point. "He was right behind me."

I was thinking unkind thoughts about his pizza and donut consumption and all the time he spent reading in a non-moving stupor, when he came into our line of sight on the path below.

She turned back to Finn. "Why? Seriously, why?"

"To stop myself. I have to keep me from meeting her here."

"What the hell for? So that we can stand here and watch her fall from the bridge? That's sick, Finn."

Confusion bubbled on his face. He was nervous and scattered and didn't know where to look. "Because she changes everything. I remember the United States. I have to be from your future. I can time travel, and the U.S. is my reality. She does *something…*"

"Exactly what, because right now you sound like a babbling idiot and I'm feeling exactly zero compassion for you."

"I can't remember!"

"Then you *are* a freaking idiot."

"Oz, I trust my gut. If I don't stop myself from stopping her, then she goes on and changes everything in my existence. And since I'm clearly from your future, and the U.S. doesn't exist…she did something. I know it."

"You don't *know* any of that, Finn. You're probably from my future but for all we know you stole someone else's time machine and took it on a joy ride. And if you intend to stop the U.S. from breaking up? I will *end* you."

She took another step toward him, hands balled into fists, but Drew finally made it up the stairs and lunged to get between them, one hand on Finn's chest as he tried to catch his breath.

"Oz, I'm just trying to protect my life," Finn said.

"At the expense of mine!"

I looked up at the Emperor. He seemed fairly amused by it all.

They don't get it, do they?

It was then Finn spotted her; she was heading toward the entry to the bridge walkway, practically bouncing on her feet. Her long black hair fluttered behind her and she pushed strands away from her face. She was smiling.

She doesn't seem sad.

"Oz, I have to stop myself."

"Yeah, but not the way you think."

Drew grabbed Finn by the arm, tightly. "I don't know what any of this is, but until Oz tells me to let go, you're not going anywhere."

Finn yanked against the hold Drew's giant hands had on him,

but he couldn't get free. Instead, he watched as another version of himself hurried from the visitors' center toward the bridge. He strained against Drew's grip a few more times, but when he saw the woman turn toward his other self, smile even wider, and then throw her arms around him, he gave up.

"Well, now," the Emperor mused out loud and not at all serious, "that was awfully quick for a suicide intervention. She seems very happy to see you."

"But I know—she changes everything," Finn muttered.

"Oz, take him back. We'll try to jog his memory again in the morning. The answers are there, floating around in that lump of Swiss cheese wedged between his ears. The woman is clearly important, but perhaps not in the way he thinks." He was watching them on the bridge and chuckling at the sight. "Apparently he kept her from jumping by performing prolonged mouth to mouth resuscitation."

Whatever had happened, it was going to happen again. There was no way for Finn to stop it now.

*

It was Oz's pointy finger jabbing him in the chest that got to Finn. The Emperor guided us from the bridge to a closer portal and we went through; once on the other side she spun toward him and let loose with words the Queen once told her were on the Bad Word List and that we did not say them without good reason, because using them was not polite.

Oz didn't care about polite. She was at least six kinds of ticked off and only the words that flew out of her kept her from punching him into another When.

"Do something with him," she said to Drew, who stood between Finn and the portal. "I don't care what, but keep him away from me."

It was then she jabbed at Finn, and his face sagged under the disappointment. "I trusted you to stay away from the portal. We have done nothing but try to help you, and this is what you do, even after you agreed not to?"

"Oz…"

"No. I don't care. Go near another portal and you *will* be stopped, do you understand? I don't even want to see you, just…no."

I wanted to go with her, back home where it was warm and there was food and no one yelling at anyone else, but she stomped across the street to the visitors' center, jumped on a public air bike, and sped away.

"I just wanted to fix things," Finn said to himself, watching her speed off.

"You wanted to *kill* someone," Drew snapped.

"No. I only wanted to stop myself. She was going to do whatever she was going to do."

"And you seem pretty sure that you stopped her from jumping off the bridge. Stopping yourself from meeting her then? It would have been murder, Finn."

"No."

"Think it through," the Emperor said. "Embrace the idea that this woman, whomever she is, may have planned to jump to her death. Let's presume you're right. By allowing her to die, by not stopping her from taking that final step off the railing, you prevent the ripple in the pond that ends with the fall of the United States. What happens after that?"

"My world goes on."

"But Oz's doesn't. In your scenario, you get your United States, but it would be at the expense of the forming of the monarchies. Look at those ripples…the U.S. falls, new countries form; families are elected to head new governments. Men and women meet and marry, and have children to carry on the royal lines. What do you think happens to those families if the U.S. never falls?"

"What happens to mine if it does?"

The Emperor lifted me up to look me in the face. "His brain is still Swiss cheese, isn't it? Even you understand."

Yeah, well, I'm not human.

"Oz will do everything in her power to stop you, because if you find a way to make that woman jump off the bridge, assuming your memory-impaired hunch is correct, then her entire world ceases to exist. That includes you, Finn. Because if you're here now and you wipe this When from time, you go with it."

8

Finn was absent from the dinner table; his place was set and the Queen had put a cold drink out for him, but she didn't question it when Oz said that she doubted Finn was coming and to start without him. They ate in uncomfortable quiet, the clicks and clinks of silverware against dinner plates broken only by the King and Queen asking about each other's day. The peppered silence was awkward and it hung in the air like a hunk of bad cheese that everyone could smell but no one wanted to bring up.

The King looked at the Queen and raised an eyebrow as if asking "What the hell?" but they let the kids stew in their own anger without prodding them about it.

None of it stopped me from waiting on the kitchen counter for my tiny taste. Their level of upset did not mean that the rules could be broken, and the rule was that if the cat is good and doesn't beg, then he gets a tiny taste when everyone else is done eating.

I worried that someone would forget, because peoples' brains often leak out important details when they're upset, but then I saw the King cutting his last bite of meat into Wick-sized pieces. He put it on a small plate and brought it to me in the kitchen, but made me jump to the floor before giving it to me.

"I don't sit on the counter and eat," he grumbled. "Neither should you."

You don't sit on the floor and eat, either. Let me sit at the table and we'll stop having this conversation.

He waited at the table while Oz and Drew did the dishes; before they could wander off to watch videos or head outside to find friends to waste time with, he sighed hard, and then told them he wanted to see them in his office in ten minutes.

"And whatever is ticking you off, leave it here. This is official. No moody teenagers allowed."

*

He didn't say that no cats were allowed. I followed them to the elevator and meowed loudly for one of them to make sure the door didn't close on my tail. It had never happened, but I wasn't sure that it couldn't, so alerting them was a matter of better safe than sorry.

Oz held the door until I was all the way in and sitting behind her where the door couldn't bite.

We could have taken the stairs, you know. It's not that far.

Drew hesitated when we reached the floor of the King's office. "Wait. Did he mean for me to come, too? Or just you? If this is just for you I don't want to annoy him by just showing up."

"Relax. He said 'teenagers,' plural. If he doesn't want you there he'll say so. No harm, no foul. Just don't take it personally if he asks you to leave and sounds blunt about it."

The King's office had never been decorated in that overblown way meant to make other people think he was twenty-three degrees of special and rich or anything, but he did have some of the cool toys. Mounted on the wall facing his desk, between the fireplace and the throne, was a video monitor that was nearly the size of the wall itself. It was hardly ever turned on, probably because looking at it too long actually hurt, but the size of it meant he could enhance things to see even the tiniest details.

News broadcasts were uncomfortable to watch, because the talking heads' heads were the size of a real person and it was like being lectured to by a teacher pulled up from the depths of someone's pre-final-exam nightmare. I could fit inside one of the news anchors' nostrils, and sometimes I wasn't sure that if they inhaled sharply that wouldn't happen. They suck in a deep breath, the kitty gets pulled through the monitor, and then everyone is unhappy. Especially the kitty.

He was sitting against the edge of his desk and the monitor was on. On it was footage of a brick wall being knocked over; he peered at it intently, and then he reversed the video to watch it fall all over again.

"Florida," he said without looking at them.

Oz leaned against the desk next to him. "They're knocking part of the wall down?"

"It looks like they may demolish the entire thing."

The Wall, something usually spoken about with a pretentious nasal snort, was a twenty-foot-tall rock wall built up around the Florida boundaries. There were a few checkpoints along its considerable length, but it had no reasonable entry.

That also meant it had no reasonable exit.

If you lived in Florida, you stayed in Florida, where the church-run government could keep you safe from the sins and temptations of the rest of the world. If you were lucky—and luck defined by being a part of the upper echelon of their church, and wealthy on top of that—you could fly out and conduct business around the world, but you'd better come back.

If you didn't come back? They'd come get you.

You might even make it home.

The King had no love for Florida and generally refused to do business with them. He held a grudge against the head of their government that he refused to explain, and had hung up on the First Minister more than once, telling him to shove things where those things normally would not fit. He also issued a formal order: all calls from the First Minister of Florida were to be handled by the Secretary of Defense, because sooner or later, if he kept calling, it would be considered an act of aggression.

"Isn't that wall supposed to keep the heathens out?" Drew asked.

The King folded his arms, considering his words first. "I believe that was the idea. Lately they've made noise about understanding that they need the fellowship of the rest of the world and keeping people from the beauty of their coastline and all they have to offer isn't fair."

"So they want an influx of tourists and the money that brings."

Oz moved closer to the monitor, peering at the footage of the wall coming down. She asked the King to zoom in, and then back it up so she could get a better perspective. He rewound it several times as she watched with her nose less than a foot from the monitor.

"Those aren't construction workers. Those are soldiers."

Drew stood next to her to watch another replay. "I thought they didn't have much of an army."

"Historically, they haven't had." The King clicked off the video and pulled up a map. "Nearly two thousand miles of wall, and they're breaking through at over a hundred spots. Officially, they're adding gates so that people can come and go."

"But they don't want tourists," Oz said.

"Don't they already have tourists?" Drew asked.

"They allow a set number of people to visit every year. Getting a permit is like winning the lottery, but typically the only people who bother to enter have family in Florida, or they're pondering emigration."

Drew frowned. "Why would anyone move there?"

"Religious conviction," the King answered.

"But there's religious *freedom* outside of Florida."

"And very little inside. There is only one recognized religion in their country, Drew. Heresy is a capital offense. If you don't cow to the party line, profess that God is the Father, Jesus is the Son, and that they are one and the same with the Holy Spirit, you've committed treason. If you believe in the Trinity but also think the state should function as Jesus would and feed the hungry without expectation of recompense, you've committed treason. If you advocate any kind of state sanctioned welfare or charity…it goes on and on."

"They'll really kill someone?"

"They wanted a Christian nation. But they ignored the actual deeds of Christ."

"I'm not familiar."

Oz turned from the monitor. "Jesus fed the hungry. He didn't hang with the righteous. He hung with the sinners, and he brought them into faith. He didn't push them away. Jesus probably would not have been in favor of a nation using his name while starving the poor and funneling more money towards the rich."

"Maybe a couple hundred years changed their minds?"

She didn't think so. "It's more likely that a couple hundred years has them bursting at the seams, and they have nowhere to go but through the wall."

"And you think it's the military breaking it down? Not citizens? Could this be an uprising, like a break for freedom?"

The King shook his head. "Oz is right. Those are soldiers breaking through the wall. If people were trying to flee, it would happen in two, maybe three key spots, and they would run like hell under a hail of gunfire. I don't trust the official line. This is not the sudden opening of their border."

"Are we responding?" Oz asked.

"We're sending troops to protect against a military incursion past the wall, but until Midlam makes it an official request, we can't do anything other than offer support. Their Queen is not ready to make that call."

"Should I call her?" Drew asked.

The barest hint of a smile tugged at the King's mouth. "I've spoken with her at length. She'll ask when she thinks the time is right."

He turned the monitor off.

"You need to be aware of what's going on. Finn is not the only puzzle to dwell on right now. He's your priority for the moment, but I think it's time for you both to be included in official matters."

"Finn," Oz huffed as she dropped into the chair. She filled him in on Finn's portal outing, every word laced with frustration.

The King was not disturbed by Finn's abrupt field trip. "He's young, impulsive, and memory impaired. You stopped him, that's what matters."

"Dad, what matters is that he was willing to let someone die because he had a hunch. How can I trust him now? How can I even look at him now?"

Drew took her spot at the desk. "Maybe deal with him the same way you deal with the really weird kid in high school. You know the one, right? The kid that thinks it's funny to make someone sit on a brownie so he can point and laugh and try to humiliate them? He doesn't mean any real harm but he's so socially awkward that you want to kick his teeth in sometimes. Or the oddball in first year that turns out all right by graduation? You tolerate him and you make yourself be nice, because deep down you know that someday he'll be all right and you'll probably even like him."

"Please tell me you were that weird kid," Oz said.

He laughed. "No. But you know, I think the Emperor might have been."

"The Emperor."

"Think about it. He's weird as hell. That whole 'Finn is Other When' stuff, and specifically forbidding Finn to touch him? Like he would explode…" He trailed off, and for a moment was lost to his own thought. Then he blinked and muttered, "Hell."

"What?"

"Maybe they *would* explode. What if Finn and the Emperor are the same person, just at different points in their life? I mean, it would explain his interest in Finn, and why he's so caught up in the not touching thing. Two selves can't occupy the same space. They touch and" —he splayed his fingers— "boom."

They both jumped when the Emperor chuckled.

"Cripes, how long have you been there?" Drew sputtered.

He was leaning against the door frame, arms folded and eyebrows knotted together, but he was more amused than annoyed. It was the same way he looked at Oz and Zed when they were little and doing things that were fun but he had already told them to not do. From time to time, he looked at me that way, but only because he was jealous at my flexibility and felt pressed to protest when I demonstrated it in front of visiting dignitaries.

"Long enough. And no, Prince Andrew, I was not that one weird kid in high school, and Finn and I are not the same person. I promise you that I have valid reasons for not allowing him to touch me, but none of them are because he and I are one and the same."

Drew wasn't convinced. "Well, sure, that's what you would have to say. You wouldn't want one of us to push you together to test it out."

Oz egged him on. "That's valid thinking, looking at either side of it. Prove they're not the same, or prove they are the same, just by seeing what happens. It might be bloody, but, well, the price of science."

"Set your hypothesis—"

The King sighed. "No one is pushing anyone else. No one is touching the Emperor, not even for science. Consider that a royal mandate."

The Emperor stepped all the way into the office. "Good. And I have a request."

"Are you asking the King, or are you asking your friend?"

He nodded toward the throne. "Foremost—my King."

Jax hesitated, unsure what to do when an official request was coming from someone he placed higher on the hierarchy than himself, but then he sat on the throne and gestured to the crown on the shelf. "Is this official-official? Because I never get to wear that thing. Not since my coronation."

"You can make it that official if it makes you feel like a real king, but it doesn't really fit you. Your head is massive."

"The crown is especially small," he argued.

"Really now."

"Fine. I'm on the throne." He pointed at Oz and Drew when they giggled. "Shut up. What can I do for you, Emperor?"

For the first time, as far as I could recall, the Emperor stood formally in front of the King. He'd tucked in his red t-shirt, and while he was still in black jeans, they were new and had sharp creases. He kept his hands out of his pockets and clasped them behind his back instead, his feet only inches apart. "If this is indeed formal…I am asking my King to provide protection for Finn."

There were more stifled giggles from Drew.

"He already has my protection."

"As your guest," the Emperor pointed out. "I am requesting official, assigned, continuous security. He needs a guard."

Oz stood up. "Look, I said I would end him but I didn't mean I would actually *end* him. And he's not like, well, dangerous to any of us. He's confused and inconsiderate, but he's truthful. I'm just pissed off at him, that's all."

"I understand that. He needs protection from himself, Oz."

She was going to argue more, I think, but the King held his hand up. "I need more than that. As a guest in my house you know I'll treat him as much like my own son as I can."

"I do know that."

"Then give me a better reason to assign guards to shadow him. And I assume you want a shadow, not someone constantly in his visual line."

"Yeah, I'm annoyed with him but I'll still keep an eye on him," Oz said.

He turned to look at her. "I hope so, Oz. Because if something happens to him, you'll never be born."

9

The Emperor found Finn sitting on the steps leading up to Union Square when it was well after dark. I watched from the door as he jogged across the street and talked to Finn (with a good twenty feet between them) and kept watching as they came back. I didn't have to go with him to know what he said. *Come on, she's not as angry with you as you think. Stay in my apartment for tonight and give yourself some space. We'll order pizza and ignore each other.*

I followed them up the short staircase and across the tile floor to the Emperor's door. It didn't matter if he saw me or not, nor if he closed the door before I could sneak in behind them. There was a flap door in the wall that let me get into his living room, one I only occasionally used because he didn't spend much time there and the level of boring I found when alone in his apartment was an actual irritant. It made my insides itch, and as hard as I tried, I could not scratch it.

However, if there was a chance for pizza, I was going in.

They were weirdly quiet while they waited for the pizza to arrive; Finn picked up an old physics book from the end table next to his chair and skimmed though it, and the Emperor read the day's news on a computer tablet. He glanced up from the headlines every now and then, looking at Finn with restrained amusement. He looked at me, too, his eyebrow arched in mock surprise, but I wasn't sure if that was because he hadn't expected me there or because Finn's presence in his apartment was unprecedented.

If anyone else had wandered in, they certainly would have been astonished. As well liked as he was, the Emperor still kept people at arm's length and never entertained. The King had spent time there, and I had, but I wasn't sure anyone else had walked through the front door since he had moved in. Maybe he hired a housekeeper. The place was clean and he never struck me as the domestic type, so someone was surely cleaning up after him.

Oh man, does the Queen come down here and clean up your crap? Seriously, dude, are you that lazy?

"I haven't forgotten you're there," he said to me, not looking up from the news. "You'll get a bite when we're done, you always do."

They ate in the living room in front of the video monitor—the news was on but the sound was low—and made stabs at small talk. The Emperor fed me bits of cheese, not making me wait until he was actually done, and I could sense it was intentional. Shift the focus off Finn, give him something to watch instead of just staring at the monitor or the floor, and make him relax.

Fine, use me. Just keep feeding me cheese. Make sure there's some sauce on it, too. That sauce is freaking tasty.

"That cat eats all day long," Finn said. "Why is he not as big as a horse?"

"He's an old man with a very high metabolism, I guess. I get yelled at three or four times a week for giving him food off my plate but it doesn't seem to hurt him at all, so I keep doing it. It makes him happy. Old men should be allowed to be happy, I think."

"Is he really as old as Oz hinted at?"

He offered me the last bit of cheese off his plate. "The King is forty-three years old, and Wick has been around at least that long. I don't think Oz can comprehend how old he must be."

"The King is that old? I mean, that's not old but he looks considerably older than you. And as that came out of my mouth, I realize it sounds backwards. Neither of you looks that old. I'll shut up now."

"I come from sterling genetics." The Emperor stood up. "Come on. I planned on doing a little work tonight. You can help."

Now there was another surprise; the Emperor actually invited someone into his lair on the same night he invited someone to stay in his apartment. I jumped from the floor to the back of his chair to ask him to take me along, but before I could open my mouth he'd scooped me up and was absently petting my head.

I trained you well.

*

Finn kept a reasonable distance between himself and the Emperor; even when they were getting into the elevator on Union Square, he made sure he got on second and moved to the other side where there would be no chance of accidental touching. When the elevator landed on the Emperor's floor and he was punching numbers on the keypad that would let them in, Finn averted his eyes.

I don't know what the Emperor called this place. It was a vast level of what used to be a parking garage, and was peppered with giant support columns. He kept a lot of equipment there, and there were tables topped with clutter and slips of papers he had scribbled notes onto, shelves loaded with tools, and he even had a very old— probably 400 years old—motorcycle propped up on two heavy metal stands. It could have been a workshop; it could have been a lab or a playground, but more and more I thought of it as his lair. He spent more time there than his own apartment, sometimes even sleeping on an air mattress he kept stowed away in a storage closet.

He also had Finn's time machine. It rested on piston-adjusted support rods, with the wing doors on both sides open, and on the floor around it were a half dozen pods that looked a lot like miniature versions of the machine itself.

Your big egg laid little eggs, Finn.

The Emperor picked one of the small pods up and sat on a nearby stool, gesturing for Finn to pull another from under the worktable. He turned the pod over in his hands, running his fingers over it, before handing it to Finn.

"This is part of the power source to your ship," he said. "There are dozens of them, and most have a dark, powdery sheen on each end, where they connect. The rest are like this, bright white. But I have no idea how to fix them."

"Batteries," Finn muttered.

"More or less. The way they fit together, I think the power cascades through one to another, and each needs to function concurrently to provide enough power to get the engine running. I think they're also the fuel source, since there doesn't seem to be any place for liquid or plasma."

Finn ran a thumbnail along the length of the pod, and it cracked open. He reached inside and pulled from it a mass of tubes with heavy red wires running between them, and they were all glazed in a thick, black, powdery coating. Mumbling that the pod was just the casing, he set it down, and stared at the tubes in his hand.

"Solar," he said after a long silence. "Well, they convert solar energy harvested from the ship's shell. For them to be this depleted, I had to be away from sunlight for a very long time."

He reached down and grabbed one of the blackened pods and opened it. The coating on the tubes was patchy, worn down to the metal underneath. Very carefully, he worked his fingers between two of the tubes and tugged until one came loose, and stared at it for a moment before tossing it to the Emperor.

"The insulating coating is fried."

He rubbed one end with the hem of his red t-shirt, leaving a black smudge on it. "A power surge?" the Emperor guessed.

"Just the opposite. If the ship wasn't getting any sunlight, these would have overheated trying to keep the engine going. Something kept me from tripping the lever…"

He trailed off, staring at the tubes in his hand.

"What, Finn? What was it?"

With a heavy sigh, Finn blinked. "I lost it. It was right there, and I lost it."

The Emperor was not disappointed. He tossed the tube back to Finn. "It's still there. Give it a day or two and we'll try to coax it out again."

10

The view from the Emperor's spare bedroom left a lot to be desired, and the window sill was too narrow for me to curl upon. The Emperor left the apartment while Finn took a shower, so he wasn't there to amuse me; after Finn fell asleep I headed upstairs to sleep in Oz's room. She had the sweet corner view, with large windows and the sill was so wide it had been made into a seat with cushions for her to sit on. I just wanted to curl up right in the middle of it and sleep, but when I made my way down the hall, her light was still on and door was open.

She was sitting on the window seat with her back against the wall, and Drew was on the opposite end.

I jumped onto her bed and stomped my way down to the foot of it.

Do your parents know you're not alone in here this late at night?

"Where have you been, Mister Wick?" she asked.

Watching.

"Dad was looking for you. He had salami and was willing to share."

I had pizza. Just as good.

I plopped myself down on the bed, intent on waiting for them to get up and give me the window seat. They went on with what they had been talking about when I came in: Drew was supposed to go home for two weeks before school started, but with Finn there he wasn't sure he would.

She assured him she could handle Finn—with both fists and a well-placed knee if necessary—but he laughed and said it wasn't a matter of should he go, it was whether or not he really wanted to.

"I don't think he considered what he was doing, going after that woman. And he's an interesting guy. I may have never gotten to go through a portal if he hadn't bolted like that. It would have been better if I could have taken time to really see stuff, but just going through and *knowing* I was four hundred years in the past? That was sweet."

"I can take you through again. I'd need Dad's permission and you would have to really learn the rules first."

"What, like don't step on a bug, because it might alter history?"

"No, you don't have to be that careful, but you have to be aware of everything around you, and what you say to other people."

"If you screw up?"

She went through the list of possibilities: you get thrown into psychiatric care because there's no possible way you are who you say you are, or you get arrested because the laws are different or you have currency for the wrong When and they think you're passing off fake money, or you're inattentive and wind up dead. Or worse, you're inattentive and cause someone else's death.

What if I went back and ate some other kitty's chicken?

Well, now I feel guilty.

"That might be the worst. Kill someone who should not have died right then and there...you really do change the future. It can start a horrible domino effect."

"What if Finn was right?"

"That he should have let the woman jump off the bridge? I don't know, but I can't believe in any scenario where he would have let that happen. What bothers me is that right now he *believes* that's exactly what he should have done, and that it would fix everything for him. He doesn't even know what needs to be fixed, but the death of some poor woman would apparently do it."

"Think you can play nice with him tomorrow?"

"If we can find him."

I know where he is.

"You don't think he went back to find her again, do you?"

I know where he is.

"I hope not. He knows where two portals are now, and if he used one—depending on what time he went through, it's probably been too long for me to just follow. I would need to know exactly what date and time he headed for."

Seriously, I know…

"Wick, what are you blathering on about? Are you hungry? I know you missed dinner. Do you want me to go get you something to eat?"

Never turn down food.

They'd figure out where Finn was sooner or later.

I wanted the salami.

*

Oz let me sit on the counter while she tore a slice of salami into pieces, and Drew opened a can of food for me; he made faces and crinkled his nose at the smell as he spooned it into a bowl, grumbling about how gross it was and how awful it had to taste. He even apologized that I had to eat it.

Dude, it's good.

He set the bowl on the counter in front of me. "Holy hell, this stinks."

Stinky goodness. You should try it.

"Complain about his food too much and he'll lean back and start licking himself," Oz said.

"Show off," Drew muttered.

I started wolfing it down while he washed his hands. He should have understood the appeal; I'd seen him take down half a gravy-soaked chicken in about four bites and my food was no different. There was chicken, and there was gravy, and I never even asked about the unidentifiable bits because it was tasty enough. If he simply asked to try a bite to see how good it was, I'd have let him.

Instead, he treated it like cooties, washed his hands, and got far across the room to look out the window rather than breathe in the meaty aroma.

*Yeah, let's see you in five or ten years trying to handle baby food
and diapers.*

By the time I reached the bottom of the bowl and was considering
asking for more, he was rocking back and forth on his feet, restless,
and asked Oz if she wanted to take a walk, get some fresh air. I
thought it was a bit too late what with it already being dark outside,
but if Zed could be out all night working I didn't think anyone would
mind if we ventured out and took a nice walk. Union Square was
well lit and they both had guards, even if they never knew where the
guards were lurking. I made my way to the edge of the counter and
reminded them I was still there, and I would like to go with them.

Oz lifted me to her shoulder and was going to let me ride there,
but Drew ran upstairs for his sweatshirt and met her at the front door;
when he eased me into the pouch I thanked him for his consideration,
and licked his wrist so he would know I appreciated it.

"Ew."

I was being nice.

"Hey, it could be worse. He could have nipped at you," Oz said.
She pushed the door open and we went outside, the slap of cool air
making me glad Drew had gotten the sweatshirt.

I liked night-time walks; even on summer days the city was
generally nice and cool, but at night there was a nip in the air that
made the tips of my ears chilly and it felt good to tuck up against a
person and warm them up, and then poke my head out to do it all
over again. When I rode around on the Emperor's shoulder at night,
I always made it a point to let my nose get good and cold, and then
I would press it against his neck, making him twitch and he always
muttered a thing or two off the bad word list and called me Jerk
Face, but he still reached up to scratch under my collar.

Riding in Drew's sweatshirt, I would have to settle for pressing
my cold nose into his wrist. It wouldn't be as shocking but it would
gross him out, and that was good enough.

They walked around Union Square, sticking to the sidewalks
where there was plenty of light; I could hear their guards moving
around us, stealthily enough that Oz and Drew didn't feel like they
were being watched, but with all the light from the streetlamps we
would have been fine without them. Even if someone had bothered

us, Drew could have protected me while Oz protected him.

Once they had gone all the way around, Oz pointed down Powell Street and suggested heading for Market.

"Looking for Finn?" he asked.

She half shrugged.

I know where he is.

"You don't owe him an apology, Oz. I mean, we obviously have to deal with him, but you're allowed to be pissed off."

"Good thing, then, because I'm still pissed off."

We were half a block from Market Street, when she veered to the right and grabbed onto a lamp post and leaned into it with one hand, pressing her other hand to her forehead.

"You all right?" He took his hands off me and let me dangle there in the pouch, and reached for her arm. "What's wrong?"

As quickly as she had looked off, she looked fine.

"It was just one quick, weird jab of dizzy," she said. "That was odd. It was like everything slid to the right for a second."

"Should we turn around and go home?"

She shook her head. "It's just as far from here if we go down Market as it is if we turn around."

"I can signal your guard. He'll have a car here in seconds."

"Really, I'm fine, Drew." She nudged him back toward the center of the sidewalk. "If it happens again, I promise, I'll let you get the guard, and then we'll get to spend happy fun times in the ER while waiting for my parents, who will be frantic."

He still wasn't happy, but he grumbled, "Yeah, not to mention what the Emperor might do," and let her keep going.

Guard dude is already ten steps closer than he was a minute ago. You won't even have to signal him.

Drew turned, looking behind us and then down the corner to our right, looking for the guards, but the closest one had ducked into a store entryway and was so much in the shadows that Drew would have needed cat-vision to find him. There were others nearby, at least three, and that was Oz's fault.

She ran away to Sausalito once. That earned her lots of supervision.

He took a few quick steps to catch up to her, holding me close to keep me from bouncing too much, and when we turned the corner Oz paused for a moment and then started running. The Emperor was down the street near the portal, leaning against the wall near the bookstore's door, and his hand was pressed hard to his chest as he struggled to catch his breath. The other hand was pressed against the wall, as if he was trying to grab on to keep from falling over.

"I am too old," he huffed when they reached him, "to run that hard."

"Too old or too out of shape?" Oz teased. "Are you all right?"

He sucked in one long, hard breath through his nose. "I may have had three or four heart attacks in the last five minutes, but I'm fine."

"Kind of late to go for a run," Drew said.

"Kind of late for you to be out walking around," the Emperor said. "You should go home." He pushed off the wall and pulled his hand away from his chest. There was a bloody handprint on his pale blue t-shirt; he looked at it and his hands, then quickly said, "No worries. It's not mine."

Both of his hands were splattered with blood, and looking closer I could see flecks of red on his wrists, and a few random spots on his neck and just under his left ear.

Drew took a step back, but Oz moved forward, until the Emperor held up a bloody hand and told her it was all right.

"Well, then whose blood is it?" Oz snapped.

"Seriously, Oz, it's fine. Go home. It's too late for you to be out wandering around, even with him."

Her eyes flicked toward the portal. "Yeah, I think we're fine, but we'll go." She reached for Drew's sleeve and tugged on it, pulling him with her, and they turned around to go home the way we'd come. Once around the corner she let go of his sleeve and reached for his hand.

"That was weird," Drew said. "Do we tell someone? Your parents? Or will your guards do something?"

She agreed that it was odd, but no, the guards wouldn't do anything. They answered to the Emperor as much as they did her parents, and unless he did something to her, they would never question him. "That was blood, right? I wasn't imagining it?"

"All over his hands and shirt."

"Damn," she sighed. "All right, I don't want to wake them, but we have to tell my parents."

"Maybe we'll get lucky and your mom will still be up."

"What, are you afraid of my dad?"

"When I'm wandering around this late at night with his daughter? Hell, yes."

You kept your sticky boy-hands to yourself. He won't hurt you. Much.

Oz reached over to pet me. "Wick, you can't be hungry already."

Wanna bet?

"I'm hungry," Drew offered.

"You're both bottomless pits. But after we talk to my mom, she'll be happy if you dig into the leftovers. Hell, maybe she'll know where Finn is."

I know where he is.

"I know your mom. If I hint that I'm hungry, she'll heat it all up *while* we're talking."

"Don't use my mom, Hollow Man. You can heat up your own food."

"I can, but you know she won't let me."

Tell her I'm hungry, too. She'll cut it up into tiny bites for me. She loves me.

The entire ride up in the elevator I thought about what she might have made for dinner that I had missed while having pizza downstairs, aside from the salami the King had been willing to share. I hoped it was pot roast; she always made a ton of that and it was tender and delicious with the perfect amount of fresh deadness and tangy gravy, and she avoided using onions in it so that I could have a bite or two. Drew loved that pot roast as much as I did and if he was willing to heat up his own leftovers, that's probably what it was.

I may have drooled on his shirt a little bit.

When the elevator door opened, Drew hesitated; the living room was not dark, as he had expected. Lights were on in the dining room, and there was music, so he was sure that there were parents up and about and they might not take kindly to him sneaking around at night with Oz.

They both wavered when the Queen laughed. Oz took a deep

breath and said, "Fair warning. They've been known to make out on the couch like no one else lives here. Clothing may be strewn about. It's kind of gross."

"Come on. That's kind of sweet."

"Yeah, sure, it's not your parents we're about to walk in on."

"If it were my parents, we wouldn't be walking in on that."

I considered ducking my face into the sweatshirt pouch, because I'd seen enough of the bouncy antics of the King and Queen, but before I could we were halfway across the living room, and they weren't on the sofa doing groping things. They were at the dining room table, playing cards spread before them, beer glasses half filled, and the Emperor was with them.

"Oz," Drew said quietly, "how the hell did he get here that fast?"

Before she could answer, the adults noticed them.

"You two are up late," the Queen said.

"We went for a walk around the block," Oz said. "Down to Market and back." She pretended to consider the Emperor for a moment and then said, "I could have sworn we saw you halfway down Market, Emperor. Like, less than ten minutes ago."

"Nope." He tossed his cards to the table. "I've been here for about an hour. Long enough to con your mother into making cookies."

He's wearing a red t-shirt now. Outside, it was blue. Before that, it was red.

"Cookies and beer?" Drew crinkled his nose.

"Ever tried it?" the King asked.

"I don't drink."

"Well," he said, gathering all the playing cards, "come back in a year. We'll treat you to warm chocolate chip cookies and ice cold chocolate stout, and then I'll take all your money in penny ante poker."

"I'll look forward to it. The cookies and poker."

"Bah." The Emperor picked up his bottle and tilted it toward Drew. "You're practically twenty. I'd give you a beer now if Jax wasn't a tight ass about it. Hypocritical tight ass, at that."

"I don't drink—"

"This one," he pointed the bottle toward the King, "was drinking when he was a lot younger than you, and he hasn't turned out half bad. As a matter of fact, he stopped doing supremely stupid things after he started drinking."

"Don't listen to him," the King said. "I was not that much younger than you, I had permission from my father, and it was not that often. Beer did not improve my thought process."

The Queen laughed. "He stopped doing stupid things because I would not tolerate them."

"Really, I don't drink."

"Good for you, sweetie," she said. "Now really, why are you both up and about?"

"We went for a walk, and then the guy with the hollow legs decided we should raid the kitchen. And don't jump up to fix anything for him. We're capable."

For a split second, she looked wounded. It passed when the King dealt more cards and when the Emperor poured more beer into her glass. Oz guided Drew into the kitchen, where he let me out onto the counter. I waited for the King to say something, but he ignored me in favor of staring at the Queen like she was a perfectly cooked cut of steak, so I stretched out to get as much of my furry glory onto the granite as I could.

Drew leaned in very close to Oz and whispered, "We did not imagine the Emperor. He was outside just a few minutes ago."

"He was, and he was right by a portal. The question is whether it was him from the past or even a week from now." She looked over me, to her parents and the Emperor sitting at the table, laughing at whatever Jax had just said. "And whose blood was all over him? And why?"

Drew got bread out for sandwiches, slapping meat and cheese on it, and he pulled extra out for me. "Honestly, Oz…as long as it wasn't mine, I'm not sure I want to know."

Oz wanted to know. She knew it was toward the top of the list of *Things We Do Not Ask the Emperor*, but she wanted to know.

*

Finn didn't show up for breakfast, but before Oz could verbally beat herself up over it, the King dropped into his chair and told her where Finn had spent the night, and if she was no longer irritated with him and was up for the company, he'd be at Union Square in an hour or so. He planned on walking around the city, alone if he needed to, but would be very happy if she and Drew would join him.

Me, too. I want to go.

I jumped into Drew's lap and was going to crawl into the pouch on his sweatshirt, but he wasn't wearing it.

You're missing something.

I pawed at his stomach.

You need to change clothes, dude.

"I'll put it on, Wick, just let me have breakfast first."

You're almost trained.

Before Drew was done eating, the Queen placed a paper bag on the table near his plate and asked him to make sure Finn got it. She knew he'd gotten dinner, the Emperor promised that, but she also knew that food first thing in the morning was not the Emperor's favorite thing and his kitchen was likely to have fairly bare cupboards.

Jax laughed—"the boy is old enough to find food for himself, sweetheart"—but Drew promised he'd make sure Finn got it, and he would guilt him into eating it.

If there's bacon in there, I'm getting some of that.

Finn groaned when Drew handed him the bag. He'd eaten and had even coaxed the Emperor into having breakfast, but he already understood a fundamental rule of the house: when Her Majesty makes you something to eat, you eat it. The rule didn't say you couldn't share, so Drew offered to take whatever Finn couldn't handle and they split the ham and cheese sandwich as they walked away from the Square.

Eating little bits from Drew's hand was awkward while in motion, but I wasn't about to turn it down when he offered some to me.

Finn wanted to walk through the South of Market neighborhood— SOMA—hoping he would recognize something, anything, and was pleased that he could pick out where the Yerba Buena Gardens were and which building housed the Museum of Modern Arts. The Old Mint building baffled him; he was sure it was a research and data center, and he stood in the street and stared at it for a long time, until

Oz reminded him that it might be something else in his time.

I hated that place. It hummed horribly and hurt my head.

Oz hated that place, too, so much that it surprised me when she didn't force Finn to move along. She humored his too-serious contemplation about it, and let him stand there to think about it. If it seemed important to him, then maybe it would jog something important loose inside his head.

From there we wandered toward the Embarcadero, and then headed toward the Bay Bridge. He expected to see Cupid's Arrow at Rincon Park, but it had been gone for hundreds of years. A restaurant he knew of was not there, but he also recalled another in its place.

"Time travel and amnesia," Oz said.

She was still annoyed with him, I could tell. She huffed through her nose and she raised her eyebrows when he wasn't looking at her, and she was just short enough with him to make me think she would rather be somewhere else. This was *take-your-brother-on-your-field-trip day* all over again. She did it because it was expected of her, but that didn't mean she liked it.

On the other hand, Drew enjoyed himself. The city was still fresh enough to him because he'd never been allowed to just wander around it when he was a child, so he was discovering things right along with Finn. They argued over the stadium—was it AT&T Park or was it just The Field—and then wondered why it was still standing, since no one had played a professional sport in it for at least a hundred years.

"There are concerts," Oz pointed out. "Lots of community events, like the biannual renaissance fair. The university holds graduation in the park. My dad's coronation was held there. So was my grandmother's funeral."

Finn's hand went to his chest, just over his heart. "Oh. I'm sorry."

"Thanks. The funeral was hard because Grandma wasn't old and it felt unfair, but the coronation was fun. It was like a week-long party and the whole world was invited. When my grandfather crowned my dad and the people in the stadium went nuts cheering, he said right into the microphone, 'Long live the King, you wanker, and long live the King Emeritus."

Drew laughed, Finn did not.

"Wait. Your grandfather was there—?"

"The monarch doesn't have to die for the next in line to inherit the throne. He abdicated and I think he's in Ireland or England right now. Granddad wanted to travel before he was too old to enjoy it. My dad turned thirty and it was like, 'Jackson, you're a big boy now. Go be King so that I can go play with my friends.' I don't think my dad really wanted to because he liked his job, but there wasn't much of a choice."

"Job? Your dad had to work?"

Oz looked at him like he was an imbecile. I recognized that look, because she frequently looked at Zed that way. "People work, Finn. He was a high school history teacher. My mom teaches fifth grade. I'll start looking for a job after this summer is over when Drew goes back to school, but Zed's already working. Granted, he only works under volunteer status, but what he does on Alcatraz is a job."

"I'm not working," Drew offered.

"School is your job," Oz said. "For the next two to four years, that's all you do."

Finn still looked perplexed. "I don't think I've ever considered someone in a royal family needing to work a real job."

"Bills still have to be paid. Food still has to go on the table."

"So you're not…"

"Rich?" she finished for him. "No. My dad is not given a ton of cash for what he does. We get to live where we do, but we also get no choice in it. There's a stipend for being the King, but anything extra? My mom earns that."

"What about you?" Finn asked Drew.

"It's not much different in Midlam. My dad is an engineer, and my mom gets a stipend for being Queen. The state pays for the house and a couple of cars, and staff for the house, but yeah, my dad pays for all the incidentals. My brother had to work all through college to save money for the traveling he knew he wanted to do after. I mean, my tuition is paid but I would work if I needed to."

"School is your job," Oz repeated.

"That's easy to say, Oz, but Mommy and Daddy aren't giving me an allowance. If things get tight, I'll absolutely get a job."

"There's no way *my* parents will allow that. You're here to get a degree and they'll make sure that happens."

Finn laughed. "Oz will make sure you get an allowance."

"Cripes, maybe I'll get paid for my grades. How much is an 'A' worth, Oz?"

"Pizza party with all your friends on the roof if you get a report card full of them. At least that's how it worked when I was in school."

"Surely college will get me ice cream along with that."

"If you're a good boy, sure. My dad rewards good boys, since he was such a wild little freak when he was a kid. Bribing kids to behave keeps his stress level lower than his parents' was."

We were headed onto the Bay Bridge, walking up the slope from Pier 26 to the upper street level. There was a lower level, but it was cut off from pedestrian traffic. The only things allowed on it were bicycles and air bikes.

"He really tried to climb this?" Drew asked.

"When he was six. It was just the beginning in a long line of stupid stunts he pulled over the years." She pointed to a tower on their right. "This is it, the one with the plaque naming it the Emperor's Bridge. And if you look up—" they all looked up "—you can see the blue line that was marked where he got stuck."

"Damn, that's like twenty feet up," Drew said.

"Doesn't sound like much, but when you see it…"

"Why?" Finn asked. "What possessed him?"

She shrugged. "He was six. Who knows?"

Finn put a foot on the base of the tower and reached up to grab a cross support. "Let's find out. What could be so interesting?"

"Finn, don't. You won't get ten feet up."

"Sure I will. And don't worry, I won't fall."

"Yeah, that's not what I'm worried about."

He pulled himself up and began to climb, making the distance with little effort. I watched him go up, but from the corner of my eye could see Oz looking down the street, waiting for the police car that was already halfway there.

*

Instead of taking us to the police station, they took us to the Emperor, who then took us to the King, who—without a hint whether he was upset or not—ordered us to the roof.

I liked the roof; it had a huge expanse of real grass I could roll around in, and it was protected all the way around by a thick, clear acrylic wall, so I could jump up on the ledge without worrying that the wind would blow me off. This was where Oz and Zed played when they were little and wanted to be outside, and where they held parties when they were older. You could see all the way around downtown from the roof, and because of the wall they could blast music and be loud without annoying everyone in the neighboring buildings. There was something going on most weekends during the school year, because their friends preferred the roof to their own postage-stamp-sized back yards, and the Queen was happy to have them all there.

The King perhaps was a bit less happy, but he reasoned that if all their friends were right there, he didn't have to worry as much about where they all were and what they were doing.

"Look to Oakland," he told them, pointing to a corner of the roof.

Finn looked, but frowned. Oz didn't bother, because she knew what the view was. Drew walked over to the corner like a happy puppy, only to be disappointed because the ball he expected wasn't there.

"Well, that sucks."

"Exactly. You can't see past those buildings. But I *knew*—and I mean I knew it like a religious conviction—that over those buildings, just past Oakland, was a place I desperately wanted to see."

"The Wastelands?" Oz asked.

He nodded. "The Wastelands. In my head they were like the old west of five hundred years ago, with dirt streets and horses and cowboys and saloons. Since I couldn't see it from here, I decided to go to the bridge and look, because if it was as wonderful as I thought, I was going to walk there and live like a cowboy. But then I got to the bridge, and I still couldn't see anything."

"How did you expect to walk that far? It would have taken weeks."

"Well, to be fair, I looked at a map and it was only three inches. I thought it would take all afternoon, but I was going to check from the bridge to make sure it was where I thought it was."

"I had places to go."

"I know. And people to disappoint."

"Indeed."

Oz wasn't ready to be done with the story. "Dad. Why not just leave the backpack?"

"I couldn't."

"Come on, you could get another backpack."

"Tell her, Jax."

"There was no way I was leaving it dangling there, Oz. I also wasn't dropping it for someone else to hopefully catch. I couldn't take that chance. What if someone missed? Or tossed it into the water? Angry people can be petty, and some of them were beyond reason with rage. So what if I was the prince? I was a kid who was not blindly obeying what the adults were telling me to do. I was afraid of what would happen if I managed to free the backpack and throw it to someone. And if I left it? Who would climb back up to get it?"

She sighed impatiently.

"My best friend was in it. I wasn't leaving him behind."

"What, you risked your life because you were carrying your teddy bear around?"

I wiggled out of Drew's sweatshirt and jumped down to rub against the King's leg.

"It was Wick. I couldn't leave the backpack, because Wick was in it."

"So you climbed."

"I climbed. I was positive that the higher I got, the better I co\
see. The problem was that when I got high enough, I panicked. T\
strap on my backpack was caught, and I couldn't move. By the\
people had noticed me and had gathered on the bridge, shouting a\
me to get down."

"But you couldn't."

"No. Well, not without wiggling out of the backpack. I did get
one arm out and then realized I couldn't just leave it there and I
wasn't tossing it down hoping someone would catch it. Then I felt
like I was losing my grip and hung onto it to keep from sliding."

"Dad."

"He couldn't leave it," the Emperor said. "And of all those
people, not one was actually doing anything to help him. They were
clustered together and near frenzy, doing nothing but shouting at
him, as if a little boy could understand the gravity of his mistake.
Thirty people or more, all yelling. It was uncomfortably loud."

"Then he showed up." The King nodded to the Emperor. "He
pushed his way through, climbed up after me, got the backpack free
and secured on my back again, and then told me to wrap my arms
around his neck, legs around his waist, and to hold on as tightly as I
could. The entire time he whispered 'You're all right, I won't let you
fall,' and I was crying so hard I couldn't see."

"I had a snot-caked shirt the rest of the day."

"When he reached the ground, he refused to let go of me. All the
sudden these people were determined to 'help' and were reaching
for me, as if they could do anything by grabbing me. He wouldn't
hand me to the police, either. He insisted he would let me go to only
one person, and that was my mother."

"She met us at the head of the bridge," the Emperor said. "The
first time I met the Queen, she was running toward me in gym shorts
and a sweatshirt, crying and near hysterics."

"She didn't let go of me for an hour. But when she did… Oz,
you've never heard her erupt so much. That was enough to scare me
into not doing anything stupid for a good year or two."

"Six months," the Emperor said. "At best."

"And you. You disappeared for weeks."

11

Since the roof was a place from which Finn could not easily run, it was there the Emperor decided to try the memory stick a second time. Oz, Drew, and the King sat in lawn chairs that blocked the path to the door—and Drew warned him that if he bolted, there would be tackling involved—and I curled up in the King's lap, mostly because he was warm and I was not.

I think Finn was still convinced that at some point the Emperor was going to hit him with the metal pipe instead of having him hold onto it; when he pulled it out of his backpack, Finn flinched, and then steadied himself against the impulse to take a few steps back. He didn't want to do this again, because when it came right down to it, he didn't want to think he was the sort of person who would chase down some poor woman just to watch her jump to her death.

"There's the rub," he said. "I may very well be the guy with no moral compass. For all I know time is littered with bodies that I left behind."

"You're not a murderer, Finn," Oz said.

His gaze was fixed on the pipe in the Emperor's hand. "I don't know that. And I don't want to remember it if I am. What if my memory comes flooding back to me, and it's nothing but blood and bits of bodies exploding around me?"

"Then we destroy your ship and keep you here," the King said. "We can deal with that."

"You can't fix evil."

The Emperor pushed the pipe toward Finn. "Maybe we can. Or maybe there's something else you're trying to not remember. Whatever it is, we're going to figure it out and deal with it."

"I'm not sure I want to know how you'd deal with it."

"You'd have a chance at redemption, Finn. But hurt one hair on Oz's head, or Zed's, or even Drew's, and I'll rip you apart myself. Make no mistake, I will inflict a considerable amount of pain on their behalf."

"You'd have to touch me to do that."

"Indeed."

Reluctantly, Finn wrapped his fingers around the bare metal, and the Emperor took a tighter grip on the rubber-coated end, the bare tip of his little finger touching metal. Finn closed his eyes, and after a few seconds of breathing in and out deeply, the Emperor began his litany of questions. He asked the same things he had before, and in return got the same answers: "I don't know."

He began to repeat the questions, his voice nearly monotone, running through the list several times until Finn's shoulders relaxed and he tilted his head back a little. His eyes were closed and the sunlight made him look pale, his eyelids flushed with pink. I could hardly tell that he was breathing, his chest barely moving with every inhale and exhale.

On the ninth or tenth time through the list, Finn began to answer.

"What year were you born?"

"Twenty-six-eighteen."

"Who was the woman on the bridge?"

"Jo."

"What's your favorite color?"

"Purple."

"How many states are there?"

"Forty."

"Who is Jo?"

"JoJo. Joanne."

"Who is Joanne?"

"Love of my life. My wife."

Oz twitched and shifted in her chair, looking first at the King and then at Drew.

"How old are you?"

"Thirty."

"How long have you been married?"

"A year."

"Where is Jo now, Finn?"

His eyes snapped open.

"Don't let go, Finn. Where is she?"

"I left her in twenty-sixteen. There was a speech…she wanted to be there but I needed to stop her. I don't know. It's like I'm seeing her twice. She's standing in the same spot, but I can see her from two different angles. I know I need to keep her from speaking, I know she felt like she needed to be there. But I can see her standing there in a massive party tent filled with metal folding chairs, and I see her twice."

"What was she speaking about?"

"She wanted…I don't know what she wanted. I can't pull that out of my brain."

The Emperor let go of his end of the pipe.

"I couldn't have wanted her to jump. She's my wife. How could I forget that? How could I forget *her?*"

*

"How can that kid be thirty years old?" the King asked the Emperor. He wasn't expecting a real answer; he was thinking out loud and trying to fit more pieces of the puzzle together. Still on the roof, the teenagers having left with Finn to find better things to do with people not so old, the King and the Emperor moved their chairs to a spot at the edge of the roof where the wall was low and watched people below.

Those are your minions. Look at them scurry like ants.

"I'm a poor judge of age, Jackson. You still look impossibly young to me."

"And you still look like the guy who plucked me off the bridge. I'm getting gray hair. Why aren't you?"

"I age well. Like fine cheese."

"Even cheese gets moldy." He reached over and took the memory stick from the Emperor, turning it over, looking down the center hole. "What is this, really?"

The Emperor snorted. "It's just a piece of pipe I found in the trash. I stuck a battery and a few wires in one end and slipped a rubber grip on it. There's a switch just under the grip. Press it and the pipe gets a mild electrical charge."

"So there's nothing special about it?"

"The power of suggestion, that's all. He could feel the tingle in his hand, presumed the stick was working, and let his guard down. Since he was concentrating on that feeling, he wasn't cluttered by all the worry."

"You like messing with people, don't you?"

"Little bit, yeah."

Tell him the whole thing. Tell him about your pinkie.

I stood on his legs, my paws on his chest, faces so close I could feel how moist the air coming from his nose was.

He should know how you helped.

"I see you there, Wick." He planted a kiss on top of my head. "You're a good boy."

Holy barf on a biscuit.

I sat down.

I'm going to stop talking to you one of these days if you keep that dog-talk crap up.

At least the King didn't pile on with the insults. He was still thinking about Finn, so I jumped over to him. "Should he go back and get his wife? Should we let him?"

"He would need to remember the exact date he left her, and she would have to be here, in the city. If he can pull that from the back of his brain, then yes, I think he should be taken back to see her."

The King nodded.

"But no, *you* should not go. I know you want to."

"I know. Risks and all that."

"Jax, You're not done, but whatever trips you make need to be worth it."

"Yeah." He stood up, putting me into the Emperor's lap. "But really, when will it ever be worth the risk? It's Oz's turn, and we both know it. It's all zooming up on us way too soon."

"She's not even eighteen yet."

"A couple of weeks, that's all. She turns eighteen, and then nineteen happens before I blink and Drew is drooling all over her. Next thing I know I'm handing the crown over, and she's this... adult."

"And then you can go traveling through time to your heart's content. And who knows? Maybe I'll go with you."

"We both know that won't happen. You'll never leave Wick behind."

12

Here's the thing. I have been the King's pet since he was a baby, but deep down he knows—he's not sure how, but he knows—that I was the Emperor's cat before that. My memory is a little fuzzy on that, but I don't doubt it. It doesn't bother the King, but once that realization came to him, I think he understood that his life was fleeting and mine might not be. He doesn't want to discuss how old I am, partly because he knows that one day he'll be gone and I'll be someone else's cat.

He hopes it will be his grandkids, or great grandkids, but there's no guarantee.

I don't even know how long I'll be their family cat. Something has tugged me in other directions before, but like Finn, I can't remember everything. All I know is that I'm here for now, and that the Emperor is content to share me. He's fine that I am officially Wick of the House of Blackshear. He still gets me when we both want to be together; he's had an apartment in the royal house for over ten years that I can get into whenever I want, and I know how to get into his lair.

In quiet moments, he's thanked me for being his anchor, but I don't really know what that means. I don't have some evil arbitrary goal of sinking him, so I can only assume it's one of those hyperbolic human things I will never understand.

After the King left we waited on the roof for a while, until he decided he wanted to poke around Finn's magical egg. I followed him, riding down in the elevator, crossing the street just behind him, and scurrying up the steps to the Square. He didn't say anything, not until we were walking from the door to Finn's ship.

"I should know how to fix this, Wick. I know how all the pieces fit together, but I can't make them work. Give me a four-hundred-year old car, I can reassemble it and get it running. The motorcycle? It took a month, but it works. Every time Zed breaks his air bike? Not a problem. I was working on things like this when I was a little boy. This shouldn't be that hard."

I crawled into the ship and jumped onto the lone seat inside. It still smelled like burning, with a faint edge of a thunderstorm wrapped around it. All the controls were laid out on a curved dashboard in front of the seat, and there was a screen above it; I could look through it, watch the Emperor move about his workspace, but from the outside I knew it was nothing but a flat white shell.

"Don't get on the dash," he told me. "One of those things might flip a switch and for all we know there's a self-destruct."

Fine. No blowing up Union Square.

"There probably isn't. Just be careful."

Yeah. You're pulling apart batteries you don't know much about and you want me to be careful.

He separated wires from the tubes Finn pulled out of the battery casing, and was turning one over in his hand. "Could be filled with anything. Lithium. Plasma. For all I know, the blood of thirty puppies."

Or acid.

"Old school lead-acid battery, maybe?"

That many tubes filled with acid in that many little pods would weigh a couple of tons.

"Probably not. I'm not sure I need to know…I just need to charge a few and see what I can hook them up to, I suppose. Maybe a video monitor. I'll either power it up and can move to the next problem, or I'll blow it up and have to start over. A bloody manual would help."

There's a place you might be able to get one, you know.

"Why doesn't he carry an operating manual in here? That would make sense, you know? Every air bike and car comes with a fracking owner's manual. You know what? If I'm ever in charge—and pray that never happens—every damned thing will come with one, detailed and in color."

Go to the humming building. And stop making up words to use instead of the ones the Queen said not to.

He set the tube down gently. "I'm not thinking straight. Tomorrow we'll probably take Finn back through the portal. I'll deal with this after that. For now, let's go get some food and go to bed. I'm tired and I'm hungry, and I know you are, too."

There we go. Procrastination suits you sometimes.

"I don't have any shrimp, though. Canned food for you. You'll forgive me for that, right?"

How about pizza? Is there leftover pizza? Or just cheese? I could go for some cheese.

"Eh, we can raid the staff kitchen. The kids always store meat and cheese in the fridge."

Sure, we'll steal the kids' snacks. That's some stellar adulting for you.

*

I woke up the next morning curled up in the big comfy chair in the Emperor's living room. He was awake already—or perhaps hadn't slept at all, which wasn't unusual—and sitting in the other chair, the one he didn't really like. His hands were cupped around his coffee mug, and he was watching news on the video monitor. I didn't look, but could hear the rumble of the talking heads reciting stories that they thought were of particular interest.

The Governor of Texas announced he was running in the next election; that sounded a bit exhausting, but entirely people-like. Surely he had a car. Maybe even an air bike. And he could probably pay someone to drive him around. Running seemed like a huge waste of energy, and yet I saw people doing it almost every day, even the King. He ran up and down Powell Street or around Union Square, as if running for its own sake made any kind of sense.

I ran every now and then, but that was usually to chase one of the fat pigeons that scurried around downtown. I wasn't even trying to catch one, because that would have been very unfair given how weighed down by the excess of human generosity they were, but I did want to play with one even if the feeling wasn't mutual.

Cats was opening in New York City for its ninety-seventh run. I might have been interested in that, but the chances of anyone taking me that far outside of the city were slim to one-quarter of a tiny fraction of none. If we were lucky, the show would come to San Francisco in a year or two. I'd seen pictures online from earlier runs; I would rather enjoy watching people dressed up like cats, I think.

The Russian oligarchy ran out of money. That amused me.

The King of England fell off his horse during a polo match but nothing was hurt other than his pride. That's what he gets for making that poor horse his sporting toy. I didn't think he would like it much if the horse decided to ride him instead. Okay, so maybe he actually asked the horse first, but I doubt it.

The First Minister of Florida announced that he would be increasing the number of tourist permits, beginning immediately. The Emperor snorted at that, and who could blame him? They destroyed Disney World a couple of hundred years ago because it wasn't pure enough, and people could come to Pacifica and visit Disneyland to see and do the same things. I kind of wanted to go, just once, just to see the giant mouse that lived there. Oz and Zed went when they were thirteen and ten and brought back pictures they had taken with him, and let me tell you, that mouse is *huge*. Like, 5000 meals huge.

Okay, to be fair, I bit a mouse once and didn't like it one bit, but come on. Just the *idea* of a mouse that big.

A memorial had been held last night to honor a family killed when their air car was knocked off the vista view road at Land's End by a toy drone; the owner of the drone was unknown, but speculation was that it had malfunctioned and fallen from the sky, startling the driver, who veered off the road and over the cliff, and into the water below. There were no survivors.

The weather talking head said that it was going to be a cool, foggy day. Big surprise there. Summer in San Francisco was usually cool and foggy. The surprise would have been hot and muggy. Or snow.

Snow would be fun. There were some pretty steep hills in San Francisco, and kids could sled and ski down them. That would be far saner than, say, trying to ride a bike down one without braking.

I didn't get to hear any sports, because the Emperor clicked the news off.

Do you ever sleep?

"Good morning, Mister Wick," he said. "Your breakfast is in the kitchen, and after you've eaten, I thought we would take a nice walk near Ghiradelli Square. We can watch boats come and go under the Golden Gate."

Zed had worked all night at Alcatraz. My gut said what the Emperor really wanted was to be there when his skiff docked. I ate quickly and used the litterbox, and was ready to go before he had his teeth brushed and hair combed. He put on a gray sweatshirt that looked a lot like Drew's red one, with the front pouch re-sewn so that I could ride in it, but it had sleeves still.

"I know, I know. The Queen made several of them. This one is a little roomier so that you have space to turn around."

She spoils me.

"To be honest, I don't know why we didn't think of something like this a long time ago. It certainly is easier to cart you around and not worry about dropping you."

Maybe because when Oz and Zed were little, no one took me many places. We stayed here and played. I didn't mind that but now that they're big it's a lot more interesting to go outside with you.

"Let me know if it gets cramped. You can still ride on my shoulder if you like."

It was cold outside; I was perfectly content to snuggle into the sweatshirt and steal the warms off his body.

*

Zed always landed his skiff near the aquatic park in front of Ghiradelli Square. It was a single-rider craft that looked a lot like a small air bike, and he could drag it out of the water and lock it up near the rack where the public air bikes were parked. When we got there, Finn was sitting on a bench at the water's edge, huddled up in a jacket borrowed from Drew, looking like a kid trying to wear his big brother's clothes. The Emperor coughed so that he would hear us approach, not wanting to startle him.

Me, I'm all in favor of making a person twitch in surprise. They always either get really mad, or look like they want to wet themselves but sooner or later think it's funny anyway. For a fraction of a second, I think Finn wanted to wet himself.

"You're up and about early," the Emperor said.

Finn relaxed and scooted on the bench to make room for us. "It sounded like Zed was going to have a difficult night. I thought he might want someone here when he got off this morning. I'm guessing you thought the same?"

"He is a remarkable young man, and he takes on far more than he should. He shouldn't have to bear it all alone."

"His parents are with you on that one." He told the Emperor about their dinner conversation; the King and Queen had planned on attending the evening memorial service and then wanted to accompany Zed to Alcatraz, to be with him when the bodies of the Miller family arrived. They knew how hard it would be, but he refused. It's hard every day, this would be no different.

Everyone knew the truth; not only would it be different, it would be unbearably hard. Still, they took him at his word that he could do his job without having them hover over him and they let him go, but Finn wanted to be sure he was all right, and when the Emperor saw the morning news he knew that someone needed to be waiting at the aquatic park when Zed headed home.

Finn stared down at the ground while Zed's skiff headed for shore; I think he wanted to give Zed that last few minutes of privacy, for his pain to be free from intrusion, but the Emperor watched Zed the whole time. When he was getting off the skiff, the Emperor got up, shuffled across the sand, and handed me to him.

With a heavy sigh, he held my fur to his face, murmuring something I couldn't make out—it could have been "hey, glad to see you" or "dude, your breath stinks"—but I don't think I needed to. I only needed to do what the Emperor knew I would do for Zed;

I pushed my head to that tender spot just under his ear, and I purred hard. We stayed like that for a minute or two while the Emperor put the skiff away for Zed, and when he finally handed me back, Finn was standing up and not looking away.

"Just breathe," the Emperor told him. "I thought it might be a good idea to go get breakfast before you go home and deal with your mother."

He didn't think the Queen would smother him, but the Emperor was right. Zed needed to decompress before facing his mother's innate need to hover and fuss over him. Zed also needed someone to talk to, someone to whom he wouldn't feel the need to protect from the details or minimize how much the entire night had pained him. He hadn't counted on Finn being there but it was less of an intrusion and more like having an extra set of ears to hear him.

We headed for the Emperor's favorite diner downtown; it was an older, run-down looking place wedged into an old alleyway between two hotels on Powell Street, with metal-trimmed tables covered by red checkered vinyl tablecloths, and the bench seats were soft and worn. It looked that way on purpose, though I wasn't a fan because everything looked like it was probably sticky, and when you have fur, sticky is not a fun thing. I also wasn't a fan of the seating. I wanted to stay in the Emperor's sweatshirt, but the server that seated us pulled up a baby's high chair covered with a large towel, and when I whined (just a tiny bit) she said, "Come on, Mister Wick, you know the deal. We can't let you sit at the table. Those are the rules."

That's only one rule.

"I could send you home, you know," the Emperor said. "It's not that far for you to walk."

Before I could complain about that notion—it was a straight shot down Powell and I would only have to cross a couple of streets before turning onto Geary, but there were a lot of mean pigeons along the way and I wasn't sure I could run faster than they could fly—the server ruffled the furs on my head and said, "But then I wouldn't be able to give him his special treat. I have some chicken and steak bites for you today."

Fine, I'll stay.

"You're such a good boy."

Oh my God.

When she clicked a tray onto the high chair I wanted to hiss at her, but then she covered it with little bits of perfectly warmed up steak and chicken, so I forgave her. A little bit.

I also forgave the Emperor for his threat to send me home when he shared a few bites of his scrambled eggs and bacon.

"All right," the Emperor said when they were almost done eating. "I know what the news said. What really happened to the Millers?"

Hundreds of years ago, there was a trail at Land's End on the west side of the city, near Ocean Beach. It had a railway running through it right along the coast, elevated a few hundred feet up from the water, and several times a day people rode through the nature trail on a small, open-seat train. Over time the soil eroded from the tracks and made it unsafe for the train, so the track was buried under a thick layer of soil, and it became a hiking path. But when the King was a teenager, a new road was laid out along the old path, which ran next to the cliff. It was fully controlled with computers and magnets, and every vehicle that went over it was micro-managed to ensure safety. Speeding was not possible, so a driver could sit back to take in all the views without worrying about missing a turn or hitting a tree.

Since it had opened to the public, there hadn't been a single accident on it involving a car. But when the Millers were on the trail with their nearly year-old twin boys, a toy drone careened through the trees, landed on the trail just in front of their car, and the burst of energy from its batteries shorted the electric wire that powered the system of magnets underground. Only 20 feet of road was affected, but the Millers were halfway through that stretch of 20 feet.

The car missed making the curve just ahead, and went off the side of the road, down the cliff, and into the water. It looked like it had been a straight slide down, and if the car had not overturned on impact they might have walked away from it. Once it hit the water, it filled up and was all the way under in seconds, and sank like a stone until it was wedged into the layers of dirt and sand under the water.

"They never had a chance," Zed said. "And it was bad enough when the rescue team got the car out and recovered the parents, but…"

"I know. Babies."

It was more than that. Zed waited nearby on his skiff in case the rescue team needed more muscle, and watched as three grown men turned away from the wreckage to compose themselves. He was curious, so he inched closer and peered into the back of the car, where the twin boys were strapped into seats next to each other.

"They were covered in mud and it was hard to see, but…they were holding hands. Those tiny fingers laced together—"

"Damn," Finn said, the word catching in his throat.

"After the memorial service yesterday their bodies were brought to the island and no one else could bring themselves to touch them. I was able to prepare the parents, but those kids are still waiting and I'm not sure I can do it, not as well as they deserve."

Finn started to say something, but stopped at the very slight shaking of the Emperor's head.

"I mean, seriously, how do I speak for lives that were that short?" Zed went on. "I can prepare them, I can wash their little bodies and do everything else, but how do you say goodbye when you've barely said hello?"

"You really don't have to do this," the Emperor said.

"I think I do."

"I'll be there if it will help," Finn said. "I'll probably cry, but I'll be there."

"I'll be there, as well. And when you're ready, I'll get Oz and Drew. They'll stand with you. Your parents will, too, if you allow them."

To that, Zed objected. Saying goodbye to babies was not something he wanted his mother subjected to. She had barely held it together during the memorial service when they were hidden away in impossibly small white coffins, but to see them there together like that was not a thing she should have to endure.

"Your mother is a very strong woman," the Emperor said.

"I know she is. But she's also so very much a *mother*. This wouldn't be fair."

She would want to hold them and never let go. The image formed in the Emperor's mind, his closest friend cradling the bodies of babies she had never known but would always love, and it broke his heart.

Don't let her do that.

"All right. Just let me know when you're ready, and I'll call Oz and Drew."

"I'll never be ready. But if we could go now and get it done, I would appreciate it."

13

They looked like they were sleeping. There was a wrongness to how they were lying on the table together with no crib slats to keep them from falling, and my first sight of them was tangled up with the thought that they looked so much like Oz and Zed had when they were babies. Eyes closed, lips pursed in the ethereal dreams that only infants know; from where I sat in the Emperor's sweatshirt the only telltale sign that they weren't simply sleeping was the absence of the slow rise and fall of their chests. A moment later, I realized that I missed the sound of an infant suckling on air, nursing in a dream. I wanted to hear it.

He was quiet about it, but I felt the Emperor's chest heave as he tried not to suck in a deep, sharp breath.

"Shamar and Tyrese Miller," Zed said, almost whispering, as he gently pulled the baby blue sheet away from them. He reached for the basin under the table, dipping his fingers in to make sure the water was still warm. He never wanted to use cold water, even on the dead, but with them he wanted it to feel soothing, and he added a bit of hot water from a pitcher that was stored under the table as well.

He let a drop of the water fall onto his wrist, checking the temperature the same way his father had tested bottles before feeding him as a baby.

"They were born on a very cold day in September, when rain fell in soft, steady drops from morning until night. Shamar was born at nine-twenty-three, Tyrese was born at nine-twenty-eight, and the rain stopped at nine-thirty."

He began to wash them, silently, though we could all see it in his eyes: *I don't know what to say for them. I don't know what to do for them.*

Oz was already crying, and couldn't help him.

Their hands.

The Emperor noticed, too. "You are loved," he murmured as he stepped to the edge of the table. Very gently, he reached down and pushed their hands closer, and then laced their tiny fingers together. "When I was a very little boy, my mother used to sing me to sleep every night. I can still hear her voice in my head, and her words tickle my brain like a soft feather."

He began to sing, so softly that at first only Zed and I could hear him. It was not so much a lullaby as it was a wish, a dream of dancing between clouds and jumping between stars, and never, ever falling.

As he sang for them, I wiggled out of his shirt and climbed onto the table. No one tried to stop me. I laid between them, my front paws on their hands, and I listened for heartbeats that weren't there and breaths that had been stolen, and I could feel the Emperor's song fill those empty places.

He's promising you something. I hope you can hear it. I hope you can find the clouds and the stars and play on them as much as you want. He wouldn't lie to you. You'll never fall again.

Finn was mouthing the words along with the Emperor.

When Zed was done, he patted their skin dry and tucked the sheet around them, up to their chins. He didn't want to take the next step, so he stood there with his eyes closed and fingers gripping the edge of the table, doing what the Emperor had told him to do earlier. He was deliberately breathing in and out, deeply, trying to soothe himself.

Oz put her hand on his. "I'll take them into the next room, Zed. It's okay."

When he opened his eyes, they were watery and rimmed with

red. He leaned over, a hand on each tiny chest, and whispered, "Mommy and Daddy are waiting for you in the next room, and Oz is going to take you to them," and then gave them each a kiss on the forehead. "I promise you, when it's time, I'll take you home to your Grandma and Grandpa. It was too hard for them to be here today, but they're waiting for you."

No one spoke again until we were outside, waiting for the ferry. Zed stood with his hands thrust deeply into his pockets, his head thrown back, his eyes closed, and he cut through the silence. "I don't think I can do this anymore. Shamar and Tyrese won't be the last, and at some point, they'll all feel like babies."

Oz and Drew agreed, he'd done enough and could walk away to find something else in life, but Finn did not.

"That pain is why you have to. It matters to you. *They* matter to you. You believe that even the dead deserve respect and kindness, and that their stories shouldn't die with them. Not many people live their beliefs so strongly that they *know* them, and you do. When the story of your life is finally told, it will take days to recite every kind act you've performed and every impact you had on both the living and the dead that can be remembered."

Zed opened his eyes and he turned toward Finn.

"Time *will* remember you, Zealand Blackshear."

As everyone filed onto the ferry, the Emperor whispered to me, "What do you know, Wick. I don't think anyone ever told him Zed's given name. He's starting to remember."

So it's time, then. Take him back to see his wife. Let him remember it all.

14

The next morning, Zed was the first to leave the apartment and he waited for us on the steps to Union Square. He looked as if sleep had been nothing but a hope and the fatigue that swirled around him might be contagious. Oz tried to convince him to go home and go back to bed, but he wasn't hearing any of it.

"Come on, I've never been through a portal. Dad offered to take me when I was little but I chickened out every time. Now I want to see what it's like, and I seriously need the distraction."

Don't blink or you'll miss the pink mist.

"Well, you'll get that." She tried to explain what he would see once on the other side: crowds of people he would have to dodge and weave through just to get from one intersection to the next, and sometimes so many people in one spot that he might not be able to make sense of why they're clustered together. The noise could be startling; cars from that era were loud, with barking engines and drivers impatiently leaning on their horns as they tried to blow off steam from being stuck, only moving only half a city block in twenty minutes. The din of voices, people doing nothing more than talking to each other, was its own sort of pollution and could cut through someone's nerves if they were used to quiet. And there was the assault of odors. "In twenty-sixteen, San Francisco had a huge homeless population and downtown had problems with public urination and defecation—so don't be surprised if someone just drops their pants while we're walking along Market Street."

"Seriously? In public?"

Hey, I've had to take care of business outside before. Don't judge.

"It will be some time before they figure out how to solve those issues," the Emperor said. He thought for a moment, giving weight to the person Zed was deep down. "You can't stop to try to help them, Zed. You have to keep moving forward and let them be, no matter how hard it is."

"Walk with blinders on," Oz said.

Finn was bouncing on the balls of his feet as we waited just outside the portal near the west end of Union Square. The Emperor reminded him of the few things he needed to know: the exact date on which we would be able to find his wife, and where she would be. She needed to be in the city, because they had no transportation options to get anywhere else.

Using a portal to get to another location wasn't possible. "The portals move us through time, not space. When you go through one, where you end up is fixed. We're leaving from Union Square, and we'll come out the other side on Union Square. If you bump into someone, apologize and move on. Don't give anyone a chance to really think about you suddenly appearing from nowhere."

"She'll be at the Civic Center," Finn said. "There's a political rally, a ramp-up for an upcoming election cycle, and something about a bloviated hot air bag running for President. A protest? I'm not sure. And there's a speech..." He trailed off, though I wasn't sure it was because he couldn't remember or was reluctant to say.

Oz didn't notice. "There's a portal closer to city hall. Should we start from there?"

The Emperor didn't think so. "Walking down a very old Market Street might be good for one or two of us." He looked specifically at Drew and added, "And someone might need time to adjust once we're there."

"Hey, I didn't barf the last time."

"That anyone saw," Oz said. "Who knows what you were doing when you lagged behind me. While I was running along Crissy Field you could have been horking up your toenails into every trash can along the way."

He knocked down a fake monk. I saw that.

He snorted a laugh through his nose. "Shuddup. I did not."

She reached for their hands in order to guide them through, but Finn said, "You don't have to do that you know. They just have to feel where the entry is, and think." He set his hand on the spot where he could feel it, and motioned for Zed and Drew to do that same. "Feel that? The buzzy tingling thing? Just push your way through it, and keep the date we're headed to in your head."

"Not feeling anything," Zed muttered.

"Forget the date, just think 'follow Finn,'" Oz said.

Drew grabbed her hand anyway. "Yeah, I'm not too sure about that. I'll let her drag me through time."

"Said every prospective husband everywhere," the Emperor mused.

"And you know this, how?" Finn asked. "Is there a Missus Emperor? An Empress?"

The Emperor feigned a look of horror. "Why would I do that to some poor woman?"

"All right. A co-emperor?"

"No. I wouldn't do that to some poor man, either. I am not relationship material."

"Ah." Finn squinted a bit. "So who broke your heart?"

The Emperor set a hand on my head. "This guy. When he left me for a young prince…well, let's just say I was devastated."

I don't blame you. I'm awesome.

The Emperor pointed to the portal, and Finn eased through. Zed grabbed Oz's other hand, and let her drag him through along with Drew.

"All right, Mister Wick, let's get this over with."

Can we hang out in the pink mist for a little bit? I want to see it.

The answer was apparently "no," because I blinked, and we were standing on the other side, the noise so loud that I flattened my ears against it, and barely noticed that Zed and Drew were helping Finn up from the ground.

Someone probably should have warned him there would be stairs there.

The crowd gathered at the Civic Center was unlike anything Zed or Drew had ever seen in person, outside of a stadium. They turned around in startled fits, trying to make sense of the noise and the cheering that was pocked with static from speakers lining the base of the trees that divided the plaza in half. We were too far back to see much of what was making everyone so excited, but they were all facing city hall and the voice seeping through the speakers was distinctively male.

So it wasn't Finn's wife that was speaking.

Where Zed and Drew were startled, Finn merely looked confused. He stretched up onto his toes to look over the crowd, muttering that he had been sure this was where he'd left her, this was one of the images floating around in his brain. "How will I find her here?"

"Yell out her name?" Drew suggested. "Or not. It's awfully loud here."

"If she's close, maybe she'll hear," Oz said.

I think Finn was about to shout; he was back up on his toes trying to take everything in, but this random woman with blueish white hair pushed her way through the closest cluster of people and tapped him on the shoulder.

"Finn, why are you still here? If you and Jo don't get moving, you'll miss the presentation. This banality" —she gestured to the crowd behind her— "isn't important right now. He's just a political blowhard. You need to get to the grant presentation."

"Um," was all he could manage, and before he could collect a coherent thought, she walked away.

Oz stepped after her, stopping her with a hand on her arm. "Finn is seriously distracted right now. Where exactly does he need to be? We'll get him there."

The woman looked past Oz; Finn was still trying to absorb everything around him, turning to look at something different every half second.

"The presentation is at Herman Plaza." She glanced at the watch on her wrist. "And it starts in half an hour, so if you all want seats, I'd leave about five minutes ago."

"We should have gone in the opposite direction," Oz said to Finn, but he wasn't paying attention. He turned one more time and took a few tentative steps forward, looking down Market Street, not paying attention to the cars or the sound of brakes squealing as he stepped into the street.

I'm not sure how bad it looked, because the last thing I wanted to see was Finn popping like a balloon, blood and guts splattering all around me, so I closed my eyes and buried my head into the Emperor's shirt. He put a hand gently on my back, his fingers scratching under my collar, and under his breath said a few things off the bad word list but then told me it was all right.

When I looked up, Zed and Drew were in the street helping Finn get up. The driver of the car was freaking out, swearing he hadn't had enough time to stop and he didn't mean to hit him, and "please dear God is he all right because the last thing I need is more points on my license," but mostly is he all right because he really didn't want to hurt anyone.

Finn apologized to him; it was his fault, he wasn't paying any attention, and no damage was done.

He obviously hadn't looked at the car's headlight.

The driver apparently didn't care about the shattered glass; he asked one more time if Finn was *sure* he was all right, and then jumped in and sped off.

Before Zed or Drew could do anything else, Finn stepped back onto the sidewalk, taking a few backward steps while he tried to assure everyone he really was fine. Zed lunged for him, but not fast enough to stop him from turning around and walking face-first into the lamppost.

The Emperor said to Oz, "And this is why we probably shouldn't have taken him through another portal while his brain is still a festering vat of fermenting primordial ooze."

"Sorry, man," Finn said to the post.

His shirt was torn and dirty from his encounter with the car, and now he had a bloody nose and his right cheek was bright red and puffy. Without looking back, he stepped around the lamp post and headed down Market Street toward the Embarcadero, walking fast enough that Oz had to jog to catch up to him, leaving the rest of us trailing behind.

It took fast walking from the Civic Center to Powell Street before we caught up to them. Finn and Oz dodged tourists who were rushing to get into an hour-long line to ride the cable car, which slowed them down, and we were right behind them by the time they stopped for a light at the Battery Street intersection.

A young woman standing next to Finn looked him over, noting the blood and the dirt-streaked shirt and jeans, and then handed him a twenty-dollar bill, telling him to get some lunch, and maybe take a few minutes to use the restroom to clean up.

Finn stared at the money in his hand, too surprised to say anything. The Emperor, though, laughed and called out "Thank you!" to her as she walked away.

Oz laughed. "Twenty bucks. Congrats. You can probably buy a burger and fries for all of us to split."

"That's not a lot?" Drew asked.

"Here? No. It'll get someone lunch, but that's about it."

Zed pointed out the obvious. "It was still a thoughtful thing to do."

The light changed and Finn shoved the money into his pocket. He began speed walking again, but when we were close to the Plaza he suddenly slowed down, and Drew walked into him, his chest slamming against Finn's back and his chin jabbing into his head. Finn fell to his knees, followed shortly by the sickening slap of his hands on the pavement.

"Son of a—" Drew grunted as he pulled him up.

Finn's hands and elbows were torn with road rash and a little bit bloody, and without thinking he wiped his hands across his shirt, leaving a faint trail that ran from his chest to his waist.

Zed reached over and ruffled Finn's hair to complete the look.

If he hadn't been so focused on the giant white tent taking up most of the Plaza, I think Finn would have hit him.

Dozens of people were milling about outside the tent; it looked like a cocktail party, with everyone dressed nicely and clutching drink cups as they made small talk. I'd been to a few of those, when the King and Queen hosted other world leaders for dinner; the people here weren't dressed quite as nicely as they did when they were trying to look good for the rest of the world, but it was far from the jeans and t-shirts I saw people in most of the time. We looked out of place, what with the Emperor and Drew wearing old sweatshirts with my riding pouches sewn on, and Finn looking like he'd been in a bare-knuckles street brawl.

Hard to tell if he could have been the victor or not.

He elbowed his way through a cluster of people hovering near the tent's door, and we followed. Inside there were at least a hundred metal chairs lined up in neat rows in front of a makeshift stage, and across the room was a woman with shiny black hair that fell nearly to her waist. I wasn't sure if she was the one we were looking for, because she looked like almost every other human I lived with, with pink skin and black hair. Drew's family was different; he had hair that was too blonde to be normal, but the rest of them had black hair and they were all considerably less pink than Oz, but there was a sameness to everyone, and it was sometimes hard to tell one from another if I didn't know them.

Finn stopped in his tracks and sucked in a sudden, deep breath.

Yep, that's her.

She was talking to another woman, and didn't notice as we came in, but Finn—another, cleaner, not-beat-up Finn—did, and he rushed over.

"They're not letting the audience in for another five minutes," he said. "I'm sorry."

He didn't recognize himself.

Finn barely glanced at him, focusing instead on the woman across the room. The whites of his eyes were suddenly red but there were no tears; it seemed as if he was straining against the impulse to hurdle over the chairs in hopes of getting to her, but knew he could not. After a moment, he exhaled as sharply as he had inhaled and said, "She can't make that speech. You have to stop her, and if you won't, I will."

"What?" Other Finn looked over his shoulder. "It's just a present—"

"It can't happen. If it does, everything will change. The country will fall apart, and—"

Other Finn took a step backward, finally seeing himself in the beat-up, disheveled, bloody man standing in front of him. "Which woman are you talking about? Because I think you're mixed up."

"Jo can't make the speech," Finn insisted. "Take her home. Now."

"She's not—"

Oz was at Finn's side, trying to grab his arm. "Finn, you were wrong. We need to leave."

He brushed her off. "Your entire future depends on this."

"This isn't mine to stop. I couldn't—"

Finn took the step forward that Other Finn had taken backward. The black-haired woman had noticed us and was moving across the room, weaving her way between those metal chairs. They clanged together as she tried to hurry. "Go home and everything will be fine," Finn said. "Stay here and everything changes."

"We're just here to—"

"Finn," Oz pleaded, but the Emperor shook his head very slightly, no.

"Take your wife home," Finn said to his other self. "Go home."

"I can't—"

"Go." Finn reached out and poked his other self in the middle of his chest. "Home."

With the sound of an electric pop, Other Finn disappeared.

*

The Emperor and I waited behind; when the other Finn vanished with the sizzle of an electric breaker popping, he hurriedly told Zed and Drew to grab Finn, and ordered Oz to get to the closest portal and to take them home. They weren't to wait for him, he would follow, but they needed to get Finn out of there *now*.

Drew and Zed were headed out before Finn's wife could make it all the way across the tent. Oz paused for a moment, to ask the Emperor if he knew what had just happened. He nodded and said he would explain it later, but for now, just go.

Jo pushed chairs out of her way and was about to run after them, but hesitated when the Emperor said, "Let them go. That particular Finn is a bit displaced."

She stopped at the door and watched as they pulled Finn away.

"Do you understand what happened?"

After several moments ticked off the clock, she turned around. "Your friends just kidnapped my husband, that's what happened."

Softly, "Jo…"

"I know, I know. I saw them. Two versions of my husband in one place, and mine popped off somewhere else. He'll be back." Then tentatively, "Won't he?"

"The tent will be filling with people soon. Do you mind going outside to talk? Just to the steps near the fountain. I swear, I don't bite."

I might.

"My cat won't, either. I promise, I just need to talk to you, so that you have an understanding of what just happened to Finn."

Her hands went to her hips, and she cocked her head ever so slightly to the right. "Sure, I'll just wander off with a total stranger who carts his cat around in the hand pouch of his sweatshirt. There's nothing uncomfortable about that."

"Please." When she twitched toward the door but still seemed reluctant, he added, "Unsticking Finn from the wrong time depends on it."

She relented after another moment of consideration, and led him out to the steps that half-circled the Plaza. She made sure he sat down first, and put herself well out of arms' reach. By the time they were both seated, the irritation had drained away; she had cocked her head to one side and asked, "Do I know you? You seem familiar."

"We haven't actually met yet."

"The tangled strings of time," she said with a bit of a laugh. "Although Finn would say it's more like a flat sheet of paper that he's poked a hundred holes through. All right. Where's he off to now?"

"He's stuck with a broken ship in twenty-four-fifteen, and we have no way to repair it and send him home."

"And yet, here you are, several hundred years in your own past."

"Here I am. It's complicated. If I try to send him home using our way of travel, he potentially vanishes into the ether because in his own time that mechanism doesn't exist yet. From here I can send him only as far as twenty-four-fifteen, unless I send him a good five years beyond his own time."

"You're caught in a paradox," she mused.

"Exactly. And I can't tell him how or why."

I leaned into his chest, feeling his heartbeat. It was increasing steadily, as was his breathing.

"Really, it's bothering me that you seem so familiar. And you have just the barest hint of a burr. Are you Scottish?"

"My burr? *You* have quite the accent," he said. "But I spend quite a bit of time in Glasgow, visiting my grandparents."

News to me.

"I was raised there! Well, in Edinburgh. Maybe that's it. You just remind me of home. I miss it."

"How long have you been away?"

"Oh, years," she said. "We left for the States when I was only fourteen. Someday I want to take Finn there and show him something other than the confined urban sprawl he seems to love so much."

"Well," he said while absently scratching my head, "he's seen quite a bit of the city four hundred years from now." His heartbeat was a steady drumbeat and it wasn't slowing down. "I know he would rather be home."

"So would I, but..." She gestured toward the tent. "We were trying to learn a bit about this century's politics, hoping to use some of their tactics to affect some change at home."

"He thinks you were about to make a speech that would lead to the demise of the United States."

She seemed startled. "Seriously? I wasn't making a speech. We were here to listen to one. What's wrong with him?"

I have a list.

"A bit of time travel induced amnesia combined with stress, I think. You were the first thing he remembered, though his memories were a bit...off."

He explained about Finn's wanting to let her jump off the Golden Gate Bridge and his certainty that she was to blame for the U.S. falling apart. Instead of being upset, she howled with laughter.

"That was a movie! I pestered that poor man to see it for weeks and we finally watched it last night. It was horrible, some warped thing about a woman who kills herself to avoid marrying a narcissistic, megalomaniacal politician. He was teasing me after, saying I would have married the bastard, chained him up in the basement, and then taken over myself. He thought I would have been a wonderful and kind but very stern dictator."

"He remembers you saying you would soar. Off the bridge."

She had no answer for that. "I've never threatened to jump off the bridge, not even as a cruel joke. It's quite the peaceful thing for me, at least when I sit anywhere along the bay and just look at it. No matter what time period we visit, we always go to the bridge. He knows I love it. And he proposed to me on the little beach at Crissy Field, at night when the bridge was lit up. I would never even mockingly tell him I would jump from it. How could I break his heart that way?"

I looked up, and he was smiling. It was soft, almost like he was trying not to, but his eyes betrayed him and I wondered if she could see it, too.

You're all squishy inside, aren't you?

"Finn says you changed everything. I think that's the trigger for his brain telling him you single handedly destroyed the U.S. He remembers a United States, and in twenty-four fifteen, that no longer exists."

"We've both said often enough that we changed everything for each other. When we met, we were both focused on going down some fairly selfish life paths and didn't care what was happening around us. I was planning on going home to Scotland to stick my head in the sand and pretend everything was fine and normal, and he was intent on finishing his degree and then going into space to stick his head in some planetary void and pretend nothing mattered."

"What happened?"

"A meteor headed for earth happened. We'd known it was coming for all of our lives, but once we realized we wanted to be together, I decided to stay and work at the university, and he decided to stay to finish his doctorate and pursue research. We eventually decided that perhaps instead of accepting the inevitable, we could stop it from destroying the planet. We're still trying. It's basically all we do, looking for different ways to keep the world from ending, even if it means spending time here, listening to dreadful politicians lie through their teeth so that we can figure out how to leech grant money off of them."

Hours later, we were still sitting on the Plaza steps; the crowd from whatever political droning that had gone on in the tent was gone, and while I was anxious to go home, the Emperor seemed reluctant to leave. He wanted to keep her talking as long as he could, and hung on every word.

I finally had to remind him that I was there.

I need to pee, dude. And eat.

"You have the most patient cat," she said, reaching over to pet me.

Yeah, well, my patience has run out.

"I'll take you home in a bit," he said. "Jo, I'm assuming you have a way home?"

"I do."

"I'll send Finn back to you, I swear. But before I can…I'll need your help."

15

Hours after Oz took the others home—but fortunately not before the Emperor found me a spot to take care of my bursting bladder, and whoever could see me from the patio tables at the coffee shop, I'm still sorry—we went through the portal that hid just behind the old Hyatt hotel near the Plaza. The Emperor timed it so that we arrived just after they did, and when he stepped through they were guiding Finn back to the Plaza. Drew had one arm and Zed had the other, and they were half-dragging, half-pulling him forward.

We caught up as they were easing Finn down to sit on the Plaza steps. He looked more than just beaten up; he looked like he'd just found out that all the steak and shrimp in the world were gone, and to rub salt into that gaping nightmare of a wound, there would never again be any good catnip or pizza. That was one of my worst fears, so I felt like I could empathize a bit.

"What just happened?" Oz demanded from the Emperor.

"Give Finn a minute," Drew said, before the Emperor could answer her. "The guy just saw himself vanish into thin air. Everyone needs a chance to think." He nudged Finn's shoulder with his own. "But man, I'm glad you didn't explode. I mean, I really wanted to know what happens when more than one version of the same person shares the same space, but I was happy enough to not see everything blow up."

Finn stared straight ahead, seeing nothing but seeing everything.

"Does anyone know what happened?" Oz went on.

"Four hundred years," Finn croaked. "It took me four hundred years to get from there to here."

Of course it did; we all went four hundred years in both directions, and Oz was about to say something, but the Emperor was shaking his head again. She sighed hard, annoyed at first because he shakes his head a lot, but then her face softened as she began to understand.

Finn wasn't talking about the portal. He was talking about his ship.

"It *literally* took you four hundred years, didn't it?"

Finn's hand went to his chest. The object under his skin that the doctor thought was an old surgical staple was a transponder; it was connected to his ship and in an emergency he could activate it and transport his way out of trouble. The failsafe built in was that only he could activate it, but when he was looking at that beat up version of himself in the tent, he realized that this seemingly half-crazed person not only knew how to use the ship but also knew where it was, and he had to protect it, even from another version of himself.

"One of me was thinking about getting to the ship and taking it anywhere else to keep him from getting to it, the other was thinking of home. Two of me, with three different ideas of where home was and one of us also thinking that *anywhere* else would be good, just to keep the ship out of his hands…the ship couldn't calculate the intended destination, so it hung up in null space while it ran through all the math. It took four hundred years for it to settle on the middle road, and then brought me here."

"Three notions of home?" Zed asked.

"Jo and I had been living in twenty-sixteen for several months. It felt a bit like home. My own time feels like home. And this When? It's all my brain knew when I was hitting that transponder."

"Why didn't you die, then?" Oz asked. "Four hundred years."

"Null space. It's that fractional slice of reality that exists just outside of time. There's nothing there, it just…is. Time doesn't exist, and yet it does. I can't explain it any better than that. I sat there in my ship, trying to reach the reset button on the dashboard, but it took time."

"Four centuries worth," the Emperor said. "Enough time to stagnate every operational property in your ship, and enough time for the solar coating on the ship's shell to discharge and for the power cells to drain."

"That ship kept me alive. It used every resource to essentially keep me in stasis."

"So we recharge everything," Drew said. "Stick that sucker out in the sun long enough to power it up, and you can go home."

"The engine was trying to run on virtually no power, Drew. It's damaged, and the parts for it are not likely to be found here."

"So go back through the portal and ask your wife to bring whatever you need. Or hell, bring a ship to take you home."

"I wish it was that easy," Finn said with a sigh.

"Then use a freaking portal!"

"Drew, they don't go forward," Oz reminded him.

"Oh, come on."

"It's very complicated," Finn said.

You might want to tell him stuff.

"The portals aren't an option," the Emperor said. "Finn, how much do you remember now?"

His eyes were clouded with sadness and fatigue, and for the first time since we'd met he looked older than Drew. "All of it. Or most of it. My memories are still pretty jumbled, but I remember everything in the ship, trying to force my hand forward to get to the switch. My brain ticked off every second of it, in spite of time not existing there."

It was the ultimate slow motion, and because the ship was sifting through every point in time looking for the place he needed to be, he watched it all unfold in front of him, his screen displaying pops and sparks of history. It was like watching a thousand movies spliced together with no discernible plot, with an image here and image there, and all the time he was trying to free himself and get back to Jo.

"I saw the U.S. fall. All I wanted was Jo. I was stuck long enough that those are the two things that wrapped around my brain. God, she must think I'm an idiot."

"Well, perhaps, but not because of that," the Emperor said.

"You need to find the guy who invented that fail safe and then let Oz kick him in the nads," Drew said.

With a heavy sigh, Finn pushed himself up, wincing when his raw hands touched the pavement. "That would be me. Clearly I needed a better way. Not that it matters now. I think you're stuck with me here."

"But your wife—" Oz started.

"I may never see her again."

"Finn, no," Drew said.

I looked up at the Emperor.

Tell him to not give up.

Finn was looking right at him, waiting for him to say something, but all he did was scratch me behind the ears, and then tell them it was time go home and get some rest.

As they walked off I told him again, *Tell him not to give up.*

"Don't worry, Mister Wick. He just needs a little more time."

He had four hundred years.

"A few more days won't hurt anything."

16

The Emperor went straight to his lair under Union Square; I wanted to go with Oz and Drew, to see if Finn had a royal meltdown or even just a bath after all the dirt and blood he accumulated, but it seemed rude to just squirm out of his sweatshirt and chase after them. He was absently stroking the fur along my back, which told me I needed to stay with him. If he weren't sinking into his feelings, he would be scratching behind my ears and under my chin.

I was hungry, too, and thought about asking him to stop somewhere for dinner, maybe share a basket of fresh fish at that awesome place on the Wharf where we could look out the window and watch boats on the bay, or go get a piece of perfectly grilled cow at the diner with the awful décor and embarrassing high chair, but I didn't think he would hear me. He stood on the Plaza watching them walk away, and he waited, his fingers slipping from my neck to my back, and I knew he was seeing something in his head that I couldn't.

I was quiet on the walk back to the Square, letting him simmer his thoughts into brain stew. Sooner or later he would share them with me like our Friday night pizza, one tidbit at a time, until we were both satisfied.

When we got to the lair—sue me, I don't know what else to call it, other than perhaps his work shop, though he seemed to do more sitting than working—he set me down on a stool and climbed into Finn's giant egg. He pulled pieces and parts out, laying them in a line on the floor, until it looked like he had gutted the entire thing. Then he stood there staring at the mess, as if he expected it to magically rise up and reassemble itself.

He looked up when the elevator buzzed. Without bothering to find out who was there, he opened the door using the remote he kept on his worktable.

Finn, still looking tired and upset but presentable—showered and in clean clothes, with long strips of gauze on his forearms, which I guessed had been put there by the Queen—waited a couple of extra seconds before slowly walking out, every movement wrapped in the soreness left from a day of bouncing off large, hard objects. He stood on the other side of the line of parts on the floor, looking down at them.

"There's no point anymore," he said.

"You have someone who needs you to go home and I don't give up so easily."

"There's no fixing this, and I can't use a portal."

He grunted, and just under his breath where I could hear it but Finn might not, I heard what he didn't actually say: *No, you can't use a portal, but giving up? That's not an option.*

Or maybe that was my thought. I don't know. I project a lot.

Finn started to fold his arms, but grimaced when he tried. Instead, he stuck his hands halfway into his pockets, trying to look relaxed. "When I first got here, Oz said that you were the go-to person if something was needed. That people just arriving to the city could come to you to find a place to live, maybe even work."

He was concentrating on the line of parts on the floor. "You have a place to live."

"I'm a guest, and guests need to leave at some point. Staying is hardly fair."

The Emperor picked up a fist-sized piece of metal. "What do you think this is?"

"It's a fuel conduit. A cracked one. Look at the line along the base, it shouldn't be there."

"So it is. But this can be fixed. A good welder can close that crack in ten minutes."

"But everything else—"

"It might not fit back in your ship perfectly, but with some maneuvering of parts and some jury rigging, it could still work."

Finn picked me up and sat down on my stool, keeping me on his lap. "I don't want to pin my hopes on a giant maybe. And let's suppose we *can* fix this. It might take years just to make the parts that can't be soldered or welded. I don't like it, but I can live with that. But I need to get out from under the King and Queen's feet. They've given me everything, from a place to stay and food to the clothes on my back. Relying on them for everything isn't fair."

"He has no idea, does he?" he said to me. Then to Finn, "You aren't underfoot. You also aren't leaving their home for someplace else, or you will crush the Queen's feelings."

"She'll understand."

The Emperor set the engine piece back down and pulled his work stool closer. "But you don't. They don't typically take random strangers into their home. There's something about you that made the Queen think she should—and make no mistake, it was her decision—and the fact that you weren't given quarters of your own elsewhere after a day or two means she, especially, does not want you to go."

"Is that why you live a couple floors down?"

"Indeed. I had a perfectly comfortable apartment just blocks away, but when she and Jax took over the royal home…she knew I didn't want to take up residence in their apartment or even on the same floor, but she wanted me close and asked me to move. She treasures people, Finn. She has a very deep need to mother them, and she's chosen you. I'll let her know you don't want to be a burden and that you asked me about finding a place of your own, but I know what she'll say. She wouldn't want you to leave any more than she wants to let us all skip Sunday dinner. You've seen how she feeds people."

"You might want to remind her that I could be a very patient axe murderer."

"You might want to consider that I likely spent more time with your wife than the few seconds it seemed like I was behind you."

Finn's grip on me tightened a bit. "Did you?"

"I spent a lovely afternoon in conversation with her and learned quite a bit. Did you know that when she first met you, she thought you were a bit of an ass?"

"I did," he snorted, letting me go. I jumped over to the Emperor's lap, just in case he got all squeezy again. "We met when I was about halfway through my doctorate and she decided I was stuck up and that I thought I was better than everyone else. The truth is I was terrified and had no idea how to talk to her. She was so much *more* than any other woman I'd known. She was funny and smart, and I could barely get two coherent words out when I was around her."

"Smart enough to help you build this ship," the Emperor said. "Smart enough to be able to explain to me in basic terms how it works. Smart enough, too, to understand that she can't just pop in with her own ship to get you. What the hell possessed you to make these things single-passenger and DNA activated?"

"The idea was to keep anyone stumbling onto one from being able to take off. Imagine someone from the eighteen-hundreds climbing in and accidentally winding up here, now."

"Fine, but no passengers?"

"The system only recognizes the DNA from one person. What if we had gone to twenty-sixteen together in my ship, only to have me disappear? Even if I'd somehow left my ship behind, she'd be stranded. She needed her own ship."

"And if something happened to hers? She would still be stranded."

"It's a work in progress, I admit that. This is still new stuff, Emperor. I'd never even seen a portal before now. I thought the ship was the only—"

Here it comes.

"That's why I can't use a portal to get home. They don't exist in my time. Not yet. They will, and when they do people will be able to move backward, but never forward to my exact timeline."

"A bit of a conundrum wrapped in a paradox. But all this"— the Emperor gestured to the ship parts on the floor— "might be salvageable. I theoretically know how to do it now. I have to."

"Have to?"

"I promised your wife, Finn."

Finn got up. "I hope it wasn't just a wish. Lie to that woman and she'll tear time apart to get to you and rip you into little pieces."

"I don't doubt it. She's very Scottish. I know better than to cross a Scottish woman, I was bloody well raised by one. And you—I know you want to go home more than anything. Staying here is giving up and I refuse to allow you to do that."

He headed for the elevator door, but stopped before getting in.

"Who are you, really, Emperor?"

"Does it matter?"

"In the grand scheme of things, no. But I suspect you're something other than what Oz and her family imagine."

The Emperor didn't say anything, but gave a slight shrug.

"I won't push it. But man, I am sure you're a whole lot like me."

"I am not you, if that's where you're going."

"Drew is disappointed by that and I didn't think you were. Still… you are a puzzle, and sooner or later, puzzles get solved."

*

I thought we would follow Finn and I jumped down, ready to head for the elevator, too, but the Emperor went back to the things strewn about the floor and picked up one of the energy modules. He cracked it open the way Finn had, looked inside, and closed it up again.

"In spite of what he thinks, I can rebuild the engine now, Wick. I can even create the framework to build a gate to send the ship through, but I still need to power these up. It's not going to be as simple as plugging them in to recharge. That would take forever."

You need a giant burst of energy.

I rubbed up against one that was on the floor, over and over, and then touched his hand with my nose.

We both jumped at the electric shock.

See?

"Static? As simple as that?"

Well, you would need a lot of it. Enough to make something crackle.

"If we can get the engine running…"

I waited for the picture to form in his head.

"A massive power surge that could be built into the gate itself. If we can get the ship to move fast enough, when it hits the gate, it hits the power grid, and that should be enough. The engine controls the gate, and the gate gets powered by every high capacity cable we can procure—we just need something to push the ship forward at a high rate of speed."

The train thingies under the streets. They move stuff pretty fast. Or those army trucks, the ones that look all squished. They're zippy.

"Mister Wick, I think we can do it. But I'd better tap into the resources quietly…it might be time to visit the Old Mint."

Bah.

I hated that building. It made an obnoxious humming sound that hurt my ears and made my furs stand on end.

Now can we go get food?

I jumped back onto his lap.

"I can do this, Wick. I can get him home."

Good.

Food?

"The question now, though… am I really ready to let him go?"

*

Half an hour later, after he'd fed us both, we headed for the balcony. He wanted fresh air and enough quiet that he could stew in his own thoughts, but Oz and Zed had beat him to it and were already sitting there, watching people down on the Square. He hesitated and I thought he was going to step back before they noticed him, but he went out anyway and dropped into the seat next to Zed.

Zed inhaled slowly and deeply. "You smell sad."

The Emperor muffled a laugh and mimicked Oz, "Oh my God, Zed, you can't just go around smelling people!"

"Can't help it. I can sense things about people by how they smell. It's my gift."

"Or your curse," Oz grumbled.

He brushed off the insult. "Everyone has a gift. They just have to find it. I'm intuitive through scent. You and Dad can see sound and sense peoples' intent from the colors that surround them. Mom is fairly empathic and can somewhat soak up someone else's pain, and soothes them while she's doing it. Even Wick there has a gift, though I can't quite articulate what it is."

I'm furry awesomeness. That's my gift.

The Emperor bit. "What's mine, then?"

Zed leaned away from him, pretending to size him up. "Yeah. You know damn well what yours is. *I'm* not sure what, but I suspect it has something to do with why you never touch anyone and why you go great lengths to keep people from touching you."

"I have valid reasons for not wanting Finn to touch me. I might even explain it someday."

"You don't owe anyone an explanation," Oz said.

"No, you really don't," Zed agreed. "But it's not just Finn. You don't touch anyone other than Wick. Ever."

"Come on. I've hugged you and carried you around a thousand times. I held your hands while crossing the street. I kissed your bumps and bruises. Both of you."

"Sure, when we were little. But that stopped when we were eleven or twelve, right about the time Oz hit puberty."

Well, to be fair, no one wanted to touch Oz then. She was not exactly pleasant for a while.

"It would have been inappropriate after that, Zed. She was entering a phase of her life where every physical contact I made with her would be heavily scrutinized by the masses, and you were soon to follow. I never would have hurt you, but people see things that aren't always there. They wouldn't have understood that I am a daily presence in your lives, or why. They only would have seen the middle aged man with adolescent children who are clearly not his own, and that raises the red flag for many people."

"People can be idiots, but I don't think that was why."

"I'm sorry if my distancing myself hurt you."

"We weren't hurt," Oz said. "And it's all right. It took a while, but we noticed it. It's not as if your touch avoidance is dinner conversation. Your quirks are yours to have, the same as Zed is entitled to annoy everyone by sniffing them."

"I don't annoy anyone."

"Really? You don't remember sniffing the Texas Governor's

daughter and telling her she reeked of lies? Or telling her brother he smelled like fear with a side of self-hatred? Everyone was pretty annoyed with you that day."

"Well, I was only, what, ten years old? I'm far more restrained now."

"Yeah, like greeting Finn with 'You smell fresh.'"

"He did. Though right now he smells like confusion."

"And what does that smell like?" the Emperor asked.

"Old gym socks, mostly."

"And sadness? What does that smell like?"

"Salt. Unshed tears." He leaned his head back, resting it against the back of the chair. "Deep, gut wrenching sorrow? That smells like a river of spent tears. There's been too much of that lately."

Oz set her hand on his arm. For a fleeting moment, I could see her mother there instead. "And you smell like, what? The sadness or the sorrow?"

"I smell like I'm drowning in both. I'm not religious, but damn I'm praying that no one dies for a while. I need a break."

"You don't have to keep doing this."

"I think he does," the Emperor said. "You have more than one gift, Zed. You also have your mother's capacity for empathy, and you care on a deep, soul twisting level. Take a break, but I don't think you can walk away from it. No one else speaks for the dead the way you do, and I think you'll be able to teach that to those who follow you."

They were quiet for a long stretch, not looking at each other. Zed stared straight up to the sky, and Oz focused on the people down below. I could hear the creak of the chairs as they breathed, and the hiss of air as the breeze kissed their fragile pink skins. The silence was like a throbbing heartbeat, until Zed took a deep breath and said, "Thank you."

"When I die—"

"No," Oz and Zed said together.

"—I want no one else speaking for me. Both of you. It would mean everything to me now to know that you'll speak for me when the time comes."

They couldn't look at him.

They don't need to think of sad things right now.

"I would freaking hug you right now if I knew it wouldn't make you jump right over the balcony," Zed said. "But man, I'm thinking about it now and it makes me a little sad, because living without someone else's touch has to suck."

"Indeed."

"And we won't tell anyone, Emperor. I mean, if people know you have a valid reason to not want to be touched, you know they're going to try, just to see what happens."

I jumped into the Emperor's lap.

I won't tell anyone, either.

"You're a good boy, Mister Wick."

Bloody hell. Stop that.

I'm not a dog.

You know, just for that, I'm telling.

Zed got up, and reached over to scratch behind my ears. "Mister Wick, you smell...wise. I don't l know why, but you do."

They watched him go inside, and when the door closed behind him, the Emperor said, "I can send Finn home, Oz. It'll take a couple of weeks to build what I need, but he can go home."

"Wow. I'm honestly not sure how I feel about that. I'm starting to genuinely like him."

"He has a life he needs to get back to."

"I know."

"I may need your help convincing your father to allow me access to everything I'll need."

"Dad would let you have anything."

"Not with Florida trying to leech beyond its borders. But the way I can get Finn home...it could be a game changer."

They sat on the balcony for another hour as he outlined his plans to build a gateway that could send Finn home, and what having that gate might mean for Pacifica.

Oz listened without interrupting, through every technical detail and every musing over things theoretical and things probable— including the possibility that he might wind up blowing San Francisco off the map—and when he was done she leaned back in her chair and said, "He won't say no to that. He can't."

17

The King did not say no. He didn't say yes, either, but the Emperor took that as consent of sorts. Before he gave blanket permission for the Emperor to go ahead, Jax wanted more information on the amount of power needed to send Finn home, and what the possibilities were of things going very wrong. Will it explode? Melt the bridge upon which the gate would be built? Did the possibility exist that anyone other than Finn could die if things did go wrong?

"That is possible," the Emperor answered to each question.

He directed Oz to help the Emperor get things ready while he took it up with the Energy Commissioner; she didn't argue, but I could see it in her face: *what energy commissioner? What exactly do you think I can do? And you were expecting this, weren't you? This feels rehearsed.*

While the Emperor and King discussed the feasibility of bringing the old solar farm back online to avoid destroying the public power grid, and pondered how quickly it could be done, Oz sat back and listened. She focused on the Emperor; it wasn't so much what he was saying but how he was saying it, as if the entire conversation was being played out for her benefit, and under her breath I heard her murmur, "What have you been up to?"

His left ear twitched; he heard her but pretended not to, and kept on with his discussion with the King.

He only wanted access to a small part of the old solar farm; two panels could harness enough to power the gate he wanted to build.

"I don't need enough power from them to cause residual heat issues, only enough to run the generators that will provide one massive burst of electricity."

After they left the King's office, the Emperor took her to the Old Mint. I hated that place; it buzzed and hummed and hurt my ears, and he knew it, but they stood outside on the street anyway while I suffered away six of my lives in his sweatshirt.

I should have gone to that school orientation thingy with Drew. Or to the museum with Zed and the Queen. Or even to the vet for a rigorous teeth cleaning and neuter-check to make sure nothing's grown back. Yeah, drop me off there instead. I'd rather let that guy with the cold hands take my temperature.

Oz didn't like it either. She made a point of avoiding being near it; to her it looked like it was wrapped in a vomit green shimmer, and it upset her equilibrium.

He stopped at the steps leading up to the front doors. "You've been inside before. Do you know its purpose?"

When she was a child, she was told that it was a repository, storage for printed pages of the most important scientific and mathematical discoveries that had been made to date. New books were a rarely printed onto paper and most information was stored as computerized data points, so as a caution against a permanent loss of power, they were painstakingly going over information that was deemed critical, printing it out, and binding all those pages into books.

"At least if the worst happens, we'll have that."

"We still have the Library of Congress," he pointed out. "It stands and is protected, so if that were the work being done...why duplicate it?"

"To have copies?"

"The Library of Congress keeps copies. Printed and bound, two of everything."

"But we need our own. If Washington refuses access, all those books might as well be lost, too."

"The Library is a neutral entity. Access is a human right."

She scowled. "Then I was lied to?"

"Misled is a better word, I think. The green shimmer that bothers you so much?"

"My dad said it was to protect everything inside. A force field?"

"Not exactly. This building is time-locked. It exists in every point of time from roughly twenty-three-hundred onward. I can walk in there today and have a discussion with someone from twenty-five-hundred. I can read material that won't be written for a hundred years, or I can look back to something left there the day the lock went live."

"Wait, so this is basically static time travel? Then we can send Finn home without risking anything."

"No. It's locked, which means if I go in there right now, on this day in twenty-four-fifteen and spend an hour there, I can meet up with someone who won't even be born for fifty years, but when I exit, it will be an hour later, on the same day, the same year I went in."

"Someone should have created a way—"

"Not for this. I can take things in, such as books or data drives, but I can't leave with anything I didn't bring in. It's to protect all the information inside. You don't want someone from a hundred years ago to be able to walk out with a book that won't exist for two hundred years."

"For the same reason I can't go forward through a portal."

"Essentially. And Oz—you can't tell Finn the purpose of this building. He can't know yet."

We headed up the steps and I buried my head against the Emperor's stomach, but as soon as we were inside, the horrible noise stopped and I no longer felt like my brain was about to render itself into goo. Once the door clicked behind us, they paused so that Oz could get a good look at the cacophony of activity going on. There were dozens of people sitting at dozens of computers, some reading intently, some typing away as if their lives depended on it. Others were scurrying around with papers in hand, and still others were weaving through the lines of computers, handing out food and drink.

"The last time I was in here there were maybe twenty people working, and only a few shelves were filled with books," Oz said.

The shelves lined the walls from floor to ceiling, and were

crammed with color-coded books. The same thing was happening on each of the four floors, men and women working furiously and not even noticing us.

"They've been busy."

"This only represents about fifteen years' worth of work," he told her.

"But I was here just a couple of years ago."

"I know. But this is roughly fifteen years of work, done over and over. They're trying to save the world, Oz. The building is time-locked so that every time they fail, they don't have to start from scratch. Hundreds of years of research, all condensed into a little over a dozen years. This is the foundation of something funded by your great grandfather, not long after he took the throne."

"This hurts my brain. And why are you showing me?"

"Because this is why we have to get Finn home. This is his life's work. If we don't get him back, in two hundred years?"

"What?"

He sighed hard.

Just tell her. She needs to know at least this much.

"In two hundred years, without Finn, the world will end."

18

The Wastelands were not, as the King once hoped, a slice of the old western United States inexplicably recreated just miles from San Francisco. Most of it was dry, barren land, chewed up and spit out by years of drought, a place from which people eventually fled rather than trying to transport in more water. When the population dwindled down to a stubborn few, the last government of the United States determined it was a good place to expand their solar energy program and thousands of giant solar panels were constructed across Nevada, feeding a tremendous amount of energy into the southwestern U.S. power grid.

The unexpected consequence of the breadth and depth of the panel construction was the abrupt death of thousands of birds; where they had been free to fly over the desert before, the blistering heat radiating from the black panels cooked them mid-flight, and they dropped from the sky like little fluffy bombs. The panels were damaged and repaired, time after time, until the birds developed a sense of danger and learned to fly around the miles of brutal heat blocking their way.

The effective migratory flight pattern change affected the ecosystem as a whole; there were still ground animals living in the desert, and without their feathery predators they grew in numbers. They expanded territory, until they reached the populated areas in southern Nevada and California. Pets vanished, disease rates went up.

When the U.S. broke apart and Pacifica came into being, one of the first things to go was the solar farm. New solar technology was significantly smaller and more efficient, built into the structures of new construction, so the farm was taken offline but not torn down, a just-in-case defense of the power grid. Protective structures were built over the panels and the infrastructure was maintained, but they had not functioned as a power source in nearly 200 years.

"This is what the plan hinges on," the Emperor said as we stood in the air conditioned protection of a military transport rig, behind the driver but where we had a clear view out the windshield. "If we can get just two of the main panels online, we'll generate and then store enough power to send you home, Finn."

There were already hundreds of workers dismantling the protective barriers from the panels, and one was already fully stripped, the relay connection clean and ready to use.

Clever boy. You've been busy.

"This is months' worth of work," Oz speculated.

He shrugged it off. "This is efficiency. They know what they're doing."

She pursed her lips thoughtfully. "Or…someone popped through a portal and went back a few months to ask my dad to get this rolling. Before Finn even got here." She turned to face him. "He wouldn't have even asked why. He'd do anything you wanted, as long as it made some sort of sense."

"I've done nothing without his permission."

"Isn't that, like, breaking the rules?" Drew asked.

"Not if it doesn't change how the timeline plays out," Oz answered. "Asking Dad to get this rolling didn't change anything. Finn still showed up, and we all spent time trying to figure him out. Except maybe for you, Emperor. How far ahead of the curve are you?"

They think you really did this last night.

"I would never ask your father to do something that would hurt any of you, you know that?"

"Of course I know that. But—"

"He met my wife, Oz," Finn interrupted. "He spent an entire afternoon with her." He was staring straight ahead, out the windshield. "He's not doing this for me, he's doing this for her. She's one of those people you instantly want to help, no matter how hard it is." He turned to the Emperor. "She would do the same for you, you know. She's much like the Queen in that. She loves you first, and it's up to you to live up to that."

"She is remarkable," the Emperor agreed.

"Don't kid yourself, Finn. He's doing this because it's the right thing to do. I just would like to have been filled in a little bit."

"You knew—"

"Emperor, you told me the basic plan, but I had no idea it was already this far along. Or was it? How does that work, going back to change things in your own timeline? Do your memories change? Do ours?"

"Does it matter?" Drew asked.

"She has every right to demand explanations from me," the Emperor said.

Zed laughed. "The Woman who will be Queen. Are we already preparing for her ruthless tyranny? Go slow. She's just practicing for something that might be a few decades away."

"Holy hell, I hope so," Oz muttered. "I still don't know how Dad does it."

Zed doesn't know the long term plan?

His hand went to my head, and he scratched behind my ears. "Your father decided a long time ago that Oz was to be incrementally included in decisions. It's helpful in how one learns to rule." He squinted, watching heat rise in wavy lines off the first set of exposed panels. "We should back away. They're getting ready to plug it in."

"Or not," Oz said. "I have a feeling you already know how this plays out. I wouldn't be here if there were any real danger."

"Oz."

She was looking out the windshield, not at him. The driver started the rig anyway, and began to back it up.

"I truly do not know the end result of any of this," the Emperor said. "You're here because you promised to keep an eye on Finn, and because this matters to you."

Finn twitched. "You what?"

"Be glad it's me, Time Boy. My dad was going to stick you with a guard twenty-four hours a day. And yes," she said to the Emperor, "it matters to me. He doesn't deserve to be stuck here without his wife."

They could meet at that noisy building.

He stopped scratching my head.

Or I suppose that would muck things up? They'd just live in there? Why can't she come here?

She should just move here. Everyone would like her.

"Wick, what's wrong?" Oz asked me.

She has a giant egg of her own. She could come live here.

"Is he all right?" she asked the Emperor. "He seems upset."

"Probably hungry."

Well. Yeah. But that's not the point. Why can't Mrs. Finn come live here? She liked me. I bet she would even give me treats.

His hand covered my head, protecting my ears, but I heard him whisper, "Sorry, Wick," just before the loud humming sliced through the air.

They all winced, and the rig driver stuck his fingers in his ears.

It was loud, but the panel was online and turning the generator that would harness its power, sending the electricity through relays that would store it across the grid.

"One more to go, and then we see if we can suck up enough power to make the gate work," Oz muttered.

"It'll either work or explode," Zed said.

"We probably should have evacuated Nevada," Drew mused.

They all turned to him.

"Well, you know. If it goes up in a giant fireball, they might be a little concerned about all that solar radiation being flung their way."

Oz squinted. "Seriously?"

"Yeah, and what if it works so well that we drain the sun? We're *all* hosed that way. It'll get, like, really cold."

"Oh my God." Oz punched him in the arm, hard. "Keep it up, funny man. We'll send you off with Finn." She pretended to consider it. "On the other hand, you'd probably like that."

He nudged her with his shoulder. "I wouldn't want to miss all this."

Hey, I think they actually like each other.

Very softly, the Emperor said, "It's about time."

If the others heard him speak, his words were lost in the sound of the rig's engine revving. The driver backed up a bit more and then asked, "Ready to go? I was told you only wanted to see the first panel fire up."

"That was enough," the Emperor said. He headed for the back of the rig and took the last seat, the one just in front of the back doors. Zed and Finn sat in the first forward seats and strapped in, and Drew left room for Oz to sit next to him. She headed for the back instead, holding onto the back of an empty seat as the rig began to move.

"You don't know how this all ends, but you know how it got started," she said.

"Would it change anything if I did?"

"Probably not, but the not knowing is going to drive me a little bit nuts."

"Ah, then." He grinned. "Short drive. Now go sit with Drew, because he looks like his feelings are hurt that you might choose to stay back here with me instead of sitting next to him. And don't let your brother make fun of you when Drew inevitably puts his arm around your shoulders."

She glanced toward him; Drew had his arm resting on the back of the bench seat.

"Zed knows I can hurt him."

Truthfully, Drew didn't look hurt at all, but she went anyway. She turned a few times to look at the Emperor, and he pretended not to notice, but when the rig landed in San Francisco and the kids had gotten off, he picked me up and sighed. "She's curious, Wick, and I'm not sure it's a good thing."

*

When Oz was little, I often curled up on her chest at night, listening to her dreams as she slept. When she got older it was much more difficult to stay up there, so I laid across her stomach and set my head right where I could hear her heartbeat, but her dreams felt so far away that it took considerable effort to hear more than wisps.

They had become private dreams, too, and instead of being a glimpse into her whimsy it felt as if I was invading her privacy.

I mostly stopped then.

But the night after visiting the Wastelands, when she excused herself from spending time with her family after dinner—even with Drew—so that she could go to bed early, I followed her. I thought that she might need company, someone she could talk to who wouldn't talk back, and someone who would listen without forgetting the whole listening part.

You people do that, you know. You're so busy thinking about what you're going to say next that you often forget when it's time to listen.

She was starting to look hard at the Emperor; if she could hear me, I could explain him. I wasn't sure she could hear me unless it was in a dream, and even though I didn't know exactly how I could do that, it was worth trying.

She curled up on her bed with a tablet reader and for a time lost herself to whatever world was woven through her book, so I stretched out next to her, half napping, half waiting. I sat on the bathroom floor while she showered and then exercised some bizarre ritual that involved removing body hair from her legs and underarms—I will never understand that, getting rid of perfectly good fur—and then I sniffed her to make sure she still smelled like herself. When she finally turned out the light and climbed into bed, I waited on the window seat until she was deeply asleep, and then jumped over to be with her.

There was no curling up on her chest anymore; age and mother nature had ruined that, so I snuggled close to her on her pillow. From there I could rest my head against hers, and when she dreamed, I would hear. If I could hear, maybe she could, too.

I expected dreams of the Wastelands, the long stretches of dust and dirt that were born out of drought, and I expected dreams of the solar panels exploding and fulfilling Drew's wisecrack of radiation and draining the sun. Instead, as she fell deeper into sleep, she dreamed about wandering into a massive room that had windows for two of its walls, where on one side of the room there were tables lined up in neat rows, four to the left and four to the right, and on the other side of the room there were ten neat little student desks. They were lined up in rows of three, with the remaining desk placed far behind the others.

In between the two sides of the room there was a large green rug, and on it there were ten small children sitting cross-legged, as if they were waiting for something to begin.

Nine of them were clustered together near the middle, chattering and laughing, and one lone little boy sat on a corner of the rug, as far from the others as he could get. His legs were bent so that he could rest his chin on his knees as he hugged his legs tightly, and he tried to ignore the slap of harsh words thrown by his classmates. Oz looked for the adult that should have been there, someone to stop the children who were taunting the little boy with black hair and sad eyes, but they were alone.

The words they threw at him were muddled, but she didn't need to hear what was said in order to understand that they wielded as weapons words meant to wound him. He stared ahead stubbornly, refusing to see the others, refusing to show them the pain that they wanted to see.

She wanted to stop them, to tell them to leave him alone and what they were doing was more than just not nice, it was horribly mean, but she could couldn't get her mouth to open. She moved closer to him, wanting to place a comforting hand on his head, to let him know he wasn't as alone as it seemed; she wanted to tell him she would make them stop if she could, but before she could figure out how, she blinked and they were outside on a school playground. The little boy sat alone on the edge of a sandbox, while the others played loudly far from him. While he sat and watched, they ran up and down a soccer field, kicking aimlessly at a ball, deliberately excluding him.

The sounds of their voices were colored with anger; she could see that, even asleep, the sound of childhood curdled with the colors of fear and rage. She watched them with sadness, until one little girl stopped, holding the ball under her foot. She grinned horribly, and then kicked, sending it toward the little boy's head.

Oz lunged and tried to stop it, but before her hands were on the ball she found herself standing at the head of a long table. The noise of dozens of children hung in the air, peppered by the clatter of silverware and drink cups. The children from the playground were seated together near the middle of the long table, four on one side and five on the other, and the little boy with black hair sat just in front of Oz, near the table's head. His elbows were on the table and he was staring down at his untouched food, head resting uncomfortably in his hands.

He barely twitched when they began throwing bits of their food at him. He inhaled deeply, and exhaled slowly, but refused to cave into their goading.

Oz tried to get close to him, but she stayed rooted in place five feet from him, her voice locked inside her head and her arms like dead weights hanging from her shoulders.

I could feel it bubbling inside her. *It's not fair. They shouldn't be so mean. You shouldn't be so lonely.*

He looked up at her. "Go home. Wake up. They think I'm a freak and they're afraid of me. You can't help."

Oz startled awake. I sniffed at her face, wanting her to know she wasn't alone, not like that little boy. She smiled when she saw me, and then pulled me on top of her, where I could feel how hard her heart was beating.

"It was just a dream, Mister Wick. Not even a nightmare."

But it made you sad.

She reached over for the bedside clock and squinted as she looked at it. It was three o'clock in the morning, and we both heard soft footsteps creeping past her cracked-open door.

"I thought I'd closed that," she said as she set me back on the bed and got up. She opened the door a bit further and peeked out, just in time to see the Emperor head out onto the balcony.

"He can't sleep again," she sighed, climbing back in bed. "I doubt he wants company if he's out there brooding this time of night."

Probably not.

"Then again, I could at least make sure he's all right."

I crawled back on top of her and purred until she let sleep overtake the idea that she should go out and talk to him.

You can't help him. Not yet.

19

On the day before Oz's 18th birthday, Finn's ship was removed from the Emperor's workshop—he had done actual work there for a couple of weeks, so I think the label finally fit—and taken to the far end of the street between Union Square and the royal home where it was perched on the back of a flatbed, magnetically driven delivery truck. The bed of the truck and the bottom of the ship had been fitted with layers of magnetic sheets so that the ship could float above the truck to avoid damaging its shell, and military guards were going to haul it to the Emperor's Bridge. It was the only place he felt the gate could be built, using the towers of the bridge as support structure, and where there was enough straight road length to build up the speed Finn's ship needed.

Once on the bridge the ship would be transferred to another truck, a high speed, rocket-fuel-propelled army vehicle that would basically fling it through the gate. It was supposed to pick up a massive amount of speed and static once in motion, and at the critical point it would abruptly stop, launching Finn through the gate.

The gate itself was unimpressive. It was made from very tall metal mesh pillars on either side of the bridge—supported by existing towers—through which enough power would be sent to possibly melt them both. At the very top of the gate, mounted to a series of rods that spanned the length between the pillars, there was a pin-point laser meant to activate a transponder in Finn's ship; between the surge of electricity and the laser, the transponder was expected to pop to life again, and send him home.

Before the laser was bolted into place the Emperor whispered to me, "We don't tell them where that transponder came from, all right? All right."

Yeah, dude, no one listens to me anyway.

Finn had been in the middle of the street with the Emperor, looking the ship over, while Oz, Drew, and Zed watched from the balcony. I curled up on a chair, far enough from the edge to keep from being blown off.

"I've never seen so many armed guards in one place before," Zed mused. He was sitting with his arms folded on the balcony railing, his chin resting on them. I wanted him to back up, but they were all close to the railing and they never moved when I asked them to.

"There were ten times that many at Dad's coronation," Oz said. "But we were little then, and they were all more open about following us around. Now they hide in the shadows and we hardly know they're there."

"I've never been sure if I prefer them hiding or not," Drew asked. "The guards openly followed me everywhere when I was under thirteen, but after that? I always knew I was being tailed but I could never find them unless something went wrong, and then all the sudden, boom, three men in street clothes were on top of me, and then one in a suit would show up two minutes later. I always wound up grounded."

"Yeah, well, you're still being followed," Oz told him.

"I suspected."

"You could still get grounded."

"I suspected," he said. "Your mom could look at me the right way and I'd probably ground myself."

Zed leaned back, his chair creaking as he pushed against it. "I kind of envy my friends. If they go out to Angel Island to do stupid things, no one will be there watching or recording. If I go, the fun stops."

"Have you not listened to the Emperor's stories about Dad as a kid? Go have fun, Zed. No one will stop you, and they don't report back to our parents. Not unless we're in danger. Dating's probably a security-induced nightmare, but you get to be a kid."

"No one can relax with the guards around, no matter what. Even then, not worth it. Can you imagine the crap fest if I get caught ramming my bike down the GGB at a hundred fifty miles an hour? That would make the news."

Finn wandered out the balcony door and dropped into the chair next to me. They nodded an acknowledgment of him.

"Yeah, well, that's dangerous. Don't do that. Pick something stupid but not *that* stupid. And don't go climbing either of the bridges. I mean, you can't fall, but they do stop you."

"Fine, so I don't do like you did, and run away to Sausalito?"

"You can totally do that. Just be home by curfew."

"What curfew?"

Drew cocked his head as he looked at Oz. "Back up. You ran away?"

"When she was six!" Zed snorted. "Hopped on a ferry and took off like it was a perfectly normal thing to do."

"I wanted a cupcake. They have cupcakes there."

"They have cupcakes here, moron."

"Well...I wanted one from there."

"How," Drew asked, "does a six-year-old princess with a dozen guards just hop on a ferry, and no one tries to stop her?"

"She had help," Zed said.

I'd heard the story a dozen times before, but I listened anyway, mostly so I'd know when to look at Drew's face as he registered what he was getting into with her.

She was only six when she ran away, but deep down?

Oz was still the same.

*

I wasn't there, but as often as I've heard the story, it feels like I was perched on the tiny princess's shoulder, going along for the ride as she made her way from her bedroom to the ferry to Sausalito. The truth is that I was curled up on the window seat in her bedroom, and woken abruptly when the Queen, along with two armed guards, stomped in, looked under her bed, in the closet, and in her bathroom.

She even asked me where Oz was, but didn't wait for an answer. The Emperor came in, muttered a few words to her, and with a sigh of "Oh my Lord," she left.

I mean, I knew where she was headed. She'd told me just before she left. As she finished tying her shoes she said simply, "I'm going to ride a ferry today, Mister Wick. I'm going to go to Salsa Lito to get a cupcake."

Ok, then.

Oz took the elevator downstairs and walked out of the building, down to the corner of Powell and Market Streets where she hopped onto a cable car and rode it all the way to the end of the line on Hyde Street. Once on the cable car she wedged herself in between two tourists and no one asked her for fare; she rode there quietly until it was time to get off, and then she walked to the Wharf, blending in with the crowd as she made her way to the ferryboat.

The ticket taker looked twice at her, but then waved her on board, and she sat in a seat outside where she could watch the city fade behind her and feel the spray of water leap over the safety rails. When the ferry docked half an hour later she strolled down the walkway, and was momentarily stopped by an older woman who sighed hard, shrugged, and let her go.

Sausalito was more confusing than she expected; she'd been there once before with her mother and brother, and remembered what the bakery looked like, but she had no idea in which direction she needed to go.

She turned right and began walking down the street, stopping to giggle at seagulls stealing food from passersby, and when she reached the retail strip she darted in and out of stores, hoping to find the place she was looking for. When she was thirsty, she stopped at a snack kiosk and asked for a drink and was given a juice box. When she was hungry, she stopped at another and asked for a hot dog and was given one along with a soft drink.

After hours of wandering (which was only two hours, but she said it felt like all afternoon) and still no bakery in sight, she wandered into a diner and sat down at the first empty booth she saw, frustrated and near tears. When she set her chin on top of her folded arms on the table, staring at the door, the server took one long look at her, marched to the door, and locked it.

Oz wasn't sure what she'd done wrong, but knew that couldn't be good, and started to cry in earnest.

The server, a woman Oz thought looked a lot like someone's grandma, sat in the seat across from her and asked gently, "Where are your parents, angel?"

"Home."

"Do they know where you are?"

She sniffed. "I told Mister Wick I was coming here to get a cupcake, but I can't find the cupcake store."

"Ah, I see. Well, we have good cake here. It's not a cupcake, but I promise you'll like it."

"Chocolate?"

"Yep, we have chocolate. I'll get you a nice big slice, and a cold glass of milk to go with it."

When she brought the cake to the table, Oz realized everyone in the diner was looking at her. The owner watched from behind the counter, people were waiting at the kitchen door, and other customers turned to look and then began whispering amongst themselves.

"I realized I was in trouble," Oz said, laughing. "This nice lady had locked me in the diner and given me cake, and then she went from table to table telling everyone they couldn't leave—and no one complained. Then I heard the old guy behind the counter telling her that he had called the police and they would be there soon. That's when I went from just crying a little to bursting into a sobbing mess. I didn't want to go to jail, and I didn't know what I had done wrong."

"They called the police?" Drew asked.

"The server recognized me and knew I shouldn't be out alone, especially at my age. A few minutes later the Emperor was knocking on the door…she let him in and I went flying at him, *begging* him to take me home and not let them throw me in jail."

The Emperor refused to bend to her will. He demanded to know if she'd paid for her ferry ticket, then any food she'd had, and when she said no, he told her that was stealing. And what happens to people who steal?

"I was crushed. He set me down and made me get back into the booth, and whatever was going to happen, it was because I had run away and worried everyone, and then stolen a bunch of stuff along the way."

The Emperor sat down with her, pointed at the door, and added, "The next person to come through that door, you have to deal with. What are you going to say, Ozzie?"

"I shrieked, 'I'm sorry!' and was crying so hard that I barely noticed that he had his arm around me and kissed the top of my head, trying to sooth me. But I was terrified—that door was going to open and there were going to be police with guns and snarling, drooling dogs, and I was going to jail for the rest of my life."

"Was the next guy through a cop?"

"Worse."

"You thought your life was over at six," Finn said. "What could be worse?"

"It was my dad."

The King, without his guards, stormed through the door just a few minutes later. He stared at her, that long, hard, *you-are-in-so-much-trouble* glare, and then launched into dad-mode. "What were you thinking? Do you know what could have happened to you? Do you?"

Oz coughed, trying to match the timber of her father's angry voice. "He got louder as he went on, and all I wanted to do was hide under the table. The entire place was dead quiet, except for my father who was yelling at me, and it bounced off the walls and slapped me, hard. No one dared so much as blink, until he added, 'You are six years old, young lady. You should know better.'"

The Emperor laughed, loudly, and said, "Says the prince who climbed the bridge when he was six."

"You," the King snapped, "stop helping."

"Never." He slid out of the booth and reached down to pick Oz up, slinging her onto his hip. "Don't you have something to tell these nice people who helped you?"

Face half buried on his shoulder, she managed to squeak out a thank you to the woman who had given her cake, while keeping a wary eye on her father.

"Jax?" the Emperor prodded.

"Yes, thank you," he said to the server and the owner behind the counter. "And I apologize for the disruption my daughter has caused."

"That's not what I meant, but it'll do for now," the Emperor said. To Oz he said, "Your daddy loves you, princess, but you scared everyone. You can't go places without getting permission first, all right?"

"Sweetheart—" the King started.

"Welcome to fatherhood." The Emperor handed Oz over to the King. "I can't wait for her teen years."

*

"Here's the thing," Oz explained. "At every point where someone should have stopped me but waved me on instead, they saw that the Emperor was a few steps behind, gesturing for them to let me go. He paid for my ticket, the juice, and the hot dog. Probably the cake, too. Within seconds of getting out the front door, before I was even ten steps toward Powell Street, someone called the Emperor and told him I was out alone. He wanted to let me go, to see what I would do and where I would go, and how well I could take care of myself."

"Where were your guards?" Drew asked.

"I only had a day guard at the time. And trust me, after that day, every time I left the house I had three, and they were all new."

"You have the Emperor," Finn pointed out. "It sounds like you don't need much guarding beyond him."

"Do you think he uses the portals to get to where he knows you'll need him?" Drew asked. "I mean, think about it. If one day he's suffering the fallout from something horrible, he can go back a day and fix it."

"Huh," Oz grunted.

Zed didn't think so. "That would violate any number of temporal rules, I would think."

Finn picked me up and pulled me onto his lap. "We should ask this guy. Eh, Wick? He would break the rules to save Oz, wouldn't he? Or the King. Or you, for that matter."

He has his purpose in life. So do I.

To Oz he said, "The Emperor is a strange man and a month ago I would have argued against it, but I really think he would do anything to protect you all. I don't understand him, but he has a kind heart."

"So kind he's willing to fling you through a giant, electrified metal gate that could very well kill you."

"Exactly."

*

Oz had one request: *don't send Finn home until after my birthday.* Ideally, not until a day or two after.

"I don't want to spend my birthday missing someone."

Zed pointed out she would just miss him later, to which she replied, "Yes, but if I know he's not leaving until after, I won't dwell on it."

I think she expected either Finn or the Emperor to argue, but they both shrugged it off.

"One day, two days, a week…I could be here for years. Other than missing my wife and getting older, it's all relative," Finn said.

The Emperor added, "To her, it will only be a few minutes after she gets home when he arrives. I don't think she'll mind."

"Nice of you to speak for her," Oz snorted.

"I spent just enough time with her to understand that she finds him amusing, and is not surprised by the things he does. To know he stayed to attend the birthday party of an eighteen-year-old girl simply to keep her from being sad? The woman I met will find it endearing."

"She would, and then be sad she missed it," Finn mused. "And then she'll ask if I danced, because what's a party without dancing?" Before Oz could assure him there would be dancing, he added, "I can't dance. At all. It's like watching someone having a seizure on purpose, because seizures are surely the 'in' thing."

"You sound old," Zed said.

"I *am* old. At least, I'm a lot older than I thought I was just a couple of weeks ago. For some reason that bothers me."

"We won't hold it against you. You can still come to my party."

Oz's eighteenth birthday party was held on the roof, and along with her forty closest friends she invited her family, the Emperor, and me.

I had intended on going anyway, because where there are teenagers there's food, and teenagers tend to be sloppy and drop a lot of tasty things, but when she extended invitations to them all she bent over to tickle my chin and said, "You, too, Wick. It's not my birthday if you're not there."

I didn't point out that she would have the birthday whether there was a party or not, and whether I was around or not, because aging is not exactly a choice. I wanted a shot at the chunks of cheese I knew would be spread out on platters, and quite possibly bits of salami and ham and beef. If she felt my presence was a requirement, I was not going to argue the point.

Once the party got rolling, the adults got out of the way and sat in chairs tucked into a corner of the roof's surround wall. I was lying near the Emperor's feet, and most of the kids hovered around the food table, not truly appreciating the massive amount of edibles splayed out before them. Music blared over the speakers set up on the far side, and there was a giant video monitor hooked up to a gaming console on the other side of the food table; three boys played pretend soldier things while others egged them on, and one lone couple was actually dancing.

Finn glanced up, surprised by the two black hovercraft that were overhead, just far enough away to keep the air blast from the engines from making everyone uncomfortable.

"Oz's birthday is a known thing," the King explained. "People would surely expect her to celebrate a milestone birthday with friends. They're up there simply to keep an eye on airspace. The perimeter is protected from the ground as well."

"Who would want to hurt Oz?"

"No one who's met her," he replied. "But anyone who thinks they have a point to make or an axe to grind? She could be their bloody illustration."

The Queen held up her pointy finger, a warning to them. "And we will not discuss this right now. I am not spending my daughter's birthday thinking about who might want to hurt her. We're here to celebrate."

"It is nice to see her actually acting like a teenager," the Emperor said. "That happens less and less."

Over near the food table Oz pushed Drew away from her side, and they were both laughing.

"She told me about her great cupcake escape," Finn said. "Hell, I don't think I worked up the nerve to sneak out until I was Zed's age, but then it was so often I'm surprised my parents didn't shackle me to a rack in my room."

"Oh, I know she's snuck out a few times since then," the Queen said. "As long as what she's doing isn't going to cause any real trouble or get anyone hurt, the guards won't tell on her."

The Emperor chuckled. "Oh, they rat her out. Just not to you."

She sighed. "I don't want to know."

"My friends and I used to sneak out to Z Island," Finn said. "We never really did anything other than hang out. We'd haul out a ton of junk food and our hover boards, and get away from our parents."

"Z Island?" the King asked.

"Alcatraz. I have no idea when people start calling it Z Island, but it's been that for all of my life."

"Because 'Alcatraz' is *so* difficult to say," the Emperor mocked. He then nodded toward the dancing couple, who were inching their way toward the dark space behind the roof door. "You have runners."

The King groaned. "Let's make the rounds, remind them where they are," he said to the Queen.

She got up, but grumbled that he was such a spoilsport and clearly did not remember being eighteen.

When they were out of earshot, the Emperor told Finn, "Be very careful about telling them things from their future. They might reason that Alcatraz becomes Z Island through colloquial use, but they don't need a hint that it could very well be because of their son."

"Did I imply that?"

"No, but...you know their futures, and they should not. Not without a very, very good reason."

"I still have massive gaps. I clearly remember the United States, and yet here we are, on the roof of the old Macy's building, and

I'm sitting with an Emperor and his cat while the King and Queen wrangle a bunch of horny teenagers."

"You also remember a forty-state U.S. In the past, the past from right now, there were fifty. Things can revive, you know." He gestured to Oz and Drew. "You know something of them, right? Their lives will be noted."

"I remember bits and pieces from high school history. I don't remember if they're together."

"Is that a question? I can't answer it. Go home and crack open a history book now and then."

"I'm a physicist, not a historian."

"Their future is your history, Finn. Their *now* is your history. Remember every detail." He leaned over and picked me up from my comfy spot near his feet, setting me on his lap. "All of it."

He'll remember the meatloaf. And the pork chops. The Queen is a good cook.

"Emperor—I know I stumbled into good fortune. The moment I got out of my ship, I could have been shot on sight. I could have been mistaken as a terrorist, or a spy, or even burned at the stake for my weird form of witchcraft. Instead, I was treated like a wanted guest. Don't think I'll ever forget that. If I live to be an old man, I will remember."

"Don't say your goodbyes yet."

"I feel like I need to begin. This feels like home, and I'm leaving it in three days."

"Time travel," the Emperor reminded him.

"If I can change how my ship functions, maybe. I'll come back if I can. Are you sure I can't use a portal?"

"After speaking with your wife? I'm sure of it. She knew nothing about them, and we don't know what will happen if someone goes forward to a time when the portals don't exist. Oz's fear of walking into nothingness? It might be worse. You might just…not be."

"And going through the gate might kill me just as easily."

"There's that chance."

"And yet, I have to. If I stay here, sooner or later I'll screw up and say something to Oz or Zed about their lives, and possibly change everything."

The Emperor nodded.

"I suspect you know exactly how that feels, too."

"Really now."

"Come on. You were an adult when you saved the King's life, and here you are thirty-seven years later looking younger than he does now. A little bouncing around in time, compressing it for yourself?"

"One, I was just a teenager, and barely that. And two…great genetics. It's that simple."

"You're old enough to be Oz's grandfather."

"Shut up!" The Emperor was laughing. "I am not. Her uncle, maybe. Old enough to be the King's brother, not his father. Not unless I spawned when I was in utero."

"Have you?"

"Have I what?"

"Spawned."

"No. There are no little emperors or empresses running around out there. I told you before, I am not relationship material."

Finn leaned forward, his elbows on his knees. "So instead of having your own, you helped raise them. Surrogates for the children you never had?"

"Oh, I've let them get away with considerably more than a parent would and I've had far too much fun."

That's because you're about as mature as they are.

"I know too much about them now and half of it is breaking my heart. In my head I can see clearly a plaque set at the entry to Z Island, proclaiming it to be a memorial to Zealand Blackshear, and it's marked with the years Zed lives. I memorized that plaque when I was a boy. And that dash in between. Why the dash? Why is it always a dash? Why not 'He lived from X year to Y year, and did fantastic things?'"

"Because life is short? That dash is important. There's not enough room on a plaque or a tombstone to do justice to the years someone lives. It's why Zed speaks for them, to give weight to that simple little mark. That dash? It's everything. The actual years don't matter, it's the dash in between. That's your *life*, Finn."

Finn reached over to scratch my head. "Let's hope it's an awfully long dash."

"Long or short, it's the most important thing—" he stopped, sucking in a deep breath. "Huh. Anyway, it's the most important thing you'll ever do."

Finn patted his lap, inviting me over. I obliged and jumped, because at some point he would remember and might reward me with something fresh and dead and delicious. "Maybe when I get home, I'll get a Wick of my own and cart him around in an old sweatshirt. Jo would love that. And if I can keep him safe and healthy for a year or so, maybe she'll even consider...spawning."

I am not going with you, no matter how much shrimp you give me.

"Then again, I once told her if I ever had a kid, I was naming it Frank, regardless of gender. She was not amused."

"Well, to be frank," the Emperor laughed.

"What's your name, Emperor?"

"Emperor will do."

"Fine," Finn grunted. "Does anyone here know your given name?"

He gestured toward me, a slight nod of his head.

"Funny."

"Aubrey knows."

"Who?"

The Emperor shifted in his chair. "Seriously? Who? The Woman who has been feeding you and fussing over you, and you ask 'who?' It never occurred to you to find out what her name is?"

"Well...no. It seemed personal and inappropriate. I asked Drew what he called her, so it's been 'Mrs. B' for the most part."

"Jackson and Aubrey Blackshear. Now tell me you know who Australia is, or I'll toss you over the ledge."

He looked offended, but I could hear the teasing in his voice. When Finn didn't answer he told me to come back to him, because clearly he did not deserve to have possession of the honorable Mister Wick.

Hey, the Emperor was just as likely to sneak treats to me. I jumped over.

"The King wanted to name his children after his favorite places to travel. The Queen drew the line at Brisbane and Wellington."

"Oz was named for an entire country?"

"If not for his position, I think the King would be living a completely different life near a beach somewhere in New Zealand, and Aubrey would be right there. Probably still teaching, but she would be happy just about any place, as long as she's with him."

"Does that have anything to do with Oz wanting to bring back the United States? Remove the family from having to rule, leaving it to the peoples' choice."

"I think Oz has many reasons."

"Is Drew a means to an end, then?"

"She won't marry him unless she loves him, I'm certain of that."

"Arranged marriages happen all the time, especially among royalty."

"But not this time. If they end up together, it will be because they both want that, and agreed that getting to know each other with the intent of someday marrying would be a good thing."

"I wasn't arguing it—"

He stopped when the Queen dropped into her chair. "What are we arguing about?"

"The merits of two teenagers arranging their own marriage," the Emperor answered.

"Oh, lord, not for many years, I hope. I already think of that boy as my son, but no. Not for a long time."

"And you were...?" the Emperor prompted.

"Stop! I was not *that* young."

"She was twenty-five. Jackson was only twenty," he told Finn.

"Drew will be twenty soon, won't he?"

"Stop it!" She pointed a finger at the Emperor. "Don't you dare remind them of that. Besides," she added, waving it off, "they're still more like cousins. I don't think she's even held his hand."

"Perhaps not in front of you, but yes, she has."

"Well, then barely that. I think she would tell me—"

"Timing," the Emperor said, nodding toward them, "is everything."

Finn and the Queen both looked across the rooftop, to where Drew and Oz were now dancing, just in time to see him lean down and kiss her. It wasn't even a smooch, it was a full on, make-Mom-squirm kiss, and if Jax had seen it, he would have said something.

"So," the Emperor then said brightly. "Should I find him quarters on my floor, or one down?"

She sighed, heavily. "You are *so* enjoying this."

"Little bit, yeah."

20

It was well after midnight when Oz drifted away from her own birthday party; most of her friends stayed on the roof to dance and play video games, but she thought it would be wiser to leave before most of her guests so that they didn't feel obligated to stay.

That was what she told her father; I think she was more disappointed by the fact that Finn refused to dance, and that was something we'd all wanted to see. And record on video. Even the Emperor danced, flailing his arms in the air and hopping up and down like he was riding a pogo stick. It lacked any form of dignity but it made the kids laugh, and his performance was probably online less than five minutes after he stopped.

I followed her to her room; I was tired of the noise and the Emperor had begun to weave his way through the stragglers, letting them know he had his eye on them, even those trying to slink off into the shadows. No one was sneaking bites of meat or cheese to me, anyway; I briefly considered jumping up onto the table and taking something, but Oz's friends were not like her family and might react without thinking—the roof had a nice barrier around it, but I didn't want to risk being the first feline to fly off the roof onto Union Square.

Sure, I would land on my feet, but I wasn't immune to physics and all my bones would turn into confetti when I hit the pavement, and then every meaty bit I'd managed to eat over the last week would explode onto the Square like a water balloon.

Delicious dead things are not to be wasted. Especially once I've eaten them.

We curled up on the window seat in her room and watched the activity on the street below. There were a dozen guards surrounding Finn's giant egg, and there were two armored security vans parked ahead of it and two more behind it, and inside each one there were more guards.

I hope they know that egg isn't going to hatch.

Drew knocked on the open door; Oz invited him in but told him to leave the door all the way open, because, "parents," and he pushed it as far as it would go, and then sat near me on the window seat. He looked to see what we were watching, and asked, "Military guard? For Finn's ship?"

"You should see how many guards are on the bridge. The gate the Emperor built might be a hundred times more valuable than Finn's ship."

"Why? It's just a giant portal, isn't it?"

She leaned away from the window, looking at him instead of the commotion below. "If it works the way he hopes, it can be used by anyone. And if anyone can use it, it can be weaponized."

"I thought anyone could already use a portal."

"Theoretically. The truth is that we don't really know much about how they work, other than if you can see them, and you can calmly think your way into one, you can come out the other side. The stories about people randomly falling through…those are just stories. I don't think it's ever happened."

"Sucks."

"Why? Were you planning on trying to somersault your way into twenty-thirty-three to go sight-seeing? Because I can take you."

"Well. No." He sighed hard. "I had this idea that maybe kids that went missing in the past had actually fallen through, and somehow we could track them down and send them home. I mean, it was just the start of an idea. I didn't really know what else to do with it."

"It would be wonderful for their families if we could."

"But?"

"But consider the timelines. We can't deliberately go back and change things in our past, because we don't know how it will affect our present. Why do you think I was so dead set on keeping Finn from stopping himself from letting Jo jump off the bridge?"

"Because it was insane, and letting her die would be wrong?"

"Partly. The thing is, if he had been right, and letting her die meant that the U.S. never fell apart—that would have meant that *our* time line would change. We exist *because* that country broke up, Drew. If he'd been right?"

"I know. We might not have even been born."

"There's the chance that we would have lived out our lives regardless and the changes would carry on in a whole new timeline, but even the idea of a When where we don't exist?"

They both startled at the sound of Finn's voice. "It never would have happened. If I'd gotten to Jo before anyone else, I think I would have remembered. One smile, that's all it would have taken."

"Well, hell, I smiled at you a couple of times," Drew snorted.

"Yeah, you're not pretty enough, Prince Andrew."

"Hey, my mom says I am."

"You're very pretty," Oz assured him. "You think you're ready, Finn? Nervous or second thoughts?"

"Terrified. The idea of dying sucks but I'm more worried about how it would feel to fry like a piece of bacon."

Bacon? Now?

"You know a few words, don't you, Wick?" He started to pull the chair away from Oz's desk, but before he could get it over to the window, the Queen came in and asked them to give her a few minutes with her daughter.

Oz watched them leave and then asked, "Am I in trouble for something? We did leave the door open."

"No, of course not." She took Drew's spot on the window bench, and obliged me with a few scratches behind my ears. "I hope your birthday was fun. Even with constantly chasing those kids out of dark corners, we enjoyed the party. Your friends are wonderful and I've missed them this summer."

"Is Dad still up there?"

"He and the Emperor are still trying to intimidate everyone. I don't think any of them are actually afraid, though, and it's turning into a game."

Oz laughed. "They know Dad is a softy. It was fun. I caught up with a lot of people and they all seem to like Drew. He was just the right amount of goofy and friendly."

"He is both, isn't he?"

"He also has so much more in common with most of my friends than I do. I didn't realize until tonight how many of them are heading to school instead of working and how many assumed I was going with them. They're excited and disappointed I didn't register for the next semester. Have to admit, it sounds appealing."

"Regrets?"

"A month ago I wouldn't have thought too hard about it, but now? I think the last couple of weeks have shown me I need to learn how to learn. I might want to go back to school just for that, if it's not too late."

"You were always a good student. And it's never too late."

Yeah. Who's going to tell the Crown Princess no?

"Mom, you're a teacher. You know how half of school is. We learn what we need in order to pass the classes, not necessarily what we really need to know or what will be useful to remember. We sort through the information we're given and try to figure out what will be on the tests, and concentrate on that. I'm not sure we really learn critical thinking. We learn to get good grades. I can do that, but I don't think I ever learned how to put all those pieces together and come up with ideas that are my own."

"I think you can, but I understand."

"Now I'm wondering if going back to school will teach me how to sift through all the little details and be objective about what's important and what's not. I know I'll need to embrace being impartial and right now I'm not."

"All this from a birthday party? Sweetheart, you were not supposed to be thinking tonight. You don't have to be an instant adult."

"I think I do. Look at all this with Finn. I was ready to blow him off after the whole bridge fiasco. I didn't care that he saw it as being for the greater good or why. I didn't want to hear it. I *refused* to hear it."

"You thought he was willing to let someone die, Oz. Compassion is never wrong."

"No, but if I could have been unbiased, I would have handled it differently. I threatened to end him."

"But you didn't. You wouldn't."

"If not for the Emperor, I might have walked away from Finn."

"And left him there in the past?"

"That's just it. I don't know. I'd like to think that I wouldn't have, but what I saw was my own life being un-invented. And then to find out his end game was really just to get back to his wife? The Emperor won't get anywhere near him, but he was still willing to bend over backwards to help and to wait for the truth."

Lightly, the Queen said, "Sweetheart, if you learn to think like the Emperor...God help us all."

Hey, he gives me cheese. She could be more like that.

"I know you're joking, but if I could think like him I'd be a better person. And none of this is why you're here right now, is it? My navel-gazing didn't send out come-see-Oz alarms."

"No, but tonight I saw Drew in a whole new light, and I needed to talk to you."

"Drew knows the door stays open."

"I trust you both. But, sweetheart—it doesn't have to be him, you know that, right? I don't want you to take a random statement your father once said in jest to be your only path. We never expected this from either of you. It was honestly just a joke."

"What? No. This makes sense to us. It's not like we can socialize the way our friends do, and even if we could, the whole random serial dating thing doesn't work."

"Of course it does. You go out and meet new people, find new interests. How do you think your father and I got together? We were introduced."

"Unless I leave San Francisco, I'm not going to meet many new people. I'm not sure I want to. When Drew and I started talking about this, hell, we were only around fourteen years old and we realized then that no matter what, we have to figure out how to be friends for the rest of our lives. We're going to be dealing with each other even if we're not together. We thought if we approached it as a friendship first, with the end goal being that we get married…we have every intention of succeeding."

The Queen scooted closer, brushing her hand across Oz's cheek. "We want you to find real love, Ozzie. Not just a comfortable, friendly union."

"Why can't it be both? He understands this life. We want the same things for both Pacifica and Midlam."

"That's a contract."

"So is marriage. He won't break my heart, Mom. And I won't break his."

Oz's phone beeped. It was a text from Drew, telling her that he and Zed and Finn were in the staff kitchen making pizza. I perked up; if there was pizza, there was cheese, and these teenagers would share.

The Queen kissed Oz on the forehead. "All right. Go be a kid while you still can. And make those boys clean up after themselves."

*

Zed was already sticking the pizzas into the oven when Oz and I reached the kitchen. The floor was dusted in flour and there was pizza sauce splattered on the stovetop, and glancing around, I was pretty sure that none of them had any plans to clean up their mess.

Drew and Finn were seated at the kitchen island, faces bathed in the glow of a portable computer. Neither looked up, but they must have heard us come in because Drew pulled out the chair that was next to him for her.

"Serious people look serious," she said, sitting next to him.

"We're looking for old pictures of the Emperor," Drew said.

Finn added, "He told me he was a teenager when he pulled your dad off the bridge. I'm just curious."

Oz turned the computer so that she could see the screen, typed quickly, and then turned it so they could see the result. On the screen was a picture of the Emperor walking down the center of the first off-ramp from the bridge, and he was holding a little boy tightly as he walked straight toward the camera. It was the first known picture of him, and another public photo wouldn't be taken for two years.

She pulled up the next one, and displayed them side by side. "But he looks pretty much the same in both."

Finn leaned in closer. "He looks about fifteen. Maybe fourteen."

Zed spun the computer so he could look. "I always thought when Dad told the story that the Emperor was an adult."

"When you're six and scared, a fifteen-year-old *is* an adult," Oz said. "But it also might explain why they're so close now. It wasn't like this giant twenty-five-year gap between them. At some point, they were pretty much on the same page."

Finn flipped through several pictures. "Maybe less time between them than you think." He turned the computer so Oz could see it better. "Your dad is about, what, twenty here? How old does the Emperor look?"

"He ages well," Zed offered.

"He doesn't look any older than Drew does now. No one ages that well."

They stopped and stared at Finn, and after a moment Oz said, "Have you looked in a mirror lately, Finn? We all thought you were around Drew's age, and you're freaking thirty years old."

"Seriously," Zed said. "And our mom. How old do you think she is?"

"That's kind of disrespectful for me to even ponder," Finn said.

"Take a guess."

"Forty-ish?"

"She would hug you for that," Oz said. "She's five years older than Dad. Forty-eight."

"Totally look at me," Drew said. "I'm only, like, thirteen."

Oz snorted. "We're talking chronological age here, Princess. Your maturity level doesn't count."

Finn didn't seem convinced. "Does he ever just disappear for a while and then come back looking older than he should? Or younger?"

She considered it, and then said, "He makes regular trips to Scotland and stays for a couple weeks at a time. Looks pretty much the same when he gets back. He's not portal hopping, if that's what you mean."

"I was wondering."

"He uses them the same way I do, mostly for kicks and not for more than a few hours at a time. He likes to take Wick on field trips to sit and people-watch, usually back about two hundred years or so."

He likes it. I'm not a fan.

"That's it? He has all these different points in time to investigate, and he just goes to sit somewhere and watch people?"

We eat fish and shrimp, too. He drinks coffee and lectures me about random things. It's not a lot of fun.

Oz had reached for Drew's hand and was absently running her thumb over his while she thought about it. After a moment, she said, "You can learn a lot about people by how they act in public, when they don't realize they're being watched. You can put history into context when you can see how people were coping."

"It's more than that," Zed said. "He watches to learn about human suffering, and goes back to see what we were doing wrong. You know most of what he does here is helping people get and then stay on their feet, right?"

"I've gathered that, but why?"

"Why not?" Zed's face clenched a bit, as if he were offended.

"No, I didn't mean it wasn't the right thing for him to be doing. He can literally do *anything*, so why that? What is it about human suffering that speaks to him? He can travel through time and witness some of the most pivotal events in history, yet he just watches people going about their daily lives? And then comes home to find places for people to live?"

Oz took the computer and closed the lid. "If you were staying longer and maybe if you were a few years younger, at some point he would probably sit you down and explain that everyone needs to have their 'thing,' some way that they give back, and you need to figure out how you'll work to improve things. He helps people find ways to live here, because when he needed it the most, someone gave him a place to sleep and fed him. My grandfather didn't ask a lot of questions, I don't think. The Emperor was here, he needed help, and it was given. That stays with a person. So really, if he does nothing else with his life, he's made Pacifica compassionate, and basically made that kindness an officially sanctioned stance."

"He pretty much ended homelessness in San Francisco," Zed added.

"Hell, his outreach is even taught in Midlam schools," Drew said. "The Emperor's Paradigm. Turns out it's cheaper to house and feed the homeless than it is to run shelters and welfare programs. And yet we haven't really done anything to change our status quo. There are a lot of people in Midlam that struggle and no one does anything about it."

"So there's zero homeless in Pacifica?" Finn asked.

"There are some," Oz said. "There will always be people who slip through the cracks. But most of the ones who show up here and stay for a day or two in the shelter are homeless by choice, and that's all right. There's still food and shelter available. Medical care is a basic human right. The resources are available for anyone who wants them."

"And it's all the Emperor's doing?"

"He started kicking the ball around when our grandfather was King, and Dad let him pick it up and run with it."

Finn tapped the closed computer lid with his fingernails. It was an annoying tap-tap-tap, and right when I was about to pounce on his hand to make him stop, he did, and then said, "He showed up when he was a teenager, right? No mention of him before the day your dad decided to scale the bridge. And then he's just…here."

"More or less."

"Where were his parents?"

Oz and Zed looked at each other.

"I've never asked," she said. "He mentions them every now and then, and I just assumed they were in Scotland and that's why he visits a couple times a year."

"Yeah, but we were also assuming he was a grown adult when Dad was six."

"Your Emperor could have been a runaway," Finn said. "Why else would he be in the city that young and alone for that long, and not one of you has even met his family?"

"Finn, they might be here," Oz said. "But…"

"There are some things you don't ask him," Zed finished for her. "I think we got in the habit of not him asking personal questions, because that would be prying."

"I'd like to ask him why he hated me when I was little," Drew said. "Is that on the list of things we don't ask about?"

"He never hated you," Oz told him, amused because we all remembered how afraid Drew had been of the Emperor. "He was just...strict."

"Strict, hell. He wanted to suck the fun out of anything I did."

Drew's earliest memory of the Emperor was when he was not quite four, on the roof in a wading pool with two-year-old Oz. Zed was a baby, not even big enough to be a sticky person, and the Emperor was walking back and forth with him slung halfway over his shoulder as he tried to coax a burp out of him. When Oz got out of the pool to get a toy, Drew grabbed a plastic cup and filled it with water, seeing his chance to throw it at her when she turned around.

"I mean, the water in the cup, not the actual cup," he explained.

He had the cup loaded and his arm cocked back, when the giant shadow of the Emperor loomed from behind, and he heard a deep growl. "No."

Drew tried to launch the water anyway, but when he did the cup was suddenly gone from his hand, and again, there was that low, angry growl. "No."

"I turned around, and damned if he wasn't already sitting down under the sun canopy with Zed, and the cup was on the ground near his feet. I wanted it back, but..."

"No," Zed growled, laughing.

"And the next summer. I snuck out onto the balcony with a couple of water balloons, and just as I was about to let one fly over the railing, it was gone. My hand was next to my head, locked and loaded, and the balloon was gone, and he said 'No.' I turned around and he was already heading back inside, and he had all of my balloons."

"He took your red rubber ball, too," Zed said. "I must have been six? We were playing on the roof and you were getting ready to chuck it at Oz. He snatched it out of your hand, pointed a finger and snapped 'No' and you looked like you had no idea what had just happened. You weren't even mad. Just, 'hey, what the hell?'"

"He didn't snap. He growled."

"Well hell, Drew," Oz said, "the question isn't why didn't the Emperor like you, it's why were you always throwing things?"

"I wasn't! But he caught me *all* the freaking time. Once, I snuck out of my room at like six in the morning and was going to go downstairs, I don't even remember why…I got halfway down the hall and there he was, standing with his hands on his hips and he had that *look*. He didn't even have to growl at me. I ran back into the bedroom and hid in the closet until your mom came looking for me."

"Big, brave Drew," Oz snorted.

"I was four or five. I thought he was going to eat me. Why else would he follow me around, looking super pissed off all the time? I wasn't plumping up enough to make a good meal."

You were a scrawny thing. Never enough meat to even make a sandwich.

Finn pointed out the most likely thing. "Maybe you were just an annoying, snotty little kid."

"I was sensitive, dammit." The timer went off, and he turned to get the pizza out of the oven. "He was just mean."

Oz reached into the cupboard for plates and passed them out, even a small one for me. "Do you remember the formal state dinner about ten years ago? We were stuck at the big round table with kids from France, Germany, and Japan, and it was boring as hell. The adults were getting drunk, and we had nothing to do. We couldn't even really talk to each other."

"I hated those dinners," Drew groaned. "We had to wear tuxes and dress shoes, and Carter never had to go."

"That's because Carter was jerk," Zed grumbled.

"Yeah, but you decided to do something about the boredom," Oz said. "If we couldn't get up and run around, we could at least have dessert."

Drew left the table to find the rolling cart they had seen earlier in the evening. It was loaded down with cake and pie, and some rubbery, jiggling things no one wanted to try. Ten-year-old logic told him it was in the kitchen, and with the kitchen door behind them and not across the room where many of the adults were lingering, he thought he could make his way, get the cart, and roll it back without any of the parents noticing.

"I was going to be a hero," he said.

He managed to get as far as the door, but when he tried to push it open it wouldn't budge. He tried again, harder, kicking at it when it wouldn't open. On his third try, it swung inward, and the Emperor was standing there.

"He just glared at me. Not a word. Since I wasn't getting into the kitchen, I went back to the table and waited for all of you to start picking on me for not getting to the cart."

"Yeah, but we didn't," Zed said. "I remember that night. Two minutes after you got back to the table, the Emperor rolled the cart out and we all got cake and ice cream."

"And I got mine last." He laughed, adding, "But damn, I think I got the biggest piece of cake."

"See?" Oz said. "He didn't hate you."

"Then why didn't I hear anything other than 'no' out of him until like, last year? And even then, it felt like a warning."

Before Drew's family left at the end of their visit in August, the King reserved a large swath of Ocean Beach for an end-of-summer family picnic. There was a barbeque grill loaded with hamburgers and chicken for the King to try to not burn, and they set up long canopies for shade. I was tethered to a pole jammed into the sand under one of them, but I didn't mind; it meant that the seagulls couldn't carry me off, and someone was always with me, feeding me bits of their burgers and chicken.

Oz and Zed played in the water with body boards, riding on short waves; every fifteen minutes a parent or a guard or the Emperor reminded them to never turn their backs on the ocean, because Ocean Beach was a place where inattentive people were swept into the water and the outcome of that was never good. Drew waited on the beach in a low lounge chair, preferring to turn his not-so-pink skin a new shade of red rather than risk the tide.

He watched as Oz came out of the water, her body board under an arm and wet hair plastered to her face. He was so focused that he didn't hear the Emperor come up behind him, and startled when he said, "You will treat her with respect, Andrew. What you're thinking…no."

Finn and Zed howled with laughter, and Oz asked, "Well, what *were* you thinking?"

Drew's not-so-pink skin turned red again.

"I know what he was thinking," Zed said. "Same thing you were."

"Shut up," Oz told him, though she was still laughing.

"Seriously, Drew. You were hauling an ice chest from the waterline back to the grill, and you'd slung it up on your shoulder. She was sitting there practically drooling. The Emperor looked at her, looked at you, then back again and said, 'His eyes are several inches higher.'"

"Oh my God, Zed!"

"He was laughing his ass off. You've never been that red before. Or since. Well, until now."

"Your abs, Drew, I swear. Not..."

"You can check out anything you like," he said.

"Considering how often you stare at her boobs, you better be fair about it," Zed told him.

Oz and Drew were both bright red, but he didn't seem to care if she knew.

Zed went on. "You grab one and I'll break your fingers."

"I'm pretty sure Oz can do that all by herself," Drew said. "Besides, I'm more afraid of what the Emperor would do. He'd probably castrate me."

"He would not," Oz said. "He's protective, that's all. The only way he would do anything to you is if he thought I hadn't wanted it."

"Do you?" Zed asked.

"That's none of your business!"

Drew arched an eyebrow, playfully. "Do you?"

Finn had been mostly quiet, but growled, "No." Then he added, "Just speaking for the Emperor."

"We're making the old man uncomfortable," Zed said.

"Not uncomfortable exactly," Finn said. "Old, maybe. I find myself taking the Emperor's train of thought here." He pointed at Drew and then Oz. "He was right. Be respectful. Both of you."

"Yes, *Dad*," Oz laughed.

Zed muttered, "I'll still break your fingers."

Oz leaned across the kitchen island and said, "What makes you think I'll tell you if he cops a feel?"

If I have to witness it, I'll tell.

Finn spared me from any potential bouncy talk. "All right. Come on. The Emperor. He doesn't hate Drew, but probably likes to torment him. He's overly protective of Oz and Zed. But what do you really know about him?"

"I don't follow," Zed said.

"Do you even know his name? I asked outright, and he wouldn't tell me."

Oz shrugged. "He's always been the Emperor. I wouldn't ask him what his first name is any more than I would the Governor of Texas or the Canadian Prime Minister. Or even my teachers. I just wouldn't ask."

"But if you want to know their names, you can look them up online. If you look up the Emperor of San Francisco, what do you get?"

"First hit? You'd get to learn about Joshua Norton. He proclaimed himself Emperor of the United States in the mid-eighteen-hundreds, and then later added Protector of Mexico to it. He wandered around in military clothing, and the people humored him, bowing as they passed him in the streets, and addressing him by his made-up title. He became a treasured icon. I mean, people seriously catered to him and even had him show up to meet dignitaries. When he died there were like ten thousand people at his funeral."

"Huh," Drew grunted. "I did not know that."

"But information about *our* Emperor?" Oz went on. "There are lots of things about what he does, but not a lot about who he *is*. I'm pretty sure that's how he wants it."

"So you have this guy who won't tell anyone his name, he's overly particular about being touched, he's grouchy and scares small children, he has time as his playground but chooses to go sit on a bench and watch people, and yet—" he shrugged lightly "—he's made a real effort to get me home, without much in the way of figuring out if I'm worth it."

"Those aren't bad things," Zed offered.

"Except for scaring small children," Drew grumbled.

"I think I may regret leaving," Finn said. "My biggest disappointment when my ship goes through the gate will be that I didn't have time to figure that bugger out. I want to know who he is."

"Then use that as a reason to fix your ship and come back," Oz said. "Historical research. Who the hell was the Emperor of San Francisco? You'll have hundreds of years of history to poke through to figure that out. Information about all of us. A week from now you could be sitting in your own living room with a thick book detailing the Blackshear Monarchy, and learn more about us than even we'll ever know. Then you can come back and taunt us with it."

"For real," Zed said. "Come back and tell me if I ever get my castle. I really want one."

"He could probably tell you that right now," Oz said.

Finn snorted. "But I won't."

"Do you really want to know more about the Emperor?" Drew asked. "Because you don't have to wait for that. Oz has all of the past at her fingertips, more or less. Go back twenty-five years or so, and just watch."

Oz flinched. "What, you want me to take him through a portal to snoop? That feels a lot like invading the Emperor's privacy."

"Not just because of him," Zed argued. "It's a chance to get a glimpse of Mom and Dad at the start of everything. The Emperor is just part of the package. Think about it, we can go see what they were like while they were our ages, before we started weighing them down with responsibility and diapers and barf. I want to see how they were before Dad became King. Like, when they were dating."

"I didn't realize you were such a romantic, Zed."

He shrugged it off, but Drew leaned over and whispered loudly to Finn, "She's lying. We all know he's a romantic. The drippy kind, even."

Oz blew out through pursed lips, half sighing, half caving in. "If we do this, we don't stay long. There are a couple of points where I know we can find them. We hit those, see what's going on, and we leave. We'll take an hour at the most. Okay?"

I pawed at Drew's stomach, trying to pull the pouch of his sweatshirt open. They were not going without me; I remembered most of the time I'd been with the King's family, but it wasn't until later that I got to go out with them, and I'd missed a lot.

Drew scooped me up, grumbling about how much my weight pulled down on the neck of his sweatshirt, but he was scratching behind my ears as he said it, so I didn't believe he was annoyed, not really.

I sniffed at him; that pervasive dog-smell was gone.

You might be worth keeping. We'll see.

On the elevator ride down, Oz warned them they'd have to move quickly, to keep the guards from stopping them. "We'll head for the portal on the Square. By the time they realize we're out, we'll be gone."

"We're allowed out of the house, Oz," Zed said.

"It's after two in the morning, lunkhead. If they catch us, they'll try to stop us. You weren't scheduled to work tonight, and we never told anyone we had after-party plans. So yeah, they'll try to stop us, but once we're through the portal, we're fine."

The elevator door slid open and she added, "I hope."

21

"Right now, Dad is sixteen years old, and about to do one of the stupidest things of his life."

We'd walked from the portal on Union Square, down Geary Street to Market, and then followed it to where it intersected with California Street. There was a coffee shop near the corner, with outside tables and a good view straight up the massively steep slope of California; she directed them there, reasoning that they would look less conspicuous waiting at a coffee shop than they would milling around on the sidewalk. Oz bought them each a hot chocolate, and they sat down.

Drew pulled the top from his cup and used his finger to pull out the whipped cream on top. He flicked it onto the lid and then set it in front of me, my own treat-filled plate.

I'm warming up to you, dude.

"Look up to the top," Oz said. Way in the distance, toward the crest of the street—which, starting a couple of blocks up, almost looked like it dropped straight down—was a tiny dot, and on that tiny dot was another tiny dot wearing a bright orange windbreaker. "Dad is about to take an old pedal bike all the way down without stopping. I don't know why. He never explained it, really, other than, 'I wanted to.'"

Zed was surprised. "I thought he made it up. How could anyone *do* that?"

Physics, dude.

"The Emperor confirmed it. Dad got on an old bicycle and screamed down California at about ninety miles an hour. I've always wondered if they both exaggerated...I want to find out."

Drew shifted uncomfortably in his seat, turning back and forth to look around. "Oz, they allowed cars on the roads back then."

"Yep." She followed to where he was looking, from the middle of the road to the place where it met up with Market Street. "There aren't too many people around and it's pretty early. He probably counted on that."

"And he's moving," Finn said.

I couldn't see quite that far, but I got the right idea; the prince who would be king pushed off with his feet, letting momentum take him down the hill. He bounced off the seat at each intersection, and by the time he was close enough that I had a clear view, he was rising over a foot off each time he hit a bump.

"If he biffs it," Drew said through clenched teeth, "he's going to be skinned alive."

"But he wasn't," Zed said.

I heard Oz suck in a sharp breath as her father reached the Battery Street intersection. She blinked rapidly, and when I looked, I could see it and feel it, too: the sudden shift, the feeling that the world had tilted off its axis, and the ghost of a bright red delivery van gunning through the light at the same time the bicycle was in the middle of the intersection.

I squinted, trying to see what wasn't there, but then it was gone and the world un-tilted itself before I could blink again.

Jax was on his brakes, the wheels on the bike stuttering in short, clipped yips as he slowed down, and then finally came to a stop just before he reached Market Street. Waiting for him at the bottom was the Emperor, his hands jammed into the pockets of his jeans, his head tilted ever so slightly to one side, and he looked every bit as angry as he would if it had been Oz or Zed.

"That was boneheaded stupid," Zed said with a bit of a laugh. "Please tell me I'm not that stupid. He's my age right now."

Finn leaned toward Oz and whispered, "The Emperor wasn't there before, was he? Did he just do something? Something felt off for a moment."

"He probably did, but I'm not sure what." She took a long sip of the hot chocolate and then asked them where they wanted to go next.

Zed slid in his chair a bit, making himself look smaller. "Can we go see Mom?"

"Yeah sure." She got up, heading toward the portal behind the old Hyatt hotel. "And no, you're not that stupid. Seriously, no one is."

*

We went forward three years. Oz knew that when her mother was studying for her post-graduate degree she had also worked the breakfast shift at a small restaurant just off Herman Plaza, and walked there every morning from her apartment just down Steuart Street. To get to work she had to cross the Plaza, so we waited near the fountain, sitting on the cement surround, huddled close to each other for warmth.

"It's freaking cold," Drew grumbled, placing his hands across my back to keep me warm. "Why didn't we bring jackets?"

"It'll warm up," Oz assured him.

The sun was barely up, and light was even dimmer for the patches of fog that hovered above. Not even six in the morning, I guessed. It might warm up, but that would be hours away.

Only Zed wasn't trying to hug himself or pushing up against anyone to share warmth. While I had the advantage of fur, he had the advantage of long nights spent out on Alcatraz, where it was often cold and wet. He was used to it, but I was not. I pressed against Drew's giant hands, hoping to somehow leech even more heat from him.

"I didn't know Mom worked when she was in school," Zed said, straining to see in the direction Oz had said she would come from. "I thought she'd always been a teacher."

What, like she popped from the womb with a ruler in one hand and a spelling guide in the other?

"She worked a lot of odd jobs before she started teaching. She had to. No one else was paying for her education. No clue where her parents were. Or are."

"I think my brain just wants her to be with Dad, even then."

"Today? She was. They're dating by now, pretty serious even, but he's only nineteen and in his second year of university. In about six months...it's going to hit the fan when he tells Grandma and Granddad that they're getting married. She'll have a job by then and he's got some romantic notion that living on a teacher's salary will be good for them."

"I bet it actually was," Finn said.

"Maybe. Mom says they weren't exactly poor, but they had to be careful. And that they had a lot of fun. Dad had never lived anywhere but the family home and he loved her tiny apartment that always smelled like boiled cabbage and egg rolls from the people downstairs." She reached over and rubbed my head. "What about you, Wick? Did you like it?"

The apartment was a single room, with a bed tucked into the corner and a sofa positioned to try to hide it. It was nice and bright even if it was small, and I could see people coming and going from a perch they hung near the window by the front door. The downstairs neighbors were pleasant and often sent food upstairs, and there was always something included for me. I also caught my first and only mouse there, and after one bite decided that it kind of sucked, so I let it go—puncture wounds and all—and watched as it scampered into a hole near the door.

I felt a bit bad about that. I hope I didn't kill it.

I liked living there well enough, mostly because Jackson was at least ten kinds of happy and I still got to see the Emperor almost every day. I never visited him where he lived because it was on a busy street in SOMA and there were cars and trucks, but he came by most days and they took me outside with them to study in the park or to watch ferry boats come and go.

There was always food and the apartment was warm, so it was fine. Jax talked about getting a job every now and then, but was always reminded that he'd promised to finish school first, and besides, who would hire the crown prince for a part time job? The security guards that followed him were part of the package, and made it more trouble that it would be worth.

The Emperor didn't have an actual job, but he was on the King's payroll. I don't think anyone knew exactly what he was supposed to do other than protect Jax from himself, but the one time he mentioned taking a part time job helping in the city's biggest shelter, the King forbade it, reminding him that he had employment, even if it didn't come with a specific job title.

He helped in the shelter anyway.

Actually, he helped so much that it mostly closed down. A few beds remained and the kitchen was kept stocked, and it was staffed with someone every day to greet people who had just gotten into the city. People could get a place to sleep for the night, but if they were staying and not just passing through, the Emperor was called and an apartment was found for them.

His efforts convinced the King: no one in San Francisco should go hungry, and no one should live without a place to call his own. If you stayed in the city, at the very least you had a place to live and vouchers for food. He guessed that most people would use the vouchers just long enough to get on their feet, and then they would find jobs and fend for themselves. And he was right; people wanted to work, and then added to his list of Things to Do was helping them find jobs.

It was a nice time for us all. Jackson studied during most of his free time, Aubrey taught sticky little people how to read and write, and the Emperor took care of those in need. We lived in that tiny apartment for two years, until the King and Queen asked them to move into the royal house, reasoning that grandchildren were on the horizon, and they wanted to be close.

That took a few more years, but we left the aroma of cabbage and moved into an apartment on the third floor, and we stayed there until Oz and Zed were little and the King wanted to retire.

I had full run of the house, always. When Jackson was small the Queen requested cat doors be installed leading into nearly every room, so that I had my choice of where to be.

She missed me when I was gone.

In fact, I'm pretty sure I was half the reason she begged him to move back home.

Curled up in Drew's sweatshirt, trying to steal the warms from his hands, I realized that there was another me not too far away, probably asleep on the Prince's bed, and he was not cold at all.

I envied him.

"There she is," Zed said, half-whispering as if she could hear from where she was at, still on Steuart Street.

Aubrey was walking quickly and looked both annoyed and exasperated, and as she neared we could see why: trailing behind her, taunting her with invitations to go find a place to engage in things of the touchy-feely and quite possibly bouncy nature, was a short, wiry man with long, dark hair and little round glasses. She sped up to a near-jog, and he was hurrying behind her.

She kept glancing over her shoulder, the irritation changing into something else, something that made the hairs on the tips of my ears tingle.

He caught up to her, grabbing her arm; she yanked it away and yelled at him to back off. She barked it like an order and he hesitated, but then lunged again. Zed twitched, but before he could get up, Oz had her hand on his arm.

"Stay put."

Aubrey pushed at his chest, trying to force him back, but he grabbed both of her arms and leaned in close, laughing as she tried to break free.

"No, Zed," Oz hissed when he tried to get up. "We can't interfere. Whatever happens, happened already, and has to. We can't stop it."

"He'll hurt her."

"If he does…he already did, Zed. If we do anything to change this—"

"She's our mom!"

"That's the point. If we stop this, she may never *be* our mother. We can't change anything, not even if he hurts her."

He wanted to argue; *I* wanted to argue. I felt Drew's hands tense and the tips of his fingers dug into my fur just a little bit. Then his entire body twitched as he fought against the impulse to jump up.

I heard "Run, Mrs. B" escape him with a whisper, but for anyone else it was lost to the sound of footsteps coming from behind us. It was fast and loud, the thud of rubber pounding on pavement. Crossing the Embarcadero, speeding across the Plaza, the Emperor was running as fast as he could.

When the Emperor was less than five feet away from them, he leapt into the air, cocking his right leg so that his knee was across his stomach, and then he kicked; his foot slammed into the other man's head and knocked him backward, making him hit the ground with an audible thump. Aubrey fell back with him, sliding on her shoulder, her head a breath away from hitting the concrete.

The hairy guy tried to get up, fueled by adrenaline and hate, but before he was up, when he was still on his hands and knees, the Emperor kicked him again, a fast snap front kick to his forehead. He skittered back, blood seeping from his nose and ears and his breakfast coated his face, but he didn't move.

No one moved. They barely breathed. The ground was splattered with vomit and blood, and the only sound I heard was Drew's pounding heartbeat, until the Emperor shuffled one step over, to get to Aubrey.

She was on her side, tears of rage and fear spilling across her face, and when she tried to move the pain sliced at any composure she might have had. The Emperor reached a gloved hand down to help her up, but she shook her head; no, she wasn't getting up that easily. He gestured for her to roll onto her back, and then held her shoulder so that she could ease down gently. When she was ready, he crouched down and let her loop her arms around his neck, and then slowly stood up, helping her off the ground.

When she was on her feet, she slid a grateful hand to his cheek, and then startled, backing away sharply.

You don't touch the Emperor. That was a rule even then. I didn't know she had ever broken it.

"We have to go," Oz said sharply. "Now. Police are going to be here soon and the last thing we need is to be tagged as potential witnesses."

*

Zed was not going to be all right until he was sure of what the aftermath of Aubrey's assault had been. While we stood in front of the portal, ready to head home, he begged Oz to take one more leap, go forward just a few days. It didn't matter that he could go home and see their mother there; he needed to see the woman who had just been attacked in the Plaza. He needed to see for himself that she was not emotionally shredded and did not walk around flinching at every odd sound she heard.

"Just give him ten minutes," Finn said. "Don't leave him with something to chew on that he'll never be able to swallow."

There was a parklet nearby, a little slice of suburbanized quiet in the heart of downtown, one she remembered from stories the Emperor had told her. They met there often after Jackson's last class of the day, when he could pepper them both with questions to help clarify what he needed to study, or to share whatever odd fact he'd learned that day.

"It was as close to school as the Emperor was going to get. He helped Dad study, and learned along with him."

That amused Drew. "I can't picture the Emperor as a student. Maybe the principal or dean, standing at the entry with a giant ruler in hand, silently threatening to bop kids in the head."

Zed laughed. "Damn, Drew, what kind of freak school did you go to?"

"Our Lady of Perpetual Nonsense. We were right down the street from the military academy and a Catholic school. They rubbed off on us."

We arrived at the parklet before anyone else did; there were four picnic tables in the center, with swings and a set of monkey bars near the table farthest away from us, and a sand box next to it. Where we entered, the tiny park was bordered with wood fencing made from thick, round posts that suggested someone expected to tether their horse to it; the wood had split in places, but it was fine enough to lean against, and sturdy enough for Oz to sit on.

"What is this now?" Zed asked.

"Daycare playground. It was closed off about fifteen years ago, but when Dad was in school it was just a tiny public park and they hung out here. If they weren't here, they were hanging in Golden Gate Park or Ocean Beach. All the same places we still go."

I was glad they didn't speculate on what their parents did at the park or the beach; I had an idea, and knew those were things better left not discussed. If Zed had thought about asking her, the notion was cut off by Aubrey's arrival. Her left arm was in a sling, and she carried a book bag in her right hand, dropping it onto the picnic table far from us. Both of her arms had vivid black bruises wrapped around her biceps, and she sat slowly, bracing herself against the table top with her free hand.

Less than two minutes later, the Emperor—dressed in all black, from his high-topped sneakers, tight jeans, and even tighter t-shirt—followed. Just outside the parklet on the other side, there was a group of teenaged girls who were overtly watching him as they passed by; he pretended to ignore them, but grabbed onto the monkey bars and swung back and forth, flexing his muscles, before swinging down and sitting at the table across from Aubrey.

"Teenaged Emperor is ripped," Oz mused. "I wonder what happened."

"Middle age," Drew chuckled.

Zed grunted. "How would you even know now? He wears clothes that actually fit. He could still be in shape."

"Don't ruin my fun," Drew said, elbowing him. "This kid is not the old man who picked on me and stole my water balloons."

Finn was standing with his arms folded across his stomach and legs crossed at the ankles, and was far more serious. "If this were the late twentieth century or early twenty-first, I'd think he was Emo or Goth. If he was wearing eye liner and had painted black fingernails, I'd be sure of it. This is not the look I expected from him."

Whatever the Emperor was talking about, Aubrey was laughing with him. Oz asked Zed if that was enough for him to know she really was all right, but then Jackson was there, dumping his books onto the table. If Zed had been ready to go before, he wasn't about to leave now, not seeing how her face lit up when Jax leaned over to kiss her.

We stayed there against the fence for another twenty minutes; I watched while they pretended to be absorbed in their own conversation, as they stole glances at their parents and the Emperor. I warned them that we should go, but they were so intent on pretending to be focused on each other that no one noticed when the Emperor looked over at them, and then got up.

No one, except for me.

By the time he had halfway crossed the parklet, Oz finally noticed, and warned them to act casual. He stopped a few feet away, hands on hips, and regarded them coolly for a moment before asking, "What are you doing here?"

"Just hanging out," Oz said.

She almost sounded sure of herself.

"Sure," he said.

Finn pushed off the fence, and held his hand out. "They've been showing me around the city. I'm Finn. You are—?"

"Nice try. Don't touch me." He looked right at Oz. "Go home."

"Excuse me?"

"Go to the closest portal, and go home."

He turned without another word, and went back to the table.

Oz exhaled sharply, exasperated. "We're going home."

Finn was laughing under his breath. "He's just guessing, and you're obeying him as if he's *your* Emperor."

"Yeah, well, he recognized that we don't belong here. That's enough. Zed, are you all right? Satisfied that Mom was not rendered into a giant, gooey pile of unending tears?"

"She seemed fine," he admitted.

When we reached the portal, she took Drew's and Zed's hands, nodding for Finn to go lead the way.

"Oh, hell no. I'm not going through first. You go."

He suspected what she did not, and he was right. Waiting for us on the other side was the Emperor, and he did not look amused. Not one bit.

22

First, he took me from Drew. Then he used his pointy finger, which meant he was serious. He pointed at Drew, and then at Finn and Zed. "You," he said to Drew. "You're moving from the guest room to the apartment across the hall from mine. Go get some of your things, the rest can wait until daylight. You two, go help him. The apartment is unlocked right now, and the keys are on the kitchen counter."

Zed muttered, "Busted," but was laughing as they walked away. *Take me with you.*

Oz didn't watch as they left; instead she searched his face, looking for the truth of how angry he was. His feelings often eluded her; he could be angry, happy, amused, or sad, but the colors she saw swirling around him never changed.

"He's either telling the truth, always," the King told her when she asked why the Emperor's colors remained steady, "or he's a sociopath. Time will tell."

She guessed that he was more irritated than he was angry, and the irritation would fall away like a breath if she didn't try to make excuses.

"How did you know? Back then?"

He turned and headed in the same direction as the others,

knowing she would follow. "I have a sense of Other When, and in that moment, that's what you were to me."

Yeah, I don't think she believes that.

She fell into step next to him, though she had to walk faster to keep up and he wasn't about to slow down for her. "We weren't trying to pry. Finn was just curious about you, and then Zed really wanted to get a sense of who Mom and Dad were before we were born, and I couldn't think of a good reason to tell him no. I've never gone back to see them, and I think I wanted to. We didn't even really let Finn go spy on you."

I can hear you laughing at her inside your head. Finn thinks you're Emo, you know. Who's laughing now?

"Did you get that? A sense of who they were?"

"You ordered us to go home before we really could, and right now I realize how ridiculous it is that I listened, because you had no way of knowing who we were. Finn even pointed out that you were just guessing, but we came home anyway."

He didn't answer.

"It had to be more than feeling like we were Other When."

Silence.

"All right, fine. So you caught us taking a field trip. It's not against the rules. We were pretty careful."

"I remember that day, Oz. Do you understand how much you resemble your mother? As does Zed?"

"I didn't think of that."

"I didn't need to know you to realize who you might be. You need to be careful, and be cautious about whom you take along. Pressure from others—"

"I get it. Finn's curiosity wasn't reason enough to pry. But I think I also got a glimpse of time being changed."

She told him about watching her father speed down California Street, with the odd, tilted feeling that everything shifted, and seeing the ghost of the van that went through the intersection at the same time he did.

"And then you were there, when you hadn't been before."

"Perhaps you hadn't noticed me."

"I'd looked around. I was trying to be careful." She stopped, forcing him to stop, too. "Wait. He died, didn't he? He was hit by that van—you went back and changed it."

His mouth opened as if he was about to answer, but then closed for a few seconds more. She met his gaze without flinching, and I could feel him wanting to look away. "I protect the timeline, Oz. I don't destroy it." He began walking again, not checking to see if she followed.

I think she just rattled you, Emperor.

No, I know she did.

Her feet made stinging sounds on the pavement as she ran to catch up. "Something convinced you to change it. Just tell me the truth."

We were just to Union Square; he crossed the street and headed for the stairs, sitting three steps up, sighing as he did. "Tell me what I was supposed to do. My best friend—I'd saved his life once and I was not about to let it end like that. So yes, I changed it. I went back a few hours, warned myself, and then called traffic control to let them know their crown prince was about to do the most senseless and immature thing he ever would. They turned all the lights to red to stop cross traffic until he was safe at the bottom on the street."

Softly, astounded, she uttered, "You interfered."

"I re-set a broken timeline." He reminded her about the Old Mint and the plethora of information available to him. "Jax was always supposed to live. I merely fixed a hiccup."

"Just how many hiccups have you fixed?"

Are you squirming now, Emperor? It feels like you want to squirm.

She can sense it was more than once.

"Only the ones that broke my heart."

She sat next to him, and I wiggled out of his grasp to sit on the sidewalk in front of them.

I won't run off.

"Sausalito?"

Tell her the truth. Tell her how heavy a tiny coffin really is.

The world weighs less.

Tell her how it would have shredded your soul to have to handle her remains after they were pressed into a tiny, perfect gem. Tell her how you couldn't bear the idea. Just tell her.

His eyes filled with tears, and he couldn't just blink them away. "You were just a baby. This perfect little girl—" His voice wavered, and he couldn't stop it. "You'd made it all the way to the Wharf, but the damned ferry guide wouldn't let you on. You wandered off, probably looking for another way—that afternoon I watched as you were pulled from the water. Your face was blue and hair plastered over your eyes, and you..."

He choked on the words. "You couldn't swim, and I knew that timeline was never meant to be. So yes, I went back and warned myself, and then made the decision to let it play out again, but with exceptions. You'd been turned away from the ferry and fell into the water after that—I was sure that if you got on, I could keep you safe. So I let you take off to have your adventure, and I followed."

"Everyone knew who you were." She spoke softly, her voice cracking. "They'd do whatever you wanted."

"They played along. From the ferry guide on down, they saw me trailing you and gesturing to let you go. I was terrified the whole time. And your parents...they have no idea. They should never know."

"You've never allowed me to keep secrets from them." Nearly a whisper.

"I know."

"But this—is it something they can know someday, but not now?"

"They can never know I changed anything. Not for you, and not for Jax."

"It won't change their trust in you."

"Your father is a good man, Oz. And I don't mean just fundamentally. I mean, he is truly a good person. Yet...if he knew time was shifted on his behalf and everything was seemingly fine after that, it plants in his head the idea that going back and changing things for the greater good is reasonable. And as King—there are a million things he would be tempted to change."

"Change them enough and you cease being good," Oz murmured.

"Change them enough, and you feel like God."

"I get it," she said. "Tell me one more thing?"

"If I can."

"Why is Drew being moved?"

She's baiting you, dude.

Relieved, he smiled. "Because he's no longer just your friend. Keeping him two doors down from you is no longer appropriate."

"So giving him his own place with tons more privacy was the better idea? Sure, give two teenagers access to a private apartment with a locking door. What could go wrong?"

"You forget something. I'm right across the hall, and am far worse for him than your parents. They love him like a son. I see him for the love-struck little hornball that he really is. And I rarely sleep."

"He's not love-struck," she said, laughing.

"Oz." He spoke gently, the way he did was she was small and sticky, when he wanted her to know he understood her, even if she didn't understand herself. "You've known each other your entire lives and for the last several years have spoken almost daily. I bet you even texted him first thing every morning, just to say hello. He didn't move here to get to know you better. He already knows you. He came because he loves you. And you wouldn't have been so eager for him to come if you didn't already love him, too. And now? You're both adults."

She let that soak in. "Meaning?"

"He's not merely a house guest. He lives here now. He needs his own space and we all need to trust you both to decide what this all means for you." Then lightly, he added, "I have never been a teenaged girl, but I imagine they have all those same confusions and impulses and wants that I had when I was your age. Whether to act on them? That's your choice."

"I'm only eighteen, Emperor. Not exactly an adult."

"Fine, you're a starter-adult. And you're leaps and bounds ahead of where your father was at your age, and he was on the cusp of being head over heels in love and thinking about marriage. That he waited two years? I was surprised."

"I'm not there yet. I'm not even *there* yet. I don't think Drew is, either."

"Good. I'm not ready for you to be there yet. The idea makes me feel old, no matter how much that boy adores you." He got up.

"Come on, morning is only a few hours away. At least pretend to sleep before your mother tries to feed you like a linebacker."

*

Around four in the morning, I crept into the Emperor's apartment, counting on him being awake. He was in his living room with an old, tattered book in hand and a glass of scotch was on the end table next to his comfy chair. I knew what he was drinking—single malt, Highlands, on the rocks, though I was certain the rocks were actually just ice cubes—because I could smell it the moment I was in the room.

Follow me.

He peered over the top of his book. "You probably didn't get fed tonight, did you? Between the party and the field trip—"

Food would be nice. But follow me.

I headed for the cat flap, and he said, "I can feed you here, you know, I have the canned food that you like. I don't know why you like it since it smells like death coughed up a hairball, but I have it."

I waited in the hallway for him to get the hint, and then headed up the stairs as he closed his door. I knew he would follow me, even when I didn't head for the staff kitchen where the cheese and salami lived, but kept going up until I had led him out to the balcony, where Oz was sitting, alone.

She needs company.

I know she heard us. Her head tilted a little, but she didn't turn to look. When the Emperor sat in the chair next to her, she said thickly, "I couldn't swim."

He jumped right onto her train of thought. "Not then."

"When I was six, probably around the time I'd gone off to find cupcakes in Sausalito, Dad had the basement pool cleaned and re-filled, and you started teaching Zed and me how to swim. I remember my parents talking about it. They didn't understand why it was suddenly so important to you that we learn. You were demanding this one thing when you'd never really demanded anything before, and you weren't going to let it go. I also started karate around then. Was that your doing, too? Making sure I could kick the crap out of anyone who bothered me?"

He inhaled slowly, deeply, taking his time.

He wanted me to swim, too, but I refused to get in the water.

Okay, not really. I watched, though. Zed loved splashing you and making you mad. I liked seeing you splash the Emperor, right in the face. He pretended to be upset but he wasn't, really. He just wanted you to pay attention.

"I was there the day you were born," he finally said. "I paced the hall outside the delivery room with your grandparents, terrified because I could hear your mother's pain through the closed door, and the few times your father came out to update us, he was near tears. You were being terribly stubborn about the whole ordeal, refusing to budge even after twenty-four hours. Your grandfather swore you'd latched onto a rib and didn't understand it was time to let go."

He was proud of that, you know.

"And then you were there. Your first cry exploded all around us—it was glorious, as if you were both formally announcing yourself and warning that we'd all better be on our toes. I was the first to hold you, after your parents did. Before your grandparents, even, which endeared me to your grandmother even less. I looked at your tiny, perfect face, and you stared right back at me, and it felt like you were saying 'hello, I already know you.'"

I remember that. She was loud.

"A switch flipped and I knew I loved you almost as much as your parents did. I never expected that. I thought I would be amused with your antics and how easily you were going to turn all the adults around you into babbling idiots, but I had no idea how protective I would feel and how deeply I would love you, just like that. I swore to you then, and to your parents, that I would do whatever I had to in order to keep you safe. Anything. And I failed. I was not going to fail again. So yes, you learned to swim, and you learned to fight, and I have annoyed you throughout your life with random what-if questions for no reason other than to teach you to think."

"You didn't fail. I'm still here."

"But you *weren't*, Oz. For that sliver of time, you were gone. And that's the cruel trick of changing time. The memories go with you. The Emperor that changed time somehow became the me of now. I don't know how, but I remember it all. Know that—the memories stick to you."

Now you know how it works.

I jumped onto his lap and curled up, hoping the wind didn't pick up enough to carry me over the side of the balcony. I wasn't worried about the birds that late at night, but the wind didn't sleep and it could be sneaky. Not there one moment, blink, and there it is, swooping down on a kitty, making him worry about the height of the balcony wall. If I hadn't thought the Emperor needed me, I would have stayed lower to the ground.

He set his hands across my back, holding me in place.

I was almost asleep when he spoke again.

"I'll never have children, Oz. Your parents have been more than gracious to allow me into your life at the intrusive levels that they have. And it's not because I saved Jax's life when he was a little boy."

"I know. You're basically brothers."

"I love you as if you were my own and you *are* my family. I need you to know that. Whatever happens with sending Finn home, if I've made a critical mistake in my calculations, or if something happens after—I desperately, selfishly need you to know."

"I already did."

"And if Finn—"

"He'll be fine. You don't make sloppy mistakes."

Tell her.

"I know Finn is curious about me, like I'm a puzzle he wants to complete before he goes home. I understand that it's mostly because he's trying to distract himself from the gorier what-if ideas, but please...don't help him with that anymore."

"All right."

"Thank you. Now go to bed, really. I'll explain to your mother why you're not at breakfast. She'll understand that you were keeping the resident insomniac company."

Oz got up. "I also won't ask why you're so pensive lately and why it feels like right now you're trying to not break in two. Whatever it is...you have to know that we love you, too, and that won't change, no matter what."

When she was gone, I head-butted his chest.

I sat through all that without horking. I deserve a treat.

He kissed the top of my head. "I promised to keep you safe, too."

You do whatever has to be done. I'll be fine no matter what.

With an exaggerated grunt, he held me a little tighter and stood up. "And now we go get the King, because that girl is not going to stay in bed. Actually—" he set me down "—you should go get some food and some sleep. I know where she's going."

You have time, right? Let the King sleep another hour. He held the door for me, and started for the family apartment instead of coming with me. *Follow me, all right?*

"Seriously, Wick, somewhere around here there's a dish filled with dry food for you. Have you ever considered actually trying it? You might like it."

Dry food is for peasants. Follow me.

I headed up the stairs. I could practically hear him rolling his eyes, the squishy clicking sound they made inside his head, but he followed me up to the roof where Drew was laying in the grass, on his back. He lingered at the door—this was neither Oz nor Zed, and intruding might be overstepping—but after some consideration (plus, I meowed loudly, so Drew knew we were there) he went over and laid down on the grass next to Drew.

He folded his arms and rested his head on his hands. "I know what Oz would be looking for if she were here staring up at the stars. She used to come out here to search for the space station or the abandoned Elysium Project. Often she hoped to see starships speeding away from Earth. I have no idea what you might be looking for."

Sleepily, Drew asked, "What's the Elysium Project?"

"It was an artificial utopian planetoid that would have existed in orbit, if it had been completed. It may be, one day."

"Ah. I know it as 'that damned space planet.' Midlam was not on board with it."

"Pacifica had hopes for it and invested heavily in its construction. It's still in the hands of the United Kingdom, and hasn't been completely discarded. Your grandchildren could live there one day."

"There's a scary thought. If I have grandkids, that means I had kids. Tiny people I can really screw up."

"You don't want children?"

"I suppose. I've never thought much about it. I'd need to actually, you know...*be* with someone."

"Someone else would help, yes."

I crawled between them, and stretched out. I thought about trying to see what was so fascinating about the night sky, but that would require exposing my belly, and I didn't trust Drew to not poke it, or even just touch it. Scratch gently under my arms, sure, but touch my tummy and you draw back a bloody stump.

If it had been Oz, I would have risked it. We found her several times, late at night, laying there the same way Drew was, flat on her back and staring up at the stars. That was long before she realized that the path she was on was fixed, when she dreamed about finding out what it would be like to go into space, and then just a few times after, when she thought she could find a way to do it all.

The Emperor never wanted to take that away from her. They laid on the grass, and mused about Elysium and what might be beyond it, never talking about the day when she would put all the dreams behind her and take on the crown, and with it the nation.

Somewhere along the line she started thinking about that on her own, though she might have had Drew's help.

Drew was quiet long enough that I thought he'd fallen asleep. His breathing wasn't quite shallow enough, but it was slow and even, and right when I thought I would get up and leave them both to sleeping on the roof he asked, "Have you ever been in love, Emperor?"

Well, now. Let's go for the really personal questions, right out of nowhere.

I didn't think he would answer. I was ready to jump up and move so that he could get up and stomp off without accidentally stepping on me, but instead he stayed still, letting the seconds tick off like heavy, weighted drops of regret, long enough that Drew squirmed a bit.

When he spoke, his voice sounded thick. "I have loved, but I have never been in love."

"No girlfriends, no one you wanted to—"

"No romantic relationships. Why?"

"I'm trying to figure out what comes next with Oz. Like, what does she expect from me? Or want? Or need? And what *shouldn't* I do?"

"I thought the two of you had already figured that out. Isn't that why you came here?"

Dude, just ask her.

"We have plans. But we never talked about how to get from making those plans to making them happen, and I honestly have no idea how she really feels. Even worse, I didn't even think about it until we went back and saw her parents together. I could *feel* how crazy they were about each other. And man, you sit at a dinner table with them and you can still feel it, even when they're not looking at each other. Like, they were meant to be, you know?"

"Indeed."

"And since we got back and you threw me out of the guest room—"

"All of two hours ago."

"—all I've been thinking about is that I know how *I* feel, but I don't think that's what people see when they look at us, and I don't want to be the one who keeps her from finding that, but I also don't want to not be the guy she does. Find it with, I mean. If that makes sense?"

"I have learned to follow many wandering trains of thought. It makes sense."

Glad you could. I thought the train derailed somewhere around 'since we got back.'

"Back home? I didn't really go out with anyone else because I didn't feel like I should, but my friends paired off like little freaks and I watched the insanity up close, and I wanted all of that. Well, except for how they treated each other, like of *course* all these girls would fall all over them and do whatever they wanted and the girls weren't any better. I didn't really fit in that way, you know? But Oz isn't like them, she doesn't act all entitled or anything and I feel like I have to keep more than a respectful distance because it's *Oz*, but then I don't know—"

"Andrew. Take a deep breath. You're overthinking."

"I *have* to overthink. Oz isn't like my other friends. And I won't treat her the way they do each other. But damn. It wouldn't take much for me to do something stupid."

"Your feelings are not stupid."

"No, but my actions? Totally could be."

"You kissed her tonight. Did she kiss you back?"

"Well, yeah, but—"

"Stop. I'll tell you the same thing I told Jax when he worried that Aubrey was so far out of his league that they might as well live on different continents. Talk to her. Be yourself, be truthful, and *talk* to her. If she wants something different than you do, she'll let you know."

"But I'm not sure…"

"Who is?" He got up, slowly. "Kiss the girl, Drew. Kiss her again. And then again. If she doesn't push you away, tell her how you really feel, and don't mince words."

"But—"

"That look you see with Jax and Aubrey? That didn't happen until he stepped up and was honest with her. Be honest, and then be prepared to wait for her heart and her brain to catch up to yours. And if it's sex that's tripping you up, she'll let you know about that as well. But talk."

He headed for the door, and I got up to follow him.

"Emperor? Do you have any regrets?"

"About?"

"Not having that."

He pulled the door open. "Every day."

*

The Emperor headed for the family's apartment to wake the King, and I went looking for Oz. He suspected that she would lose the battle with sleep and sneak out again; I didn't know where she was going and I wanted to see. I went into her bedroom first, and the bed was unmade and still warm, so I ran down the stairs and saw her just as she slipped out the front door. I bolted through the cat flap and followed.

Instead of heading to the portal on Union Square, she walked close to the building where she was less likely to be seen from the balcony or windows and made her way toward the one on Market

Street. I raced after her to catch up, and just before she was about to enter it she heard me and turned.

I want to go, too. Take me with you.

She didn't want to; I could see that. But she also wasn't going to leave me standing there on the sidewalk alone in the middle of the night. With an exasperated "Fine," she tucked me under her arm and carried me through. We popped out into the dark of night, without even light from the lamp posts to give us a little bit of clear vision.

Well, I could see. I don't think Oz could. She knew her way, regardless, and headed toward the Plaza, lingering at the curve where Market turned to Steuart. There were working lampposts there, and I could see what she had come for: half a block down, just outside Aubrey's apartment, the young Emperor was waiting. He was leaning with his back against the wall, staring at his phone, but he saw movement from the corner of his eye, and turned his head to see what it was.

I think we should go. He won't like this.

Oz stood her ground, but she shifted me to her shoulder, either to give me a better view or to have her hands ready to sucker punch him.

Let's not hit him. He is still the Emperor, after all.

When he reached her, he waited a moment, regarding her with the same cool indifference he had before, trying to make her squirm. When she didn't react, he sighed and said, "Didn't I tell you to go home?"

"Did I say that I would?"

"Yeah, you kind of did. I heard you tell your friends it was time to leave. So, what? You took them home and came back?"

"Something like that. But that was also weeks ago, wasn't it?"

He shoved his phone into his pocket, and his hands went to his hips. I recognized that posture. It was his *I have a dozen things to say to you and none of them will come out kindly, and I'm a bit irritated right now* stance. He used it a lot when she was little, and the beat of quiet before he spoke always made her squirm, and then when she was older, think.

She had to understand it; he was upset and trying to not go off on her.

You looked at Jax like that a lot, too. Or do. I dunno, my brain hurts.

"Look, you shouldn't be here. You don't want them to see you and to start asking questions. Jax will figure it out, and he shouldn't."

"He has no way—"

"You *look* like her. He can time travel. It wouldn't take him but a minute to do the math."

"But—"

"All right, then don't rob them of the joy of meeting their first child for the actual first time. They're not married yet and shouldn't know that they will be. And if they know you're on the horizon—unless something horrible has happened and you have a purpose other than curiosity for being here—things might change. Spare them. Go home. Or visit some other When. Just not here."

She looked past him; down the street, walking hand in hand and giggling at their own private joke, were her parents. Aubrey was leaning into Jax and she reached across herself to squeeze his arm with her free hand. Then they stopped, under the light, just long enough for a few stolen kisses.

He turned to look, too, and softened a bit.

"Come on, I'll walk a bit with you."

She fell into step next to him. "It's a little late for them to be out, isn't it?"

"I could say the same for you."

"It could be the middle of the afternoon for me. You don't know."

"Indeed, I don't. And yes. It's late, and yes, I'm their excuse. The Queen is not amused by this romance and would be fairly unhappy if she knew he was out this late alone with her."

"Wait. Really?"

"Don't tell me. If she likes Aubrey later, I'll find out for myself."

"Well, no, that's not what I was thinking. I just—"

"Didn't realize they had hormones and feelings? I'm fairly certain my parents never did, either. Yet, here I am."

At that, she laughed. He led her past the portal on Market Street toward the one on Union Square; it didn't surprise me, his wanting to linger for a bit. He was even more inquisitive when he was younger than he was in middle age, and I could practically hear the gears of his brain squeaking as he thought of a hundred things to ask her, even when he knew he should not.

We were at the far end of the royal house, with Union Square just ahead, when he stopped. "I'll distract them long enough for you get to the portal without being seen. And I'm sorry, I do understand that you just wanted to see them, even if you never had the chance to speak to them."

"That was just a small part of it. I came because I wanted to see you."

He reached up to scratch the top of my head. "I'm sure you will, just step through the portal."

"How old are you, Emperor?"

The smile he fought tugged at the corners of his mouth. "So you really do know who I am. I'm eighteen. Why?"

"You were fifteen when you saved the prince's life. He's nineteen now."

"Funny how that works. Now go."

He turned abruptly and hurried off. I knew she wanted to go after him, but I also knew she shouldn't, so I started to slip my way off her shoulder, forcing her to catch me.

Don't feel bad. Even then he could be a bit of a—

We were halfway up the steps when she groaned, "Oh great."

Standing just outside the portal was the Emperor, our Emperor. And next to him was the King. She hesitated and I thought she was going to turn and run, but instead she hoisted me a bit closer and stomped all the way up.

"All right," the Emperor said. "So far I've told you to go home twice, and to bed twice. If you won't listen to me, listen to your father."

"To be fair, you were only my age when you told me to go home, so I don't think that counts."

Ha. She's not wrong.

Jax didn't seem all that interested in shoving her through the portal to go home. Instead, he stepped away from it and sat down on the capstone of one of the giant planter boxes that dotted the corners of the Square. He was looking down the street, where the young Emperor and his own younger self had turned the corner with Aubrey, and we could hear their laughter.

"My God, we were young," he breathed. "Don't think I've never done this exact same thing, Oz. I took a few ill-advised trips to witness my own parents' beginnings."

"You spied on Grandma and Grandad? I have a hard time imagining that."

What, like you didn't just do that?

"They were always so reserved. I don't think I ever saw them touch at all, not until she was dying. I had a hard time imagining how they ever could have been together, and I certainly couldn't imagine how it started at all. So I went, hid as much in the shadows as I could, and saw bits and pieces as they fell in love. They were still reserved, but… I could see it. And then I mourned it, because it felt like somewhere along the way they lost it."

They just didn't let you see it. He made her laugh, really hard. So hard once she threw up, right there in the trash can next to the throne.

"I was determined that I would never love so secretly that my kids would feel like they needed proof. If you did, I'm sorry."

"I didn't, Dad. If anything, it's the opposite."

"You two are still fairly handsy," the Emperor teased. "Imagine living through the start of it all, Oz. All the smooching, the drooling, the groping—"

"That's enough," the King said.

"And yet, for some odd reason she just wanted to come here and ask me my age."

Across the street, the young Emperor was walking backwards, mocking his friends with obnoxious kissing sounds. When they made it to the door, as Jax and Aubrey went in, he turned and waved.

The Emperor returned the gesture. "In five minutes all hell will break loose when the Queen finds us heading for the roof in the middle of the night, and Jax has to explain why he was not in his room when she looked for him hours earlier."

"Yeah, and you laughed your ass off about it. You got to go home, and I had to stand there and take it."

"Why *were* you out so late at night, Dad?"

"I was nineteen, Ozzie. I don't need to explain."

"Remember that," the Emperor said. "A month from now when you catch her in Drew's apartment at three in the morning—she's an adult. She doesn't need to explain."

"You. Shut up."

"Why? Because your daughter now knows what a hornball you were?" To her he said, "He was a teenaged boy. They're all hornballs. She was a grown woman, and she loved him."

"I don't need to hear this," Oz said.

"Neither do I," the King said. "You're enjoying this, aren't you?"

"Little bit, yeah."

"Home," the King sighed.

Just before he went through the portal, the Emperor leaned over and whispered to Oz, "I'm on your side in this. Whatever you feel for Drew is entirely appropriate and you have every right to show him. But make no mistake, if he hurts you, I will—to quote you—end him."

"Thank you," she said when she was on the other side. "But right now? I need to go scrub the image of my parents pawing at each other out of my brain." She handed me to him. "Really. Just…ew."

23

Two days later, at holy-bejeezus-o'clock in the morning, the Queen was trying to convince Finn that he needed to eat. On the table in front of him was a plate heaping with scrambled eggs and bacon and toast, and he stared at it like it was about to come to life and swallow him whole.

I watched from the counter; the King had already told me to get down three times, and each time the Queen waved him off, telling him I wasn't hurting anything.

Everyone else picked at their food, too. The King went through the motions of eating by taking temperamental-toddler-sized bites and the Emperor sat there breaking apart pieces of bacon until he had a layer of pork confetti strewn across his eggs, but he didn't eat any of them. I don't think she cared whether they ate or not, but Finn was leaving and she was not sending him off with an empty stomach.

Finn, on the other hand, thought an empty stomach was the wiser choice, because there was a very real chance he would throw it all back up before leaving the house.

"One of two things will happen. Either I'll die in a horrible explosion when my ship hits the gate, or I'll suddenly be home, trying to explain to my wife why I thought letting her jump off the Golden Gate Bridge was a sterling idea."

The Queen was flitting around the kitchen—she wasn't eating, either, and no one dared tell her she needed to—and she grabbed a bottle of orange juice from the refrigerator and set it in front of Finn. "Sweetheart, it's not like you planned on throwing her off the bridge yourself."

"The frame of mind I was in? I'm not sure."

She stood behind his chair and bent over to plant a kiss on the top of his head. "Oz can see the truth in you, Finn. You never would. I promise you that."

I'll take a head kiss since you're handing them out.

"Hush, Wick. You'll get something to eat when we're done."

That's not what I asked for. Besides, at this rate no one will ever be done and I'll die of old age while the bacon gets cold.

"Your wife was amused, Finn," the Emperor said. "Expect to be made fun of for a long time to come, but she won't be angry or hurt."

I jumped from the counter to the table, risking the King's ire.

Yeah, if you're not going to eat that, can I have your bacon?

The Emperor grabbed me and pulled me to his lap before the King could react, but I still felt the daggers from his unhappy glare. Finn broke a piece of his bacon in half and held it out to me, and he grinned when I took it.

It worked! Dang, dude, you need to stay! I have you trained!

After I'd eaten that piece, the Emperor gave me a few of the ones he'd already broken up.

"You spoil him," the King grumbled.

"Always." The Emperor leaned down and whispered into my ear, "I promise. Always."

24

The Ferry Building was blocked off to the public and the actual ferries were being held back in Sausalito, Vallejo, and Oakland, which was sure to cause some public grumbling. The walkway on the back side of the building closest to the bridge was cluttered with cameras pointing to various spots on the bridge, and there were several video monitors so Oz and her family could watch, both from a distance and up close, as Finn and the Emperor made the final preparations for his ship to go through the gate. I wanted to be on the bridge with them, hanging halfway out of the Emperor's sweatshirt as he gave Finn his last instructions, but I was on the cold cement walkway, waiting with everyone else.

I'd been with them the night before, as the Emperor drummed into Finn the sequence he needed to follow and thought that for continuity's sake—for luck—I should be there, but just before he got into the transport van with Finn he handed me off to Drew.

Drew let me sit on a stool he'd pulled from inside the Ferry Building, and he lined me up right in front of a monitor so that I could watch. Oz stood protectively behind me, and I could see her reflection in the screen. She switched from watching on the monitor to looking at the bridge a dozen times in just a few minutes, torn between what she wanted to really see.

From the dock, Finn's ship looked like a bright white spot floating just about the bridge's railing. On the monitor, with the wing door open and the empty seat waiting there for Finn to strap himself into, it felt ominous. The camera mounted to my right followed as the Emperor walked with from the ship to the gate, which was set up halfway to Treasure Island, and displayed them on the monitor just below it. The Emperor did a lot of gesturing, pointing to the top and the sides of the gate, but there was no sound, so I could only guess what they were talking about.

This side of the gate will kill you first if you run into it; this other side will hurt worse. So don't run into them, all right? There's a laser bolted to the rods on top but it's not the exploding kind of laser, so don't worry when it hits the ship, unless it really does blow up. Then you can worry.

The ship was closer to us, not far from the on-ramp, so we also watched them walk back to it, and they moved much slower than they had been. Finn's gait was peppered by micro-hesitations and he clearly wanted to throw up over the side of the bridge. The Emperor was in no hurry, either, and the distance between him and Finn narrowed quite a bit, but he was still very careful to not get close enough that there would be an incident of accidental touching.

Then they were at the ship, and we watched as Finn climbed in and strapped himself down, a harness over his chest and belt over his hips. The Emperor leaned down to say something to Finn, and the expression on his face changed from nauseated worry to abrupt surprise.

But then the Emperor slammed the door closed, and walked away.

Finn's ship became a static image on the screen; we looked up and watched as the Emperor climbed back into the transport van, and as every guard that had kept watch over the ship and the gate left the bridge. Fifteen minutes later the only living thing on the Emperor's Bridge was Finn; it had been cleared from both ends, in San Francisco and in Oakland, because no one knew for sure if the amount of electricity going to the gate would stay contained within it, or blow up.

It wasn't until then, while we waited for the Emperor, that I started to worry. I wasn't even sure why, but it felt important enough to worry about; Finn had heard me ask for bacon and he'd given it to me. That meant he needed to be all right.

Ten minutes later the Emperor came out the back door of the Ferry Building. He looked pale, his black hair like strands of spilt ink as it whipped around his face in the breeze. He barely glanced at me and didn't look at anyone else at all; he looked at the monitor, and then up at the bridge, then lifted his communicator and spoke into it.

"All right, Finn, power it up."

Your hand. It's kind of shaky.

The whine of the engine reverberated all the way to the dock. It sounded like angry bees couched in distant thunder, and it was not a happy noise.

"As soon as you're in motion, you need to have your hand hovering over that big red button in the center of the console."

Finn's voice crackled through the speaker. "I know. The absurdly large red round thing. Can't miss it. When my screen flashes, hit it."

"No hesitations. Your hand needs to be moving before you're even thinking about it."

"No worries. Three. Two. One." The ship began to move. "And thank you. All of you."

With that, Finn's ship was rocketing toward the gate, and with the press of a single one of the Emperor's fingers on a remote switch, the gate lit up and Finn shot through it, the sound like a crack of lightning that swelled and then echoed for several seconds.

When the echo died off, all that remained was ringing in my ears and a desperate need to know if it worked. Using the remote, the Emperor changed the angle on the cameras, looking down past the gate. There was nothing there. No ship, no burn marks, no sign that Finn had ever been there, other than the gate itself.

In the time it took to blink, he was gone.

Into his communicator the Emperor said, "All right. Bury the cables under the street and create an access point. The King wants them available to use."

"That's it?" Drew muttered.

I got up and head-butted the Emperor's hip.

Tell us he's okay.

"Yeah, that's it," he said. "He made it through."

The King moved closer to the monitor, staring at the emptiness behind the gate. "You're sure?"

"The bridge didn't blow up and there aren't pieces of his ship littering the far side of the gate. We have to assume he made it."

The Queen grabbed onto the King's arm, and leaned into him. "I'll miss him. No one else has ever liked my meatloaf the way he did."

The King smiled, but his eyes didn't look as happy as his mouth.

I'm not sure what they expected, but that's what was supposed to happen. Finn was there, and then he was not. That was the plan. It was what they *wanted*. Without saying anything else, they fell away one by one, all but Oz, Drew and the Emperor. The guards left with the King and Queen, and for a moment the quiet on the dock was so loud I could feel it buzzing on my whiskers.

Finally, Oz broke the silence. "Just before you closed the door to his ship, you said something to him, and he looked very surprised."

"He did, didn't he?"

"Emperor."

"It was like I'd told him 'happy birthday, you're getting a puppy—but not until next year. And then only if you eat your vegetables every night.'"

"*Emperor.*"

He wanted to keep it for himself, that look of complete surprise on Finn's face. He blinked slowly, like his eyelids were too heavy to hold up but he had to because no one wants to stand there with their eyes closed when there are other people around. You might trust them, but who knows what they'll really do?

No one thought Oz or Drew would touch him, but people are people and sometimes people can't resist doing the things they're not supposed to.

"I told him I would see him in three days."

"You're going there? How? They're pulling the power cables from the gate and the portals don't go forward."

"I'm not going anywhere. And neither are you. The portals are now forbidden, and I'm going to ask you to not press me on that."

"All right. So he's coming here. Without the gate."

"Indeed."

"How?" Drew asked.

"He'll invent the portals," the Emperor answered, as if it were so simple.

Drew exhaled sharply. "Wow."

Oz was less impressed. "So he's not coming back in three days."

"He is. But it will be three days for us, a few years for him. I just needed him to know he hadn't seen the last of us."

"Yet in three days he's going to expect to see you, and when he doesn't? That's not fair, Emperor."

"It was a weak moment, I admit that."

She waited for an explanation; they stared at each other until even I was uncomfortable, and I can out-stare almost anyone.

Just when I thought she was about to give up, he blinked. "Give me your hand."

She hesitated, but then finally extended her hand, palm-side up. Very carefully, he set his hand on top of hers, watching her face, waiting for that moment when she understood.

After a moment her eyes went wide and flooded with tears, and she reached out, wrapping him in a tight hug he hadn't asked for and normally would have stepped away from, but his arms went around her and he buried his face against the top of her head.

"I'm sorry," she said against his shoulder. "I am so, so sorry."

25

That night, I did something I rarely did with the Emperor: as he slept, I curled up on his chest, riding the rise and fall of each breath and heartbeat, and I listened for his dreams. I did it frequently for Oz and Zed when they were little, nestling near their heads and peeking into the things their minds created late at night, and more recently when I was trying to make Oz hear me, but the Emperor didn't often sleep, and when he did he tossed and turned too much for a cat to be safe near him.

The dreams he had when he was new to the city had sometimes worried me. He was adrift in most of them, wrapped in a tight cocoon of loneliness, wanting desperately to not be the last human alive yet not feeling like he was a part of anything. I tried to tell him, whispering in his ear, that there were friendly people around him, and the prince's father respected him. He would never really be alone.

I couldn't convince him; he knew what I didn't completely understand, that he could be alone in a room filled with people, and he would run before letting any of them get too close.

Getting close meant getting *close*, and he couldn't afford to risk that.

"It's not that they would touch me, Wick," he once said, "but that they would then know me."

Now he dreamed about home.
I can take you there. I think I remember how.
He wanted home to come to him.
I couldn't give him that.

*

The day after Finn left, a one-hundred-twenty-three-year-old woman named Henryetta Briggsman, who walked from her apartment a block down from the royal family house to the Plaza every day, just to enjoy the sunshine or fog or rain—it didn't matter because she loved it all and she didn't care how long it took her to get there and back—died in her sleep. She was found by her caregiver, curled up in bed with a very old and page-worn book in hand, her recently adopted cat curled up on her pillow next to her face, and soft music filtered through her radio.

Zed went back to work, reasoning that she deserved to be spoken for, and he had cared about her; any number of people could prepare her body, but he needed to speak to her life—he had known her, and he loved how positive she was, secure enough to bring home a kitten when she herself was long past the century mark—and he wanted to send her off with the same kindness in which she had lived.

He brought the cat home with him, to watch over until he could deliver him to her caregiver. I would have welcomed the cat to stay, but he was tiny and scared, and the caregiver loved him and wanted him. Zed brought him home just before dinner time, when the Queen had demanded that everyone—including the Emperor—sit down to have a real family meal.

The King made it clear: "You will give her this, because she's a little bit sad and having you all here will make her happy. And when dinner is over, you're not leaving. Stay and pay attention to her, and so help me if she cries, I'll behead whoever is responsible."

Zed knew that a kitten, even for an evening, would make her smile. The little ball of fluff was no bigger than half of me, and I was never a big guy. He huddled in the corner of a plastic pet carrier, mewling in a tiny, frightened voice, and Zed had to reach inside to get him.

"He's friendly," Zed told the terrified ball of fur, nodding toward me. "He won't eat you."

Well, not this close to dinner. After that, it depends on what we had.

"He's beautiful," Oz cooed, reaching out to stroke the top of his head. "What's his name?"

"Major."

I heard the Emperor suck in a breath; he quietly excused himself and got up from his chair, leaving the room. Aubrey started to follow, but Oz stopped her.

"He's exhausted, Mom. Let him be."

She still wanted to go after him, but instead picked me up, kissed the top of my head, and said, "Go keep an eye on him, Wick. I promise, I'll save you some food."

Give some to the Major. I think I've been in the army. It's hard work and makes a guy hungry.

I followed the Emperor to the balcony and jumped up onto his lap. He was too close to the edge for my taste, but I couldn't supervise him well enough if I sat in my usual spot. He stared at the sky, barely blinking, and his hands settled on my back, holding me close.

The King's gonna behead you now, you know.

"I won't let you fall, Wick."

I know you won't.

"You won't let me fall, either."

Not if I can help it. Your head, on the other hand…if it rolls, I won't be able to stop it and staple it back on for you. You're on your own with that.

"I know he's coming back. Intellectually, I know he made it home and that he'll come back. But what if he doesn't? What then, Mister Wick?"

We grow old and die, same as always.

"I went to the Old Mint this morning. I rechecked the data and compared the newest reports with the last I'd seen. The gate—that was new. I should have just fixed his ship. That's all I was ever meant to do, just fix the ship and send him home. I shouldn't have changed anything, not yet. Not without his permission."

I stood up, my front paws on his chest, and looked him in the eyes.

You're still here. I'm still here. Oz is still here. Oh! I saw her with Drew in his living room last night and they had music playing and they were dancing. Not even that weird up and down spastic hopping rabbit dancing that you do. They slow danced and there wasn't even any space between them. I think he was going to kiss her but I left before that because it didn't seem like I should stay. I mean, they had the door open but I think that was because they were afraid you'd break it down if they didn't.

He bopped heads with me, softly. "You are indeed my anchor. Whatever happens, for that I am forever grateful."

Take me back to dinner. The Queen wants you there and she'll make you feel happier. Plus, you'll get to keep your head, and there's real live fresh dead meat, and I don't want that little wad of fur to get it all. Life's too short to skip the good stuff.

"He'll come back," the Emperor said, getting up. "They both will."

*

By the time we'd gone back to the living room, the Emperor had made up his mind to be as pleasant as he could, and shoved to the back of his mind the things that were bothering him. He played with the kitten (though he refused to call him by name, instead calling him "Puffball," which seemed to fit) and let him sit on his shoulder until he mewed loudly to be saved, because the Emperor's shoulder was almost six feet from the ground and was a scary place for a baby to be. He then talked to Zed about how different it felt to speak for Mrs. Briggsman, how it was a happy thing and not weighed down by the guilt he'd felt saying goodbye to the Miller babies. Mrs. Briggsman had lived the life she wanted and left when she was ready. When he really thought about it, most of the people he prepared and spoke for were like that: older and content. The tragedies were the anomalies, and he thought he could learn to deal with them.

He engaged Drew without growling, and learned that his mother had taken his father's name—officially changing the name of the

Royal House, which was unheard of in Midlam and caused a bit of scandal—because she thought that the House of Van Hoff sounded a bit more regal than the House of Mor, and because it *really* pissed her father off. The Emperor teased him (when the King and Queen were not within earshot, because the King did not like to discuss Drew and Oz's plans) about eventually changing his own name, but Drew didn't take the bait. He reminded the Emperor that he didn't have to change his name, but wasn't opposed to it. His only concern about names was what Midlam and Pacifica would become once they merged.

"The United States of Oz," the Emperor suggested, which was met by exaggerated groans.

When dinner was over, he chased the teenagers from the kitchen, insisting that he and the King would clean up while they entertained the Queen in the living room. The King grumbled but relented, because it was supposed to be all about the Queen, anyway, and she wanted to spend time with the kids. I watched from the counter, risking the King's ire and really risking that he might squirt me with water from the sink faucet, but he let me be while he dried off and then put away each dish that the Emperor handed him.

Well, this is no fun, not if it doesn't bother him.

I left them to finish without my supervision.

In the living room, the Queen was showing old pictures to the kids on the video monitor; there were embarrassing naked baby pictures that Zed threatened to delete, and there were pictures of Oz at karate tournaments and Zed playing basketball, and a few of them in the basement swimming pool with the Emperor—prompting Drew to wonder out loud why he swam with a shirt on— but none went back any older than Oz's infancy.

"Come on," Oz said, "I know you have pictures from when you were kids."

The Queen flipped through a list of folders that were on the computer. "None of my childhood photos are on here, but I'm sure your dad's are." She settled on a folder that was labeled as his late teen years and clicked on it.

When the first picture loaded, Drew uttered, "Holy hell."

From behind us the Emperor said, "Hey. I was not *that* bad

looking." He leaned against the dining room entry, arms folded, looking at a giant picture of himself.

In the photo, his hair curled over his ears and forehead, and he had a mustache and goatee; he was still in his all-black phase, and it made him look quite sinister.

"How old were you here?" Oz asked.

"Nineteen, I think. Just before your parents' wedding."

"A week before," the Queen said. "Jax had dragged you off to get fit for a suit, and his mother ordered you to get a haircut and to shave. We wanted a picture before you did it, to commemorate the loss of all that hair."

"Ah, she did. I'd forgotten."

The King dropped into his favorite chair. "She told you to scrape that awful mess off your face, and if your hair was still touching your ears the morning of the wedding, she would have them removed."

"And I believed her."

The Queen flipped through several more pictures, until she found one she in particular wanted to see. It was of the three of them huddled together in front of the Christmas tree on Union Square; they were bundled in jackets and gloves, and the Emperor stood between them with his arms draped across their shoulders, pulling them close. Their noses and ears were red-tipped from the cold, but I don't think they cared. It was our first Christmas in the tiny one room apartment that smelled like cabbage, and they were all happy just to be together in that one moment.

"Zoom in," the Emperor told her. He pointed to a bulge in his jacket. "Look close. Wick's ears are sticking out just above where my zipper stops. We carted that poor cat around even then."

You kept me warm. I wanted to be there. Then you and I watched while they tried to ice skate on the little rink set up on the Square. Jax was really bad at it.

"He was our furry little mascot," the Queen said. "You used him to flirt shamelessly, too."

He was as bad at that as Jax was on ice skates.

She kept flipping through photos, letting the kids laugh at their youth and awkwardness. She came across one and stopped; it was of her and Jax, sitting at a coffee shop table. They sat close, leaning toward each other, speaking with a seriousness that made it clear they paid no attention to anyone else in the room.

"I don't remember this," she said.

The Emperor did. "It was the day you two met. I left the table after fifteen minutes, and neither of you noticed. I took the picture because it was adorable. There were at least twenty other people in that coffee shop, but the two of you were utterly alone."

Zed looked a bit closer. "Dang, Dad. You were *really* young."

"I'd just turned eighteen," he said. "But I knew. I'd known her for less than an hour, and I knew."

Oz glanced back to where the Emperor was standing; he pointed at her and then Drew, raised an eyebrow, and said, "Eighteen for only a week, and you were ready to battle the world to be together."

"When you know, you know," Jax said.

"Huh."

The King turned in his chair to glare at him. "You. Shut up."

"I'm just saying. I was only seventeen then and didn't even know what I wanted for breakfast. There you were, meeting the love of your life, and I remember it, Jax. You fought your mother over it. Loudly and often, until your father told her to either accept Aubrey, or accept losing you. You had one foot out the door and would have left if she'd kept fighting you."

Before the King could say anything, the Queen tagged onto the Emperor's thought. "She thought I was too old for him." To Oz and Zed she said, "She was right, I think. But that never would have stopped us. His age didn't matter to me."

Jax groaned as he leaned back. "You don't have to help him."

"Help with what?" Drew asked.

Zed talked over him. "What was Grandma's problem? You didn't just start dating and announce right off the bat you were getting married."

"She was concerned, sweetheart," the Queen replied. "He was her only child, and very young. I was just enough older that it worried her."

"And Aubrey was doing nasty, nasty things to her little boy," the Emperor said.

"She *presumed*," Jax said. "And really? In front of my kids?"

The Emperor looked to Oz and Zed. "You know they've had sex, right?"

King Jackson went red, but Oz and Zed laughed, Drew was too stunned to say anything, and the Queen was outright amused. For a moment I thought Jax was going to stand up and punch the Emperor, but the laughter overrode his irritation, and he gave into it.

"Don't listen to him. You were both ordered online."

"Perhaps the assembly instructions were," the Emperor said.

They spared him from more embarrassment at the Emperor's hands. Zed had to take the kitten to Mrs. Briggsman's caretaker and Drew left to call his parents; Oz kissed them both and said she was going to read before going to bed, or perhaps surf online to find the shop she'd been purchased from.

"Hey, I might want a refund!" the King called after her.

"You," the Queen said to the Emperor, not at all upset, "are horrible."

"Little bit, yeah."

The King was not angry, but he was also not exactly happy. "Do you really think they needed to know I was having sex at eighteen?"

"Honestly? Yeah, I kind of do. Virginity as a virtue is an outdated concept, Jax. Your daughter especially needs to know that she won't be a huge disappointment to you if her relationship with Drew takes her in that direction."

"It's also not something she needs to be in a hurry to get rid of."

"Jax, relax." The Queen got up and kissed him. "We don't get a say in it any more than your mother did. Oz is not going to have to win that fight with us. Now I'm going to go soak in a hot bath. You can either stay here and play with the Emperor, or join me."

She kissed him again and headed down the hall.

"Sure, stay here and play with me," the Emperor teased.

"If I ever decide to sit here and bicker with you instead of jumping into a hot bath with her…shoot me." He pushed himself up, but lingered for a moment. "I know what you're doing. I know that you're right. But that's my baby girl and I really don't want to face it any more than my mother did."

"I know."

"And I understand it makes me a hypocrite."

"No, not particularly."

The sound of water rushing through pipes caught his attention and I thought he was going to leave, but instead he sat on the arm of his chair. "You moved Drew to keep them from having to sneak around, didn't you? I wanted to believe it was to keep him from being so close to Oz all the time, but…"

"Sooner or later he would have moved on his own, and likely somewhere else in the city. Keeping him in the building spares Aubrey from the pain your mother felt on those nights when she had no idea where you were. And Oz doesn't have the buffer you had. I was your excuse most of the time, telling her that you were with me, studying or watching videos. I presumed you did not want Oz and Drew to feel like they needed to lie to you in order to have privacy."

"No, I don't."

"You'll never be completely ready for this, Jax."

His shoulders sagged. He looked down at his hands; his fingers were laced together and he was absently brushing his thumbs together. It was the human equivalent of dropping his tail and flicking it, wanting something but not being exactly sure if pouncing was a good idea or the first move in bringing on a lot of pain.

"I should be," he finally said, looking up. "And I want this for her, I really do. I want my kids to feel what I felt when you introduced me to Aubrey. I want every single bit of that for them, from that first kiss on. I want Oz to look at him and wish the rest of the world would fall away and leave them alone. I *lived* for those moments. But I don't know how to let go."

"If it were Zed?"

He flinched. "You think I'm sexist?"

"No. I think that it would be easier with Zed because you've been a teenaged boy and can relate to him. But Oz? You're the first man she loved and it hurts to know that she just might love someone else a little more enthusiastically."

Jax nodded.

"But…she won't love him *more*. You didn't love your mother any less when you fell in love with Aubrey. Apples to oranges."

"Yeah. Well."

"You truly want this for her."

"I know that—"

"No." He sat in Aubrey's chair and picked up the controller and flipped through a series of pictures until he reached one we'd already seen. In it, he was sitting at the parklet picnic table holding a guitar, and opposite him was Aubrey and a girl I did not recognize. She was not as pink as they were, and had long, dark hair that she tucked neatly behind her ears. His head was thrown back in laughter, and she was smiling, her hand held to her chest the way people do when they're both shocked and amused. "Remember her? Aisha Salazar? I broke her heart."

"She moved to Vegas, didn't she?"

"After I left her a sobbing mess in the middle of Union Square. Jax…everything you had with Aubrey, we wanted. Desperately. But I couldn't get near her. I couldn't risk it and I couldn't make her understand why. I would give almost anything to be able to go back and tell that girl that I loved her and then actually be able to do something about it. You don't want Oz to carry with her the weight of loving someone and having to walk away. She'd have to carry it forever, and it comes with the added burden of 'if only.'"

"Turn it off," Jax murmured.

He did as the King asked, and turned the monitor off. "You don't have to be comfortable with what Oz is headed for. Just don't make it difficult. Don't risk either of those kids walking away from each other because they feel like you don't think it's appropriate. And Andrew? The boy keeps a massive piece of wood to block open his door, all for the sake of propriety. He forgoes privacy, so that *we* won't worry."

The Emperor stood, then bent over to pick me up.

"He respects your daughter, Jax. He respects you. Don't be the reason he leaves her in the middle of Union Square with her heart in her hands, broken because he refused to take it."

*

He carried me downstairs, silent the entire way. Drew's apartment door was blocked open and he was on his sofa talking into his phone, but he didn't look happy. The Emperor knocked softly to get his attention, then pushed the wood block aside with his foot and said, "You deserve your privacy, Andrew," and then pulled the door closed, making sure it clicked softly instead of slamming.

You like him, don't you? You like him and Oz. They make you feel squishy inside.

Once inside his apartment he set me on the seat of the comfy chair and offered to get me something to eat, and then he brought it to me and allowed me to snack right there in the best spot in the place. He turned the video monitor on and switched it from news and entertainment to the computer, and started combing through pages of words about Florida that didn't interest me. I finished eating, took a bath, and then curled up to sleep.

When I woke up two hours later he was still reading Florida reports and was fidgety and restless. It was going to be another one of those nights—if he went into his bedroom to do more than change clothes I'd be surprised—so I got up to give him the comfy chair and headed for the cat flap. Oz was probably asleep, but I could stretch out on her window seat or even the foot of her bed.

"She'll dream tonight, Wick," he said, knowing where I was likely to go. "Help her make it at least pleasant."

Fine, but if she has any bouncy dreams, I'm leaving.

Oz was sleeping on her side in the middle of the bed, clutching a pillow to her chest. I curled up next to her, my forehead touching hers, one paw on her shoulder. I didn't hear anything coming from her, so I let myself fall half asleep, knowing the other half would listen when it was time.

Don't drool on me, okay?

I waited for an hour, snoozing in fits and starts, until I heard her. Once I could hear, I peeked.

She stood at the edge of a large red carpet, the kind with tiny loops that are fantastic for sharpening claws upon, and the room she was in was massive. It was long and wide, with high ceilings; the walls were dirty white, except for one that had mirrors that ran nearly floor to ceiling, and there was a pervasive smell of sweat and mentholated muscle cream.

She inhaled deeply; it was a familiar smell, and she liked it.

Even in a dream, it hurt my nose.

Standing at the center of the carpet was a young teenaged boy, perhaps thirteen, his black hair slick with sweat and stuck to his forehead and ears. He was dressed in a white karate uniform trimmed with the same black as the belt he wore, and he had on white mat shoes and thin white gloves. Oz was puzzled over the gloves and shoes, muttering, "I trained barefoot. The only gloves I had were made from foam to protect my hands."

Sitting on the floor to her right, at the edge of the carpet and against the other wall, were three other teenagers dressed in white gis. They were all sweaty and tired, and the youngest of them— Oz guessed he was around sixteen—had a bloody nose and punch-reddened cheek. "You fought them all, didn't you?" she asked the boy in the center, but he didn't answer.

Instead, he looked past her. There was movement behind her, but she couldn't make herself turn to look, not even when whomever it was began to speak.

"You all performed acceptably. I'm pleased." The voice was male, and clearly an adult. "Three on one is never easy, and you worked well together."

"But we lost," the boy with the bloody nose said. "To *him*."

"This time. And now it's my turn." A man wearing black gi pants and a red gi top, held closed by a black belt bearing six red stripes, stepped onto the carpet. He was wearing full protective gear; his feet and hands were covered in vinyl-dipped foam, he had a protective helmet on, and had even covered his shins.

The boy had no gear. Oz peered closer; he wore a black belt, too, and she counted the stripes on it.

"Not possible," she muttered. "He's way too young to be a fourth degree."

The instructor and the boy bowed to each other, and began to fight. It was fast, blow after blow landing hard, and the boy connected with spinning kicks and jumping back fists. Oz sucked in a breath when she saw the instructor drop his left hand just a bit; the boy saw the opening, too, and jumped into the air, slamming a quick round kick to the side of his head and then he landed on his feet before the sick thud faded from the air.

The instructor staggered, but did not fall. The boy refused to let up and covered the distance between them, catching him with a forward palm strike to his face. Then with one quick swipe of his foot, his instructor was on the ground, calling for a break.

The boy's white gloves were splattered with blood, and the instructor spit out his mouth guard. "That's some damn fine combat," he said as he slowly, painfully got back up. "I'm honestly not sure I can ever beat you again. You're only going to grow stronger and faster. I'm recommending you to the testing panel. Congratulations."

He bowed to his young student, who didn't look as pleased at his victory as the instructor did.

Oz wanted to congratulate the boy; she stepped forward, but as soon as her foot touched the carpet, she was in another room. It was gloomy and not well lit; the walls on one side were covered with loaded bookshelves, and dust motes floated from the books like soft sneezes. In front of her was a window; she looked out expecting sunshine, but instead it led to another part of the building.

She was looking at a long tunnel, its walls made of brushed metal. It stretched on as far as she could see, and along its entire length there were entry points with no doors, one facing another, and in the ceiling above each set of doors there was a red light. Shadows moved between the entryways, shrouded in a smoky cloud.

Behind her came a sigh and she turned. The boy from the dojo was sitting at a long and wide desk; there were several open books in front of him and he was writing furiously, occasionally stopping to turn a page.

"I know you," she said. "I've dreamed about you before."

He didn't look up.

"This is school for you now, isn't it? No other kids tormenting you. You're on your own. But why?"

She moved closer. To her left there was a giant white board, and the math that filled it was nothing she understood. She looked at the books on his desk; trigonometry and physics, chemistry and biology, and a thin, worn book on ancient poets. She wanted to ask him what he was studying, but a woman's voice from the other room called him to dinner. Irritated at the interruption, he tossed his pen to the desk and got up; Oz followed him out the door, hoping to see but not intrude, but found herself outside, standing on a sidewalk.

It was all familiar, but nothing looked the way she expected. She began to walk, looking for signs, until she reached an intersection. "Market and Battery," she whispered to herself. It was San Francisco, but far removed from what she expected. This street was shiny and new, shadowed by the tall metal and glass skyscrapers that lined it, and lit by massive lamp posts that jutted from the sides of each building.

It could have been night, for all the darkness above. It could have been day, for all the light breaking through the shadows.

There were people ahead, and she walked toward them, hoping to ask where she was. When she was. There was an older man, perhaps in his late forties though she couldn't easily make out his features, and he was with a teenaged boy. She knew who it was, the boy from the dojo and the solitary classroom, but he was much taller and his hair had grown, curling over his collar in the back, shading his eyes and ears. He was thin but moved with a subdued power, holding his speed so that his father could keep up.

Then grief slapped at her, and she stopped.

They both looked sad, and the father's face was red from battling the tears he refused to shed. She knew it was a fight he was going to lose; she could feel him bleeding pain from where she stood, and wanted to turn from it to spare him from being seen, but she was rooted in place and couldn't move.

When they were less than thirty feet from her, the boy turned to his father and grabbed him into a tight hug. It went on for a long time, and when they finally pulled apart the man put his hands to his son's cheeks and pulled his head down so that he could place a long kiss on his forehead. When the boy kissed him back, the tears began, so he kissed his father again and reluctantly let go.

He turned toward Oz and took a few steps.

"You might be able to help me now," he said. He took one more step and was swallowed whole by the portal she had not seen.

Oz let go of the pillow she'd been holding and startled awake. I sniffed at her face to let her know I was there and that she was all right, it was just a dream. She rubbed my head and sat up, hearing the footsteps outside her door.

It's just him. He can't sleep. Nothing new about that.

Her door was cracked open and she looked into the hallway. The Emperor was out on the balcony, his feet on the rail, hands folded on his stomach, and he was looking to the sky.

He doesn't need company. Go back to bed.

She went outside anyway. It was cold on the balcony, but she went out in the shorts and t-shirt she'd been sleeping in, and dropped into the chair next to him.

"I hope I didn't wake you," he said.

"Only if you were the one who opened my door."

"I sometimes check on you and Zed at night. I'm sorry."

I jumped into his lap to steal his warms.

They aren't babies anymore. You're one night-time check away from being really creepy.

"It's fine," she said. "Can't sleep?"

She knew the answer to that; we all knew the answer. The Emperor rarely slept; it wasn't because he hated the idea of wasted hours lost to slumber, but it eluded him much of the time. Instead, he read books or studied data that the King didn't have enough time to wade through. He watched newscasts from around the world and dove into massive historical texts. When he needed to be tired enough to sleep, he worked out hard in the gym or swam fast laps in the pool, trying to exhaust himself into even the hope of sleep.

There was a time when he walked the city at night, but after the Queen convinced him to take their old apartment, he kept his roaming to either the halls of the home or to his lair. He knew she would feel better if he kept close to home, and wandering around wasn't helping to ease his insomnia.

"Can't sleep," he told Oz.

"Worried about Finn?"

"Little bit. Mostly just restless. Same as usual. And you should go back to bed."

"I will in a minute." She leaned her head back and closed her eyes. "If I stay out here long enough, I'll get super cold. Then I'll run back, jump under the covers, and it will feel toasty warm. That'll make me sleepy again."

"If only my bed wasn't so far from the balcony."

"You're kind of overdressed for it, anyway."

"Fine. You leave, I'll strip down to my underwear, freeze for fifteen minutes, and then run to the guest room."

She snorted a laugh. "And I hope so hard that you run into Mom when you do."

"I'll cover my nipples with my hands to spare her the embarrassment."

"If she wasn't embarrassed when you started ratting my dad out about his sex life, I don't think your tiny little man-nipples will do it."

"Ah, I do enjoy making your dad uncomfortable. And the older you and Zed become, the more opportunities I have. Your mother, on the other hand."

"You can't rattle her so easily."

He turned to look at her. "Oh, I could, Ozzie. I could make her turn six shades of red and then some. But I won't. Your father is fair game and if he can ever find something to use as payback on me, he's welcome to it."

"You knew Mom first, right?"

"I met her first, then introduced them."

"Does she have anything on you?"

With a deep chuckle, he picked me up and stood, dropping me onto Oz's cold legs. He never answered her, but that laugh was enough. She turned to watch him go back inside, and as the door slowly shut behind him.

I probably imagined it, but I could still hear him laughing as he headed down the stairs.

"I wonder what was he like when he was little," she said as she got up.

Go back to bed and sleep, I'll tell you.

"I'm betting young Emperor did *something*. Surely I can find out what it was."

She did as she'd said she would: she ran back into her bedroom and dove under the covers with me, and it was as gloriously warm as she'd said. I'd thought I would follow the Emperor and tell him about her dream, so he would know she hadn't had a nightmare, if that's what he worried about, but the warms were too inviting and I fell asleep under the blankets, pressed up against her spare pillow, and I stayed there all night.

Two days later, lunch was had in the King's office. He asked Oz and Drew and the Emperor to meet him there, and because it sounded very official and the Queen promised sandwiches, I tagged along. It wasn't even that I was sure I would get bites of their food; it sounded so official that I thought the King might wear his crown, and I couldn't remember ever having seen that, not since his coronation.

They were situated in uncomfortable looking metal chairs all pointed toward the giant video monitor, and they stared at a map of the North American Continent. It was marked up with squiggly red lines and bright orange arrows, and everyone looked terribly serious.

"They have air power," Oz said absently. "Ancient air power." She pointed to a spot on the right side of the screen and added, "Those shadows—Dad, remember when that air show came to San Francisco? Someone flew an old airplane under the Golden Gate, an old fighter. Those shadows look a lot like that." She squinted, trying to see the date stamp on the picture. "This was taken a week ago."

"Three to four-hundred-year-old technology," the Emperor mused.

"But why?"

"Florida is quite a bit behind the rest of us and doesn't have even hover tech yet," the King said. "At least nothing beyond toys, like basic bikes and boards. These airplanes could literally fly under our sensors. I don't think we've been equipped to look for them for the last hundred years."

"They could have had the tech," Drew grunted. "They were offered the tech. It meant tearing up their infrastructure to accommodate it, and they refused."

"They wanted it," the Emperor told him. "It would have taken fifty years and tens of billions of dollars to implement. Low tech was far less expensive, and frankly if not for the capabilities of our mosquito drones and satellites...brilliant."

"Those have internal combustion engines," Drew pointed out. "Where are they getting the fuel? It's not from Midlam and I'm guessing not from Pacifica, either."

"Asia," Oz said.

"And there's nothing illegal about that," the King said. "We purchase small quantities for some of our older vehicles, too. The dilemma is addressing the fact that they are clearly assembling an air force when none existed before. They've torn down a good chunk of their wall and allowed millions of their people to leave."

"Have they?" Oz asked. "Or is what you've seen still a matter of soldiers tearing down the wall and scouting past it?"

The image on the monitor changed. We were looking at a picture taken from a ground camera; it was a miles-long line of people marching along a roadside. Men, women, and children; the men were all older, and the children were very young.

"They're calling it a humanitarian emigration," the King said. "Too many to feed."

"So they're dropping the whole let's-invite-tourists excuse?" Oz asked.

"No. They're actively advertising in Midlam for tourism and have petitioned to be allowed to advertise in Pacifica. But they're also admitting they can't feed the masses."

Drew grunted again. "They've been offered food. Midlam offers them food a dozen times a year. We've even offered it for free, when it was clear they were balking at the cost. They don't want to pay for it, but they refuse any sort of charity."

"I know. Midlam's military has responded, cautiously."

"Are those people officially refugees?" Drew asked.

Carefully, the King answered, "They aren't considered active targets."

"How many are we taking?" Oz asked.

"If they come…we could accommodate two to three million, easily. Midlam is poised to take as many as two million. But should we?"

He knew the answer. He wanted to see if Oz did.

"Of course."

"And what if any of them are plants? What if some of those people are meant to enact terrorism here or in Midlam?"

"It doesn't matter. You take in the people who say they need help while beefing up your security to make sure nothing goes wrong. If our defense force is up to par, they'll ferret out potential terrorists."

"If they miss one?"

"That would suck," Drew muttered.

"What else?" the Emperor pressed. "What else about all of this makes the little voice in the back of your brain speak up?"

Oz gestured to the monitor. "Florida is counting on both Midlam and Pacifica to assume that they won't start anything if we're taking in so many of their people. They're either truly sending their citizens away because they can't feed them, or they're sending them as acceptable collateral damage. Smoke and mirrors."

"Why? Drew asked. "What can they gain?"

Oz picked up a computer pointer from the desk and aimed it at the monitor. With it she moved one of the long red lines from the Florida border to halfway to Texas, and another from its northern border to New York.

"That's what. Land mass."

They stared at it for a long, quiet minute, and then Drew asked, "Has New England asked for help?"

"Their military is talking to ours."

"And Midlam? Has my mother officially requested aid?"

"We're sending troops." He turned the monitor off. "Understand, we're treading lightly here. There hasn't been an overt threat made. But it's suspicious, and the heads of both Pacifica's and Midlam's military agree, something is going on. I want you both to be aware as things unfold."

Drew scowled. "Why?"

Oz was looking at the King, and she was anything but happy. "Because if they die, if your mother and my father *die*, we're next in line. We have to be ready to step up, and right now neither of us is."

The Emperor shifted uncomfortably. "Jax. Don't do that."

"Do what?"

"Die. I forbid it."

"All right then," the King said. "The Emperor has spoken, and I've been forbidden. Living shall continue."

Oz got up. "I'm with him. No dying. No one's ready for that."

She and Drew left, closing the door behind them.

"You're watering this down for them, you know that, right?" the

Emperor asked the King. "At some point you have to tell them that Midlam is headed for war with Florida, no ifs about it. We know they have planes flying and we know they've dropped test bombs in the Atlantic."

"I need them to start thinking about it, and seeing as how this is all in Shazia Van Hoff's hands right now? Yeah, Midlam's going to war, but—" He turned the monitor back on, and flipped through image after image of satellite photos, pictures that showed Midlam's army mobilizing, and pictures of Florida's military creating lines of attack "—they need to be kids, at least for now."

"Jax, they don't have that luxury."

The King rubbed at his temples, like he was trying to force back in a headache that wanted out. "They're both idealists. They have this grand vision of uniting Pacifica and Midlam into one big happy place, with pixies and fairies and everyone holding hands and singing. I don't want to rip that away from them just yet."

The Emperor took the remote from the King and turned the monitor off. "They might still have that, someday. When she becomes Queen, if they really do marry—"

"If."

"It might not be the utopia they hope for, but they can still do this."

"I want the fairies," the King said. "I want the magic. I want what's in my daughter's head."

The Emperor slapped at his legs and he stood. "Fine. Then let's go get a drink or two. Maybe six. You'll see fairies."

"Finn comes back tomorrow. Do you really want to be hungover?"

"I don't get hangovers. I'm Scottish. I can handle my booze."

"You're as Scottish as I am Canadian."

"Don't flatter yourself. You're not that polite." He bent over to scratch behind my ears. "No cats in the bar, Mister Wick. Go find the kids or the Queen. Someone will give you food if you ask nicely."

I don't even have to be all that nice.

I followed them out; they went left, down the stairs to the giant glass doors that led to outside, and I went right, up the stairs that led to the family apartment and where I hoped the Queen was waiting for me with plates of shrimp and cheese and dead meaty things.

*

The Queen was at her desk in the little nook off the kitchen, shuffling through a stack of papers. I hopped up onto the desk to say hello and to give her a head bonk, but I didn't ask for anything to eat because she was clearly busy getting things ready for the school year, planning for the thirty sticky people she would be stuck with in her classroom.

I'm not going to like it when you're not home all day.

"Sweet Wick." She kissed the top of my head. "Go look on the counter. There's a little plate with some bites of roast beef for you."

This is why I love you. You understand me.

I ate that and headed for the staff kitchen a floor down, because if Oz and Drew were there, I could probably score something else. They weren't, but there were flecks of shredded cheese on the floor, probably from when they made pizza, but I didn't eat it because I couldn't be sure who dropped it there or when.

"Never eat random things off the floor," the Emperor once told me. "You're the royal kitty. Someone might try to harm you by putting down bad food."

I tried to bury it, swiping at the floor with my paw, but it was still there a minute later so I left and went back upstairs to look in Oz's bedroom. The door was open and they were both on the window seat, computers on their laps, and each was staring at their screens while they mumbled to each other.

I had nowhere else to go, really—Zed was at work and wasn't always free with the treats anyway—so I jumped up on the bed and curled up, half-listening while Drew talked her through the digital maze of registering for school. Their voices became a gentle lull, and I fell asleep while he explained to her that she didn't need to decide exactly what she wanted to study right off the bat; she could take a few classes and then decide, the way he had. He'd spent his first two college years exploring math and science and history, and even spent a semester diving deeper into classic science fiction, which was his first true literary love. If he could figure out a way to turn it into a degree, he'd drop political science in a heartbeat.

She thought he should; he had stories in his head that probably needed to get out, and he might even be able to write books.

"I've read some really old sci-fi," she told him. "Heinlein and Vonnegut and Bradbury—you could really make a go of it. Your brain works that way."

"Sure, that sounds exactly like something you would want your husband doing instead of work."

"What I want for my future husband is for him to find his bliss. It sounds creative, and he needs to be creative. To balance me, you know?"

"I don't know, Oz. I'm kind of unbalanced as it is."

There was something about Zed and graduating high school early, but I was mostly asleep by then, and it was dark outside when I woke up. They were still there, but the computers were on her desk. Drew was leaned against the window frame on one side and Oz was on the other, their legs stretched out on the seat until their feet touched. Music was playing, sort of muted and meant to be in the background; it was very old and instrumental and not what I expected Oz to listen to.

"Where's Finn popping up?" Drew asked her.

They were staring out the window, probably looking at Union Square, but for all I know they were ogling at their own reflections and admiring how pretty they were.

Finn was supposed to come back through a portal on the Square; while he waited, the Emperor had been to the building that hums a dozen times, collecting new information with each outing. He took me with him on his last visit, and the walls were now covered—nearly every inch, and some of the floor space as well—with books that contained all the research Finn's people were doing two hundred years in the future.

He read out loud to me, whispering so that he would not bother anyone else. Finn planned on shutting down all the portals just before coming back, including the one on Union Square. Once they were gone, he would open a new, bigger portal that was not so close to the stairs, so there needed to be no one standing at the center of the Square.

Once that new portal was open, he wanted me to stick close to him. Stay by his feet, or stay in his sweatshirt pocket, he didn't care where, but he wanted me with him and not with anyone else.

I didn't know why, but it seemed important to him.

"This has been a hell of a month," Drew said. "I can't believe so much has happened."

"It didn't all get done in a month," she said. "The solar farm going back online? The gate being built? None of that happened in less than five or six months, and even that seems like they'd be rushing it."

"You think the Emperor went back through a portal and got things rolling early?"

"Maybe. Probably."

"What was that whole thing the other day when he asked for your hand?"

No, Oz. No.

After thinking about it she said, "It's not mine to tell. Let's just say I understand him a tiny bit better."

She started to say something more but stopped at the sudden loud noise coming from across the hall. There were hard footsteps and doors banging, and she started to get up, I think to run to make sure everything was all right, when the Emperor's voice boomed down the hall.

"He's sozzled six different ways, Aubrey. Good luck getting him to bed."

Oz relaxed, and leaned back against the window frame.

"What?" Drew asked.

"They're drunk," she snorted. "It happens maybe once a year, usually on someone's birthday…though they both got so hammered after my grandmother died that I think Dad was hungover for a week."

"And the Emperor?"

"He was very quiet for a long time after that. My grandmother hadn't quite liked him as much as my grandfather did, but there at the end? She asked for him more than once, and I think realized how good he was to the family."

"So he mourned by getting your dad drunk?"

"It's what brothers do, I suppose. Go out and get drunk, and cry on each other's shoulders where no one else will see."

"I'm not sure my brother would do that for me."

"Your brother is moody and self-absorbed, but if you needed him he'd be here in a heartbeat and if you were both legal, he'd get you as drunk as you wanted to be."

"He's no Zed, but…yeah. He probably would if he could. Maybe. He's most likely joining the military soon so any commiserating would have to wait until he could get leave time."

"Carter Van Hoff, soldier boy. I can't picture it."

"Yeah, well, he hasn't said anything to my parents, so no telling yours."

"Seriously, until Finn is back and life returns to some sense of normal, I wouldn't tell them if he was joining the Boy Scouts."

"That would be tragic, a twenty-three-year-old signing up to learn how to tie knots with a bunch of twelve-year-old boys. No, he'd rather sign up to learn to blow things up with a bunch of kids our age."

"There's a strong history of military service among British royals, you know."

"I'm not criticizing. I just don't think he's doing it because he wants to. I think he's run out of ideas about what he wants to do with his life."

You're not even twenty, dude. Like you know, either.

"What about you, Wick? Do you know what you want beyond dinner?"

Hey, I think I used to be in the army. And I was an officer. I've done my time.

Their feet were still pushed together, sole to sole, and when the music changed they started rocking their feet back and forth with the beat of the song. It started before either of them realized they were doing it, but when they did they both laughed, and I had flashbacks to Jax and Aubrey sitting at their favorite parklet table, shoulder to shoulder, swaying to the beat of music the Emperor played on a guitar. It was odd and adorable then, and almost as odd and adorable with Oz and Drew, with the same potential for inducing vomiting in innocent bystanders.

That's sweet. Really. Too sweet. Please stop.

When the song ended, they stopped, and Drew said abruptly,

"You know, I kinda think I want to be more like the Emperor."

What, drunk?

"Where did that come from?"

I know where he keeps the beer. I could show you.

"It's just—the more I get to know him, the more I realize he's not the guy I was afraid of when I was little. He was intentionally scary then because we were kids and he had that whole stern adult thing going on, but now? Don't get me wrong, I still think he's, like, six degrees of weird, but he matters and he makes a difference. And someday he'll need someone to pick up where he leaves off."

"I really don't want to think about that."

Bet he doesn't, either.

She went on. "But...he's been talking lately like he's looking ahead to the inevitable, too, almost like he's been saying goodbye. I don't like it, but there it is. He's thinking about it."

"He's not that old."

"I know. Trust me, I seriously know. But damn, Drew, he has a harsh parental streak that confounds me sometimes and pisses me off other times."

"I don't want to be your dad," Drew snorted. "No, I meant the way he helps people. He doesn't even ask why they need help, he just does what they need and trusts that the rest follows. I want to be that. The guy willing to help without expecting anything in return."

"So you don't just want to do good. You want to be good. Really, what brought that on? I mean, you are a good person, Drew. Don't think you aren't."

Hey, even I've warmed up to you.

You can stay, as long as you never smell like dog again.

"The other night, after we went back to see what he was up to, I went up to the roof to just kind of hang out since I couldn't sleep and he found me there. We had an actual conversation and it wasn't like he thought he was talking to some stupid teenager. He was pretty open—I even asked him some things that were really too personal and he answered. I don't know...it just made me realize the one thing I hadn't really figured out. Who I want to be. Beyond what I study. I mean, I get it, why my brother is heading into the army because he still doesn't have it figured out, but I have to."

"We have time for that. Both of us do."

"Yeah, but there's more to our lives than what our births decided we'd be. It's one thing to know I don't want to ever be King. It's another to I know I absolutely want to be your Prince Consort. Yet another to still want the other part of the plan, to unite Pacifica and Midlam. It's a whole other thing to understand what I want to be in the middle of all that. I want to be your Prince but I also need to be something for myself."

She looked surprised. She smiled, just a little, like she was trying hard not to. "You absolutely want to be my Prince? As in, let's go from just getting to know each other to being…us?"

He turned on the window seat, his feet dangling to the floor. "We already know each other. Don't we?"

"I think we do."

"Look, one of the things he told me was to man up and be honest with you."

That made her laugh. "He actually told you to man up?"

"Well, not in those exact words, but yeah."

"Funny, he pretty much said the same thing to me. He pointed out that we spent so many years talking, so why else would you have moved here, and why did I want you to? We've already spent a lot of time getting to know each other."

"And we've spent enough time this summer getting familiar. I mean, without the groping and…stuff. Because I wouldn't expect that, not yet. I get it, I know there are limits and…stuff."

"And stuff," she snickered.

He was on his feet; his eyes were wide and he shoved his hands into his pockets as if he didn't know what to do with them. "I love you. I know the plan was to take our time getting there, but the Emperor is right, I have to be honest with you and not wait for you to make some huge decision. I know I might have gotten there ahead of you—"

"You didn't."

"—and I don't expect for you to say it back, but it's the truth and I owe you the truth."

She stood up. "What else did he tell you?"

Cripes, don't tell her. Just do it.

"Um. That I should kiss you. And then kiss you again. He didn't tell me what to do after that."

You're telling her. Yeah, Romeo's got nothing on you.

Well, I suppose that's all right. The dude did die after, what, three days of mooning over some thirteen-year-old girl?

She didn't give him the chance to say anything else, which was probably good because he was heading straight into babbling-idiot territory. Instead, she grabbed his shirt near the collar and pulled him close, then planted one hell of a kiss on him.

Before he could catch his breath, she did it again.

Great. I get to live through this again.

Come up for air. Geez.

"All right," she said when she finally let him go. "Where do we go from here?"

"The hell out of your bedroom," he sputtered.

"Balcony?"

"Balcony. Yes. Fresh air."

Yeah, that's not going to help. Trust me. I've had to see this before.

"You can come, Wick."

Planned on it.

I followed Drew down the hallway, and he held the balcony door open for me. The Emperor had beat them to it, though. He was sitting with his feet up on the rail, his head against the back of the seat cushion. He looked like he was sleeping, but I knew better; his breathing wasn't slow enough and his ear twitched when he heard us. I jumped into his lap and head butted his chest so that he would know I was with them.

Run. They're getting all smoochy. They LUV each other. Run before they make you hurl.

"I'm not as think as you drunk I am," he said, opening his eyes.

"You're not as funny as you think you are, either," Oz said. "What are you doing out here? I figured you'd be plastered to your living room floor, watching the ceiling spin."

"Sobering up. The cool air helps, and I want to be clear headed in the morning so that I can stomp through the halls and wreak havoc on your father's hangover."

"You're evil."

"Little bit, yeah."

"You know," Drew said, "I usually look forward to breakfast, but I think tomorrow it's going to kind of suck. Mr. B is not going to be any sort of happy."

"No worries," the Emperor said. "If history is any proof, tomorrow morning His Majesty will dine alone in his office, nothing but toast and coffee, because the office is fairly soundproof. And the nice thing about a soundproofed room is that no one else has to hear him swear."

"What did you do?" Oz groaned.

"His computer *might* be set to blast the sound of an air horn every five minutes from the time he sits down."

Drew snorted loudly. "You aren't just a little evil. You've practiced."

"Little bit, yeah."

"Ask him about Easter dinner when I was seven years old. He's been practicing a long time," Oz said.

"Hey, I did *not* tell your mother to stuff the chicken with carrot chunks."

"No, you managed that on your own, and then asked if were having rabbit for dinner, and oh, by the way, is it the one you saw hopping down the hallway that morning?"

"Man, that's harsh," Drew said. He didn't sound like he thought it was all that bad, though, and was chuckling under his breath.

"Hey, you ate the chicken, young lady. And then acted like you were picking hair out of your teeth. Zed is the one who was traumatized."

"He wouldn't eat baked chicken for three or four years." Oz startled at the sound of buzzing nearby, and leaned forward and looked up, toward the roof line. "Orange blur? Was that a bird? It's a little late for the pigeons to be out begging. Or is Zed up there playing with a plane or a drone?"

The Emperor strained to see what she was looking at. "It will be a long time, if ever, before Zed touches a drone."

She stood up, leaning over the edge of the balcony, making my heart beat faster because there was nothing there to catch her if she fell, and I wouldn't put it past those pigeons to group together and snatch a person or a kitty. Her head turned as she looked in all directions, until she pointed down at the security vans on the street between Union Square and the royal house.

"It's a drone, hovering near the front van," she said.

The Emperor handed me to Drew and got up, leaning over the edge with her. "The same type that crashed in Land's End." He watched for another full minute and added, "Exactly the same type. Same size, same brand."

His shoulders sagged, and Oz set her forehead on her arm, sucking in a deep breath, as they came to the same conclusion.

"Are you sober enough yet, Emperor?"

"I am now. You get a giant pot of coffee and I'll go wake your father. We'll meet in his office—and I'll turn the computer alarms off, just to be nice."

"What just happened?" Drew asked, lifting me with him as he stood.

"The Millers," she said. "That wasn't an accident. They were straight up murdered."

26

By the time we made it to his office, the King was already at his desk. He was bleary-eyed and looked like he was only half awake, his hair crushed down on one side and sticking straight up on the other; he sat there holding his head up by smashing his cheeks into his hands, elbows digging into the desk top. When Oz set a mug of coffee in front of him he mouthed "thank you," but he didn't move other than to close his eyes. I jumped onto the desk and curled up near him, in case he wanted to pet me to calm his nerves from being jarred out of his inebriated sleep.

The Emperor was in front of the giant video monitor and Oz stood next to him. She mirrored his stance, arms folded and head cocked the way he did when he was either annoyed or concerned, and watched as he flipped through picture after picture. Most of them looked to me to be the same images they'd combed through before, of people leaving Florida in long lines, marching one after the other, and of airplanes and giant gaping holes in the wall.

Drew dropped into the floppy chair, the good one that the Emperor usually got to sit in. He could see the monitor from there, and watched as Oz took the remote from the Emperor and then pulled up the picture of the field of airplanes in Florida.

Once she had that up, she pulled up another picture and put it side by side with the other. "This one," she said, pointing to the one on the left, "is the older image I looked at earlier. The other was taken this afternoon."

"They look the same," Drew said.

She touched the monitor and pulled the new picture over, until it was on top of the old. "Identical. Even the shadows are similar. Those planes haven't been moved."

"Boneyard?" Drew asked.

"We know Florida has been flying," the Emperor said. "They've been dropping test bombs into the Atlantic Ocean." He pulled up a third picture, one of the long line of people leaving Florida. "Their people will arrive in Midlam's heartland soon." He clicked to a new image. "They're walking out of Florida, but using mass transit once they reach populated cities."

"Still mostly women and children?" Oz asked.

"Older men, as well," the Emperor said. "They seem to be headed for the Missouri or Kansas region. All of them."

The King finally sat back, and they turned at the sound of his chair creaking. "The drone you saw tonight. How obvious was it?"

"I noticed the color from its sound first, when it flew by the balcony," Oz said. "It went by quickly, but it registered with me enough to keep looking for it. Then we spotted it near the security detail down on Geary. It hovered near the vans and looked like it was pointed to look in the windows."

The Emperor added, "It was large enough that Oz originally wondered if Zed was flying one off the roof, but then Zed wouldn't have been using it to peek into those vans." He gestured for Drew to get out of his chair, and sat down hard when he did. "The question is, why?"

Drew moved to one of the other chairs. "They have three and four-hundred-year old tech. The drones that we play with as kids now were pretty close to high-tech a few centuries ago. It's not surprising that's what they would have now."

"Keep going with that thought," the King said.

"They know that what they have is old, and know that we know that. So it would make sense to them to fly drones in Pacifica that would be dismissed as some ten-year-old kid's toy, because who would think of it as spy gear? If they have anything newer, they're not going to tip their hand."

Oz agreed. "And how better to test that theory than to use one to stage an incident that could easily be mistaken for an accident, and then see what happens? All the while, distracting us with fake military exercises and the sudden emigration of a significant portion of their population?"

"North Korea," Drew muttered. "Like, around the early twenty first century. It was a tiny country with a dictator constantly trying to compensate for…something. He made a lot of noise, like a little kid on the playground trying to be all tough in front of the bigger kids. No one took him seriously, even throughout all of his showcase nuclear testing. Not until he actually used one."

"Florida as a modern day North Korea," the Emperor muttered. "Interesting."

The King opened the top right drawer on his desk, and pulled from it the official phone that he never used. "I'll call for a sweep of our air space and advise Midlam to do the same. You two, go to bed. Finn comes back tomorrow and I know you want to be coherent for that."

Oz hesitated, but a drunk King and barely sober Emperor were not people she wanted to argue with. She nodded and then reached for Drew's hand, pulling him along with her. When they were gone and the door had clicked behind them, the King said, "I want your take on this. Is she on the money? Were the Millers intentionally killed?"

"I don't think we'll ever know, but I also think she's more right than not. The Land's End drone was probably not a toy, and whether or not it crashed on purpose, the end result was that it killed an entire family. They're openly spying on Pacifica, Jax, and we didn't notice it until after the gate we used to send Finn home was activated. They may have seen the entire thing."

"Would they understand what they saw?"

"There's no denying that his ship was there, and then it was gone. Whether they would interpret that for what it was, or even made a guess that we'd executed someone in a fairly public and barbaric way, who knows?"

The King still had the phone in hand, and briefly rested his chin on it. "Then that's the chatter we'll go with. As of three days ago,

Pacifica executed a suspected spy, and will continue to do so as we ferret out the guilty. Publicly, and with no advanced warning."

"Do you want to be *that* king? The one who kills without the benefit of an open trial?"

"That drone flew past my daughter, and undoubtedly took a series of photographs. If anything, I want the message that Florida's First Minister hears to be obvious—she is protected, and I will execute anyone who tries to harm her or her boyfriend."

"So he's not just the Prince of Midlam anymore."

"I want it clear, Emperor. He might be the Prince of Midlam, but he is in my house and is as protected as my own children. What I want the Minister to hear is that without question, I will kill on their behalf if I have to. He's not exempt. I don't think you would do any less, either."

The Emperor pushed himself up, and then picked me up from the desk. "Indeed," he said. "I would do that, and more." He ruffled the fur on my head and then told me to go chase after the kids and make sure they behaved. He had errands to run before it was too late, and the King was too tired and grumpy to be decent company.

"The King just wants to go back to bed," Jax groaned, but he was already pressing things on his phone, so I did as I was told and went to find Oz and Drew.

*

They weren't on the balcony or in her bedroom, so I plodded down the stairs—someone really should build me my own little elevator—and found them in Drew's living room. The door was open, and he'd put a chunk of wood in front of it to keep it from swinging closed. They were sitting on the floor with their backs resting against the sofa, and Oz was scrolling through a list of movies on the video monitor.

You know that sofa is for sitting, right?

She kept scrolling, but she wasn't really paying any attention to what she was doing. "So here's a part of the riddle," she said, making me wish I had been there for the start of the conversation.

"For the hell of it, I went back to a couple weeks after the Emperor basically chased us all home."

"Just because you could?"

"I think because Finn has turned him into this enigma for me. The guy playing around on the monkey bars was just too young to be the Emperor at the same time my dad was nineteen. So I went back and point blank asked him how old he was and he said he was eighteen. I pointed out that he'd been fifteen when he picked my dad off the bridge, and all he said was 'funny how that works' and then he left. Then later he admitted in front of all of us that he was nineteen when my parents got married."

Drew grabbed the remote from her hand. "I can't read that fast. And yeah, it's funny, but it's not surprising. Time travel, Oz. It's what you guys do. And you probably shouldn't tell me much more, because it'll annoy the snot out of him if he finds out."

Yeah, I've seen him blow his nose. You don't want to do that.

"I don't think it's a secret. And he shouldn't expect me to keep secrets from you, anyway."

"You have every right to keep things from me, especially if it's not something that affects me. Someday you'll have to keep a lot from me, like it or not. There's going to be a time when you won't be able to share matters of state with me—and for all we know the Emperor *is* a matter of state."

State of confusion, maybe?

"You know, I never really thought twice about him until we saw him outside the portal with blood on his shirt, and I didn't even care about that very much until Finn decided he was a puzzle. He's always just been my sort-of uncle who lives downstairs, and sometimes I can't explain him. He taught me how to swim and helped my dad teach me how to ride a bike. He stared boys down so hard they almost melted right in the middle of the roof during the parties Zed and I had. I didn't really consider how much *more* he might be, and now it's like this little itch at the back of my brain. I'm trying not to scratch it, but it's just not going away."

Drew pretended to consider her. "Maybe shove a thin stick up your left nostril, and kind of twist it along through your sinuses. You might be able to reach the backside of your brain that way. Wiggle it back and forth, that ought to do it."

"The next eighty, ninety years with you are going to be like this, aren't they?"

"Unless the solar panels soak up all the sun's energy before then, I hope so."

Do I need to leave? Because experience tells me that this is when the groping starts. I don't want to be stuck here when the groping starts.

To my relief, Drew jumped up, and then helped her up. "Look, when you don't scratch an itch you can't reach, it just gets worse until it damn nears drives you crazy and you have to get someone else's help. And right now, I don't want anyone else helping you scratch. So which When do we head for?"

She didn't let go of his hand. "Some point when he's older than eighteen."

"You realize that if you pick a random point, you might wind up following him around on a perfectly normal day and find him doing normal things. Do you really want to follow him around, just to find out that he eats a grilled cheese sandwich every day at one o'clock at the same diner, and the only odd thing is that sometimes he has fruit instead of fries with it? He might be a very boring person."

"Day to day, maybe."

Drew was sure that it didn't matter what he said; sooner or later that itch had to be scratched, and it might as well be sooner. I scrambled up, patting him on his leg to make sure he remembered I was there and that I wanted to go, too. After all, I'd been told to make sure they behaved, and I couldn't do that if they were ten or fifteen years in the past without me.

*

They walked around downtown for half an hour while Oz tried to think of a good When to take Drew to, a point in time she was sure they would find the Emperor. I could hear the soft footsteps nearby, the sound of her guards following in the shadows, trying to keep up. She couldn't hear them, but she knew they were there and also understood they wouldn't follow too closely; that gave her enough time to get to the portal behind the old Hyatt, which was between two buildings and just far enough around a corner that she could get us through it before they could catch up.

"It's the one time none of them will get into trouble for losing track of me," she told Drew. "They can't follow me through, and I'm technically allowed to go freely, so…"

She wasn't, not really. She was supposed to let someone know she was going, and exactly which When she planned on visiting. She was allowed to go through portals on her own, but not as freely as she'd have Drew think.

She pulled him through to the summer when she was ten years old. Drew and his brother were visiting without their parents; Carter refused to do anything they wanted to, and in hindsight she couldn't blame him. He was fifteen, Drew was twelve, and Zed was only eight. Drew probably would have preferred to tag along with his older brother, but he also didn't mind playing with Oz and Zed, so when the Emperor offered to take them—along with a cadre of security— to the small beach at the Presidio, he went.

"I remember that summer," he told her as they made their way up the Embarcadero, heading in the direction of the Golden Gate Bridge. "Didn't we try to bury Zed?"

"We didn't try. We actually buried him," she snickered.

"So we're going to go watch ourselves play in the sand, and watch him watching us? This should be exciting. Tomorrow can we go somewhere and watch paint dry?"

"Hey, I can take you home, you know. I picked this for a reason. When we were sticking Zed into the hole we'd dug, the Emperor disappeared for a few minutes. When he came back, he was out of breath and sweaty. I remember looking up at him and thinking he wasn't as mad as he seemed, he was just hot."

"Oz, he was super pissed. We had Zed in all the way to his hips and he was crying because the weight of all that wet sand hurt."

"Yeah, but the Emperor was yelling at the guards, not us. We were just being stupid, and they did nothing to stop us. We really could have hurt him."

"Those were my guards mostly," Drew said. "Zed was screaming and they were arguing that they weren't our babysitters, they were just supposed to provide protection. And the Emperor went super

Scottish on them—I could barely understand a word he said. But at least I didn't hear him growl 'no' at me that day."

"The gist was that they were spectacular failures. And I'm betting you never saw them again."

He had to think about it. Growing up he'd had a rotation of personal security, changing so often that he stopped counting on anyone being there more than a few weeks at a time. He'd learn a name, get used to them, and then they were gone for months at a time, until they rotated back. When he hit his teens, he never saw the guards, even when he knew they were there. The only person who was a fixture was the nanny, Patti, and she spent more time watching daytime videos than she did watching them. When his father was at work and his mother was in meetings or holding court, he and his brother had free reign.

"Maybe that's why the Emperor scared me so much," he told her. "I wasn't used to that level of supervision. Or really even hearing the word 'no.'"

Maybe that's why your brother is such an asterisk.

"He's why we didn't have a nanny or even a regular babysitter," Oz said. "My dad, you know, same as your mom. It's a twenty-four hour a day job most of the time and he feels grateful to be home for dinner. My mom was gone until school had been out for two or three hours dealing with students' crap. The Emperor picked us up every day, played with us on the roof, made sure we did our homework before Mom got home, so that was one less thing for her to deal with—I really think he would have made dinner for us if that wasn't totally her domain. He taught us to swim, carted me back and forth from karate lessons until I was sixteen, made Zed practice piano. Still does."

Drew stopped in the middle of the sidewalk. "Are you sure you want to do this, Oz? He's like…hell, he's more than a sort-of uncle. He's your bonus dad. What more do you need to know?"

"I'm not sure. But think about it, Drew—we saw him near a portal covered in blood and we still don't know what that was about. I don't know what it is I need to know, I just know I need to figure it out."

He wanted to go back. Nearly every muscle was straining to turn around, and the hand he used to support me was twitchy. Instead, he took a couple of breaths and said, "All right then. We'll go find him."

It was a long way to the beach at the Presidio, and they walked much of it in silence. For a while it felt awkward, like they both knew they should turn around and go home but neither would admit it, and I was about to voice my displeasure at the discomfort of being with them when Oz playfully butted her shoulder against his arm. Two seconds later, he did the same to her.

Hit harder. First person to fall down loses.

"Don't worry, Wick. If we're here long enough, I can get you something to eat. I have cash for this When."

Fine. But you're going the wrong way to get the really good fishy snacks. There's nothing down this way except for rude birds and disappointment.

It took an hour to get from the portal to the path just past Yacht Harbor. It cut through a strand of trees that separated the beach from the docks where people parked their boats. On the beach side there were two buildings, one that had restrooms for people on the inside and water stations for dogs on the outside—and I suppose cats as well, but I wasn't drinking from it if I didn't have to—and the other one was a snack shack, where people could buy drinks and sandwiches, but no fish or shrimp bites. There were six tables in front of the shack, grouped in a tight cluster.

They picked a table on the side farthest from the beach, but where they had a good sightline in three directions. On the beach were three kids surrounded by at least eight adults, and the kids were flinging sand everywhere. I could hear them squealing with young laughter and it set off music in my head. I remembered it; I missed it.

Hey, those are little yous! I recognize them.

"I wonder where Carter is," Drew said as he sat down. "I know he never wanted to be anywhere we were, but I can't see him passing up the beach. There might be girls here."

Oz was focused on the Emperor. He was sitting on a bench on the sand side of the break wall, his arms resting along the back of it, and he was watching as the kids dug into the sand. "Carter," Oz said, a bit distracted, "was probably hanging out near the modern art museum, flirting with the girls who took root at the Gardens every day. Or he was at Ocean Beach, pretending to be a surfer. This beach is too small for the ratio of little kids to women that he preferred."

I wiggled until I was sitting on Drew's lap, but still tucked into his sweatshirt. I rested my paws on the table, and tried to see what Oz was looking at. The Emperor hadn't moved yet, but he was looking around.

"God, he was such a douche when he was a teenager," Drew said. "He's not any better now. He chases girls like his life depends on it. Everything behind him is littered with broken hearts."

"And you? Surely you didn't spend all your time in your bedroom, reading and playing video games."

"When I wasn't doing that, I was talking to you online." When she looked skeptical he said, "Well, yeah, I hung out with friends. We did things in a big group, mostly. A lot of my friends started hooking up with each other when we were around fifteen or sixteen, but I didn't."

"With all the girls that surely let you know they were interested? Never?"

The Emperor was now leaning forward, his elbows on his knees. He had his phone in hand and kept glancing between its screen and the kids, who had gotten a considerable amount of sand out of the hole they were digging.

"No. Why? Did you? Someone had to have asked you out a time or two or ten."

She snorted. "Way too much trouble to even bother. Always knowing there were guards watching my every move? Never knowing if someone was interested in me for me or because of the family I was born into? I hung in a group with friends, too. We had tons of safe, family-friendly parties at home on the roof. And then there was you…"

"Yeah. One time I thought about taking a date to a school picnic, but it felt like cheating. I don't cheat."

She looked away from the Emperor. "I would have been fine if you'd dated, Drew. You've always been entitled to your own life."

"Come on. We've been talking about our future since you were about twelve years old. Marriage since you were fourteen. I think you would have minded. *I* would have minded."

Oh my god they're going to start with the lip-smashing right here and now.

Oz suddenly shifted her gaze from him to over his shoulder. He and I looked, too, until she told us to stop. In the space between the snack shack and the restroom there was a man dressed in black security gear, his hand resting on the butt of his holstered gun, and he was pressed against the restroom wall. He watched the children playing in the sand, focused and waiting.

"Oz," Drew whispered, "I think he was one of my guards when I was little. Like, five or six. For sure he wasn't one this summer."

I looked over to the Emperor. He'd gotten up, but wasn't looking in our direction.

Oz patted Drew's arm, signaling him to get up, and told him to go around the other side of the snack shack. She led him into the strand of trees, and they waited behind one of the biggest ones, where they could be shielded but still could see right between the buildings.

Pretend you're smooching. No one will watch—

Everything suddenly slipped. The world tilted, and I felt a stab of dizziness. The Emperor was walking onto the beach, toward the kids, but he was also walking away from them, toward the restroom.

I blinked once, twice. He was only moving toward the restroom. I looked up at Oz, and from the confused look on her face, I was pretty sure the world had tilted for her, too.

While the Emperor headed into the restroom, the guard unholstered his gun, sliding a scope on the top, screwing a longer piece on its barrel. On the beach, twelve-year-old Drew was running from the spot where he had been helping to bury Zed's legs; he was laughing, his squeaky in-between voice cracking in the air.

His guard trailed behind him slowly, bored, allowing the pre-teen to have his fun.

"Oh my God, Drew…he's aiming at you."

"It's okay. He didn't shoot me. I'm not dead," he whispered, though I could feel the tension build in him. Every muscle on him tightened, his breathing quickened. We were so focused on young

Drew that we didn't notice when the Emperor slipped out the back door of the restroom's building, not until he was sneaking up behind the gunman.

When he was just a few feet behind, he made a hissing sound. The gunman turned, startled, giving the Emperor his opening. He grabbed the guard's wrist, turning hard and fast, plowing his free arm into the gunman's bicep until his arm snapped. Before he could scream, the Emperor had a hand over his mouth and was dragging him behind the building.

The gunman flailed; he tried to swing behind his own body with his uninjured arm, and for a moment broke free. He lunged at the Emperor, broken arm flapping at his side, teeth bared and he was practically growling. The Emperor slammed his arm forward, catching the guard in the face with the palm of his hand, the sound of it coming at us like a sharp, wet slap.

He stumbled back and then, while trying to right himself, spun on his heel and fell backward into the Emperor's grasp. With one terrifying, horrible crunch, the Emperor grabbed his head and then snapped his neck; he fell to the ground, bloody and broken and not moving.

Breathing hard, the Emperor slumped against the back wall of the snack shack. He took great gulps of air, and then forced himself to breathe through his nose, calming himself as he pulled a handkerchief from his pocket. He wiped the blood from his hands, and then tugged at the hem of his t-shirt while he checked it for stains. When he was sure he wasn't bloody, he took his phone from his other pocket and poked at its screen, his hands steady. The call lasted only a few seconds, and then he headed back to the beach, his gait steady, as if nothing had happened.

I looked up at Oz. She had the side of her hand jammed into her mouth to stifle the noises she wanted to make. Drew had his sweatshirt clenched in fists on either side of me, and I realized that the pouch was pulled uncomfortably tight across my chest.

When the Emperor was standing in front of poor, crying Zed, his hands on his hips as he was ordering the others to dig him out, Drew finally unclenched.

"What just happened, Oz? Did I just see what I think I did?"

Oz was slow to take her hand from her mouth, but when she did she breathed, "Yeah, I think so. The Emperor just killed the guy who was about to end you."

*

We hid behind the trees until Oz spotted a security van turning into the parking lot on the far side of the break wall. She poked at Drew's side and told him to get moving, and she led the way down the line of trees to the head of the path, where they could still see well enough to get an idea what was going on.

The van drove up over the walking path and parked at the side of the restroom; farther down, the kids were being ushered into an air car, their fun for the day ending with Zed's rescue from premature and incomplete burial. The Emperor waited in the parking lot until the car was on the road and heading toward home, then he began walking toward us.

We crossed the street and headed in the same direction. Oz took Drew's hand, and told him to try walking as naturally as possible, do nothing to attract his attention. They moved at a dallying pace, until the Emperor's fast stride put him far enough ahead that they felt safe, and they followed.

He followed the wide sidewalk around Marina Green, and then went down the path behind Fort Mason, making his way past the aquatic park, where he turned and headed for Ghiradelli Square. He scrambled up the steps on the east side, and was past the fountain and headed to a closed-off walkway on the far side by the time we were even close to catching up.

"There's a portal there," Oz said, breathing hard from the effort of keeping up. She pulled Drew along, peeking around the corner before following him. He was already gone, and she tucked a finger under my chin to make me look up at her. "Wick, I'm begging you, when we get through, be as quiet as you can. If you meow, he'll notice us."

Fine. It's not like you listen to anything I say, anyway.

We went through, and once on the other side spotted him turning the corner. We started after him, but just as we were about to hit the corner she held up her hand to signal Drew to stop; she heard the

Emperor's voice, and he was close by. One finger held to her lips, a reminder to be quiet, she peeked quickly, and then Drew did as well.

The Emperor was ten feet away, and with him was another version of himself. They looked to be the same age; the only difference I could see was that the Emperor we had followed was in jeans and a pale yellow t-shirt, and the other wore a faded gray hooded sweatshirt. Drew ducked back and we listened to the same voice going back and forth. One assured the other that the immediate threat had been taken care of, the other said that the threat was still very real and he'd only cut off one of the arms.

"I'll cut off as many arms as I need to in order to get to the head. What I don't understand is why they were going after Andrew."

"The boy is meant to live. So how was it that he didn't? And why here in San Francisco, and not in Chicago?"

"Why would anyone want a boy his age dead at all?"

Oz patted Drew on the arm and nodded toward the portal, whispering that it was time to go. They were cornered with no way to move past the walk way, so they might as well go home. He nodded and pushed away from where he had been leaning against the wall and reached for her hand.

And then the Emperor walked around the corner.

They froze, as if not moving made them invisible. He put his hands on his hips, cocked his head to the right just a bit, and he sighed, "Really, how many times do I have to tell you to go home?"

She breathed in pretty hard, but she was trying hard to look composed. "I went home. And that was years ago."

"Years for me. For you, what? A day? A week?" He nodded toward Andrew. "And you brought him? For what, a stroll down memory lane?"

"I'm not breaking any rules, Emperor. Besides, you just went back to talk to yourself."

The anger that flashed across his face surprised me. I expected stern, but he was seriously pissed off. "I did what was necessary. And you surely know I've had to do this from time to time, but—" he was practically spitting "—*only* to protect the timeline."

Oz was as defiant as he was angry. "And all I'm doing is watching. I'm not going back to hurt anyone or change anything."

"Is that an accusation?"

Drew set his hand on her arm, pulling gently. "Oz. Let it go. To this Emperor you're a ten-year-old little girl and he'll do anything to keep protecting her, including verbally slapping down her eighteen-year-old self. I don't know what exactly happened back there but I'm pretty sure he saved my life. I don't have to know why. I just have to be grateful." He turned to the Emperor. "We'll go home. No argument."

At that, the Emperor laughed, though he wasn't amused at all. "She's been arguing with me since she was born. I don't think she's going to stop now."

She started to turn, but hesitated. "Emperor. How old now?"

"You're ten. Do the math."

With that, he pointed to the portal and told them to go, and the same flash of anger they'd seen minutes before convinced Oz to listen. Once on the other side, she stopped and then said, "After that I was sure he would be right here when we got home."

They shouldn't have relaxed. When they turned the corner to get to the stairs, the Emperor was sitting at the fountain's edge, and he was not any degree of happy.

"I'm not going to tell you again, Oz," he said.

He's really mad, guys. His accent is back. He's NOT goin' tell yew again.

"We just—"

"You've gone eighteen years without wondering so much about me. Why now? And why not just *ask* me?"

I would have been looking everywhere but at him, but Oz stared right back.

"Because I don't know what the question is yet."

Drew was not as certain as she was. "Look, Finn started—"

The Emperor was on his feet. His jaw clenched, and I could hear his teeth grinding. "Finn should have been shut down the moment he started to press, and he should not have been taken through a portal, not again, and *especially* not to bloody spy on me."

"I'm sorry," Drew said. "I kind of suggested it."

"I don't care. I'm not asking you. I'm telling you. This stops now. I don't care if you take Drew back a hundred years to sit on a bench and watch the people go by or four hundred to grope each other in the back of a car, but you will not follow me again. Do you understand?"

Drew said he wouldn't, but Oz wasn't letting go as easily. "What happened back there?"

With his next breath, the Emperor let the anger fade away. There was no point; Oz had no fear of him, and no reason to think his irritation would change how he thought about her. "You already know that, don't you?"

"I know what we saw. We were behind the snack shack, hiding in the trees. You came around the backside of the building and beat the snot of out of an armed guard, and you broke his neck. I'm also pretty sure he was going to kill Drew. And that he succeeded."

Drew flinched. "Wait. What?"

"I fixed the timeline," the Emperor said.

"How many times? I get the first two I know about, but this? Was it because he was just a boy?"

"I did it because he wasn't supposed to die at twelve years old."

"I was freaking *dead?*"

She leaned into him. "All right. Maybe the question I should have asked is why would anyone want Drew dead?"

"The better question, indeed. And there are no ready answers." When she didn't let the redirection dissuade her, he relented. He sat back on the fountain's edge and said, "Five or six times. Always to correct something I know should not have happened."

"When it broke your heart," she said softly.

"The hiccups. They always broke my heart."

Drew carefully pulled me from his sweatshirt and handed me to the Emperor. "She just wanted to know you. Really know you. But the truth is, she knew you all along and even told me who you were just a few weeks ago."

"Remind me what I said," Oz asked.

"Icon of the city. Protector of us all. Isn't that enough?"

Oz closed her eyes, sucking in a deep breath, and when she let it out she said, "I'm an idiot. Emperor, I'm sorry. I really am."

"I know. Now go home. And I mean it, I'm not telling you again."

You didn't just save Drew for the timeline. You saved him for her.

She can feel it, and that's gonna make a girl ask a few questions.

He watched them go, until they were down the stairs and out of his sight. "She'll get her answers soon enough. She knows who I am...I think the question she's looking for is 'why?'"

27

Every street that surrounded Union Square was blocked off with giant neon yellow signs that said CLOSED BY ORDER OF THE KING in big black block letters. People were directed to walk two blocks in every direction to detour around it, and there was a lot of grumbling—by 8 a.m. the Emperor had taken six calls from traffic enforcement about it—but it wasn't going to last forever and on the last call he answered he directed the officer reporting to him to tell all the whiners to get their panties out of a wad and be grateful they only had to walk a few extra blocks.

If the people upset by having to detour could have seen the lawn chairs lined up on the sidewalk across from the Square, blocking the entrance to the royal house, they would have complained louder. Closing the streets so the King and Queen can sit outside in the shade of their building? What the hell?

Surely someone in a nearby building was looking out the window and would record the odd goings-on, especially once Finn popped up out of nowhere. It didn't appear that anyone had captured his first appearance on video, but there was no fanfare building up to that. There had been no street closures, no inconveniences for the masses. People would look for something this time.

By nine o'clock the Emperor was in his seat, and by nine-thirty he had turned off his phone, tired of the complaints. Jax, he mumbled, mostly to himself but it could have been to me, was not the sort of King who inconvenienced the masses on a whim. They should understand that and show a little patience the one time he does it, even if he won't offer an explanation. He stared at the Square, waiting impatiently even though he expected nothing to happen until after ten, but when Oz and Drew came out at nine-fifty, followed shortly by Zed and the Queen, he tore himself away.

He got out of his chair, partly because they were outside where people could see, and one does not remain seated when the Queen shows up, and partly because he especially did not remain seated when a woman shows up.

I wondered if he would do the same thing for Oz when she was older. In public, I was certain; in private, I had my doubts. He always jumped to his feet when the Queen entered the room, but if she was busy in the kitchen or busy cleaning out my litter box, he didn't have a problem with dropping into the closest chair.

The Queen took the chair next to the Emperor. "Jax," she told him as he sat back down, "is intentionally indisposed."

He hadn't expected the King to be present, and knew he was waiting several miles away at the Cliff House on Ocean Beach. There was a portal there; he would be able to see when it went offline, and would know that within minutes he could either head home, or he would hear a horrific eruption of noise coming from downtown.

He didn't want Oz there. He didn't want any of them near the Square, but there was no dissuading her and the Queen was not going to leave her daughter even if the worst happened.

Even the Emperor tried to talk them into going with the King. "I'm willing to risk my life for this. No one else needs to."

"You don't *need* to," Oz pointed out. "Finn knows where to find everyone. But we should be there, you know? Besides, he's opening a portal, not setting off a bomb."

Not on purpose, anyway.

So they waited, lined up along the street in horribly uncomfortable chairs, until the Emperor, twitchy and nervous, stood up quickly and declared he was going up to the Square; waiting by the door offered a horrible view, and he wanted to see, clearly, what was going to happen.

Oz scrambled after him, even though the Queen yelled at her to stop. A few minutes later—the Queen resigned to the inevitable—they were all waiting at the edge of the Square, on the far side from the existing portal, and I ran after them because there was no way I was sitting by myself.

There were pigeons around. I'd chased enough of them to understand they might want to indulge in a little feathery group revenge.

Just after ten, Drew turned to Zed and said, "You know this is going to be super boring for us. We won't see anything until Finn is actually coming out of the portal."

Zed thought that he would smell it; if not the actual portal, then the changes in Oz and the Emperor, either their excitement or their terror.

Oz leaned toward him, and in a whisper asked, "What's the Emperor smell like today?"

Zed inhaled deeply. "Christmas."

The crackling sound from the portal grew louder, enough that everyone could hear it, and the Emperor stood up, watching intently as its colors brightened—I don't know if Drew or Zed could see that—and then winked out in a shrinking crimson star. His hand went to his chest and his breath quickened, and I did as he had asked: I jumped down from my seat near Oz and made sure I was at his feet.

I had an inkling why, a nagging voice in the back of my head that felt like a memory was trying to wiggle its way forward, but I didn't dwell on it. He wanted me near him, so there I was.

Then just twenty feet away, there was a bright blue light that hung in midair and expanded from the size of a pin prick to the size of a human head and then to the size of two doorways, and it stretched from the ground to well over their heads, thinning out and pulsating, the hum of it pricking at my ears.

Drew and Zed and the Queen scrambled to their feet, seeing for the first time a portal right in front of them. She reached for Zed's and Oz's hands, ignoring the fact that each of the kids uttered things off the bad word list.

The Emperor grabbed a communicator from his back pocket and said excitedly into it, "It's stable, Jax. You can come back."

"Finn there?"

"Not yet, but this was the iffy part. The portal is here and stable."

The King had a police air car—hyper-speed-equipped with clear air space the whole way—waiting for him; before the Emperor could get the communicator back into his pocket he was likely in the back seat and flying at the highest safe speed possible to get back to the Square. The Emperor had told him earlier that he had roughly ten minutes if he wanted to actually be there when Finn stepped through—but Finn would understand if he couldn't be.

"Are you kidding? Finn will be the official first contact from the future. I'll be there."

The sirens screamed all the way down Market Street and then abruptly went quiet when the car turned onto Powell. It came to a screeching halt at Geary, and the King sprang out and ran for the Square, nearly tripping on the top step, and made it just in time to see a well-worn leather shoe slip out of the blue shadow.

The Emperor held his breath; I could feel it from where I sat at his feet. He didn't breathe until this thin, older man had stepped all the way through, pausing as he took a deep breath, and he grinned widely as he looked right at the Emperor.

It was Finn, and he was at least forty years older than he'd been just three days ago.

He took a step forward, holding his arms out. "My God…Dash, it really is you," he choked out.

The Emperor finally exhaled, and then met Finn halfway, pulling him into a tight hug, and he managed to sob a single word.

"Dad."

28

Oz was the only one who didn't twitch in surprise. She held a hand up to stop the rest of them from moving forward to greet Finn, and said, "Give them a minute." She made them wait until Jo stepped through the portal; her joy was explosive as she shouted "William!" and sprinted for the Emperor. Oz didn't let anyone move until the Emperor's face had been covered in kisses and he had been hugged so hard he likely couldn't breathe, not until he bent over to pick me up. When his face went from elated to sad, she moved.

Finn's hand was on my head, petting, looking for that sweet spot behind my ears, and Jo reached for the Emperor's arm. "Not yet, sweetheart," she said to him.

"Not yet for what?" Oz demanded.

The silence that followed was unbearable. I tried to wiggle out of the Emperor's hands, but he wasn't letting me go. Seconds ticked off as the Emperor's heart beat went up, and I could feel Jo's grip on his arm tighten. She wasn't pulling or tugging; she wanted him to know she was there, and in almost as much pain as he was.

The last thing she wanted was to take me from him.

No one loved him more; no one could.

This is okay. Let me go, dude.

"When the portal turns pink, Wick is supposed to go through," the Emperor croaked. His eyes were rimmed red, and he pulled me closer, clutching me to his chest.

Finn clipped a tiny red box to my collar, and then flicked a switch on it.

"Why?" Oz tried to step between the Emperor and his father, but Finn was busy turning my collar so that the box rested on the back of my neck.

"Wick is the test to make sure that the world still exists two hundred years from now," Finn said. "When the portal turns pink, it means that the last person in San Francisco has gone through and relocated somewhere else. We'll send him to a week beyond that, and if he comes back, then we know we succeeded."

"*If?*"

Jo stroked my chin, and I felt her sadness. "We can't send a person through."

"You don't have to send *him*, either." She tried to reach me, but the King was behind her, his arms around her, hugging hard and holding her back.

"He'll come back," he said, as gently as he could.

She was struggling and Jo was crying. "We don't want anything to happen to him. But he's been trained—"

"I don't care!"

The Emperor kissed the top of my head. "It's okay, buddy." His breath ruffled my fur, warm and moist. "We can't send Wick through now," he told Finn. "I removed one of his transponders and embedded it in the gate to make sure your ship would be able to go through it. I know I was only supposed to fix your ship, and I could have, but…building the gate gives us transporting possibilities. And Wick can't go through without that transponder."

"I suspected as much. He has a failsafe. This is only to help him remember what he's supposed to do."

Finn flicked one more switch.

And then I remembered.

I knew I would do this as far back as when I was first brought to this When of San Francisco, the day he asked the old King to care for me. Finn explained it to me then; I was going to live with the royal family, but I would see Will all the time and I would keep him safe just by being there. When the time came, when I had lived as long as three other cats could even hope for, I would head back toward home through a new portal. I would be alone when I got there, but all I had to do was wait a few minutes, look around, and then go back to where they would be waiting for me.

He didn't have to tell me that I might not make it past the portal entry. I knew that.

I was fine with that.

I was older than any of them realized; if I'd reached the end of the line, it was probably time.

It's all right. I can do this. I just walk through, take a look around while the camera on my neck takes pictures, then I come back. I used to practice it, remember? There's a Wick-sized portal in the back of Oz's closet that I used to go through, until I forgot what it was for.

"All those books in the Old Mint," Oz sputtered. "You've done this how many times? A hundred? A Thousand? It's *never* worked! Don't kill him for a maybe!"

Tell her the truth. Tell her that if I die, you probably will too. You can't live without me here, Emperor. Tell her you wouldn't let me go if it wasn't that important.

"It's different this time," Finn said. "This time Dash created the gate instead of only repairing my ship, and that changed everything."

"Dash who did what?" Drew asked.

They ignored him.

"In every recorded previous attempt, we tried changing the trajectory of the meteor that might crash into earth, in approximately thirty minutes from the time we left. We tried a hundred different ways to move it off course. But this time we had the schematics for the gate, and we built a half-dozen of them. A year ago those gates were launched into space and tested with debris, and it worked. Every piece we put through the first gate held. The meteor should enter the first gate and not earth's atmosphere, and if it holds—"

"But you can't guarantee it."

Jo wanted to be gentle with the truth. "No. We can't, which is why we can't send a person through. Wick is how we'll know if it worked, and if we can go home."

I can do this. Piece of cake. Or shrimp. When I get back, I want shrimp. And cheese. I can have that, right?

"Wick is my anchor," the Emperor whispered. He lifted me so that we were looking at each other's faces. "And you're right. If you die, I will, too. Sooner rather than later."

He set me down.

"Without Wick, I don't have even a year here. Half that. I won't be able to eat. I won't be able to sleep. Not at all, Mom. I already have trouble sleeping, but without him it will get progressively worse, until I won't sleep even a minute. Without my anchor, I'll wither and die, and that's not a metaphor. It's the truth. I won't survive. I'll go in his place."

We can go together.

"No, Wick. I promised I would keep you safe, and you're safe with Jax and Oz. You don't need an anchor to hold you here."

When Jo tried to reach for him, crying his name, Finn pulled her back.

"If I stay without him, I'm just as dead as if that portal leads out into empty space, but it will take longer and hurt more."

It hit Finn all at once, and his face sagged with the weight of understanding. He still had his arms around Jo, and rested his head on her shoulder. "I don't want to watch my son slowly die. And if Wick doesn't come back, he will. You know he will. It's why we sent Wick ahead in the first place, to be William's anchor and to save his life. I have you. You have me. He has no one else to keep him from being unstuck from this time and I don't think we're enough. He's been without us for too long."

"Oz." The Emperor picked me back up and held me out to her, and as she took me he pulled her close, setting his forehead against hers. "Just listen to my thoughts. Most of it won't make sense, but it's everything you need to know about me, and you can sort through it all later. If I don't come back...help Zed speak for me. Tell him the highlights, and save the lowlights for yourself."

They stood there, with me in between them, for several minutes. When they pulled apart, he kissed her on the forehead.

"I've wanted to do that a million times for the last six or seven years."

"You're coming back," she whispered. "If I have to rip that portal apart, you're coming back."

The hum of the portal changed.

"It's pink," the King said.

He let go of Oz, kissed Finn and Jo, and then without looking back he stepped into the pink mist.

29

We waited.

When it was dark outside and fog had wrapped around the city with icy fingers that poked and flicked, we were still there on the Square, waiting for the Emperor to step back through the still-pink portal. We would wait, the King said, until either the Emperor came back or the portal winked a new color to let us know it had closed on the other side. Finn warned him it might not change, but it didn't matter; we would wait.

Jo cried until she physically couldn't anymore; when she wasn't leaning against Finn, she was leaning against Aubrey, who was soaking up as much of the pain as she could. She could feel it, pain compounded against anguish, and swallowed her own tears so that Jo could let hers come freely.

She had touched the Emperor once; she understood more than most. She loved him, too, and was willing to pull as much pain from his mother as she could. I could see it in her eyes, the searing ache and agonizing loss, and knew it was multiplied by not only the possible loss of her friend, but the knowing of how much it would hurt if it had been Oz or Zed.

Drew and Zed dragged the chairs from the sidewalk up to the Square so that everyone could be more comfortable, and we sat in front of the portal as if it were a campfire that we hoped would soon give off warmth. Oz stared at it, only blinking when her eyes burned, and I was sure she was sifting through all the thoughts the Emperor had given her; it was his entire life, from the moment after his birth when he was fully aware until just before he stepped through.

I could hear the last thing he thought to her. *Love them and treat them well. They're all that will be left of me in this world, no matter the When.*

I watched her while half-listening to the conversation going on next to me. When they could speak around their pain, Finn and Jo explained everything they could, but I already knew most of it. Years before Finn was even born, NASA had spotted an object in space that, if their math was right, was headed for earth. If it hit, it would end all life, save for a few stubborn bacteria.

Finn invented the portals in hopes that he could relocate as many people as possible before the meteor hit; he bounced his way through time, using his ship to punch small tears in the fabric between null space and reality. He then built gate-like portals around those tears and seeded them with transporters. When he was confident that they worked, he guided people through, taking them to so many different points in time that the surplus in population wouldn't be noticed.

He couldn't save the world, but he could save most of San Francisco.

"The portals aren't so much a way to travel through time as they are a way to be transported through it," he told the King.

This wasn't news to him. He knew, and his hand went to the spot just under his hairline where he could feel the small transponder that had been placed there when he was still a baby.

It was news to Oz, though, and enough of their discussion filtered through her concentrated fog that she finally looked away from the portal.

"Wait. What?"

The King reached for the Queen's hand, and he looked to her for permission to tell. She nodded, and with a deep breath he said, "Just behind your right ear, under your scalp, there's a small bump about the size of a grain of rice. It's the reason you can use the portals. It connects your brain to them, and when you go through it activates the transporters and allows you to move through."

"I thought because I could see—"

"Partly," Finn said. "Your synesthesia is why they have sound. I needed to give you a way to find the portals easily, without the rest of the world being able to see where they are. That low crackle is why you can see them when others can't, and the transponder is why you can take people through with you, but no one else can just fall through. Or go through on purpose."

He'd taken thousands of people through the portals, but they couldn't just turn around and go back, not without his help. That seeming unkindness was to make sure they wouldn't try to return to a dead world—or worse, to nothing at all.

"I'm sorry, Ozzie," the Queen said. "You would have been told—"

Oz shook her head. "It doesn't really matter now, does it?"

"Be angry," the King told her. "I was. A lifetime of being made to feel just a bit more special than the average person, only to learn it was foisted on me? You're allowed to be upset by the manipulation of the truth."

"Why bother? I mean, what difference does it make if I can trip through time or not? It's not like I did anything more than go off on little diversions. I wasted it and I didn't exactly make a difference to anyone."

Finn's tension softened. "But you did, Oz. That's how I met you, because you understood the portals, and it's why you were able to accept me so easily. Without you, my arrival might have been very different. I wasn't changing that."

Zed was the first to find something to smile about. "Even knowing she wanted to hurt you after the whole throw-the-wife-off-the-bridge thing?"

"Even so."

Oz was less amused, but her gaze had shifted to Drew, who was frowning hard and staring at his own feet.

"Drew. What?"

He took a deep breath, squinting hard before finally looking at Finn. "Okay. So. The Emperor created the gate that got you home, right? And you move people through portals using some kind of transporter, right? And the gate works the same way?"

"More or less."

"Okay. So he used a gate to transport you home. And you're using six gates to hold a meteor in place, but why?"

The explanation was long and mostly boring, but by using fairly simple terms Finn was able to paint him a picture. The gates were lined up one after the other, with the first having a transponder that would be embedded in the rock using a high-speed laser, the same way the Emperor had used one of mine to send Finn home. After that, each gate was to transport the meteor back and forth; if it worked the meteor would be held forever between the second and third gate, with the rest being fail-safes.

"So they're just neatly lined up?"

Finn nodded.

"Okay. So you have six gates in a row but you're really only using, what, three of them? Since you're transporting it back and forth, why didn't you move the other three gates so that they're not in a line but kind of curved, so the transporter would push the meteor's trajectory away from earth by going through *all* of the gates? I mean, like, don't rely on it begin held there forever, but transport it off. You know, so it goes on its merry way and isn't just hanging there to wipe out the planet on some random future day if the gates fail. And then you have them for later, to move if you need them again."

"It's probably more complicated than that," Zed said.

Finn was on his feet. "But it's not. It's not, and I'm an idiot." He grabbed Jo's hand. "Come on, we've still got work to do." To Oz he said, "Stay here and keep an eye on the portal. And keep Wick safe, because if something happens to him, William is going to be crushed."

As they ran off, Drew asked, "Did I help, or did I make it worse?"

"Prince Andrew," Zed said, punching him on the arm, "You may have just saved the Emperor's life."

"I don't get it."

"The Old Mint building is time-locked," Oz explained. "If Finn can go in and find someone from the exact day he needs, and give them all the information they need to know *before* they deploy the gates…they can make those changes, and do exactly what you suggested. Transport the meteor away from earth."

"Huh. I'm not sure what a time lock is, but whatever. You'd think that if they're smart enough to do that, they're smart enough to point the freaking gates away from the planet in the first place."

"You'd think."

"Do you think the Emperor made it through?" Drew asked.

Zed got up and went to edge of the portal, brushing away Oz's warning to not get too close. "If the meteor hit, would this have disappeared? Or would there be an entry without there also being an exit? What if he stepped in, and there was nothing to go to?"

"That's exactly why I was never allowed to go forward in time," Oz said.

"I can still smell him."

That startled her. She got up and rushed to his side. "How?"

"I just can. It's like he's there, but I just can't see him. And he smells…he's terrified."

"Oh my God."

"He never made it through?" Drew said, less a question than a fear.

"There's no exit point," Oz groaned.

Zed turned away from the portal. "What do we do, Oz? We can't leave him there."

She was crying, giant tears rolling down her face. "I don't know. I'm not sure I can get him out, and if he's stuck there, even if Finn can alter his own time line to fix the gates…he's there, right in between then and now."

"Transporter signals degrade over time," Drew muttered.

"What?"

"Well, in science fiction they do. Keep someone in a transporter field for too long and their atomic structure kind of…fades away. Like a body can't hold itself together."

I sniffed at the portal. I couldn't smell what Zed did, but I didn't think he was making it up, either.

I'm his anchor.

My job is to hold him in place. Maybe I can hold his bits and pieces together, too.

Before Oz could grab me, before any of them could, I stepped forward, into the portal, and into a bath of pink.

30

Hold still. I'm going to climb you like a tree, so that you can grab onto me and keep me in one place. I think I would be okay down here but I'd feel better if you had a good hold on me. Plus, we might be here a while. It might take them some time to figure out how to get us out. I know you can't talk. Just listen.

I'll tell you a story. Listen to that instead of being afraid that you're stuck. Or maybe just remember. That's like playing in a swimming pool, right? Only it's full of memories that you can pull out like splashed drops. Think about how we got here.

Remember when Finn brought me home? Probably not, you were so little. He found me limping along in the Castro somewhere around nineteen-sixty-eight. He had food and offered some to me when I stopped and meowed because I smelled it, and I was so hungry that I went up to him even though he was a stranger and strangers hadn't been very nice to me. They were always chasing me away from food and water, sometimes even throwing things at me. But Finn wasn't angry, he acted like he was happy to see me and he offered me something to eat, and I was so, so hungry that I risked getting that close to a human. He had a sandwich, and I think he picked out all the beefy bits for me when he saw how hungry I really was. He didn't keep any of it for himself. I even got to lick the bread. And one of the first things he said to me, after saying "Poor, hungry baby" was that I reminded him of a cat named Wick and that he had liked that cat very much.

After he fed me I followed him, and kept telling him I needed a home. He didn't understand what I was saying, but he heard me. He said that he was pretty sure I had no place to live, seeing how thin I was and how unkempt my fur had become. And he was right; I had gotten too tired to take care of myself so I'd slacked off on basic hygiene. He picked me up and said that he had a little boy who would love me a lot, and that I would be safe with his family. That's when he took me through my first portal.

I was safe, too. Your mom loved me from the moment she saw me, and she gave me a gentle bath that I didn't fight because I was so tired and it felt so good, and then she fed me tiny meals nearly ten times a day for a long time, to make sure that I got healthy. She sat on the floor with us every day, and told you over and over to be gentle with the kitty. Be soft and kind and he'll love you.

And I did. You named me Major and we played army almost every day until you started going on time trips with your father. You built tiny cities out of blocks and I knocked them down while we saved the pretend people from our pretend evils. Then you built houses for everyone, and we didn't knock those down because that was mean, and we never, ever wanted to be mean.

I was your Major and you were my General. We were an army of two and we were going to save the world.

And then when I realized you could understand me? I don't even remember how old you were, but it couldn't have been more than four or five, because you were trying so hard to tell your parents what I wanted, and they thought you were making things up, and that's when I told you to tell them I was going to run across the sofa and jump onto the table, and when I did, they laughed because I did that every day. So I told you to tell them I was going to hiss at them, and they didn't laugh so much when I did it.

Still, I don't think they really believed it until you were about six, and after kissing your mother goodnight you told her not be afraid of the bad things in the sky, because Major said that daddy would fix it all, and Major never lied, not even when you had to go to the doctor and get shots. I promised you that even though it would hurt a tiny bit, the hurt would be over so fast that a few minutes later you wouldn't even remember why you'd been afraid of it. She remembered you being brave, telling her that I'd said that right before you rolled up your sleeve and told the doctor to take his best shot.

They really started listening then, didn't they? Finn began taking you through the portals more often and told you it was for special field trips, so that you would learn more about history, when the truth is that he was looking for a place in time where we would all be comfortable and happy together. He thought he knew the When he wanted to live in, but he had to be sure because it wasn't for just him. And then you started going off on your own without permission, when you got it into your head that you wanted to watch your favorite bedtime story happen, the one about the time when his friend, the Emperor of San Francisco, saved the life of a little prince stuck on the bridge with a cat in his backpack.

The problem was that while you were waiting there, the Emperor never came. There were dozens of people yelling at that little boy to get down, but none of them were helping. He was crying and you became more and more afraid he would fall, and that Emperor was nowhere around, so you finally pushed through all those people and you got him yourself, and then you held him tight while you marched him to his mother.

And man...you were so afraid when you got home and realized that you had to tell your father where you'd gone and what you'd done, because you had just changed the timeline and it wasn't something little like breaking a tree limb or squashing a bug. You'd waited for the Emperor as long as you thought was safe, but then you had to climb and get the prince, because if something happened to him your dad wouldn't have anyone to help him later when he was lost in time with no memory. Then there would be no princess named Oz, no eulogist named Zealand or goofy prince named Andrew. He would show up in a When he didn't know, and he would be utterly alone.

That was the first time you ever saw your father cry, I think. He just sank to the floor and started crying, because he knew then that his son was the Emperor, and that his life was going to be a lonely one.

But you already knew that, didn't you? You couldn't touch someone without peeking into his or her head or letting them see your thoughts, even if you didn't want to. You were going to be alone anyway, so if you could live your lonely life being someone who could be something good? You wanted that. I wasn't thrilled with being given to the prince's family, taken back to when he was just a baby, while I waited for you, but I understood why. You were taking all these trips as a teenager so you could get to know the prince as he grew up, and you needed me to be there because the whole being unstuck from your own time made you sick. Time always wants to fix itself, and you being somewhere Time thought was wrong made it itch a lot, and that itch had to be scratched. That made you queasy and you couldn't sleep. But your parents figured it out, because you were never sick when you went away with your dad, and then he went a few more times alone and when he started staying longer, he started feeling it, too.

Eventually, you didn't feel well even when he was along. He realized the connections mattered; you loved him, he knew that, but you spent every day with me, almost all day, and we were bonded.

Finn had you to anchor him when he was lost in time, even if he didn't know it. And then later he knew to send everyone with someone else, but you had no one. Just me.

I'm your anchor, William.

I can hold you in place, right here.

I'll stay with you here in the pink as long as it takes. I'm not letting you fade into the mist. It might hurt, but we're going to wait here and it might be a million years, but they'll get us out.

They will.

I promise.

I've never lied to you.

We'll go home, and have pizza and shrimp and other delicious dead things, and you won't ever have to worry again about the world ending.

You're going to get old, Emperor. As old as me, maybe.

I was dying when Finn rescued me. You kept me alive.

You're my anchor, too.

31

We slept.

I could have moved around a bit, but the Emperor couldn't manage it very well, so I stayed curled up in his arms, resting against his chest, waiting for someone to rescue us from the mist. His eyes were closed, but I could feel when he was awake and when he was asleep, though I honestly could not tell if we slept in micro-minutes or for hours at a time.

I swear, I will never again ask if I can hang out in the pink mist.

His chest rose and fell quickly; he was trying to laugh.

For one abrupt moment, when I saw a bright light flash from the other side of the portal, I thought they were coming for us. The light came and went, and then nothing. I tried to look past him, to see if there was anything behind us, but I couldn't stretch far enough and was afraid if I tried too hard, I would fall.

Any other time, I was sure I could land on my feet.

For all I knew, physics didn't apply when stuck in the pink mist. Maybe time didn't, either.

*

There was another bright flash. It lasted a fraction of a moment longer than the last one, and it felt warm.

"We moved," I heard the Emperor think.

Or the planet blew up.

"Yeah, thank you for that thought."

I hung my head over his forearm, looking to where I knew the portal door was in front of us, and it had changed. I could see the building across the street, the sun pinging off the windows and I could see shadows of people zooming past.

Open your eyes. There's something out there.

"I see it."

Then it went dark, and he felt movement again.

Not to alarm you, but that looks like where we lived when you were little.

His heart rate picked up, and his breathing along with it. "He opened the other portal again. We're looking through two doors."

And just like that, it slammed shut, and we were yanked backwards, hard. He kept his arms around me as he flew back, and while I cringed at the sound his breath made while being sucked in so hard, it was music to hear Oz's voice above his breath.

"Welcome back."

32

There was shrimp and there were beefy things, and it felt like someone's birthday all over again. I didn't even complain when I was passed from lap to lap and told what a good boy I am. We were on the roof just as the sun was going down and the cool air began to feel cold. The people sat in chairs in a circle, and each one of them had nice things to say to me as they fed me bits of perfectly cooked dead meaty things. Maybe it was my birthday, I don't know. I'd never celebrated one but it felt that's how mine should be.

Aside from all the attention I was given, it was a lot like Oz's birthday had been, minus all the teenagers who were too stingy to share the food. There was not-as-loud music, and a table laid out with food that was not pizza, but instead of only the adults being tucked into the corner while they watched the kids, the kids pulled up chairs to sit with them. The chairs were circled around a fire pit, but the pit had shimmering lights and it blew hot air instead of fire, so it was safe for me to be near. I could even walk along the flat top edge of it, balancing as I went around, making a great show of not falling off.

Oz and Drew drifted away after they had properly admired me. They were over near the food, standing a little too close to each other to make the King happy, but there was nothing going on that made me want to close my eyes or hurl. Drew had his hands shoved safely into his back pockets and was bent over just a little bit, like he was thinking about kissing or maybe even head butting her. Oz was laughing at something he said, so I was pretty sure the head butting was out, and if he was going to go in for the kiss he was going to have an audience. Maybe even a critique, because the Emperor looked over at them, perhaps a bit wistfully, and then excused himself to go talk to them.

I followed; he was going to be closer to the food and I'd gotten all I was going to get from everyone else for a while. Besides, if Drew did kiss her and the Emperor told him it sucked as far as he could tell, I wanted to see Drew's reaction up close.

Instead, the Emperor asked Drew to give him a minute with Oz, which disappointed me a little bit; Drew backed away from her and said, "Sure, but whatever she said I did, I didn't really."

The Emperor cocked his head just slightly, hands on his hips the way he had when Drew was small and sticky, when he wanted to scare him. "You mean, whatever she says you obviously want to do, you haven't yet worked up the nerve?"

"Bite me, old man." Drew was laughing as he left them.

"All right, then," the Emperor said, pointing to a spot on the ground near the roof wall. They sat down, leaning against it, and I sat right in front of them, staring, because staring seemed like a fine thing to do. "That boy is no longer afraid of me."

"Not in the least."

"That's a shame. I did enjoy staring him down when he was a little boy. I didn't have to say a word. He'd stop, his eyes would go wide, and off he'd run."

"He was pretty sure that your diet consisted of the brains and bones of little children back then."

"That's oddly specific."

"He has an oddly specific imagination."

"Good for him. He'll need it to keep up with you. And I need to apologize." He bent his legs, draping his arms over his knees, fingers hanging like tempting, wiggly toys. He stared at me without really seeing me. I knew the cadence: slow breath in, slow breath out, then confession. "The burden of my memories is too much to give someone without warning. I've only given so much one other time and I wouldn't have imposed them on you if I hadn't been certain I was about to die."

Oz stretched her legs out, fingers laced together as she rested her hands on her stomach. He seemed sad, but she was relaxed. "It's not a burden. It was noisy and unsettling for the first couple of hours, but once I realized how much there was and how out of sequence I was processing things, I sort of shoved it all into a box in my brain and taped the lid closed. It's not mine, so I'll resist peeking into it."

He swallowed a hot ball of regret, and I could hear it slide down his throat. "Nevertheless…those things are with you forever and for that I am sorry. One person should never know another so well."

"It's all right. I won't betray you."

"And you've almost always been respectful about my privacy, avoiding asking the things you knew you shouldn't. Now here I am, shoving it all into your head in a matter of minutes, with no time to prepare yourself for it. It will always be there. But…I think if anyone can contain that box, it's you."

His feet slid on the grass and he met her pose, a bit more relaxed, with his legs crossed at his ankles, but I could still feel the sadness slither around him in loose coils.

"Who was the other person?" she asked. "My mother?"

"No. Your grandmother. You know she disapproved of me, don't you?"

Dude. She thought you were Satan. Or an alien overlord.

"I never understood that. You saved Dad's life. I've read all the newspaper articles about it and heard people's notions that he would have gotten down safely one way or the other, but even Grandma was certain he would have fallen if not for you."

"And she was grateful. But over the first few years, he aged and I did not, and she couldn't make sense of that. Your grandfather kept her in the dark about me and why I was here—and he knew much of it, possibly far more than I did, because my father needed his help—but she had a keen sense that I was Other When. She resented it. She wanted to know what else was out there, what was coming, and no one would tell her.

"Then when she became ill…it was cruel. Death ate away at her so slowly, in these horrible, startling fits that grabbed her limb by limb, creeping from her fingers and toes inward, as if it was consuming her soul. She was in terrible pain, yet the only times she really cried were for the things she would never know. She wanted desperately to know your father would be happy, and what would become of her grandchildren. She wanted to know if she'd created a treasured legacy or if she was leaving the world a bitter woman, resentful for all the kindnesses she had withheld. I had answers that I had every right to keep to myself, but I also knew that I could put those things into her mind as if they were her own memories and give her peace.

"When I thought she was close to the end I laid my hand on her forehead and I gave her everything I knew, everything that I hoped would make her passing bearable. When I was done she said that she knew me, and she truly did, as much as anyone can."

Oz swallowed, hard.

Don't cry. It was happy. I was there. She loved him for that.

"She held on for a week, and didn't tell a soul. I've never given that much to anyone other than her, and now you. Not even my own parents."

Quietly, Oz asked, "What about my mom?"

"Aubrey? No. Why would I?"

"We were there when you saved her from the douchebag that attacked her in the Plaza. She touched you on the cheek, and it clearly startled her. It didn't make sense until you touched my hand. I knew then that she had heard something from you."

He twitched, just a little.

Ha. You didn't know they'd been there.

"She only got a glimpse. My real name, my When, and a very small bit of why I was there. She swore her secrecy even though I told her she didn't need to keep anything from Jax. He wouldn't let either of us tell him. He had somewhat of an idea why I was there and had grasped long before then that not knowing everything was probably in his best interests. He also understood why she became my protector of sorts after that. And also why when they took over the family apartment, she wanted me there. I don't live downstairs from you because of some overwhelming need to be roommates with my best friends. I'm there because it soothes something in her."

"And you just don't say no to my mom."

"Truly. She is genuinely empathic, Oz. Not simply the 'somewhat' that Zed believes. She will soak up someone's pain and make it her own, until she can heal it."

"Her gift."

"Her burden. And I am deeply sorry I've made my life yours." She started to say something, but he held up a finger to stop her. "I am also sorry because when I was giving you my memories, I inadvertently heard things that were floating in the front of your mind."

"If you heard that I wanted to drop kick your mom for what she planned to do to Wick, I'm sorry."

That made him chuckle. "She'll forgive that. She'd probably love you for it, because Wick matters to her. No. Most of what I heard was about Drew. That you truly do love him and how much you don't want to talk to your parents about it because you know when that part of your life begins it will upset them. And Drew saying that he wanted to be like me. Don't encourage him. My life is not one someone should aspire to."

He didn't have to explain.

"He wants the part where he's selfless and dedicated to helping others. Not the loneliness."

"That sprang from the loneliness."

"But it won't with him. I won't let him be lonely. And you—you don't have to stay that way. You can obviously control how much you let someone see when you touch them. When Finn left, you only let me know that he was your father and how much it hurt to hold that from him, and how much it hurt to have left your parents behind when you were a boy. I had a hint of how hard it was. But that's it. If you can control that, you can be with someone."

He turned to look at her, regret hidden in the tiny bit of a smile that he managed. "It's more than that. It's the unguarded moments. Oz, watch your parents. See how often they touch without even thinking about it. All those random kisses just because they're passing each other in the hallway and the way she trails her fingers over his arm simply because he's right there and she can't stop herself. Those moments just happen and there's no guarding from the chatter that everyone has running through their heads all the time."

"I didn't say it would be easy. But it's obviously like a window. You can close it."

"It's a window that works both ways. I might be able to close off my thoughts quickly, but it's far too much to ask of someone else."

Pointedly, Oz sighed, "You've never even tried. Other than with your parents, I'm guessing."

"I could never risk that much truth. I can touch my parents and not give them free admission to my thoughts, and they learned how to close their minds to me when I was just a little boy. To expect someone else to is asking far too much. The private moments between couples would never allow for that."

"All right, that's fair enough. But the game has changed, you know. Who you are is no longer a secret. Neither is why you were here."

Dude, no. Don't let her see your heart bleed. Don't make me hear it.

"It's never been an option with anyone, and even if I could shut the window and teach someone else to do the same...I have an expiration date." He leaned his head back, looking up to the stars, and he swallowed hard. It was the onus of his life, that he wouldn't even be born for two hundred years; it was also the onus of his father in not knowing who the Emperor was. "All the stories he told me when I was a child—and he made up many of them because I wanted more than his few weeks here gave him—and he had no clue, so there was always unfettered access to information and I sought it out. He had made this Emperor to be a nearly mythological, magical person for me, so I read everything I could about him and memorized as much as possible. Including the date of his death."

That was part of the reason Finn sank to the floor and cried like a baby when he realized who his son was. He knew, in that flash of clarity, that he'd never hidden anything from Will about the Emperor, always thinking that one day he would take his son to meet his hero. It was also why he explored other Whens, looking for a different time in which he could settle his family, because he knew that less than a year after sending Finn home, the Emperor would steadily grow ill, and would die.

"I have six months, Oz. There's not enough time to begin living."

I waited for Oz's tears. I braced for her anger. I could feel the bubble of grief forming and expected outrageous indignation, and was ready to spring onto her lap to purr for her. Instead, she snorted a laugh through her nose, and said, "You're not going to die, Emperor."

I don't want him to, either.

"Ozzie—"

"Those books you read when you were little, the ones that haven't even been written yet? They don't know that you changed the paradigm. *That* history ends with Wick going through the portal and never coming back, leaving you here and broken. But now? He's right here, still with you, still your anchor."

Still saving your sorry asterisk. You can thank me later.

"You lost him in a different timeline," she said. "His absence is why that Emperor died. But *you* won't."

From the time he stopped being a sticky little person until that moment, I'd only seen the Emperor cry perhaps four or five times, and at least two of those were negated when he fixed hiccups in the timeline. Now he was sitting next to Oz, staring up at the stars, and giant tears leaked from the corners of his eyes, dripping into his ears.

Oz wasn't finished. "You have time. I'm guessing you're still a year younger than my dad, even though you look like it's about five or ten? And looking at Finn and Jo—they have to be in their late seventies and they're pretty freaking spry. Neither one looks much older than my mom. How long of a life could that other Emperor have expected, if he had remained in his own When? A hundred fifty? More? What's your projected, healthy life span?"

His voice croaked. "One-eighty or thereabouts."

"So you're still basically a teenager. Lots of time to find someone to grow old with."

He wiped at his eyes, and finally looked at her. "I am not a teenager."

Scottish, dude. Iyam NOT a teenayger.

You need to work on that.

"Fine. But you're not middle aged, either. Now *please* tell me how you were fifteen when my dad was six, and then my age when he was nineteen. I get that it's because of the portals, but my brain can't make sense of it."

My brain had a hard time when it was happening. He left right after handing the Prince over to his mother and it was weeks before we saw him again. He kept that pattern up for over ten years: he would be here for a week or two, then gone for long stretches. The older Jax became the longer the Emperor stayed, but there were always periods where we didn't see him.

He was going home, staying for a day or two at most, and then coming back weeks after he'd left. By the time he'd aged two years, Jax was only a few months from turning eighteen.

After that, he stayed.

"I am legitimately a year younger than your dad," he told her. "I stayed because it was time, and because going home was just…difficult." He nodded toward Jo and Finn. "My mother had to step away from their work for several years when it became clear I couldn't stay in school with other children. She spent her days teaching me, and yes, you can thank her for my accent, then evenings helping him with process notes and documentation, just to keep on schedule. It was unintentional, but I became a distraction. They truly did try hard to carve out time for me, and if they had been doing anything else…"

"Saving the world and all that."

"They didn't just let me go. It killed them, but when I wanted to stay here they gave me up. And they knew what the end would be. They knew that they would come back, and I—"

"You're not going to die. They're here now, and you can be a family."

"Ah, but their When still exists. They'll have to go home."

Oz nodded, but didn't look happy. She turned her head to look at them, and he reached out, hesitating at first, but then set his fingers under her chin and gently made her turn back to him.

"You have to go with them!"

You know, it's rude to talk in your heads to each other while I'm right here.

"I have no life there. I never had friends. I was never happy. There's no one who misses me, other than them. And the portals will be reopened. If I survive, I can visit. They can visit. I can even take you there someday. But this is my home."

"They'll be heartbroken."

He shook his head. "They'll understand. I was never meant to go back. And you—if you would, spend some time learning to close that window in your head. And help me teach Zed. You two are the closest to children I'll have, and you're right, my secret is out. You know who I am and don't need to withhold everything in order to keep it all from Finn anymore. I won't refrain from hugging you and planting kisses on the tops of your heads anymore. I don't care if you think you're too old. I have time to make up for."

"We'll never be too old for that, Emperor."

He looked over at Drew, who was standing behind Aubrey, obviously waiting for the Emperor to be done with Oz. "You know… that boy will wait for you as long as you need him to. You don't need to worry about what he expects. He understands that what he might want and what you're ready for are two different things. He'll wait."

Oh hell, please, no bouncy talk. Not now.

"There's more to it than that."

"I know. But you're entitled to those feelings. And those urges—"

"Oh, God, I am *not* talking about sex with you!"

"—you're also entitled to not act on them if you're not ready to. He'll wait, because he wants it to be you and he wants you to be sure."

"No, really, I'll stick my fingers in my ears if I have to."

I'll howl if it helps.

"You could always go talk to your dad. I know he has a few things he wants to say to you but isn't sure how. You and I? We're on equal footing here. It might be easier to talk to me."

"I haven't even talked to *Drew*. But yeah…I hadn't considered the equal footing thing. I'm sorry."

"It's fine. And I mean that, Oz. As much as I understand what you want, I'm proof that one can live without that and still be happy. And I am happy, I want you to know that."

He's even happier when there's pizza.

Or that might be me.

"Bonus dad," she said. "Drew told me you were my bonus dad, and he was right. My actual dad? I know this scares him."

The Emperor got up, and reached a hand down to help her up, but said, "Slam that window closed," before he touched her. When she was on her feet, she threw her arms around his waist and hugged him. "This terrifies him, Oz, but that's all right. He remembers what young love feels like. He knows it's healthy, even if he's not ready for you be that grown up."

His hand was still at the small of her back as they took a few steps toward the fire pit, when she stopped. "Do we end up together, Emperor?"

"Nah. You're far too young for me."

"Yeah, very funny." She took two steps, and then stopped again. Under her breath she said, "William Jackson Blackshear."

He spun on his heel and stood between her and the rest of them, standing uncomfortably close to her. "Stop. No."

"Your name will come out. Your parents—"

"I haven't figured that out yet. Someone will eventually ask, I'm sure, and I don't know how long we can avoid an answer. That wasn't a thing we ever discussed. When Finn remembered who he was, he knew he shouldn't tell you his last name, but in all the months of preparing me to be here, we never talked about it."

King Jackson at six o'clock.

When the Emperor turned to look, the King asked if everything was all right. He explained that he had dumped far too much information into Oz's head, and wanted to be sure she was all right.

"Are you?" the King asked her.

She nodded. "Other than having all of him swimming in my head now, sure. It also means I have a lot of them"—she gestured to Finn and Jo— "in there, too." She looked at them for a long moment. "That entitles them to family privilege, doesn't it?"

"The Emperor *is* family, Oz. You know that."

"I mean officially. And I'm serious. Make him and his parents legally binding members of the House of Blackshear."

The Emperor chuckled. "You want to *adopt* me?"

Me, too, please. I want a crown.

"I wouldn't try to argue with her," the King said. "You know she's going to bring this up with her mother, and ten minutes after that the papers will be filed. You and I will not be consulted." He shrugged. "It's just a formality at this point, don't you think?"

When the King turned around the Emperor whispered to her, "You think quickly. And thank you."

"Eh. I just want to call you Uncle Willie."

"You wouldn't."

Her laughter trailed behind her.

The King is right. You don't get a vote. I bet he can even get the Old King to come home for a bit to sign the papers to become your official second daddy. And you have to call him that.

He picked me up. "I'm not averse to holding you over my head until the pigeons notice and take you for a ride, Major Wick."

You see those women over there? They would do mean and nasty things to you if you did. They love me. And it's just Mister now, if that's all right. I don't want to be in the army anymore.

"That's fine. You've earned your retirement. You're a good boy."

Dude, I swear to Bast, I will pee on you right here and now.

"Ah, but you *are* a good boy. Everyone knows it. Just accept it already."

Fine, but there better be pizza for me later. You can buy my affection with pizza.

"You're a cheap date, Wick."

Yeah, but I'm not easy. Remember that.

33

"In static time, here, you were in the portal for roughly ten hours," Finn told the Emperor. "In relative time? Well, we had to send someone back to the last possible moment to tell me to leave the other portal online, and then we had to go back and time it just right—"

"We tried to pull you through with us," Jo added. "When that didn't work, Oz decided to just reach in and grab you."

"Again," Zed said. "She tried a couple of times."

"She couldn't quite get a grasp on you," Finn said. "But relatively, if you could have felt time passing? You were probably stuck there for a week or more. I thought we had you on the other side at one point, but you were there and gone before I could blink."

Hey, I think we saw that.

"Indeed. We saw sunlight, and people moving far too fast. Then nothing. Then…Oz."

But did it work? Is there a future to go home to?

"What's he saying, sweetheart?" Jo asked.

Drew twitched. "What? Wick?"

"Wick wants to know if the gates worked. Does Earth survive?"

"You can freaking *talk* to *Wick*?"

"We all talk to Wick," Oz snickered. "Pipe down."

The King was looking at me closely, almost sadly, so while Finn explained Drew's idea of moving the gates and then having to go back through the portal to be there at the right time—which frankly didn't interest me; all I cared was that it worked—I jumped onto his lap, stretched up, and licked his chin.

I'm still your kitty, too. I won't go anywhere.

He looked to the Emperor.

"No, Wick, we won't. We'll stay here. This is our When now."

"William." That didn't sound like Jo, but I was surprised to hear anyone else using his name. I turned on the King's lap; the Queen was looking at us with a touch of upset. "Don't you dare do that to your parents. They've waited how many years for you to be able to go home?"

"Aubrey. This *is* my home."

"He can visit us." Jo's voice was soft and not as sad as I would have expected. "Or we can come here. I know he can't go back."

Finn looked at the Emperor, trying to gauge how he would react. "Or…we can stay."

The Emperor did not agree. "Absolutely not. You know too much."

"So do you, and you manage."

"But your work—"

"Is done. Dash, we've spent our entire adult lives focused on one thing, and it's done. We sacrificed far too much—including you— and I think it's time we were able to put our focus somewhere else."

"Like explaining how the Emperor can talk to cats?" Drew blurted out.

Well, you all could, if you just listened to me.

"It's his gift," Zed explained, amused. "Oz sees sound, I smell emotions, your head is so high in the clouds you see what we don't, and he can converse with the cat."

"Oh yeah, sunshine? What do I smell like right now?"

"Onion rings and hamburger, mostly. There's an undercurrent of horny desperation, but I wasn't going to mention that."

"Zed."

"Sorry, Mom."

Finn went on. "Anyway. I don't see a reason we shouldn't stay, at least for now. There's work here I can do."

"Dad, you can't."

"Physics is physics, no matter the When." To the King he said, "I owe you. The future owes you."

"There's no debt, Finn. If anything, we're even. You can certainly stay, but not because you owe us anything."

"In the grand scheme of things? Billions of lives depended on my work, and in the end it was what happened *here* that saved them. You knew that was the end game, too, I know that now. You let it play out, knowing what was at stake."

"I was given an idea after you arrived. No more than that."

"Well, I have an idea of what good I can do here, now."

"Dad."

Finn ignored him. "You're about to go to war."

"*Dad.*"

The King handed me back to the Emperor, and he leaned forward, elbows on his knees, and the look on his face alone was enough to keep Oz and Drew and Zed from asking questions.

"Midlam is under an undeniable threat," he agreed. "We're providing some support. But we're not at war."

"You will be."

I wiggled away from the Emperor, because I was afraid he was going to grip me so hard that my beefy treats would come up.

"Dad, you can't tell them anything. You can't interfere. You can't change the timeline."

You just don't want them to stay because if your mom stays here she'll mom you to death.

"I'm not, not really. The focus of my work will be on something you already created. The gate. You said then it was a game changer, and you were right. This country is about to head into war, and that gate can change everything."

"How so?" the King asked. "Transport the enemy into oblivion?"

"Nothing so horrid, though that would work. The technology that opened the portals was a way to move people and objects through time, but not space. I could send someone from twenty-six-fifty to nineteen-ninety-nine, but they would end up in the same geographical spot they left. But with the gate? With a little work, I can send someone through space. I had the framework when I built my first ship. It's what sent me to the ship and then into null space."

"Transport someone from here to there. San Francisco to Chicago."

"Exactly. But better—I may be able to send someone through both time and space. Leave here at lunch, be there for breakfast."

"Or leave here after the battle, get there before it starts."

"Catch the enemy first."

"That's a dangerous game to play," Drew said.

"And it's a process that doesn't exist yet," Finn added. "We have the portals. We have the gates. I just need to figure out how to make them work without having a receiver on each end."

"And will this change your timeline at all?" the Queen asked.

"It's already changed," Finn replied. "Wick is alive. From here on out, it's essentially a new timeline."

"You don't know that yet," the Emperor argued.

The rooftop door opened, and everyone turned as one of the King's guards ran to him.

He listened closely to what was whispered in his ear and then barked, "Clear the roof." He grabbed his chair and dragged it until it was behind the roof entry, and everyone followed, stacking their chairs before heading into the stairwell. We watched from there as a white and blue hover car turned from the air above Stockton Street, lifted over the edge of the roof, and landed with a jolting thud.

The King was the first out the door, in spite of his guard's objections, and we followed in a cluster behind him. I flattened my ears against the high-pitched whirr of the engine, and hid behind the Emperor's legs until it stopped and the car door started to lift.

Drew uttered, "Mom," and started to move toward the car, but the woman who stepped out gently shook her head, and then looked away from him. She had clenched in her hand a clump of white cloth, holding it so tightly that her fingers were almost as white, and before the King and Queen could greet her, she unfolded it, and handed it to him.

"Shazia?" He looked at the thick material he was holding. "What's this?"

She stared at the cloth, biting her lower lip. When she finally looked up, she said, "Florida attacked Chicago this morning."

Drew pushed his way past the Emperor. "Where's Dad?"

His mother exhaled sharply and her eyes flicked toward him, but she kept focus on the King.

"I—we were blindsided. They flew six planes over Wisconsin, and none of their aircraft registered on our systems. I'd moved ninety per cent of our troops to stage near the Florida border—there weren't nearly enough left in Chicago to mount a reasonable defense. I never considered they had the means to launch a northern attack."

"Where's Dad?" Drew asked again, his voice thin.

Oz slipped her arms around him, half holding him back, half holding him up, trying to comfort him against what she felt was coming.

"They blanketed the city. It took less than an hour, and Chicago was left in ruin. I didn't know what else to do, other than run."

Aubrey reached for Drew's arm, touching him right at his elbow, and she laid her other hand on Oz's shoulder. Whatever pain he was about to be engulfed in, she was already trying to take.

When the King had nothing to say to her, Shazia Van Hoff went on. "I've left orders with the head of our Department of Defense to expect coordination from Pacifica, and to accept orders from the head of your military, and from you."

She finally looked at Drew. "I am so sorry, Andrew."

He fell back against Oz, deflated.

"King Jackson, I am formally surrendering Midlam to Pacifica, and of this moment, I abdicate to you and accept your rule."

"And now," Finn said quietly, "we're at war."

ABOUT THE AUTHOR

Max Thompson is a long time feline blogger and life coach columnist for *Mousebreath!* Magazine. He lives in Northern California with his typist, writer K.A. Thompson, another human known mostly as "The Man," and the royal pain in his asterisk, Buddah Pest.

He can be found online at
http://psychokitty.blogspot.com and at
http://facebook.com/thepsychokittyspeaksout